Contents

Fielder's Choice

AN ANTHOLOGY OF BASEBALL FICTION

Introduction

In explaining his devotion to baseball, novelist Philip Roth revealed, "I loved the game, with all my heart," not merely for the enjoyment of playing it, but also for the mythic and aesthetic dimensions that it gave an American boy's life, especially one whose grandparents could hardly speak English. For a man whose attachment to America was strong but whose roots were only inches deep, Roth discovered, as others before him, that baseball was the secular church that reached into every class and region of the nation and bound millions upon millions "of us together in common concerns, loyalties, rituals, enthusiasms, and antagonisms."

Baseball also taught him geography. However much his teachers instructed him about the stockyards and the Haymarket Riot, Chicago began to exist for him as a real place and to matter in American history only when he became aware of Phil Cavarretta, star first baseman of the Chicago Cubs. The size and spread of the continent came alive when, as a boy in Newark,

New Jersey, he had to stay up until 10:30 P.M. to listen to the radio report of a Cardinal-Dodger game, and when Cardinal pitcher Mort Cooper threw a third strike past Pee Wee Reese in "steamy" Sportsman's Park in faraway St. Louis.

Two of the most cataclysmic events of Roth's boyhood— the death of President Roosevelt and the bombing of Hiroshima —reached him while he was out playing ball. Not surprisingly, his ability as a player was limited. He was cut from his high school team the day before the coach gave out the uniforms.

"But this misfortune," Roth explained, "did not necessitate a change in my future plans. Had I been cut from the school itself, *then* there would have been hell to pay in my house. . . . As it was, my family lost no more faith in me than I actually did in myself. They probably would have been shocked if I had made the team."

Similarly, Roger Kahn was also an aspiring and amateur player. In *The Boys of Summer* Kahn tells of his fright when, as a young sportswriter covering the Brooklyn Dodgers, he was asked to stand at the plate and pretend he was a batter while Dodger pitcher Clem Labine worked on his control, which had been giving him problems. "Although Labine was not regarded as very fast and was complaining about his arm, the ball exploded with a sibilant whoosh, edged by a buzzing as of hornets. I had never heard a thrown ball make that sound before. It seemed to accelerate as it came closer, an impossibly fast pitch that made the noises of hornets and snakes. I was paralyzed as I watched it approach. Then, at what seemed the last millisecond, the spinning ball grabbed air and hooked away from my head and over the plate. I didn't want to play this game. I had never wanted to play *this* game."

So wide is the chasm between the amateur and professional player that few writers made the team, or even came close. Inevitably, the reader is the winner. The professionals have neither the head, nor the time, for the romance. It is those who didn't make the club who expanded the considerable realm of baseball literature. The shelf now sags and, like Roth, the latest wave of contributors are the fringe players, and fans, or both. If sports have become the opiate of the people, as charged, then baseball was the original narcotic, and among those with the most severe addiction were the amateurs.

"I was a fan from the time I was a kid and went to Ebbets Field whenever I could," said Bernard Malamud, who gave us *The Natural,* one of the best baseball novels. "I used to sit in the 50-cent bleachers on Sundays. This was in the days of Dazzy Vance, Max Carey, and Zack Wheat. I saw Babe Ruth hit a homer or two at Yankee Stadium, and was present the day Lou Gehrig took over first base from Wally Pipp. The whole history of baseball has the quality of mythology."

And Robert Coover, growing up in East St. Louis, Illinois, sat nights at his kitchen table, equipped with nothing more than a pair of dice and pads of paper. With each roll, Coover created and recorded his own league, filled with imaginary players, later presented to us in the fascinating and absorbing *The Universal Baseball Association, Inc., J. Robert Waugh, Prop.* Like Philip Roth, Chaim Potok, Bernard Malamud, Mark Harris, and others, Coover drew from baseball, employing it as the vehicle for his literary fantasy.

It has been thirty years since publication of the last volume devoted wholly to baseball fiction. The game has, of course, undergone some change. We now have the designated hitter, artificial turf, and the new symmetrical and largely antiseptic stadiums—the reigning American architecture of the 1960s and 1970s. But as you will discover, the most significant and startling differences have been provided by the writers whose works are often more exciting and varied than the game itself.

Jerome Holtzman
Evanston, Illinois

The Universal Baseball Association, Inc.

ROBERT COOVER

J. Henry Waugh, a fifty-six-year-old accountant, eats delicatessen food, drinks in a neighborhood bar, picks up B-girls, and enjoys country music. But his consuming concern is the Universal Baseball Association, a mythical league that comes alive nightly on his kitchen table. Mr. Waugh is the founder, proprietor, president, historian, statistician, disciplinarian, and conscience of his association. A full schedule of games is played, each action being determined by a roll of the dice. From the novel *The Universal Baseball Association, Inc.*

Bottom half of the seventh, Brock's boy had made it through another inning unscratched, one! two! three! Twenty-one down and just six outs to go! and Henry's heart was racing, he was sweating with relief and tension all at once, unable to sit, unable to think, *in* there, *with* them! Oh yes, boys, it was on! He was sure of it! More than just another ball game now: *history!* And Damon Rutherford was making it. Ho ho! too good to be true! And yes, the stands were charged with it, turned on, it was the old days all over again, and with one voice they rent the air as the Haymaker Star Hamilton Craft spun himself right off his feet in a futile cut at Damon's third strike—zing! whoosh! *zap! OUT!* Henry laughed, watched the hometown Pioneer fans cheer the boy, cry out his name, then stretch—not just stretch—*leap up* for luck. He saw beers bought and drunk, hot dogs eaten, timeless gestures passed. Yes, yes, they nodded, and crossed their fingers and knocked on wood and rubbed their palms and kissed their fingertips and clapped their hands, and laughed how they were all caught up in it, witnessing it, how he was all caught up in it, this great ball game, event of the first order, tremendous moment: *Rookie pitcher Damon Rutherford, son of the incomparable Brock Rutherford, was two innings—six outs—from a perfect game!* Henry, licking his lips, dry from excitement, squinted at the sun high over the Pioneer Park, then at his watch: nearly eleven, Diskin's closing hour. So he took the occasion of this seventh-inning hometown stretch to hurry downstairs to the delicatessen to get a couple sandwiches. Might be a long night: the Pioneers hadn't scored off old Swanee Law yet either.

A small warm bulb, unfrosted, its little sallow arc so remote from its fathering force as to seem more akin to the glowworm than lightning, gleamed outside his door and showed where the landing ended; the steps themselves were dark, but Henry, through long usage, knew them all by heart. Cold bluish street-light lit the bottom, intruding damply, seeming to hover unrelated to the floor, but Henry hardly noticed: his eye was on the game, on the great new Rookie pitcher Damon Rutherford, seeking this afternoon his sixth straight win . . . and maybe more. Maybe: immortality. And now, as Henry skipped out onto the sidewalk, then turned into the front door of Diskin's Delicatessen, he saw the opposing pitcher, Ace Swanee Law of the hard-bitten Haymakers, taking the mound, tossing warm-up pitches, and he knew he had to hurry.

"Two pastrami, Benny," he said to the boy sweeping up, Mr. Diskin's son—third or fourth, though, not the second. "And a cold six-pack."

"Aw, I just put everything away, Mr. Waugh, the boy whined, but he went to get the pastrami anyway.

Now Swanee Law was tough, an ace, seven-year veteran, top rookie himself in his own day, one of the main reasons Rag Rooney's Rubes had finished no worse than third from Year L through Year LIV. Ninety-nine wins, sixty-one losses, fast ball that got faster every year, most consistent, most imperturbable, and most vociferous of the Haymaker moundsmen. Big man who just reared back and hummed her in. Phenomenal staying power, the kind old Brock used to have. But he didn't have Brock Rutherford's class, that sweet smooth delivery, that virile calm. Mean man to beat, just the same, and to be sure he still had a shutout going for him this afternoon, and after all, it was a big day for him, too, going for that milestone hundredth win. Of course, he had a Rookie catcher in there to throw to, young Bingham Hill, and who knows? maybe they weren't getting along too well; could be. Law was never an easy man to get along with, too pushy, too much steam, and Hill was said to be excitable. Maybe Rooney had better send in reliable old Maggie Everts, Law's favorite battery mate. What about it? Haymaker manager Rag (Pappy) Rooney stroked his lean grizzly jaw, gave the nod to Everts.

"How's that, Mr. Waugh?"

"Did you put the pickle?"

"We're all out, sold the last one about thirty minutes ago."

A lie. Henry sighed. He'd considered using the name Ben Diskin, solid name for an outfielder, there was a certain power in it, but Benny spoiled it. A good boy, but nothing there. "That's okay, Benny. I'll take two next time."

"Working hard tonight, Mr. Waugh?" Benny rang up the sale, gave change.

"As always."

"Better take it easy. You been looking a little run-down lately."

Henry winced impatiently, forced a smile. "Never felt better," he said, and exited.

It was true: the work, or what he called his work, though it was more than that, much more, was good for him. Thing was, nobody realized he was just four years shy of sixty. They were always shocked when he told them. It was his Association that kept him young.

Mounting the stairs, Henry heard the roar of the crowd, saw them take their seats. Bowlegged old Maggie Everts trundled out of the Haymaker dugout to replace Hill. That gave cause for a few more warm-up pitches, so Henry slowed, took the top steps one at a time. Law grinned, nodded at old Maggie, stuffed a chaw of gum into his cheek. In the kitchen, he tore open the six-pack of beer, punched a can, slid the others into the refrigerator, took a long greedy drink of what the boys used to call German tea. Then, while Law tossed to Everts, Henry chewed his pastrami and studied the line-ups. Grammercy Locke up for the Pioneers, followed by three Star batters. Locke had been rapping the ball well lately, but Pioneer manager Barney Bancroft pulled him out, playing percentages, called in pinch-hitter Tuck Wilson, a great Star in his prime, now nearing the end of his career. Wilson selected a couple bats, exercised them, chose one, tugged his hat, and stepped in.

Henry sat down, picked up the dice, approved Everts' signal. "Wilson batting for Locke!" he announced over the loudspeaker, and they gave the old hero a big hometown hand. Henry rolled, bit into pastrami. Wilson swung at the first pitch, in across the knuckles, pulling it down the line. Haymaker third-sacker Hamilton Craft hopped to his right, fielded the ball, spun, threw to first—*wide!* Wilson: safe on first! Henry marked the error, flashed it on the scoreboard. Craft, one of the best, kicked the bag at third sullenly, scrubbed his nose, stared hard at Hatrack Hines, stepping now into the box. Bancroft sent speedster Hillyer Bryan in to run for Wilson.

"Awright! now come on, you guys! a little action!" Henry shouted, Bancroft shouted, clapping his hands, and the Pioneers kept the pepper up, they hollered in the stands.

"Got them Rubes rattled, boys! Let's bat around!"

"Lean into it, Hatrack, baby! Swanee's done for the day!"

"Send him down the river!"

"Dee-ee-eep water, Swanee boy!"

"Hey, Hatrack! Just slap it down to Craft there, he's all butter!"

The dice rattled in Henry's fist, tumbled out on the kitchen table: *crack!* hard grounder. Craft jumped on it this time, whipped the ball to second, one out—but young Bryan broke up the double play by flying in heels high! Still in there! Bancroft took a calculated risk: sent Hatrack scampering for second on Law's second pitch to Witness York—*safe!* Finishing his sandwich, Henry wondered: Would the Rookie Bingham Hill, pulled for inexperience, have nailed Hines at second? Maybe he would have. Pappy Rooney, the graybeard Haymaker boss, spat disdainfully. He knew what he was doing. Who knows? Hill might have thrown wild.

Anyway, it didn't matter. Pioneer Star center-fielder Witness York stepped back in, squeezed his bat for luck, swung, and whaled out his eleventh home run of the season, scoring Hines in front of him, and before Law had got his wind back, big Stan Patterson, Star right fielder, had followed with his ninth. Wham! bam! thank you, ma'am! And finally that was how the seventh inning ended: Pioneers 3, Haymakers 0. And now it was up to Damon Rutherford.

Henry stood, drank beer, joined in spirit with the Pioneer fans in their heated cries. Could the boy do it? All knew what, but none named it. The bullish roar of the crowd sounded like a single hoarse monosyllable, yet within it, Henry could pick out the ripple of Damon's famous surname, not so glorified in this stadium in over twenty years. Then it was for the boy's father, the all-time great Brock Rutherford, one of the game's most illustrious Aces back in what seemed now like the foundling days of the Universal Baseball Association, even-tempered fire-balling no-pitches-wasted right-handed bellwether of the Pioneers who led them to nine pennants in a span of fourteen years. The Glorious XX's! Celebrated Era of the Pioneers! Barney Bancroft himself was there; he knew, he remembered! One of the fastest men the UBA had ever seen, out there guarding center. Barney the Old Philosopher, flanked by Willie O'Leary and Surrey Moss, and around the infield: Mose Stanford, Frosty Young, Jonathan Noon, and Gabe Burdette, timid Holly Tibbett behind the plate. Toothbrush Terrigan pitched, and Birdie Deaton and Chadbourne Collins . . . and Brock. Brock had come up as a Rookie in Year XX—no, XIX, that's right, it would have to be (Henry paused to look it up; yes, correct: XIX), just a kid off the farm, seemed happy-go-lucky and even lackadaisical, but he had powered his way to an Ace position that first year, winning six straight ball games at the end of the season, three of them shutouts, lifting the long-suffering Pioneers out of second division into second place. A great year! great teams! and next year the pennant! Brock the Great! maybe the greatest of them all! He had stayed up in the Association for seventeen years before giving way to age and a troublesome shoulder. Still held the record to this day for total lifetime wins: 311. 311! Brock Rutherford . . . well, well, time gets on. Henry felt a tightness in his chest, shook it off. Foolish. He sighed, picked up the dice. Brock the Great. Hall of Fame, of course.

And now: now it was his boy who stood there on the mound. Tall, lithe, wirier build than his dad's, but just as fast, just as smooth. Smoother. More serious somehow. Yes, there was something more pensive about Damon, a meditative calm, a gentle brooding concern. The calm they shared, Rutherford gene, but where in Brock it had taken on the color of a kind of cocky, almost rustic power, in Damon it was self-assurance ennobled with a sense of . . . what? Responsibility maybe. Accountability. Brock was a public phenomenon, Damon a self-enclosed yet participating mystery. His own man, yet at home in the world, part of it, involved, every inch of him a participant, maybe that was all it was: his total involvement, his oneness with UBA. Henry mused, fingering the dice. The Pioneer infielders tossed the ball around. Catcher Royce Ingram talked quietly with Damon out on the mound.

Of course, Pappy Rooney cared little for the peculiar aesthetics of the moment. It was his job not only to break up the no-hitter, but to beat the kid. Anyway, old Pappy had no love for the Rutherfords. Already a Haymaker Star and veteran of two world championships, four times the all-star first baseman of the Association, when Dad Rutherford first laced on a pair of cleats for the Pioneers, Rag Rooney had suffered through season after season of Haymaker failure to break the Pioneer grip on the UBA leadership, had gone down swinging futilely at Brock's fireball as often as the next man. So maybe that was why it was that, when the Haymaker right fielder, due to lead off in the top of the eighth, remarked that the Rutherford kid sure was tough today, Rooney snapped back: "Ya don't say. Well, mister, take your goddamn seat." And called in a pinch hitter.

Not that it did any good. Henry was convinced it was Damon's day, and nothing the uncanny Rooney came up with today could break the young Pioneer's spell. He laughed, and almost carelessly, with that easy abandon of old man Brock, pitched the dice, watched Damon Rutherford mow them down. One! Two! Three! And then nonchalantly, but not arrogantly, just casually, part of any working day, walk to the dugout. As though nothing were happening. *Nothing!* Henry found himself hopping up and down. One more inning! He drank beer, reared back, fired the empty can at the plastic garbage bucket near the sink. In there! *Zap!* "Go get 'em!" he cried.

First, of course, the Pioneers had their own eighth round at the plate, and there was no reason not to use it to stretch their lead, fatten averages a little, rub old Swanee's nose in it. Even if the Haymakers got lucky in the ninth and spoiled Damon's no-hitter, there was no reason to lose the ball game. After all, Damon was short some 300-and-some wins if he wanted to top his old man, which meant he needed every one he could get. Henry laughed irreverently.

Goodman James, young Pioneer first baseman making his second try for a permanent place in the line-up after a couple years back in the minors, picked out a bat, stepped lean-legged into the batter's box. Swanee fed him the old Law Special, a sizzling sinker in at the knees, and James bounced it down the line to first base: easy out. Damon Rutherford received a tremendous ovation when he came out—his dad would have acknowledged it with an open grin up at the stands; Damon knocked dirt from his cleats, seemed not to hear it. Wasn't pride. It was just that he understood it, accepted it, but was too modest, too *knowing*, to insist on any uniqueness of his own apart from it. He took a couple casual swings with his bat, moved up to the plate, waited Law out, but finally popped up: not much of a hitter. But to hear the crowd cheer as he trotted back to the dugout (one of the coaches met him halfway with a jacket), one would have thought he'd at least homered. Henry smiled. Lead-off man Toby Ramsey grounded out, short to first. Three up, three down. Those back-to-back homers had only made Law tougher than ever. "It's when Ah got baseballs flyin' round mah ears, that's when Ah'm really at mah meanest!"

Top of the ninth.

This was it.

Odds against him, of course. Had to remember that; be prepared for the lucky hit that really wouldn't be lucky at all, but merely in the course of things. Exceedingly rare, no-hitters; much more so, perfect games. How many in history? two, three. And a Rookie: no, it had never been done. In seventeen matchless years, his dad had pitched only two no-hitters, never had a perfect game. Henry paced the kitchen, drinking beer, trying to calm himself, to prepare himself, but he couldn't get it out of his head: *it was on!*

The afternoon sun waned, cast a golden glint off the mowed grass that haloed the infield. No sound in the stands now: breathless. Of course, no matter what happened, even if he lost the game, they'd cheer him, fabulous game regardless; yes, they'd love him, they'd let him know it . . . but still they wanted it. Oh yes, how they wanted it! Damon warmed up, throwing loosely to catcher Ingram. Henry watched him, felt the boy's inner excitement, shook his head in amazement at his outer serenity. "Nothing like this before." Yes, there was a soft murmur pulsing through the stands: nothing like it, electrifying, new, a new thing, happening here and now! Henry paused to urinate.

Manager Barney Bancroft watched from the Pioneer dugout, leaning on a pillar, thinking about Damon's father, about the years they played together, the games fought, the races won, the celebrations and the sufferings, roommates when on the road several of those years. Brock was great and this kid was great, but he was no carbon copy. Brock had raised his two sons to be more than ballplayers, or maybe it wasn't Brock's work, maybe it was just the name that had ennobled them, for in a way, they were—Bancroft smiled at the idea, but it was largely true—they were, in a way, the Association's first real aristocrats. There were already some fourth-generation boys playing ball in the league—the Keystones' Kester Flint, for example, and Jock Casey and Paddy Sullivan—but there'd been none before like the Rutherford boys. Even Brock Jr., though failing as a ballplayer, had had this quality, this poise, a gently ironic grace on him that his dad had never had, for all his raw jubilant power. Ingram threw the ball to second-baseman Ramsey, who flipped it to shortstop Wilder, who underhanded it to third-baseman Hines, now halfway to the mound, who in turn tossed it to Damon. Here we go.

Bancroft watched Haymaker backstop Maggie Everts move toward the plate, wielding a thick stubby bat. Rookie Rodney Holt crouched in the on-deck circle, working a pair of bats menacingly between his legs. Everts tipped his hat out toward the mound, then stepped into the box: dangerous. Yes, he was. The old man could bring the kid down. Still able to come through with the clutch hit. Lovable guy, old Maggie, great heart, Bancroft was fond of him, but that counted for nothing in the ninth inning of a history-making ball game. Rooney, of course, would send a pinch hitter in for Law. Bancroft knew he should order a couple relief pitchers to the bull pen just in case, but something held him back. Bancroft thought it was on, too.

Rooney noticed the empty bullpen. Bancroft was overconfident, was ripe for a surprise, but what could he do about it? He had no goddamn hitters. Even Ham Craft was in a bad slump. Should pull him out, cool his ass on the bench awhile, but, hell, he had nobody else. Pappy was in his fifteenth year as Haymaker manager, the old man of the Association's coaching staffs, and he just wasn't too sure, way things were going, that he and his ulcer were going to see a sixteenth. Two pennants, six times the league runner-up, never out of first division until last year when they dropped to fifth . . . and that was where his Rubes were now, with things looking like they were apt to get worse before they got better. He watched Everts, with a count of two and two on him, stand flatfooted as a third strike shot by so fast he hardly even saw it. That young bastard out there on the rubber was good, all right, fast as lightning—but what was it? Rooney couldn't quite put his finger on it . . . a little too narrow in the shoulders maybe, slight in the chest, too much a thoroughbred, not enough of the old man's big-boned stamina. And then he thought: shit, I can still beat this kid! And turning his scowl on the Haymaker bench, he hollered at Abernathy to pinch-hit for Holt.

Henry realized he had another beer in his hand and didn't remember having opened it. Now he was saying it out loud: "It's on! Come on, boy!" For the first time in this long game, the odds were with Damon: roughly 4-to-3 that he'd get both Abernathy and—who? Horvath, Rooney was sending in Hard John Horvath to bat for Law. Get them both and rack it up: the perfect game!

Henry hadn't been so excited in weeks. Months. That was the way it was, some days seemed to pass almost without being seen, games lived through, decisions made, averages rising or dipping, and all of it happening in a kind of fog, until one day that astonishing event would occur that brought sudden life and immediacy to the Association, and everybody would suddenly wake up and wonder at the time that had got by them, go back to the box scores, try to find out what had happened. During those dull-minded stretches, even a home run was nothing more than an HR penned into the box score; sure, there was a fence and a ball sailing over it, but Henry didn't see them—oh, he heard the shouting of the faithful, yes, they stayed with it, they had to, but to him it was just a distant echo, static that let you know it was still going on. But then, contrarily, when someone like Damon Rutherford came along to flip the switch, turn things on, why, even a pop-up to the pitcher took on excitement, a certain dimension, color. *The magic of excellence.* Under its charm, he threw the dice: Abernathy struck out. Two down, *one to go!* It could happen, *it could happen!* Henry reeled around his chair a couple times, laughing out loud, went to urinate again.

Royce Ingram walked out to the mound. Ten-year veteran, generally acknowledged the best catcher in the UBA. He didn't go out to calm the kid down, but just because it was what everybody expected him to do at such a moment. Besides, Damon was the only sonuvabitch on the whole field not about to crap his pants from excitement. Even the Haymakers, screaming for the spoiler, were out of their seats, and to the man, hanging on his every pitch. The kid really had it, okay. Not just control either, but stuff, too. Ingram had never caught anybody so good, and he'd caught some pretty good ones. Just twenty years old, what's more: plenty of time to get even better. If it's possible. Royce tipped up his mask, grinned. "Ever hear the one about the farmer who stuck corks in his pigs' assholes to make them grow?" he asked.

"Yes, I heard that one, Royce," Damon said and grinned back. "What made you think of that one—you having cramps?"

Ingram laughed. "How'd you guess?"

"Me too," the kid confessed, and toed a pebble off the rubber. Ingram felt an inexplicable relief flood through him, and he took a deep breath. We're gonna make it, he thought. They listened to the loudspeaker announcing Horvath batting for Law. "Where does he like it?"

"Keep it in tight and tit-high, and the old man won't even

see it," Ingram said. He found he couldn't even grin, so he pulled
his mask down. "Plenty of stuff," he added meaninglessly. Damon
nodded. Ingram expected him to reach for the rosin bag or wipe
his hands on his shirt or tug at his cap or something, but he
didn't: he just stood there waiting. Ingram wheeled around,
hustled back behind the plate, asked Horvath what he was
sweating about, underwear too tight on him or something? which
made Hard John give an uneasy tug at his balls, and when, in
his squat behind the plate, he looked back out at Rutherford,
he saw that the kid still hadn't moved, still poised there on the
rise, coolly waiting, ball resting solidly in one hand, both hands
at his sides, head tilted slightly to the right, face expressionless
but eyes alert. Ingram laughed. "You're dead, man," he told
Horvath. Henry zipped up.

Of course, it was just the occasion for the storybook spoiler.
Yes, too obvious. Perfect game, two down in the ninth, and a
pinch hitter scratches out a history-shriveling single. How many
times it had already happened! The epochal event reduced to
a commonplace by something or someone even less than commonplace, a mediocrity, a blooper worth forgetting, a utility ballplayer never worth much and out of the league a year later. All
the No-Hit Nealys that Sandy sang about . . .

>*No-Hit Nealy, somethin' in his eye,*
>*When they pitched low, he swung high,*
>*Hadn't had a hit in ninety-nine years,*
>*And then they sent him out agin*
>   *the Pi-yo-neers!*

Henry turned water on to wash, then hesitated. Not that he
felt superstitious about it exactly, but he saw Damon Rutherford standing there on the mound, hands not on the rosin bag,
not in the armpits, not squeezing the ball, just at his side—
dry, strong, patient—and he felt as though washing his hands
might somehow spoil Damon's pitch. From the bathroom door,
he could see the kitchen table. His Association lay there in
ordered stacks of paper. The dice sat there, three ivory cubes,
heedless of history yet makers of it, still proclaiming Abernathy's
strike-out. Damon Rutherford waited there. Henry held his

breath, walked straight to the table, picked up the dice, and tossed them down.

Hard John Horvath took a cut at Rutherford's second pitch, a letter-high inside curve, pulled it down the third-base line: Hatrack Hines took it backhanded, paused one mighty spellbinding moment—then fired across the diamond to Goodman James, and Horvath was out.

The game was over.

Giddily, Henry returned to the bathroom and washed his hands. He stared down at his wet hands, thinking: he did it! And then, at the top of his voice, "WA-*HOO!*" he bellowed, and went leaping back into the kitchen, feeling like he could damn well take off and soar if he had anyplace to go. "*HOO-HAH!*"

And the fans blew the roof off. They leaped the wall, slid down the dugout roofs, overran the cops, flooded in from the outfield bleachers, threw hats and scorecards into the air. Rooney hustled his Haymakers to the showers, but couldn't stop the Pioneer fans from lifting poor Horvath to their shoulders. There was a fight and Hard John bloodied a couple noses, but nobody even bothered to swing back at him. An old lady blew him kisses. Partly to keep Rutherford from getting mobbed and partly just because they couldn't stop themselves, his Pioneer teammates got to him first, had him on their own shoulders before the frenzied hometown rooters could close in and tear him apart out of sheer love. From above, it looked like a great roiling whirlpool with Damon afloat in the vortex—but then York popped up like a cork, and then Patterson and Hines, and finally the manager Barney Bancroft, lifted up by fans too delirious even to know for sure anymore what it was they were celebrating, and the whirlpool uncoiled and surged toward the Pioneer locker rooms.

"Ah!" said Henry, and: "*Ah!*"

And even bobbingly afloat there on those rocky shoulders, there in that knock-and-tumble flood of fans, in a wild world that had literally, for the moment, blown its top, Damon Rutherford preserved his incredible equanimity, hands at his knees except for an occasional wave, face lit with pleasure at what he'd done, but in no way distorted with the excitement of it all:

tall, right, and true. People screamed for the ball. Royce Ingram, whose shoulder was one of those he rode on, handed it up to him. Women shrieked, arms supplicating. He smiled at them, but tossed the ball out to a small boy standing at the crowd's edge.

Henry opened the refrigerator, reached for the last can of beer, then glanced at his watch: almost midnight—changed his mind. He peered out at the space between his kitchen window and the street lamp: lot of moisture in the air still, but hard to tell if it was falling or rising. He'd brooded over it, coming home from work: that piled-up mid-autumn feeling, pregnant with the vague threat of confusion and emptiness—but this boy had cut clean through it, let light and health in, and you don't go to bed on an event like this! Henry reknotted his tie, put on hat and raincoat, hooked his umbrella over one arm, and went out to get a drink. He glanced back at the kitchen table once more before pulling the door to, saw the dice there, grinned at them, for once adjuncts to grandeur, then hustled down the stairs like a happy Pioneer headed for the showers. He stepped quickly through the disembodied street lamp glow at the bottom, and whirling his umbrella like a drum major's baton, marched springily up the street to Pete's, the neighborhood bar.

N-o-O-O-o Hit Nealy!
Won his fame
Spoilin' Birdie Deaton's
Per-her-fect game!

The night above was dark yet the streets were luminous; wet, they shimmered with what occasional light there was from street lamps, passing cars, phone booths, all-night neon signs. There was fog and his own breath was visible, yet nearby objects glittered with a heightened clarity. He smiled at the shiny newness of things springing up beside him on his night walk. At a distance, car head lamps were haloed and taillights burned fuzzily, yet the lit sign in the darkened window he was passing, "DIVINEFORM FOUNDATIONS: TWO-WAY STRETCH," shone fiercely, hard-edged and vivid as a vision.

The corner drugstore was still open. A scrawny curly-headed kid, cigarette butt dangling under his fuzzy upper lip, played the pinball machine that stood by the window. Henry paused to watch. The machine was rigged like a baseball game, though the scores were unrealistic. Henry had played the machine himself often and once, during a blue season, had even played off an entire all-UBA pinball tourney on it. Ballplayers, lit from inside, scampered around the basepaths, as the kid put english on the balls with his hips and elbows. A painted pitcher, in eternal windup, kicked high, while below, a painted batter in a half-crouch moved motionlessly toward the plate. Two girls in the upper corners, legs apart and skirts hiked up their thighs, cheered the runners on with silent wide-open mouths. The kid was really racking them up: seven free games showing already. Lights flashed, runners ran. Eight. Nine. "THE GREAT AMERICAN GAME," it said across the top, between the gleaming girls. Well, it was. American baseball, by luck, trial, and error, and since the famous playing rules council of 1889, had struck on an almost perfect balance between offense and defense, and it was that balance, in fact, that and the accountability—the beauty of the records system which found a place to keep forever each least action—that had led Henry to baseball as his final great project.

The kid twisted, tensed, relaxed, hunched over, reared, slapped the machine with a pelvic thrust; up to seventeen free games and the score on the lighted panel looked more like that of a cricket match than a baseball game. Henry moved on. To be sure, he'd only got through one UBA pinball tourney and had never been tempted to set up another. Simple-minded, finally, and not surprisingly a simple-minded ballplayer, Jaybird Wall, had won it. In spite of all the flashing lights, it was—like those two frozen open-mouthed girls and the batter forever approaching the plate, the imperturbable pitcher forever reared back—a static game, utterly lacking the movement, grace, and complexity of real baseball. When he'd finally decided to settle on his own baseball game, Henry had spent the better part of two months just working with the problem of odds and equilibrium points in an effort to approximate that complexity. Two dice had not done it. He'd tried three, each a different color, and the 216 different combinations had provided the complexity, all right, but he'd nearly gone blind trying to sort the colors on each throw. Finally, he'd compromised, keeping the three dice, but all white, reducing the total number of combinations to 56, though of course the odds were still based on 216. To restore— and, in fact, to intensify—the complexity of the multicolored method, he'd allowed triple ones and sixes—1-1-1 and 6-6-6—to trigger the more spectacular events, by referring the following dice throw to what he called his Stress Chart, also a three-dice chart, but far more dramatic in nature than the basic ones. Two successive throws of triple ones and sixes were exceedingly rare— only about three times in every two entire seasons of play on the average—but when it happened, the next throw was referred, finally, to the Chart of Extraordinary Occurrences, where just about anything from fistfights to fixed ball games could happen. These two charts were what gave the game its special quality, making it much more than just a series of hits and walks and outs. Besides these, he also had special strategy charts for hit-and-run plays, attempted stolen bases, sacrifice bunts, and squeeze plays, still others for deciding the ages of rookies when they came up, for providing details of injuries and errors, and for determining who, each year, must die.

A neon beer advertisement and windows lit dimly through red curtains were all that marked Pete's place. Steady clientele, no doubt profitable in a small way, generally quiet, mostly country-and-western or else old hit-parade tunes on the jukebox, a girl or two drifting by from time to time, fair prices. Henry brought his gyrating umbrella under control, left the wet world behind, and pushed in.

"Evening, Mr. Waugh," said the bartender.

"Evening, Jake."

Not Jake, of course, it was Pete himself, but it was a long-standing gag, born of a slip of the tongue. Pete was medium-sized, slope-shouldered, had bartender's bags beneath his eyes and a splendid bald dome, spoke with a kind of hushed irony that seemed to give a dry double meaning to everything he said— in short, was the spitting image of Jake Bradley, one of Henry's ballplayers, a Pastimer second baseman whom Henry always supposed now to be running a bar somewhere near the Pastime Club's ball park, and one night, years ago, in the middle of a free-swinging pennant scramble, Henry had called Pete "Jake" by mistake. He'd kept it up ever since; it was a kind of signal to Pete

that he was in a good mood and wanted something better than
beer or bar whiskey. He sometimes wondered if anybody ever
walked into Jake's bar and called him Pete by mistake. Henry
took the middle one of three empty barstools. Jake—Pete—lifted
a bottle of VSOP, raised his eyebrows, and Henry nodded. Right
on the button.

The bar was nearly empty, not surprising; Tuesday, a working night, only six or seven customers, faces all familiar, mostly
old-timers on relief. Pete's cats scrubbed and stalked, sulked and
slept. A neighborhood B-girl named Hettie, old friend of Henry's,
put money in the jukebox—old-time country love songs. Nostalgia
was the main vice here. Pete toweled dust from a snifter, poured
a finger of cognac into it. "How's the work going, Mr. Waugh?"
he asked.

"Couldn't go better," Henry said and smiled. Jake always
asked the right questions.

Jake smiled broadly, creasing his full cheeks, nodded as
though to say he understood, pate flashing in the amber light.
And it was the right night to call him Jake, after all: Jake Bradley
was also from the Brock Rutherford era, must have come up
about the same time. Was he calling it that now? The Brock
Rutherford Era? He never had before. Funny. Damon was not
only creating the future, he was doing something to the past,
too. Jake dusted the shelf before putting the cognac bottle back.
He was once the middle man in five double plays executed in one
game, still the Association record.

Hettie, catching Henry's mood apparently, came over to kid
with him and he bought her a drink. A couple molars missing
and flesh folds ruining the once-fine shape of her jaw, but there
was still something compelling about the electronic bleat her
stockings emitted when she hopped up on a barstool and crossed
her legs, and that punctuation-wink she used to let a man know
he was in with her, getting the true and untarnished word. Henry
hadn't gone with her in years, not since before he set up his
Association, but she often figured obliquely in the Book and
conversations with her often got reproduced there under one
guise or another. "Been gettin' any hits lately?" she asked, and
winked over her tumbler of whiskey. They often used baseball
idiom, she no doubt supposing he was one of those ball-park

zealots who went crazy every season during the World Series and got written up as a character—the perennial krank—in the newspapers, and Henry never told her otherwise. Since she herself knew nothing at all about the sport, though, he often talked about his Association as though it were the major leagues. It gave him a kind of pleasure to talk about it with someone, even if she did think he was talking about something else.

"Been getting a lot," he said, "but probably not enough." She laughed loudly, exhibiting the gaps in her teeth. "And how about you, Hettie, been scoring a lot of runs?"

"I been scorin', boy, but I ain't got the runs!" she said, and whooped again. Old gag. The other customers turned their way and smiled.

Henry waited for her to settle down, commune with her drink once more, then he said, "Listen, Hettie, think what a wonderful rare thing it is to do something, no matter how small a thing, with absolute unqualified utterly unsurpassable *perfection!*"

"What makes you think it's so rare?" she asked with a wink, and switching top knee, issued the old signal. "You ain't pitched to me in a long time, you know."

He grinned. "No, but think of it, Hettie, to do a thing so perfectly that, even if the damn world lasted forever, nobody could ever do it better, because you had done it as well as it could possibly be done." He paused, let the cognac fumes bite his nostrils to excuse the foolish tears threatening to film his eyes over. "In a way, you know, it's even sad somehow, because, well, it's done, and all you can hope for after is to do it a second time." Of course, there were other things to do, the record book was, above all, a catalogue of possibilities . . .

"A second time! Did you say *perfection* or *erection?*" Hettie asked.

Henry laughed. It was no use. And anyway it didn't matter. He felt just stupendous, not so exultant as before, but still full of joy, and now a kind of heady aromatic peace seemed to be sweeping over him: ecstasy—yes, he laughed to himself, that was the only goddamn word for it. It was good. He bought another round, asked Pete: "How is it you stay in such good shape, Jake?"

"I don't know, Mr. Waugh. Must be the good Christian hours I keep."

And then, when the barkeep had left them, it was Hettie who suddenly turned serious. "I don't know what it is about you tonight, Henry," she said, "but you've got me kinda hot." And she switched top knee again: call from the deep.

Henry smiled, slowly whirling the snifter through minute cycles, warming the tawny dram in the palm of his hand. It was a temptation, to be sure, but he was afraid Hettie would spoil it for him, dissipate the joy and dull this glow, take the glory out of it. It was something he could share with no one without losing it altogether. Too bad. "It's just that nobody's bought you two straight drinks in a long time, Hettie," he said.

"Aw," she grumbled and frowned at her glass, hurt by that and so cooled off a little. To make up for it, he ordered her a third drink. He'd had enough, time to get back, had to make it to work in the morning, old Zifferblatt had been giving him a hard time for weeks now and just looking for a chance to raise hell about something, but Pete poured him one on the house. Not every day you pitched perfect games and got VSOP on the house. "Thanks, Jake," he said.

"Henry, hon', gimme some money to put in the jukebox."

Coins on the bar: he slid them her way. Stared into his snifter, saw himself there in the brown puddle, or anyway his eye.

> *It was down in Jake's old barroom*
> *Behind the Patsies' park;*
> *Jake was settin' 'em up as usual*
> *And the night was agittin' dark.*
> *At the bar stood ole Verne Mackenzie,*
> *And his eyes was bloodshot red . . .*

"The Day They Fired Verne Mackenzie": Sandy Shaw's great ballad. Dead now, Verne. First of the game's superstars, starting shortstop on Abe Flint's Excelsiors back in Year I, first of the Hall of Famers. But he got older and stopped hitting, and Flint, nice a guy as he was, had to let him go. And they all knew how Verne felt, even the young guys playing now who never knew him, because sooner or later it would be the same for them. Hettie leaned against him, head on his shoulder, humming the jukebox melodies to herself. He felt good, having her there like that. He sipped his brandy and grew slowly melancholy, *pleasantly* melancholy. He saw Brock the Great reeling boisterously down the street, arm in arm with Willie O'Leary and Frosty Young, those wonderful guys—and who should they meet up with but sleepy-eyed Mose Stanford and Gabe Burdette and crazy rubber-legged Jaybird Wall. Yes, and they were singing, singing the *old* songs, "Pitchin', Catchin,' Swingin'" and "The Happy Days of Youth," and oh! it was happiness! and goddamn it! it was fellowship! and boys oh boys! it was significance! "Let's go to Jake's!" they cried, they laughed, and off they went!

"Where?" Hettie mumbled. She was pretty far along. So was he. Didn't realize he had been talking out loud. Glanced self-consciously at Pete, but Pete hadn't moved: he was a patient pillar in the middle of the bar, ankles and arms crossed, face in shadows, only the dome lit up. Maybe he was asleep. There was only one other customer, an old-timer, still in the bar. The neon light outside was probably off.

"To my place," he said, not sure it was himself talking. Could he take her up there? She leaned away from his shoulder, tried to wink, couldn't quite pull it off, instead studied him quizzically as though wondering if he really meant it. "Hettie," he whispered, staring hard at her, so she'd know he wasn't kidding and that she'd better not spoil it, "how would you like to sleep with . . . Damon Rutherford?"

She blinked, squinted skeptically, but he could see she was still pretty excited and she'd moved her hand up his pantleg to the seam. "Who's he?"

"Me." He didn't smile, just looked straight at her, and he saw her eyes widen, maybe even a little fear came into them, but certainly awe was there, and fascination, and hope, and her hand, discovering he could do it, yes, he could do it, gave a squeeze like Witness York always gave his bat for luck before he swung, and she switched knees: *wheep!* So he paid Jake, and together—he standing tall and self-assured, Hettie shiveringly clasped in his embrace—they walked out. As he'd foreseen, the neon light was out; it was dark. He felt exceedingly wise.

"What are you, Henry?" Hettie asked softly as they walked under the glowing nimbus of a mist-wrapped street lamp. His raincoat had a slit in the lining behind the pocket, and this she reached through to slip her hand into his coin pocket.

"Now, or when we get to my place?"

"Now."

"An accountant."

"But the baseball . . . ?" And again she took hold and squeezed like Witness York, but now her hand was full of coins as well, and they wrapped the bat like a suit of mail.

"I'm an auditor for a baseball association."

"I didn't know they had auditors, too," she said. Was she really listening for once? They were in the dark now, next street lamp was nearly a block away, in front of Diskin's. She was trying to get her other hand on the bat, gal can't take a healthy swing without a decent grip, after all, but she couldn't get both hands through the slit.

"Oh, yes. I keep financial ledgers for each club, showing cash receipts and disbursements, which depend mainly on such things as team success, the buying and selling of ballplayers, improvement of the stadiums, player contracts, things like that." Hettie Irden stood at the plate, first woman ballplayer in league history, tightening and relaxing her grip on the bat, smiling around the spaces of her missing molars in that unforgettable way of hers, kidding with the catcher, laughing that gay timeless laugh that sounded like the clash of small coins, tugging maybe at her crotch in a parody of all male ballplayers the world over, and maybe she wasn't the best hitter in the Association, but the Association was glad to have her. She made them all laugh and forget for a moment that they were dying men. "And a running journalization of the activity, posting of it all into permanent record books, and I help them with basic problems of burden distribution, remarshaling of assets, graphing fluctuations. Politics, too. Elections. Team captains. Club presidents. And every four years, the Association elects a Chancellor, and I have to keep an eye on that."

"Gee, Henry, I didn't realize . . . !" She was looking up at him, and as they approached the street lamp, he could see something in her eyes he hadn't seen there before. He was glad to see it had come to pass, that she recognized—but it wouldn't do when they got to bed, she'd have to forget then.

"There are box scores to be audited, trial balances of averages along the way, seasonal inventories, rewards and punishments to be meted out, life histories to be overseen." He took a grip on her behind. "People die, you know."

"Yes," she said, and that seemed to excite her, for she squeezed a little harder.

"Usually, they die old, already long since retired, but they can die young, even as ballplayers. Or in accidents during the winter season. Last year a young fellow, just thirty, had a bad season and got sent back to the minors. They say his manager rode him too hard." Pappy Rooney. Wouldn't let go of the kid. "Sensitive boy who took it too much to heart. On the way, he drove his car off a cliff."

"Oh!" she gasped and squeezed. As though afraid now to let go. "On purpose?"

"I don't know. I think so. And if a pitcher throws two straight triple ones or sixes and brings on an Extraordinary Occurrence, a third set of ones in a bean ball that kills the batter, while triple sixes again is a line drive that kills the pitcher."

"Oh, how awful!" He didn't tell her neither had ever happened. "But what are triple sixes, Henry?"

"A kind of pitch. Here we are."

Even climbing the stairs to his place, she didn't want to release her grip, but the stairway was too narrow and they kept jamming up. So she took her hand out and went first. From his squat behind the box, the catcher watched her loosening up, kidded her that she'd never get a walk because they could never get two balls on her. Over her shoulder, she grinned down upon him, a gap-tooth grin that was still somehow beautiful. Anyhow, she said, I *am* an Extraordinary Occurrence, and on that chart there's no place for mere passes! The catcher laughed, reached up and patted her rear. "You said it!" he admitted, letting his hand glide down her thigh, then whistle up her stocking underneath the skirt. "An Extraordinary Occurrence!"

She hopped two steps giddily, thighs slapping together. "Henry! I'm ticklish!"

He unlocked the door to his apartment, switched on a night

light in the hall, leaving the kitchen and Association in protective darkness, and led her toward the bedroom.

"We're at your place," she said huskily when they'd got in there, and squeezed up against him. "Who are you now?" That she remembered! She was wonderful!

"The greatest pitcher in the history of baseball," he whispered. "Call me . . . Damon."

"Damon," she whispered, unbuckling his pants, pulling his shirt out. And "Damon," she sighed, stroking his back, unzipping his fly, sending his pants earthward with a rattle of buckles and coins. And "Damon!" she greeted, grabbing—and that girl, with one swing, he knew then, could bang a pitch clean out of the park. "*Play ball!*" cried the umpire. And the catcher, stripped of mask and guard, revealed as the pitcher Damon Rutherford, whipped the uniform off the first lady ballplayer in Association history, and then, helping and hindering all at once, pushing and pulling, they ran the bases, pounded into first, slid into second heels high, somersaulted over third, shot home standing up, then into the box once more, swing away, and run them all again, and "Damon!" she cried, and "Damon!"

Alibi Ike

RING W. LARDNER

His first name was Frank X. Farrell, and I guess the X stood for "Excuse me." Because he never pulled a play, good or bad, on or off the field, without apologizin' for it.

"Alibi Ike" was the name Carey wished on him the first day he reported down South. O' course we all cut out the "Alibi" part of it right away for the fear he would overhear it and bust somebody. But we called him "Ike" right to his face and the rest of it was understood by everybody on the club except Ike himself.

He ast me one time, he says:

"What do you all call me Ike for? I ain't no Yid."

"Carey give you the name," I says. "It's his nickname for everybody he takes a likin' to."

"He mustn't have only a few friends then," says Ike. "I never heard him say 'Ike' to nobody else."

But I was goin' to tell you about Carey namin' him. We'd been workin' out two weeks and the pitchers was showin' somethin' when this bird joined us. His first day out he stood up there so good and took such a reef at the old pill that he had everyone lookin'. Then him and Carey was together in left field, catchin' fungoes, and it was after we was through for the day that Carey told me about him.

"What do you think of Alibi Ike?" ast Carey.

"Who's that?" I says.

"This here Farrell in the outfield," says Carey.

"He looks like he could hit," I says.

"Yes," says Carey, "but he can't hit near as good as he can apologize."

Then Carey went on to tell me what Ike had been pullin' out there. He'd dropped the first fly ball that was hit to him and told Carey his glove wasn't broke in good yet, and Carey says the glove could easy of been Kid Gleason's gran'father. He made a whale of a catch out o' the next one and Carey says "Nice work!" or somethin' like that, but Ike says he could of caught the ball with his back turned only he slipped when he started after it and, besides that, the air currents fooled him.

"I thought you done well to get to the ball," says Carey.

"I ought to been settin' under it," says Ike.

"What did you hit last year?" Carey ast him.

"I had malaria most o' the season," says Ike. "I wound up with .356."

"Where would I have to go to get malaria?" says Carey, but Ike didn't wise up.

I and Carey and him set at the same table together for supper. It took him half an hour longer'n us to eat because he had to excuse himself every time he lifted his fork.

"Doctor told me I needed starch," he'd say, and then toss a shovelful o' potatoes into him. Or, "They ain't much meat on one o' these chops," he'd tell us, and grab another one. Or he'd say: "Nothin' like onions for a cold," and then he'd dip into the perfumery.

"Better try that apple sauce," says Carey. "It'll help your malaria."

"Whose malaria?" says Ike. He'd forget already why he didn't only hit .356 last year.

I and Carey begin to lead him on.

"Whereabouts did you say your home was?" I ast him.

"I live with my folks," he says. "We live in Kansas City—not right down in the business part—outside a ways."

"How's that come?" says Carey. "I should think you'd get rooms in the post office."

But Ike was too busy curin' his cold to get that one.

"Are you married?" I ast him.

"No," he says. "I never run round much with girls, except to shows once in a while and parties and dances and roller skatin'."

"Never take 'em to the prize fights, eh?" says Carey.

"We don't have no real good bouts," says Ike. "Just bush stuff. And I never figured a boxin' match was a place for the ladies."

Well, after supper he pulled a cigar out and lit it. I was just goin' to ask him what he done it for, but he beat me to it.

"Kind o' rests a man to smoke after a good workout," he says. "Kind o' settles a man's supper, too."

"Looks like a pretty good cigar," says Carey.

"Yes," says Ike. "A friend o' mine give it to me—a fella in Kansas City that runs a billiard room."

"Do you play billiards?" I ast him.

"I used to play a fair game," he says. "I'm all out o' practice now—can't hardly make a shot."

We coaxed him into a four-handed battle, him and Carey against Jack Mack and I. Say, he couldn't play billiards as good as Willie Hoppe; not quite. But to hear him tell it, he didn't make a good shot all evenin'. I'd leave him an awful-lookin' layout and he'd gather 'em up in one try and then run a couple o' hundred, and between every carom he'd say he put too much stuff on the ball, or the English didn't take, or the table wasn't true, or his stick was crooked, or somethin'. And all the time he had the balls actin' like they was Dutch soldiers and him Kaiser William. We started out to play fifty points, but we had to make it a thousand so as I and Jack and Carey could try the table.

The four of us set round the lobby a wile after we was through playin', and when it got along toward bedtime Carey whispered to me and says:

"Ike'd like to go to bed, but he can't think up no excuse."

Carey hadn't hardly finished whisperin' when Ike got up and pulled it.

"Well, good night, boys," he says. "I ain't sleepy, but I got some gravel in my shoes and it's killin' my feet."

We knowed he hadn't never left the hotel since we'd came in from the grounds and changed our clo'es. So Carey says:

"I should think they'd take them gravel pits out o' the billiard room."

But Ike was already on his way to the elevator, limpin'.

"He's got the world beat," says Carey to Jack and I. "I've knew lots o' guys that had an alibi for every mistake they made; I've heard pitchers say that the ball slipped when somebody cracked one off'n 'em; I've heard infielders complain of a sore arm after heavin' one into the stand, and I've saw outfielders tooken sick with a dizzy spell when they've misjudged a fly ball. But this baby can't even go to bed without apologizin', and I bet he excuses himself to the razor when he gets ready to shave."

"And at that," says Jack, "he's goin' to make us a good man."

"Yes," says Carey, "Unless rheumatism keeps his battin' average down to .400."

Well, sir, Ike kept whalin' away at the ball all through the trip till everybody knowed he'd won a job. Cap had him in there regular the last few exhibition games and told the newspaper boys a week before the season opened that he was goin' to start him in Kane's place.

"You're there kid," says Carey to Ike, the night Cap made the 'nnouncement. "They ain't many boys that wins a big league berth their third year out."

"I'd of been up here a year ago," says Ike, "only I was bent over all season with lumbago."

II

It rained down in Cincinnati one day and somebody organized a little game o' cards. They was shy two men to make six and ast I and Carey to play.

"I'm with you if you get Ike and make it seven-handed," says Carey.

So they got a hold of Ike and we went up to Smitty's room.

"I pretty near forgot how many you deal," says Ike. "It's been a long wile since I played."

I and Carey give each other the wink, and sure enough, he was just as ig'orant about poker as billiards. About the second hand, the pot was opened two or three ahead of him, and they was three in when it come his turn. It cost a buck, and he throwed in two.

"It's raised, boys," somebody says.

"Gosh, that's right, I did raise it," says Ike.

"Take out a buck if you didn't mean to tilt her," says Carey.

"No," says Ike, "I'll leave it go."

Well, it was raised back at him, and then he made another mistake and raised again. They was only three left in when the draw come. Smitty'd opened with a pair o' kings and he didn't help 'em. Ike stood pat. The guy that'd raised him back was flushin' and he didn't fill. So Smitty checked and Ike bet and didn't get no call. He tossed his hand away, but I grabbed it and give it a look. He had king, queen, jack and two tens. Alibi Ike he must have seen me peekin', for he leaned over and whispered to me.

"I overlooked my hand," he says. "I thought all the wile it was a straight."

"Yes," I says, "that's why you raised twice by mistake."

They was another pot that he come into with tens and fours. It was tilted a couple o' times and two o' the strong fellas drawed ahead of Ike. They each drawed one. So Ike throwed away his little pair and come out with four tens. And they was four treys against him. Carey'd looked at Ike's discards and then he says:

"This lucky bum busted two pair."

"No, no, I didn't," says Ike.

"Yes, yes, you did," says Carey, and showed us the two fours.

"What do you know about that?" says Ike. "I'd of swore one was a five spot."

Well, we hadn't had no pay day yet, and after a wile everybody except Ike was goin' shy. I could see him gettin' restless and I was wonderin' how he'd make the get-away. He tried two or three times. "I got to buy some collars before supper," he says.

"No hurry," says Smitty. "The stores here keeps open all night in April."

After a minute he opened up again.

"My uncle out in Nebraska ain't expected to live," he says. "I ought to send a telegram."

"Would that save him?" says Carey.

"No, it sure wouldn't," says Ike, "but I ought to leave my old man know where I'm at."

"When did you hear about your uncle?" says Carey.

"Just this mornin'," says Ike.

"Who told you?" ast Carey.

"I got a wire from my old man," says Ike.

"Well," says Carey, "your old man knows you're still here yet this afternoon if you was here this mornin'. Trains leavin' Cincinnati in the middle o' the day don't carry no ball clubs."

"Yes," says Ike, "that's true. But he don't know where I'm goin' to be next week."

"Ain't he got no schedule?" ast Carey.

"I sent him one openin' day," says Ike, "but it takes mail a long time to get to Idaho."

"I thought your old man lived in Kansas City," says Carey.

"He does when he's home," says Ike.

"But now," says Carey, "I s'pose he's went to Idaho so as he can be near your sick uncle in Nebraska."

"He's visitin' my other uncle in Idaho."

"Then how does he keep posted about your sick uncle?" ast Carey.

"He don't," says Ike. "He don't even know my other uncle's sick. That's why I ought to wire and tell him."

"Good night!" says Carey.

"What town in Idaho is your old man at?" I says.

Ike thought it over.

"No town at all," he says. "But he's near a town."

"Near what town?" I says.

"Yuma," says Ike.

Well, by this time he'd lost two or three pots and he was desperate. We was playin' just as fast as we could, because we seen we couldn't hold him much longer. But he was tryin' so hard to frame an escape that he couldn't pay no attention to the cards, and it looked like we'd get his whole pile away from him if we could make him stick.

The telephone saved him. The minute it begun to ring, five of us jumped for it. But Ike was there first.

"Yes," he says, answerin' it. "This is him. I'll come right down."

And he slammed up the receiver and beat it out o' the door without even sayin' good-by.

"Smitty'd ought to locked the door," says Carey.

"What did he win?" ast Carey.

We figured it up—sixty-odd bucks.

"And the next time we ask him to play," says Carey, "his fingers will be so stiff he can't hold the cards."

Well, we set round a wile talkin' it over, and pretty soon the telephone rung again. Smitty answered it. It was a friend of his'n from Hamilton and he wanted to know why Smitty didn't hurry down. He was the one that had called before and Ike had told him he was Smitty.

"Ike'd ought to split with Smitty's friend," says Carey.

"No," I says, "he'll need all he won. It costs money to buy collars and to send telegrams from Cincinnati to your old man in Texas and keep him posted on the health o' your uncle in Cedar Rapids, D.C."

III

And you ought to heard him out there on that field! They wasn't a day when he didn't pull six or seven, and it didn't make no difference whether he was goin' good or bad. If he popped up in the pinch he should of made a base hit and the reason he didn't was so-and-so. And if he cracked one for three bases he ought to had a home run, only the ball wasn't lively, or the wind brought it back, or he tripped on a lump o' dirt, roundin' first base.

They was one afternoon in New York when he beat all records. Big Marquard was workin' against us and he was good.

In the first innin' Ike hit one clear over that right field stand, but it was a few feet foul. Then he got another foul and then the count come to two and two. Then Rube slipped one acrost on him and he was called out.

"What do you know about that!" he says afterward on the

bench. "I lost count. I thought it was three and one, and I took a strike."

"You took a strike all right," says Carey. "Even the umps knowed it was a strike."

"Yes," says Ike, "but you can bet I wouldn't of took it if I'd knew it was the third one. The score board had it wrong."

"That score board ain't for you to look at," says Cap. "It's for you to hit that old pill against."

"Well," says Ike, "I could of hit that one over the score board if I'd knew it was the third."

"Was it a good ball?" I says.

"Well, no, it wasn't," says Ike. "It was inside."

"How far inside?" says Carey.

"Oh, two or three inches or half a foot," says Ike.

"I guess you wouldn't of threatened the score board with it then," says Cap.

"I'd of pulled it down the right foul line if I hadn't thought he'd call it a ball," says Ike.

Well, in New York's part o' the innin' Doyle cracked one and Ike run back a mile and a half and caught it with one hand. We was all sayin' what a whale of a play it was, but he had to apologize just the same as for gettin' struck out.

"That stand's so high," he says, "that a man don't ever see a ball till it's right on top o' you."

"Didn't you see that one?" ast Cap.

"Not at first," says Ike; "not till it raised up above the roof o' the stand."

"Then why did you start back as soon as the ball was hit?" says Cap.

"I knowed by the sound that he'd got a good hold of it," says Ike.

"Yes," says Cap, "but how'd you know what direction to run in?"

"Doyle usually hits 'em that way, the way I run," says Ike.

"Why don't you play blindfolded?" says Carey.

"Might as well, with that big high stand to bother a man," says Ike. "If I could of saw the ball all the time I'd of got it in my hip pocket."

Along in the fifth we was one run to the bad and Ike got on

with one out. On the first ball throwed to Smitty, Ike went down. The ball was outside and Meyers throwed Ike out by ten feet.

You could see Ike's lips movin' all the way to the bench and when he got there he had his piece learned.

"Why didn't he swing?" he says.

"Why didn't you wait for his sign?" says Cap.

"He give me his sign," says Ike.

"What is his sign with you?" says Cap.

"Pickin' up some dirt with his right hand," says Ike.

"Well, I didn't see him do it," Cap says.

"He done it all right," says Ike.

Well, Smitty went out and they wasn't no more argument till they come in for the next innin'. Then Cap opened it up.

"You fellas better get your signs straight," he says.

"Do you mean me?" says Smitty.

"Yes," Cap says. "What's your sign with Ike?"

"Slidin' my left hand up to the end o' the bat and back," says Smitty.

"Do you hear that, Ike?" ast Cap.

"What of it?" says Ike.

"You says his sign was pickin' up dirt and he says it's slidin' his hand. Which is right?"

"I'm right," says Smitty. "But if you're arguin' about him goin' last innin', I didn't give him no sign."

"You pulled your cap down with your right hand, didn't you?" ast Ike.

"Well, s'pose I did," says Smitty. "That don't mean nothin'. I never told you to take that for a sign, did I?"

"I thought maybe you meant to tell me and forgot," says Ike.

They couldn't none of us answer that and they wouldn't of been no more said if Ike had of shut up. But wile we was settin' there Carey got on with two out and stole second clean.

"There!" says Ike. "That's what I was tryin' to do and I'd of got away with it if Smitty'd swang and bothered the Indian."

"Oh!" says Smitty. "You was tryin' to steal then, was you? I thought you claimed I give you the hit and run."

"I didn't claim no such a thing," says Ike. "I thought maybe you might of gave me a sign, but I was goin' anyway because I thought I had a good start."

Cap prob'ly would of hit him with a bat, only just about that time Doyle booted one on Hayes and Carey come acrost with the run that tied.

Well, we go into the ninth finally, one and one, and Marquard walks McDonald with nobody out.

"Lay it down," says Cap to Ike.

And Ike goes up there with orders to bunt and cracks the first ball into that right-field stand! It was fair this time, and we're two ahead, but I didn't think about that at the time. I was too busy watchin' Cap's face. First he turned pale and then he got red as fire and then he got blue and purple, and finally he just laid back and busted out laughin'. So we wasn't afraid to laugh ourselfs when we seen him doin' it, and when Ike come in everybody on the bench was in hysterics.

But instead o' takin' advantage, Ike had to try and excuse himself. His play was to shut up and he didn't know how to make it.

"Well," he says, "if I hadn't hit quite so quick at that one I bet it'd of cleared the center-field fence."

Cap stopped laughin'.

"It'll cost you plain fifty," he says.

"What for?" says Ike.

"When I say 'bunt' I mean 'bunt,' " says Cap.

"You didn't say 'bunt,' " says Ike.

"I says 'Lay it down,' " says Cap. "If that don't mean 'bunt,' what does it mean?"

" 'Lay it down' means 'bunt' all right," says Ike, "but I understood you to say 'Lay on it.' "

"All right," says Cap, "and the little misunderstandin' will cost you fifty."

Ike didn't say nothin' for a few minutes. Then he had another bright idear.

"I was just kiddin' about misunderstandin' you," he says. "I knowed you wanted me to bunt."

"Well, then, why didn't you bunt?" ast Cap.

"I was goin' to on the next ball," says Ike. "But I thought if I took a good wallop I'd have 'em all fooled. So I walloped at the first one to fool 'em, and I didn't have no intention o' hittin' it."

"You tried to miss it, did you?" says Cap.

"Yes," says Ike.

"How'd you happen to hit it?" ast Cap.

"Well," Ike says, "I was lookin' for him to throw me a fast one and I was goin' to swing under it. But he come with a hook and I met it right square where I was swingin' to go under the fast one."

"Great!" says Cap. "Boys," he says, "Ike's learned how to hit Marquard's curve. Pretend a fast one's comin' and then try to miss it. It's a good thing to know and Ike'd ought to be willin' to pay for the lesson. So I'm goin' to make it a hundred instead o' fifty."

The game wound up 3 to 1. The fine didn't go, because Ike hit like a wild man all through that trip and we made pretty near a clean-up. The night we went to Philly I got him cornered in the car and I says to him:

"Forget them alibis for a wile and tell me somethin'. What'd you do that for, swing that time against Marquard when you was told to bunt?"

"I'll tell you," he says. "That ball he throwed me looked just like the one I struck out on in the first innin' and I wanted to show Cap what I could of done to that other one if I'd knew it was the third strike."

"But," I says, "the one you struck out on in the first innin' was a fast ball."

"So was the one I cracked in the ninth," says Ike.

IV

You've saw Cap's wife, o' course. Well, her sister's about twict as good-lookin' as her, and that's goin' some.

Cap took his missus down to St. Louis the second trip and the other one come down from St. Joe to visit her. Her name is Dolly, and some doll is right.

Well, Cap was goin' to take the two sisters to a show and he wanted a beau for Dolly. He left it to her and she picked Ike. He'd hit three on the nose that afternoon—of'n Sallee, too.

They fell for each other that first evenin'. Cap told us how it come off. She begin flatterin' Ike for the star game he'd played and o' course he begin excusin' himself for not doin' better. So she thought he was modest and it went strong with her. And she believed everything he said and that made her solid with him—that and her make-up. They was together every mornin' and evenin' for the five days we was there. In the afternoons Ike played the grandest ball you ever see, hittin' and runnin' the bases like a fool and catchin' everything that stayed in the park.

I told Cap, I says: "You'd ought to keep the doll with us and he'd make Cobb's figures look sick."

But Dolly had to go back to St. Joe and we come home for a long serious.

Well, for the next three weeks Ike had a letter to read every day and he'd set in the clubhouse readin' it till mornin' practice was half over. Cap didn't say nothin' to him, because he was goin' so good. But I and Carey wasted a lot of our time tryin' to get him to own up who the letters was from. Fine chancet!

"What are you readin'?" Carey'd say. "A bill?"

"No," Ike'd say, "not exactly a bill. It's a letter from a fella I used to go to school with."

"High school or college?" I'd ask him.

"College," he'd say.

"What college?" I'd say.

Then he'd stall a wile and then he'd say:

"I didn't go to the college myself, but my friend went there."

"How did it happen you didn't go?" Carey'd ask him.

"Well," he'd say, "they wasn't no colleges near where I lived."

"Didn't you live in Kansas City?" I'd say to him.

One time he'd say he did and another time he didn't. One time he says he lived in Michigan.

"Where at?" says Carey.

"Near Detroit," he says.

"Well," I says, "Detroit's near Ann Arbor and that's where they got the university."

"Yes," says Ike, "they got it there now, but they didn't have it there then."

"I come pretty near goin' to Syracuse," I says, "only they wasn't no railroads runnin' through there in them days."

"Where'd this friend o' yours go to college?" says Carey.

"I forget now," says Ike.

"Was it Carlisle?" ast Carey.

"No," says Ike, "his folks wasn't very well off."

"That's what barred me from Smith," I says.

"I was goin' to tackle Cornell's," says Carey, "but the doctor told me I'd have hay fever if I didn't stay up North."

"Your friend writes long letters," I says.

"Yes," says Ike; "he's tellin' me about a ballplayer."

"Where does he play?" ast Carey.

"Down in the Texas League—Fort Wayne," says Ike.

"It looks like a girl's writin'," Carey says.

"A girl wrote it," says Ike. "That's my friend's sister, writin' for him."

"Didn't they teach writin' at this here college where he went?" says Carey.

"Sure," Ike says, "they taught writin', but he got his hand cut off in a railroad wreck."

"How long ago?" I says.

"Right after he got out o' college," says Ike.

"Well," I says, "I should think he'd of learned to write with his left hand by this time."

"It's his left hand that was cut off," says Ike, "and he was left-handed."

"You get a letter every day," says Carey. "They're all the same writin'. Is he tellin' you about a different ballplayer every time he writes?"

"No," Ike says. "It's the same ballplayer. He just tells me what he does every day."

"From the size o' the letters, they don't play nothin' but double-headers down there," says Carey.

We figured that Ike spent most of his evenins answerin' the letters from his "friend's sister," so we kept tryin' to date him up for shows and parties to see how he'd duck out of 'em. He was bugs over spaghetti, so we told him one day that they was goin' to be a big feed of it over to Joe's that night and he was invited.

"How long'll it last?" he says.

"Well," we says, "we're goin' right over there after the game and stay till they close up."

"I can't go," he says, "unless they leave me come home at eight bells."

"Nothin' doin'," says Carey. "Joe'd get sore."

"I can't go then," says Ike.

"Why not?" I ast him.

"Well," he says, "my landlady locks up the house at eight and I left my key home."

"You can come and stay with me," says Carey.

"No," he says, "I can't sleep in a strange bed."

"How do you get along when we're on the road?" says I.

"I don't never sleep the first night anywheres," he says. "After that I'm all right."

"You'll have time to chase home and get your key right after the game," I told him.

"The key ain't home," says Ike. "I lent it to one o' the other fellas and he's went out o' town and took it with him."

"Couldn't you borry another key off'n the landlady?" Carey ast him.

"No," he says, "that's the only one they is."

Well, the day before we started East again, Ike come into the clubhouse all smiles.

"Your birthday?" I ast him.

"No," he says.

"What do you feel so good about?" I says.

"Got a letter from my old man," he says. "My uncle's goin' to get well."

"Is that the one in Nebraska?" says I.

"Not right in Nebraska," says Ike. "Near there."

But afterwards we got the right dope from Cap. Dolly'd blew in from Missouri and was going to make the trip with her sister.

V

Well, I want to alibi Carey and I for what come off in Boston. If we'd of had any idear what we was doin', we'd never did it. They wasn't nobody outside o' maybe Ike and the dame that felt worse over it than I and Carey.

The first two days we didn't see nothin' of Ike and her except out to the park. The rest o' the time they was sight-seein' over to Cambridge and down to Revere and out to Brook-a-line and all the other places where the rubes go.

But when we come into the beanery after the third game Cap's wife called us over.

"If you want to see somethin' pretty," she says, "look at the third finger on Sis's left hand."

Well, o' course we knowed before we looked that it wasn't goin' to be no hangnail. Nobody was su'prised when Dolly blew into the dinin' room with it—a rock that Ike'd bought off'n Diamond Joe the first trip to New York. Only o' course it'd been set into a lady's-size ring instead o' the automobile tire he'd been wearin'.

Cap and his missus and Ike and Dolly ett supper together, only Ike didn't eat nothin', but just set there blushin' and spillin' things on the tablecloth. I heard him excusin' himself for not havin' no appetite. He says he couldn't never eat when he was clost to the ocean. He'd forgot about them sixty-five oysters he destroyed the first night o' the trip before.

He was goin' to take her to a show, so after supper he went upstairs to change his collar. She had to doll up, too, and o' course Ike was through long before her.

If you remember the hotel in Boston, they's a little parlor where the piano's at and then they's another little parlor openin' off o' that. Well, when Ike come down Smitty was playin' a few chords and I and Carey was harmonizin'. We seen Ike go up to the desk to leave his key and we called him in. He tried to duck away, but we wouldn't stand for it.

We ast him what he was all duded up for and he says he was goin' to the theayter.

"Goin' alone?" says Carey.

"No," he says, "a friend o' mine's goin' with me."

"What do you say if we go along?" says Carey.

"I ain't only got two tickets," he says.

"Well," says Carey, "we can go down there with you and buy our own seats; maybe we can all get together."

"No," says Ike. "They ain't no more seats. They're all sold out."

"We can buy some off'n the scalpers," says Carey.

"I wouldn't if I was you," says Ike. "They say the show's rotten."

"What are you goin' for, then?" I ast.

"I didn't hear about it bein' rotten till I got the tickets," he says.

"Well," I says, "if you don't want to go I'll buy the tickets from you."

"No," says Ike, "I wouldn't want to cheat you. I'm stung and I'll just have to stand for it."

"What are you goin' to do with the girl, leave her here at the hotel?" I says.

"What girl?" says Ike.

"The girl you ett supper with," I says.

"Oh," he says, "we just happened to go into the dinin' room together, that's all. Cap wanted I should set down with 'em."

"I noticed," says Carey, "that she happened to be wearin' that rock you bought off'n Diamond Joe."

"Yes," says Ike. "I lent it to her for a wile."

"Did you lend her the new ring that goes with it?" I says.

"She had that already," says Ike. "She lost the set out of it."

"I wouldn't trust no strange girl with a rock o' mine," says Carey.

"Oh, I guess she's all right," Ike says. "Besides, I was tired o' the stone. When a girl asks you for somethin', what are you goin' to do?"

He started out toward the desk, but we flagged him.

"Wait a minute!" Carey says. "I got a bet with Sam here, and it's up to you to settle it."

"Well," says Ike, "make it snappy. My friend'll be here any minute."

"I bet," says Carey, "that you and that girl was engaged to be married."

"Nothin' to it," says Ike.

"Now look here," says Carey, "this is goin' to cost me real money if I lose. Cut out the alibi stuff and give it to us straight. Cap's wife just as good as told us you was roped."

Ike blushed like a kid.

"Well, boys," he says, "I may as well own up. You win, Carey."

"Yatta boy!" says Carey. "Congratulations!"

"You got a swell girl, Ike," I says.

"She's a peach," says Smitty.

"Well, I guess she's O. K.," says Ike. "I don't know much about girls."

"Didn't you never run round with 'em?" I says.

"Oh, yes, plenty of 'em," says Ike. "But I never seen none I'd fall for."

"That is, till you seen this one," says Carey.

"Well," says Ike, "this one's O. K., but I wasn't thinkin' about gettin' married yet a wile."

"Who done the askin', her?" says Carey.

"Oh, no," says Ike, "but sometimes a man don't know what he's gettin' into. Take a good-lookin' girl, and a man gen'ally almost always does about what she wants him to."

"They couldn't no girl lasso me unless I wanted to be lassoed," says Smitty.

"Oh, I don't know," says Ike. "When a fella gets to feelin' sorry for one of 'em it's all off."

Well, we left him go after shakin' hands all round. But he didn't take Dolly to no show that night. Some time wile we was talkin' she'd came into that other parlor and she'd stood there and heard us. I don't know how much she heard. But it was enough. Dolly and Cap's missus took the midnight train for New York. And from there Cap's wife sent her on her way back to Missouri.

She'd left the ring and note for Ike with the clerk. But we didn't ask Ike if the note was from his friend in Fort Wayne, Texas.

VI

When we'd came to Boston Ike was hittin' plain .397. When we got back home he'd fell off to pretty near nothin'. He hadn't drove one out o' the infield in any o' them other Eastern parks, and he didn't even give no excuse for it.

To show you how bad he was, he struck out three times in Brooklyn one day and never opened his trap when Cap ast him what was the matter. Before, if he'd whiffed oncet in a game he'd of wrote a book tellin' why.

Well, we dropped from first place to fifth in four weeks and we was still goin' down. I and Carey was about the only ones in the club that spoke to each other, and all as we did was to remind ourself o' what a boner we'd pulled.

"It's goin' to beat us out o' the big money," says Carey.

"Yes," I says. "I don't want to knock my own ball club, but it looks like a one-man team, and when that one man's dauber's down we couldn't trim our whiskers."

"We ought to knew better," says Carey.

"Yes," I says, "but why should a man pull an alibi for bein' engaged to such a bearcat as she was?"

"He shouldn't," says Carey. "But I and you knowed he would or we'd never started talkin' to him about it. He wasn't no more ashamed o' the girl than I am of a regular base hit. But he just can't come clean on no subjec'."

Cap had the whole story, and I and Carey was as pop'lar with him as an umpire.

"What do you want me to do, Cap?" Carey'd say to him before goin' up to hit.

"Use your own judgment," Cap'd tell him. "We want to lose another game."

But finally, one night in Pittsburgh, Cap had a letter from his missus and he come to us with it.

"You fellas," he says, "is the ones that put us on the bum, and if you're sorry I think they's a chancet for you to make good. The old lady's out to St. Joe and she's been tryin' her hardest to fix things up. She's explained that Ike don't mean nothin' with his talk; I've wrote and explained that to Dolly, too. But the old lady says that Dolly says that she can't believe it. But Dolly's still stuck on this baby, and she's pinin' away just the same as Ike. And the old lady says she thinks if you two fellas would write to the girl and explain how you was always kiddin' with Ike and leadin' him on, and how the ball club was all shot to pieces since Ike quit hittin', and how he acted like he was goin' to kill himself, and this and that, she'd fall for it and maybe soften down. Dolly, the old lady says, would believe you before she'd believe I and the old lady, because she thinks it's her we're sorry for, and not him."

Well, I and Carey was only too glad to try and see what we could do. But it wasn't no snap. We wrote about eight letters before we got one that looked good. Then we give it to the stenographer and had it wrote out on a typewriter and both of us signed it.

It was Carey's idear that made the letter good. He stuck in somethin' about the world's serious money that our wives wasn't goin' to spend unless she took pity on a "boy who was so shy and modest that he was afraid to come right out and say that he had asked such a beautiful and handsome girl to become his bride."

That's prob'ly what got her, or maybe she couldn't of held out much longer anyway. It was four days after we sent the letter that Cap heard from his missus again. We was in Cincinnati.

"We've won," he says to us. "The old lady says that Dolly says she'll give him another chance. But the old lady says it won't do no good for Ike to write a letter. He'll have to go out there."

"Send him tonight," says Carey.

"I'll pay half his fare," I says.

"I'll pay the other half," says Carey.

"No," says Cap, "the club'll pay his expenses. I'll send him scoutin'."

"Are you goin' to send him tonight?"

"Sure," says Cap. "But I'm goin' to break the news to him right now. It's time we win a ball game."

So in the clubhouse, just before the game, Cap told him. And I certainly felt sorry for Rube Benton and Red Ames that afternoon! I and Carey was standin' in front o' the hotel that night when Ike come out with his suitcase.

"Sent home?" I says to him.

"No," he says, "I'm goin' scoutin'."

"Where to?" I says. "Fort Wayne?"

"No, not exactly," he says.

"Well," says Carey, "have a good time."

"I ain't lookin' for no good time," says Ike. "I says I was goin' scoutin'."

"Well, then," says Carey, "I hope you see somebody you like."

"And you better have a drink before you go," I says.

"Well," says Ike, "they claim it helps a cold."

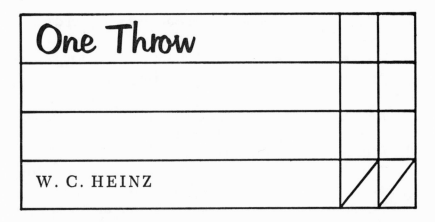

One Throw

W. C. HEINZ

I checked into a hotel called the Olympia, which is right on the main street and the only hotel in the town. After lunch I was hanging around the lobby, and I got to talking to the guy at the desk. I asked him if this wasn't the town where that kid named Maneri played ball.

"That's right," the guy said. "He's a pretty good ballplayer."

"He should be," I said. "I read that he was the new Phil Rizzuto."

"That's what they said," the guy said.

"What's the matter with him?" I said. "I mean if he's such a good ballplayer what's he doing in this league?"

"I don't know," the guy said. "I guess the Yankees know what they're doing."

"What kind of a kid is he?"

"He's a nice kid," the guy said. "He plays good ball, but I feel sorry for him. He thought he'd be playing for the Yankees soon, and here he is in this town. You can see it's got him down."

"He lives here in this hotel?"

"That's right," the guy said. "Most of the older ballplayers stay in rooming houses, but Pete and a couple other kids live here."

He was leaning on the desk, talking to me and looking across the hotel lobby. He nodded his head. "This is a funny thing," he said. "Here he comes now."

The kid had come through the door from the street. He had on a light gray sport shirt and a pair of gray flannel slacks.

I could see why, when he showed up with the Yankees in spring training, he made them all think of Rizzuto. He isn't any bigger than Rizzuto, and he looks just like him.

"Hello, Nick," he said to the guy at the desk.

"Hello, Pete," the guy at the desk said. "How goes it today?"

"All right," the kid said but you could see he was exaggerating.

"I'm sorry, Pete," the guy at the desk said, "but no mail today."

"That's all right, Nick," the kid said. "I'm used to it."

"Excuse me," I said, "but you're Pete Maneri?"

"That's right," the kid said, turning and looking at me.

"Excuse me," the guy at the desk said, introducing us. "Pete, this is Mr. Franklin."

"Harry Franklin," I said.

"I'm glad to know you," the kid said, shaking my hand.

"I recognize you from your pictures," I said.

"Pete's a good ballplayer," the guy at the desk said.

"Not very," the kid said.

"Don't take his word for it, Mr. Franklin," the guy said.

"I'm a great ball fan," I said to the kid. "Do you people play tonight?"

"We play two games," the kid said.

"The first game's at six o'clock," the guy at the desk said. "They play pretty good ball."

"I'll be there," I said. "I used to play a little ball myself."

"You did?" the kid said.

"With Columbus," I said. "That's twenty years ago."

"Is that right?" the kid said. . . .

That's the way I got to talking with the kid. They had one of those pine-paneled taprooms in the basement of the hotel, and we went down there. I had a couple and the kid had a Coke, and I told him a few stories and he turned out to be a real good listener.

"But what do you do now, Mr. Franklin?" he said after a while.

"I sell hardware," I said. "I can think of some things I'd like better, but I was going to ask you how you like playing in this league."

"Well," the kid said, "I suppose it's all right. I guess I've got no kick coming."

"Oh, I don't know," I said. "I understand you're too good for this league. What are they trying to do to you?"

"I don't know," the kid said. "I can't understand it."

"What's the trouble?"

"Well," the kid said, " I don't get along very well here. I mean there's nothing wrong with my playing. I'm hitting .365 right now. I lead the league in stolen bases. There's nobody can field with me, but who cares?"

"Who manages this ball club?"

"Al Dall," the kid said. "You remember, he played in the outfield for the Yankees for about four years."

"I remember."

"Maybe he is all right," the kid said, "but I don't get along with him. He's on my neck all the time."

"Well," I said, "that's the way they are in the minors sometimes. You have to remember the guy is looking out for himself and his ball club first. He's not worried about you."

"I know that," the kid said. "If I get the big hit or make the play he never says anything. The other night I tried to take second on a loose ball and I got caught in the run-down. He bawls me out in front of everybody. There's nothing I can do."

"Oh, I don't know," I said. "This is probably a guy who knows he's got a good thing in you, and he's looking to keep you around. You people lead the league, and that makes him look good. He doesn't want to lose you to Kansas City or the Yankees."

"That's what I mean," the kid said. "When the Yankees

sent me down here they said, 'Don't worry. We'll keep an eye on you.' So Dall never sends a good report on me. Nobody ever comes down to look me over. What chance is there for a guy like Eddie Brown or somebody like that coming down to see me in this town?"

"You have to remember that Eddie Brown's the big shot," I said, "the great Yankee scout."

"Sure," the kid said. "I never even saw him, and I'll never see him in this place. I have an idea that if they ever ask Dall about me he keeps knocking me down."

"Why don't you go after Dall?" I said. "I had trouble like that once myself, but I figured out a way to get attention."

"You did?" the kid said.

"I threw a couple of balls over the first baseman's head," I said. "I threw a couple of games away, and that really got the manager sore. I was lousing up his ball club and his record. So what does he do? He blows the whistle on me, and what happens? That gets the brass curious, and they send down to see what's wrong."

"Is that so?" the kid said. "What happened?"

"Two weeks later," I said, "I was up with Columbus."

"Is that right?" the kid said.

"Sure," I said, egging him on. "What have you got to lose?"

"Nothing," the kid said. "I haven't got anything to lose."

"I'd try it," I said.

"I might try it," the kid said. "I might try it tonight if the spot comes up."

I could see from the way he said it that he was madder than he'd said. Maybe you think this is mean to steam a kid up like this, but I do some strange things.

"Take over," I said. "Don't let this guy ruin your career."

"I'll try it," the kid said. "Are you coming out to the park tonight?"

"I wouldn't miss it," I said. "This will be better than making out route sheets and sales orders."

It's not much ball park in this town—old wooden bleachers and an old wooden fence and about four hundred people in the stands. The first game wasn't much either, with the home club winning something like 8 to 1.

The kid didn't have any hard chances, but I could see he was a ballplayer, with a double and a couple of walks and a lot of speed.

The second game was different, though. The other club got a couple of runs and then the home club picked up three runs in one, and they were in the top of the ninth with a 3–2 lead and two outs when the pitching began to fall apart and they loaded the bases.

I was trying to wish the ball down to the kid, just to see what he'd do with it, when the batter drives one on one big bounce to the kid's right.

The kid was off for it when the ball started. He made a backhand stab and grabbed it. He was deep now, and he turned in the air and fired. If it goes over the first baseman's head, it's two runs in and a panic—but it's the prettiest throw you'd want to see. It's right on a line, and the runner is out by a step, and it's the ball game.

I walked back to the hotel, thinking about the kid. I sat around the lobby until I saw him come in, and then I walked toward the elevator like I was going to my room, but so I'd meet him. And I could see he didn't want to talk.

"How about a Coke?" I said.

"No," he said. "Thanks, but I'm going to bed."

"Look," I said. "Forget it. You did the right thing. Have a Coke."

We were sitting in the taproom again. The kid wasn't saying anything.

"Why didn't you throw that ball away?" I said.

"I don't know," the kid said. "I had it in my mind before he hit it, but I couldn't."

"Why?"

"I don't know why."

"I know why," I said.

The kid didn't say anything. He just sat looking down.

"Do you know why you couldn't throw that ball away?" I said.

"No," the kid said.

"You couldn't throw that ball away," I said, "because you're going to be a major-league ballplayer someday."

The kid just looked at me. He had that same sore expression.

"Do you know why you're going to be a major-league ballplayer?" I said.

The kid was just looking down again, shaking his head. I never got more of a kick out of anything in my life.

"You're going to be a major-league ballplayer," I said, "because you couldn't throw that ball away, and because I'm not a hardware salesman and my name's not Harry Franklin."

"What do you mean?" the kid said.

"I mean," I explained to him, "that I tried to needle you into throwing that ball away because I'm Eddie Brown."

Bang the Drum Slowly

MARK HARRIS

Bruce Pearson of the New York Mammoths opens
the season with the knowledge he is suffering from
an incurable disease. Though only a fringe player—
he is the Mammoth's third-string catcher—Pearson's
admirable conduct, in the face of death, has a uni-
fying and inspiring effect on his teammates, who go
on to win the pennant. The story is told by Bruce's
best friend, pitcher Henry "Author" Wiggen. From
the novel *Bang the Drum Slowly*.

In the morning he did not feel too good, Monday, Labor Day.
"I will call Doc," I said.

"No," he said.

"Does it feel like the attack?" I said.

"Yes and no," he said. "I feel dipsy. Maybe I will feel better
opening the window," and he went and opened it and sat by
it and breathed it in and went and put a chew of Days O Work
in his mouth and went back and spit down a couple times.

"Maybe it will rain," I said.

"Not soon," he said. "Maybe by night," leaning out and
looking both ways and up. He knew if it would rain or not,
which I myself do not know without looking at the paper and
even then do not know because I forget to look. In the end I
never know if it will rain until it begins. But he knew by the
way the clouds blew, and he said he felt better now, and he
shut the window and called Katie, saying he felt dipsy today,
and he said in the phone, "No, I do not think he did" and

clapped his hand over the phone and begun to say something to me, and I said, "No. Tell her no. Tell her I forgot," and she eat him out, and he said, "But Katie," and then again, "But, Katie, but," until she hung up, and I did not look, and he went on talking, like he was still talking to her, and finally he said, still bluffing, "Well, OK, Katie, and I love you, too" and hung up, all smiles, and we went out to the park and he still did not feel too good, and he told Dutch, and Dutch said, "Well, we can not do without you, but we will try. Will we not try, boys, and make the best of a bad blow?" and the boys all said "Yes siree bob" and "You said it, boss" and "Sure enough" and all, and they hustled out, and me and Bruce laid on the table and listened with Mick.

There was plenty of scrap left in Washington yet. They did not know they were beat. You probably could of even found a little Washington money in town if you looked hard enough, not much, but some, for the town did not know what the Mammoths knew, not knowing the truth, not knowing Washington was beat on August 26, which I personally knew laying in bed and listening to the boys, and knew for sure when Goose shot the light out, knowing what it done to a fellow when he knew, how it made them cut out the horseshit and stick to the job. Washington hustled, jumping Van Gundy for a run in the second and another in the fourth, and we laid there, not moving, only listening, Mick folding towels but not hurrying like he hurries when he is nervous, only sitting there folding one after the other and setting it on the pile and creasing it out and reaching over slowly for the next, the 3 of us as calm as we could be like we were looking at the front end of a movie we already seen the back end of, and you knew who done it, who killed who, and we thought, "Washington, you are dead and do not know it."

George opened our fifth with a single, and they played Perry for the bunt, which he crossed them up and slammed through first and into the opposite field, and it was Pasquale that bunted instead and caught all Washington flat-footed, George scoring and Perry going clear to third and Pasquale winding up at second, for George dumped Eric Bushell in the play at the plate, and they passed Sid to get at Canada, and then they passed *Canada,* not meaning to, and Bruce said he felt better now, and we went down and warmed.

We warmed close to the wall. I remember every now and then he stuck out his hand and leaned against it, and I said, "Still feeling dipsy?" and he said, "No, only a little," and he crouched down again, first sitting on his heels and then flatting out his feet behind him and resting on his knees and looking back over his shoulder to see where Dutch was looking, for Dutch will fine a catcher for catching on his knees. "Maybe it will rain," I said, and he looked up and said "I hope so."

"I am warm," I said, though I was not, and we sat on the bench in the bullpen.

"It is a big crowd," he said. "It is Labor Day, that is what it is," and he took out a chew and broke it in half and give me half a chunk, saying, "Chew a chew, Arthur," which he always asked me and I always turned down except I took it then and chewed it and did not like it much, having no use for tobacco nor liquor, and every time I spit it dribbled down my chin. "Keep your teeth tight shut when you spit," he said.

It run long, for we begun hitting quite a bit, and he said, "You must be getting cold by now," and I said no. "It is getting cold," he said, and he reached around behind him for his jacket except it was not there, and I jiggled the phone, saying, "Send up a jacket for Bruce," and 3 boys sprung up off the bench and raced down the line, Wash and Piney and Herb Macy, and the crowd all begun yelling and pointing, never seeing such a thing before as 3 men all racing for the bullpen like that, and Krazy Kress sent down a note saying, "Author, what the hell??????" and I looked up at the press-box and give Krazy flat palms, same as saying, "What the hell what?"

We started fast in the second game. It was raining a little. Sid hit a home run in the first with Pasquale aboard, Number 42, the first home run he hit since August 17, according to the paper, and Bruce shook his hand at the plate, and Sid stopped and told Bruce, "Wipe off your bat," and Bruce looked at his bat and at Sid, not understanding, not feeling the rain, and Sid took the bat and wiped it off, and Bruce whistled a single in left, the last base hit he ever hit, and made his turn and went back and stood with one foot on the bag and said something to Clint, and Clint yelled for Dutch, and Dutch went out, and they talked. I do not know what about. Dutch only said to me, "Pick up your sign off the bench," and he sent for Doc, and Doc sat in the alley behind the dugout and waited, and the boys sometimes strolled back and sat beside him, asking him questions, "What does he have?" and such as that. They smoked back there, which Dutch does not like you to, saying, "Smoking ain't learning. Sitting on the bench and watching is learning," but he said nothing that day. You knew he wouldn't.

Washington begun stalling like mad in the third, hoping for heavy rain before it become official, claiming it was raining, though the umps ruled it was not. Sy Sibley was umping behind the plate. They stepped out between pitches and wiped off their bat and tied their shoe and blew their nose and gouged around in their eye, saying, "Something is in my eye," and Sy said, "Sure, your eyeball," and they stepped back in. As soon as they stepped back in again I pitched.

He never knew what was coming, curve ball or what. "Just keep your meat hand out of the way," I said, and he said he would but did not. It did not register. He was catching by habit and memory, only knowing that when the pitcher threw it you were supposed to stop it and throw it back, and if a fellow hit a foul ball you were supposed to whip off your mask and collar it, and if a man was on base you were supposed to keep him from going on to the next one. You play ball all your life until a day comes when you do not know what you are doing, but you do it anyhow, working through a fog, not remembering anything but only knowing who people were by how they moved, this fellow the hitter, this the pitcher, and if you hit the ball you run to the right, and then when you got there you asked Clint Strap were you safe or out because you do not know yourself. There was a fog settling down over him.

I do not know how he got through it. I do not even know how yours truly got through it. I do not remember much. It was 3–0 after 4½, official now, and now we begun stalling, claiming it was raining, claiming the ball was wet and we were libel to be beaned, which Washington said would make no difference to fellows with heads as hard as us. Eric Bushell said it to me in the fifth when I complained the ball was wet, and I stepped out and started laughing, "Ha ha ha ho ho ho ha ha ha," doubling over and laughing, and Sy Sibley said, "Quit stalling," and I said I could not help it if Bushell was going to say such humorous things to me and make me laugh. "Tell him to stop," I said. "Ha ha ha ho ho ho ha ha ha."

"What did he say?" said Sy, and I told him, telling him very slow, telling him who Eric Bushell was and who I was, the crowd thinking it was an argument and booing Sy. "Forget it," said he. "Get back in and hit."

"You mean bat," said Bushell. "He never hits," and I begun laughing again, stepping out and saying how could a man bat with this fellow behind me that if the TV people knew how funny he was they would make him an offer.

"Hit!" said Sy. "Bat! Do not stall."

"Who is stalling?" said I, and I stepped back in, the rain coming a little heavier now.

I threw one pitch in the top of the seventh, a ball, wide, to Billy Linenthal. I guess I remember. Bruce took it backhand and stood up and slowly raised his hand and took the ball out of his mitt and started to toss it back, aiming very carefully at my chin, like Red told him to, and then everybody begun running, for the rain come in for sure now, and he seen everybody running, but he did not run, only stood there. I started off towards the dugout, maybe as far as the baseline, thinking he was following, and then I seen that he was not. I seen him standing looking for somebody to throw to, the last pitch he ever caught, and I went back for him, and Mike and Red were there when I got there, and Mike said, "It is over, son," and he said "Sure" and trotted on in.

In the hospital me and Mike and Red waited in the waiting room for word, telling them 1,000 times, "Keep us posted," which they never done and you had to run down the hall and ask, and then when you asked they never *knew* anything, and for all you could tell they were never *doing* anything neither, only looking at his chart, standing outside his door and looking at his chart and maybe whistling or kidding the nurses until I really got quite annoyed.

He was unconscious. Around midnight he woke up, and they said one of us could see him, the calmest, and I went, and he only said "Howdy," but very weak, not saying it, really, only his lips moving. He looked at me a long time and worked up his strength and said again, "Howdy, Arthur," and the doctor said, "He does not know you," and I said he did, for he always called me "Arthur." Then he drifted off again.

They told me take his clothes away, and I took them, his uniform and cap and socks and shoes, and I rolled them up with his belt around them and carried them back out. Red and Mike went pale when they seen me. They went pale every little while all night, every time a phone rung or a doctor passed through. "Relax," said I. "He is not dying."

"You never seen anybody die," said Red.

"I seen them in the movies," I said.

"It ain't the same," he said.

"He will not die," said Mike. "He will only pass on."

We went out and got something to eat. It was still raining, and we walked a long ways before we found a place open. It was very quiet in the streets. We ate in one of these smoky little places, everything fried. The paper said MAMMOTHS COP 2, GOLDMAN SWATS 42ND, and there was a picture of Sid crossing the plate and Bruce shaking his hand. "Then he hit," I said.

"And then he did not know what happened without going back and asking Clint," said Red.

"It is sad," said Mike. "It makes you wish to cry."

"It is sad," said Red. "It makes you wish to laugh."

We went back in the waiting room and stretched on the couches and slept. While we were asleep somebody threw a blanket over me, and over Red and Mike as well. I don't know who. When we woke up the sun was shining, and I went down the hall and asked, and they looked at his chart and said he was fine, and I heard him singing then, singing, "As I was a-walking the streets of Laredo, as I walked out in Laredo one day, I spied a young cowboy all wrapped in white linen, all wrapped in white linen and cold as the clay," and I run back for Red and Mike, and they heard me come running and went all pale again, and I said, "Come with me," and we went back down the hall again. You could hear him even further down now, for he sung louder, "It was once in the saddle I used to go dashing, once in

the saddle I used to go gay, first down to Rosie's and then to
the card house, shot in the breast and am dying today." We
stood and listened and then run in, and he stopped singing
and tried sitting up, but he was too weak, and we said, "Get on
up out of there now and back to work," and "This sure is a lazy
man's way of drawing pay for no work," and he said, "Did anybody bring my chews?"

"I will go get them," said Mike, and he went back to the
hotel and brung them, and clothes as well, saying, "I hope I
brung the right combination," and Bruce said "Yes." He never
cares about the combination anyhow, only grabs the nearest.
If I did not shuffle his suits around he would wear the same one
every day.

We hung in the hospital. Dutch called from St. Louis
around supper, glad to hear that all was well again, and he told
Red why not come out now, as long as the worst was over.
"Business before pleasure," said Red, and he went.

He was so weak he even got tired chewing, shoving it over
in his cheek and leaving it there, and his hands shook. He could
not hold the newspaper nor his knife and fork but would eat a
little and lay back again, saying, "No doubt I will pep up and
be back in action again in no time," and we said he would, me
and Mike and the doctors and nurses as well, though we knew
he would not. Maybe I never seen a man die and wouldn't know
if I did, but I knew when a man was not libel to be back in
action very soon.

I picked up the club in Pittsburgh on Friday, and I pitched
on Saturday and won, Number 22, which give us a sweep of
the 2 in Pittsburgh, 6 wins in 7 starts, according to the paper,
9 in the last 11, and 14 in the last 17, counting back to August
26, Goose's birthday, the night the boys all knew the truth. The
cushion was 6½, and it was now only a matter of time. We
needed 3 to clinch.

Him and his father and Mike were in the clubhouse when
we hit Chicago, and the boys all went wild to see him, not
phoney wild, neither, but the real thing, admiring him, and he
stood up and said, "Howdy, boys," and they pumped his hand
and told him how they missed him, and he got dressed, and he
was white and thin, and he was cold, always cold, and he sat

on the bench all wrapped in jackets, getting up off the bench every so often and going back and laying down awhile, and then coming back out.

We whipped Chicago twice. Nothing in the world could stop us now. Winning makes winning like money makes money, and we had power and pitching and speed, so much of it that if anybody done anything wrong nobody ever noticed. There was too much we were doing right. It was a club, like it should of been all year but never was but all of a sudden become, and we clinched it the first night in Cleveland, Blondie Biggs working, and we voted the shares, 30 full shares and a lot of tiny ones, $1,500 to Mike and the same to Red, and $1,250 to Piney for playing the guitar, and $1,000 to Diego Roberto for talking Spanish to George, and little slices to batboys, big hands and big hearts like you have when you win, not stopping rolling then but rolling still and winning though we did not need to win but could of relaxed and played out the string, yet hating to relax either because we were playing ball at last like it was meant to be played.

He went with us all the way. He dressed every day, and then he sat, no stronger than ever, thin and white and his cheeks all hollow, but his spirit high. Sometimes he picked up a bat and swung it a couple times and sat down again.

The Series opened in New York on a Wednesday, and I pitched and won, and Van Gundy Thursday, and after the Thursday game Bruce went home. "It is practically copped," he said. "I see no sense in trucking all the way out there and back."

"No," said the boys. "Come along for the ride."

"No," he said, "I will see you in the spring. I will be back in shape by spring," and we said he would, saying, "See you in the spring, Bruce. See you in Aqua Clara."

"See you," said he, and I went with him and his father and put them on the plane. He could barely carry his bags. "Arthur," he said, "send me the scorecard from Detroit," and I said I would.

But then I never sent it. We wrapped the Series up on Sunday, my win again, and I took a scorecard home with me and tossed it on the shelf and left it lay. Goddam it, anyhow, I am just like the rest. Wouldn't it been simple instead of writing a page on my book to shoved it in the mail? How long would it of took? Could I not afford the stamps?

Tuesday I got this letter from Arcturus saying Katie was up there raising holy hell and I better do some sensational explaining. I did not know what in hell to do now. I clipped it in the lampshade, and every night I looked at it. After about 3 nights I seen they took the letter "s" out of Perkinsville and tacked it on the end of Wiggen—

MR. HENRY W. WIGGENS
PERKINVILLE, NEW YORK

I figured one way to start off was bawl the daylight out of them for not spelling, and I hardly got warm when the phone rung. It was his father, and he was dead. That was October 7.

In my Arcturus Calendar for October 7 it says, "De Soto visited Georgia, 1540." This hands me a laugh. Bruce Pearson also visited Georgia. I was his pall-bear, me and 2 fellows from the crate and box plant and some town boys, and that was all. There were flowers from the club, but no *person* from the club. They could of sent somebody.

He was not a bad fellow, no worse than most and probably better than some, and not a bad ballplayer neither when they give him a chance, when they laid off him long enough. From here on in I rag nobody.

Rhubarb

H. ALLEN SMITH

April in New York. Weather. Scenery. The first cat-owned big-league baseball team in recorded history was ready to open its season.

Clarissa Wood insisted that she supervise preparation of the owner's field box, situated immediately behind the home team's dugout at Banner Field. She wanted a cat-sized throne done in platinum and black velvet set up in the middle of the box. She wanted to order a cedar tree from Mount Lebanon in Syria and have a scratching post made from it and placed in a conspicuous position. She contended that Rhubarb's jewel-encrusted sanitary tray should be placed in a small enclosure at the back of the box, out of sight of the populace.

One by one her ideas were knocked down.

Len Sickles had a good deal to say about the arrangements. He told Eric that whenever the new owner of the Loons was present at Banner Field for a baseball game, he, the owner, would have to be within easy reach of the Loon players. That, said Len, was a primary consideration.

"These goons of mine," the manager explained, "are playing ball like they were the nine Apostles. They are inspired. They believe that this cat brings them luck. And they insist that Rhubarb's gotta be somewhere close to the dugout, so they can run up and touch him."

Whereupon Eric invented a gadget. Rhubarb's pedestal was built into the structure of the box and against the back wall of the dugout. A small hole was cut into the wall, communicating between dugout and owner's box, a hole just big enough to accommodate a man's hand. Of necessity the hole was down near the floor of the owner's box, and Rhubarb, if placed beside it, where the players could reach through and touch him, would have been out of sight all the time. The gadget solved the problem. It was a cat elevator. Normally Rhubarb's pedestal extended above the roof of the dugout, giving the cat a clear view of the playing field and giving the fans a clear view of the cat. If an emergency arose, a tight spot, a clutch, a situation in which a player felt the need of touching Rhubarb, he turned a crank and the pedestal would sink, with Rhubarb on it. The player who wanted to touch Rhubarb for luck poked his hand through the aperture to do the touching, then withdrew it and cranked the pedestal back into its normal position. This arrangement obviated use of the silver cage, a situation that gave Eric some worry. He decided that some physical restraint would have to be put on the cat, so a strong fishline was hooked to a heavy staple in the wall of the box with a snap fastener at the other end of Rhubarb's collar.

As for the sanitary tray, Eric vetoed Miss Wood's scheme for hiding it away out of sight.

"Rhubarb owns this ball club," he told her. "That means he owns this ball park—every inch of it. If he wants to go he can walk right out to home plate, or the pitcher's mound, and go. The fans will love it."

Miss Wood was incensed over the very thought of such a thing. "In the first place," she said, "someone would have to go with him and have him on his leash. I assure you, Mr. Yaeger, from the bottom of my heart, that a cat will not do such a thing while on a leash. Furthermore, who is going to take him out there in front of all those rowdy people?"

"I wouldn't mind doing it myself," Eric assured her. "I have my hammy moments."

"You are being most unreasonable," she said. "The very idea of that sweet kitty-cat having to do his business in front of the public horrifies me. What if he does own the park? Mr. Rockefeller owns Rockefeller Center, but *he* doesn't go on the skating rink."

"He would draw a good crowd if he did," said Eric. "He would get more skaters."

St. Louis was to oppose the Loons on opening day, and Eric led Rhubarb's entourage to Banner Field two hours before game time. Doom carried the cat and was flanked by Willy Bodfish and Clarissa Wood. Willy was unhappy, having had to cancel a date at his dentist's. Polly Pinckley accompanied Eric, clutching Ration Book Number Three in her hand. She insisted on carrying it wherever she went in the belief that she would shame Eric into abolishing the Office of Guava Jelly Administration.

The party went first to the executive quarters, and Rhubarb was introduced for the first time to his own private office. He seemed bored by it. Then Eric led the way to the Second Guess Club, a large room where the sports writers gathered before and after games. For this momentous occasion the sports writers were reinforced by a horde of feature writers, all of whom were clamoring for the right to sit in the owner's box. Some of these feature writers tried to pull an old dodge on Eric.

"My city editor," one young woman said to him, "assigned me to sit in the box with Rhubarb. I've simply *got* to do it. If I don't I lose my job. My city editor said so. And I've simply got to keep my job, Mr. Yaeger. I'm the sole support of my old mother who's dying of heartburn, and——"

"Nuts, sister!" Eric brushed her off. "I used to work on newspapers myself."

A sports columnist came forward escorting the Mayor. His Honor had been preparing for the ceremonial job of throwing

out the first ball. He had been preparing for it at the bar, and
it showed on him.

"Let me see the beautiful pussy!" boomed the Mayor.

"Shhh!" said Polly.

"I feel deeply honored," the Mayor plowed on. "I might
even say I feel deeply honored. Indeed I do. Deeply. Rhubarb,
my boy, I salute thee! You have become the *second* citizen of
our great metropolis. I salute the second citizen! Hello, pussy!
You ole pussy, you! I'm your Mayor! Yes sir! Lord Mayor of Dick
Whittington! That's me! And I got a piece of advice for you, cat.
I quote what that little jerk used to squeak: 'Patience and
formaldehyde!' Where's the goddamn ball!"

"Your Honor," said Eric, "why don't you step over to the
bar and have yourself a pleasant toddy? It's on Rhubarb. He
owns all this, you know, including the toddies. Have a couple
of snifters on a cat. It'll strengthen your throwing arm, improve
your aim."

"Will it?" bayed the Mayor. "Adoo, adoo, kind friends, adoo!
Off weedershine! Hoista mananna!"

The Mayor headed for the bar.

"It looks to me," murmured Polly, "as if His Honor is going
to throw *up* the first ball."

A press photographer called Eric to one side.

"Listen, Mr. Yaeger, I got a marvelous idea. I want to get
something unusual in the way of a picture."

"Good God, man!"

"I mean unusualer than the others. Now, I studied up this
idea. Instead of having the Mayor throw out a baseball, why
don't we let him throw out a meat ball? Leave the cat go after
it. You could have him throw it out towards first base, and I'll
be waiting out there and I'll get an unusual shot."

"Son, you have a fair sort of idea there, but didn't you just
see His Honor? He'd have meat smeared all over Section 18."

The photographer was disappointed and went away grumbling and placed Eric in a prominent position on his son-of-a-
bitch list, meaning that someday he'd try to snap a picture of
Eric while Eric was picking his nose.

It was time to get down to the field. The stands were
already packed as Eric came up through the Loons' dugout

with Rhubarb in his arms. A roar of welcome greeted them. Eric walked across the grass toward the St. Louis dugout, stopping near home plate to hold the cat above his head, so all could see. The roar redoubled in volume.

At the visitors' dugout Eric came up against an unpleasant situation which he should have anticipated. St. Louis was the traditional enemy of the Loons, and Eric quickly recognized a strong undercurrent of animosity toward the cat. Several of the players, presumably the more superstitious members of the St. Louis team, ducked into their dugout and disappeared. Eric heard one man growl, "Git the goddamn Joner outa here!"

Dick Madison, the St. Louis manager, furnished the tip-off on what to expect. The St. Louis gang was going to use ridicule as its chief weapon against Rhubarb. Madison minced up to Eric, took off his cap, and executed a low sweeping bow. Then he stepped back into the dugout and returned with a mousetrap. It was probably the biggest mousetrap ever manufactured—being about four feet long and two feet wide. It was already set and baited with a wedge of yellow cheese that probably cost around a dollar eighty-five. Madison clowned his way out toward home plate and daintily set the trap down on the grass. Then he stood up and gestured with his right arm, indicating that Rhubarb was to help himself to the cheese, a present from his host of St. Louis admirers. The crowd roared with laughter.

Meanwhile the St. Louis players had quietly gathered at the dugout entrance. Now they formed a conga line and started to dance. Each man was carrying a long cattail, and the fans were highly amused at the line of capering players curved and circled around the field. Eric wasn't greatly amused.

"Cute," he said acidly to Dick Madison. "Very very cute!"

"Ah, shuddup!" said Madison. "Go scratch yourself a hole in the ground, you cat nurse, and crawl in it and cover yourself up!"

Eric felt like popping him one, but he had his arms full of cat. He chose the course of discretion and hurried back across the grass to the Loons' dugout. Here he encountered an explosive situation. Len Sickles was having difficulty keeping the Loons in hand. They wanted to open proceedings by swarming onto the field and beating the brains out of their opponents for making fun of their owner.

They gathered excitedly around Eric, and some of them talked reassuring baby talk to Rhubarb.

"Yes, Rhubarb!" crooned Benny Seymour, the coach. "You sweet liddle Rhubarb you! You sweet thing! Pay no attention to them filthy bastards, honey! We'll fix 'em for you! Yes sir, we will!"

Others expressed similar sentiments. Eric was somehow pleased with it all. The boys were one hundred per cent back of Rhubarb.

The others were already in the owner's box, and Eric took Rhubarb to his pedestal. The cat was behaving like a gentleman. He sat on the pedestal for a while, looking around at all the color and activity and noise, and then he hopped over into Eric's lap and went to sleep.

Eric had to wake him up when the time came for the game to start. The line-ups were being announced over the loud-speaker system. The announcer called attention to the presence of the new owner of the Loons. Eric put the cat back on the pedestal, and Rhubarb stretched himself and yawned for the edification of the crowd.

Across the way two men held the Mayor up, pointed him in the direction of the field, and told him to throw. He threw, and the ball went into Section 5 behind the Mayor and hit a woman in the eye. Almost everyone in the park was watching Rhubarb, so the Mayor's inadequate performance attracted little attention and he was given no opportunity to repeat it.

Rhubarb now appeared to take an interest in the proceedings. He sat up and watched the Loons take the field. Goff was pitching, and the St. Louis center fielder, Peterson, was the first man to face him. Peterson connected with the first ball thrown to him.

A split second after the bat cracked against the ball something cracked in the owner's box. Rhubarb shot forward, the fishline snapped, and the yellow cat streaked into right field.

It was the fastest Eric had ever seen Rhubarb move. The ball went to the right of the first baseman, and Rhubarb was on it before the right fielder could reach it. The fielder ran up, then

stopped in bewilderment. Rhubarb was trying to seize the baseball in his teeth, and the fielder's perplexity was so great that
he could do nothing but stand there helplessly. Meanwhile
Peterson was quickly circling the bases.

Then a new element of confusion entered the picture. Someone in the St. Louis dugout played the visitors' trump card. They
turned loose a bulldog. At the same moment someone in the
right-field bleachers tossed a terrier over the fence.

Both dogs went for Rhubarb full tilt.

The stands, the dugouts, the players on the field, the game
officials—everyone was in an uproar.

Rhubarb looked up from the ball and saw the bulldog
coming at him. He feinted, pretending that he was about to flee
in the direction of his box.

The bulldog was lost. He swerved, and as he swerved
Rhubarb hit him, clawing and biting. The dog let forth a scream
of anguish just as the terrier arrived on the scene. That shriek
did something to the terrier. He put on the brakes, skidded to
an amazed halt, took another quick look just to make sure, then
wheeled around and started for what he hoped would be some
secluded spot fifty miles away. But Rhubarb was after him like
a bullet, leaving the bulldog lying on the field, yelping and
bleeding. Now came the terrier's turn. The cat ripped and
whipsawed him up one side and down the other.

People were beginning to pour onto the field, and the din
was deafening, yet above it all sounded a howl of pain that came
from no dog. The High Commissioner had jumped over the wall
of his box; he had taken about five quick steps with his eyes
fixed on the distant ruckus. He had stepped squarely into the
big mousetrap, and the thing had almost torn his leg off.

Willy Bodfish was the first occupant of the owner's box
to reach the scene of combat, and he succeeded in prying Rhubarb loose from the terrier. The fallen dogs were removed from
the arena, and back in the box Eric got Rhubarb into his cage
while police were herding the more excited fans off the field.
There was an immediate and acrimonious conference in front
of the Loons' dugout involving the umpires, the High Commissioner (free of the trap but sorely wounded), officials of the
league, managers of both teams, and most of the players.

Dick Madison was hot with fury—so enraged that he simply jumped up and down on the ground.

"That's my kid's dog!" he screamed in anger. "That cat's killed him! Leave me at him!"

They finally had to seize and restrain Madison. Len Sickles, too, had his dander up and was howling that he was going to punch Dick Madison's head off.

"I saw it!" yelled Sickles. "Everybody saw it! You turned that dog loose outa your own dugout!"

There was a prolonged and angry consideration of ground rules. The High Commissioner stood by, glaring at Dick Madison, for he had seen where that damned trap came from. The umpires, after a whispered conference with the High Commissioner, announced that Peterson was not entitled to a home run. He was not entitled to anything. Madison went into a new tantrum bordering on epilepsy over this fresh manifestation of man's inhumanity to man. His players milled around with fists clenched, eager to start a fight. Madison wanted to take his team and leave, go back to St. Louis, and never again have any relations with the Loons.

The argument over Peterson's status—whether or not he was entitled to at least a hit—went on for fifteen minutes.

"It was an act of God," said the High Commissioner.

"Then, by God, we get a home run out of it!" bellowed Madison.

"You'll get a bust in the nose out of it," yelled the High Commissioner. "What the hell do you mean by leaving that trap out there for me to fall into? Look what it did! Ripped my pants leg clear off! I oughta kill you and then bar you from baseball for the rest of your lousy life! Peterson gets no hit. I rule that Peterson must return to the plate and we start all over again. And"—he gave Eric an ominous glance—"if that cat gets onto the field again, I'll outlaw you and the cat and your whole damn team so you won't even be able to get into the Piedmont League!"

"That cat won't get onto the field again," said a stranger, stepping forward. "I seize this cat in the name of the law."

The stranger looked around for a cat to seize in the name

of the law, but Rhubarb was some thirty feet away in his cage.

"Now what?" said Eric.

"Hand over the cat," said the stranger. He pulled back his coat and exhibited a shield. "I happen to be the sheriff of this county. Judge Loudermilk of Surrogate Court commands the appearance of one Rhubarb Banner forthwith, for examination before trial, in the case of Tatlock versus Banner."

"You're crazy!" cried Eric. "You can't examine a cat before trial! What'll you examine him for, fleas?"

"All I know is I got my orders," said the sheriff. "The cat goes, and he goes right now."

"Furthermore," Eric argued, "this doesn't look legally proper to me. Maybe you've got a subpoena. But you can't come out here and seize Rhubarb like this."

"I've got a subpoena," said the sheriff, "and if that cat was a human I'd serve it on him and be done with my duty. But this cat ain't a human. It's a case where I got to make up my own rules as I go along. Judge Loudermilk wants Rhubarb Banner, and Rhubarb Banner he gets. Let's get going."

And so Rhubarb and Eric and Polly and Doom and Clarissa and Willy trooped out of the stands and got into automobiles and drove to downtown Manhattan. Back at Banner Field the opening game of the season was started anew, and the Loons, deprived of a cat to touch, lost it by a score of 12–0.

Leroy Jeffcoat

WILLIAM PRICE FOX

On Leroy Jeffcoat's forty-first birthday he fell off a scaffold while painting a big stucco rooming house over on Sycamore Street. Leroy was in shock for about twenty minutes but when the doctor brought him around he seemed all right.

Leroy went home and rolled his trousers and shoes into a bundle with his Sherwin-Williams paint company cap and jacket. He tied the bundle with string to keep the dogs from dragging it off and put it in the gutter in front of his house. He poured gasoline over the bundle and set it on fire. That was the last day Leroy Jeffcoat painted a house.

He went uptown to the Sports Center on Kenilworth Street and bought two white baseball uniforms with green edging, two pairs of baseball shoes, a Spalding second baseman's glove, eight baseballs and two bats. Leroy had been painting houses at union scale since he got out of high school, and since he never gambled or married he had a pretty good savings account at the South Carolina National Bank.

We had a bush-league team that year called the Columbia

Green Wave. The name must have come from the fact that most of us got drunk on Friday nights and the games were always played on Saturdays. Anyhow the season was half over when Leroy came down and wanted to try out for second base.

Leroy looked more like a ball player than any man I've ever known. He had that little ass-pinched strut when he was mincing around second base. He also had a beautiful squint into or out of the sun, could chew through a whole plug of Brown Mule tobacco in four innings, and could worry a pitcher to death with his chatter. On and on and on . . . we would be ahead ten runs in the ninth and Leroy wouldn't let up.

But Leroy couldn't play. He looked fine. At times he looked great. But he knew too much to play well. He'd read every baseball book and guide and every Topp's Chewing Gum Baseball Card ever printed. He could show you how Stan Musial batted, how Williams swung, how DiMaggio dug in. He went to all the movies and copied all the stances and mannerisms. You could say, "Let's see how Rizzuto digs one out, Leroy." He'd toss you a ball and lope out about forty feet.

"All right, throw it at my feet, right in the dirt." And you would and then you'd see the Old Scooter movement—low and quick with the big wrist over to first.

Leroy could copy anybody. He was great until he got in an actual game. Then he got too nervous. He'd try to bat like Williams, Musial, and DiMaggio all at once and by the time he'd make up his mind he'd have looked at three strikes. And at second base it was the same story. He fidgeted too much and never got himself set in time.

Leroy played his best ball from the bench. He liked it there. He'd pound his ball into his glove and chatter and grumble and cuss and spit tobacco juice. He'd be the first one to congratulate the home-run hitters and the first one up and screaming on a close play.

We got him into the Leesboro game for four innings and against Gaffney for three. He played the entire game at second base against the State Insane Asylum . . . but that's another story.

When the games ended Leroy showered, dried, used plenty of talcum powder and then spent about twenty minutes in front of the mirror combing his flat black hair straight back.

Most of the team had maybe a cap and a jacket with a number on it and a pair of shoes. Leroy had two complete uniform changes. After every game he'd change his dirty one for a clean one and then take the dirty one to the one-day dry cleaner. That way Leroy was never out of uniform. Morning, noon, and night Leroy was ready. On rainy days, on days it sleeted, and even during the hurricane season, Leroy was ready. For his was the long season. Seven days a week, three hundred and sixty-five days a year, Leroy was in uniform. Bat in hand, glove fastened to belt, balls in back pocket, and cut plug going. And he never took off his spikes. He would wear a set out every two weeks. You could see him coming from two blocks away in his clean white uniform. And at night when you couldn't see him you could hear the spikes and see the sparks on the sidewalk.

The Green Wave worked out on Tuesday and Thursday in the evening and we played on Saturday. Leroy worked out every day and every night. He'd come up to Doc Daniels' drugstore with his bat and ball and talk someone into hitting him fly balls out over the telegraph wires on Mulberry Avenue. It could be noon in August and the sun wouldn't be any higher than a high foul ball, but it wouldn't worry Leroy Jeffcoat. He'd catch the balls or run them down in the gutter until the batter tired.

Then Leroy would buy himself and the batter a couple of Atlantic ales. Doc Daniels had wooden floors and Leroy wouldn't take his baseball shoes off, so he had to drink the ale outside.

Doc would shout out, "Leroy, damn your hide anyway. If you come in here with those spikes on I'm going to work you over with this ice-cream scoop. Now you hear?"

Leroy would spin the ball into the glove, fold it and put it in his back pocket.

"Okay, Doc."

"Why can't you take those damn spikes off and sit down in a booth and rest? You're getting too old to be out in that sun all day."

Leroy was in great shape. As a rule, house painters have good arms and hands and bad feet.

He would laugh and take his Atlantic ale outside in the sun or maybe sit down in the little bit of shade from the mailbox.

Later on, he would find someone to throw him grounders.

"Come on, toss me a few. Don't spare the steam."

He'd crowd in on you and wouldn't be more than thirty feet out there.

"Come on, skin it along the ground."

You'd be scared to throw it hard but he'd insist.

"Come on, now, a little of the old pepper. In the dirt."

Next thing you'd be really winging them in there and he'd be picking them off like cherries or digging them out of the dust and whipping them back to you. He'd wear you out and burn your hands up in ten minutes. Then he'd find somebody else.

Leroy would go home for supper and then he'd be back. After dark he'd go out to the street lamp and throw the ball up near the light and catch it. The June bugs, flying ants and bats would be flitting around everywhere but he'd keep on. The June bugs and flying ants would be all over his head and shoulders and even in his glove. He might stop for a while for another Atlantic ale, and if the crowd was talking baseball he'd join it. If it wasn't and the bugs were too bad he'd stand out in the dark and pound his ball in his glove or work out in the mirror of Doc Daniels' front window. In front of the window he became a pitcher. He worked a little like Preacher Roe but he had more class. He did a lot of rubbing the resin bag and checking signs from the catcher and shaking them off. When he'd agree with a sign he'd nod his head slow . . . exactly like Roe. Then he'd get in position, toss the resin aside, and glare in mean and hard at the batter. He took a big reach and stopped and then the slow and perhaps the most classic look toward second base I've ever seen—absolutely Alexandrian. Then he'd stretch, wind, and whip it through. He put his hands on his knees . . . wait. It had to be a strike. It was. And he'd smile.

And read a sports page? Nobody this side of Cooperstown ever read a page the way Leroy Jeffcoat did. He would crouch down over that sheet for two hours running. He'd read every word and every figure. He went at it like he was following the puzzle maze in *Grit*, trying to find the pony or the seventeen rabbits. He had a pencil about as long as your little finger and he'd make notes along the margin. When he finished he'd transfer the notes to a little black book he carried in his back pocket. Leroy would even check the earned run average and the batting and fielding average. I don't mean just *look* at them . . . he'd *study* them. And if he didn't like them he'd divide and do the multiplication and check them over. And if they were wrong he'd be on the telephone to the *Columbia Record* or else he'd write a letter.

Leroy was always writing letters to the sports writers. Like he'd read an article about how Joe DiMaggio was getting old and slipping and he'd get mad. He'd take off his shoes and go inside Doc Daniels', buy a tablet and an envelope, get in the back booth and write. Like: "What do you mean Joe DiMaggio is too old and he's through. Why, you rotten son of a bitch, you just wait and watch him tomorrow."

Next day old Joe would pick up two for four and Leroy would take off his spikes and get back in that back booth again. "What did I tell you? Next time, you watch out who you're saying is through. Also, you print an apology this week or I am going to personally come up there and kick your fat ass. (Signed) Leroy Jeffcoat, taxpayer and second baseman, Doc Daniels' Drugstore, Columbia, S.C."

This would be a much better story if I could tell you that Leroy's game improved and he went on and played and became famous throughout the Sally League. But he didn't.

He got a little better and then he leveled off. But we kept him around because we liked him (number one), that white uniform edged in green looked good (number two), and then, too, we used him as an auxiliary man. A lot of the boys couldn't make it through some of those August games. When you start fanning yourself with a catcher's mitt, it's hot. All that beer and corn whisky would start coming out and in most games we would wind up with Leroy playing.

One game, Kirk Turner, our right fielder, passed out right in his position in the short weeds. We had to drag him into the shade and Leroy ran out to right field and began chirping. He caught a couple and dropped a couple. At bat he decided he was Ted Williams and kept waiting for that perfect ball that Ted described in the *Saturday Evening Post*. The perfect ball never came and Leroy struck out twice. In the seventh he walked. It was his first time on base in weeks and he began dancing and giving the pitcher so much lip the umpire had to settle him down.

Our last game of the year and the game we hated to play was with the South Carolina State Penitentiary down the hill.

First of all, *no one* beats The Pen. Oh, you might give them a bad time for a couple of innings but that's about all. It's not that they're a rough bunch so much as it's that they play to win. And I mean they really play to win.

Anyhow, we went down and the game started at one-thirty. The high walls kept the breeze out and it was like playing in a furnace. Sweat was dripping off my fingertips and running down my nose.

Billy Joe Jasper pitched and in the first inning they hit him for seven runs before Kirk Turner caught two long ones out by the center field wall.

We came to bat and Al Curry, our catcher, led off. Their pitcher's name was Strunk and he was in jail for murder. The first pitch was right at Al's head. He hit the dirt. The crowd cheered. The next pitch the same thing; Al Curry was as white as a sheet. The next pitch went for his head but broke out and over the inside of the plate. Al was too scared to swing and they called him out on the next two pitches.

Jeff Harper struck out next in the same manner. When he complained to the umpire, who was a trusty, he went out and talked to Strunk. It didn't do any good.

I batted third. It was terrifying. Strunk glared at me and mouthed dirty words. He was so tall and his arms were so long I thought he was going to grab me by the throat before he turned the ball loose. I kept getting out of the box and checking to see if he was pitching from the mound. He seemed to be awfully close.

I got back in the box. I didn't dig in too deep. I wanted to be ready to duck. He reached up about nine feet and it came right at my left eye. I hit the dirt.

"Ball one."

From the ground: "How about that dusting?"

"You entering a complaint?"

"Yes."

"I'll speak to him."

The umpire went out to see Strunk and the catcher followed. They talked a while and every few seconds one of them would look back at me. They began laughing.

Back on the mound. One more beanball and once more in the dirt. And then three in a row that looked like beaners that broke over the plate. Three up. Three down.

At the end of five innings we didn't have a scratch hit. The Pen had fourteen runs and the pitcher Strunk had three doubles and a home run.

We didn't care what the score was. All we wanted to do was get the game over and get out of that prison yard. The crowd cheered everything their ball team did and every move we made brought only boos and catcalls.

At the end of seven we were still without a hit.

Leroy kept watching Strunk. "Listen, I can hit that son of a bitch."

I said, "No, Leroy, he's too dangerous."

"The hell he is. Let me at him."

Kirk Turner said, "Leroy, that bastard will kill you. Let's just ride him out and get out of here. This crowd makes me nervous."

But Leroy kept on insisting. Finally George Haggard said, "Okay, Leroy. Take my place." So Leroy replaced George at first.

Strunk came to bat in the eighth and Leroy started shouting, "Let him hit! Let him hit, Billy Joe. I want to see that son of a bitch over here."

He pounded his fist in George's first baseman's glove and started jumping up and down like a chimpanzee.

"Send that bastard down here. I want him. I'll fix his ass."

The crowd cheered Leroy and he tipped his hat like Stan Musial.

The crowd cheered again.

Strunk bellowed, "Shut that nut up, ump."

The umpire raised his hands, "All right, over there, simmer down or I'll throw you out."

The crowd booed the umpire.

Leroy wouldn't stop. "Don't let him hit, Billy! Walk him.

Walk that beanball bastard. He might get a double; I want him over here."

Billy Joe looked at Al Curry. Al gave him the walk sign. Two balls . . . three balls. . . .

"You getting scared, you bastard? Won't be long now."

The crowd laughed and cheered.

Again the Musial touch with his cap.

Strunk shouted, "Listen, you runt, you keep quiet while I'm hitting or I'll shove that glove down your throat."

Leroy laughed, "Sure you will. Come on down. I'll help you."

Four balls. . . .

Strunk laid the bat down carefully and slowly walked toward first. Strunk got close. The crowd was silent. Leroy stepped off the bag and Strunk stepped on. Leroy backed up. Strunk followed. Everybody watched. No noise. Leroy stopped and took his glove off. He handed it to Strunk. Strunk took the glove in both hands.

Leroy hit him with the fastest right I've ever seen.

Strunk was stunned but he was big. He lashed the glove into Leroy's face and swung at him.

Leroy took it on the top of his head and crowded in so fast Strunk didn't know what to do. Leroy got him off balance and kept him that way while he pumped in four lefts and six rights.

Strunk went down with Leroy on top banging away. Two of us grabbed Leroy and three got ahold of Strunk. They led Strunk back to the dugout bleeding. He turned to say something and spat out two teeth. "I ain't through with you yet."

The crowd went wild.

Someone shouted, "What's his name? What's his name?"

"Jeffcoat . . . Leroy Jeffcoat."

They cheered again. And shouted, "Leroy Jeffcoat is our boy." And then, "Leroy Jeffcoat is red hot."

Leroy tipped his hat Musial-style, picked up George Haggard's glove and said, "Okay, let's play ball."

Another cheer and the game started.

The Pen scored two more times that inning before we got them out. We came to bat in the ninth behind 21 to 0. Strunk fanned me and then hit Coley Simms on the shoulder. He found out that Leroy was batting fifth so he walked the next two, loading the bases so he could get a shot at him.

So Leroy came up with the bases loaded and the prison crowd shouting, "Leroy Jeffcoat is our boy."

He pulled his cap down like Musial and dug into the box like DiMaggio. The crowd cheered and he got out of the box and tipped his cap.

Strunk was getting madder and madder and he flung the resin down and kicked the rubber. "Let's go, in there."

Leroy got in the box, whipped the bat through like Ted Williams and hollered, "Okay, Strunk, let's have it."

Zip. Right at his head.

Leroy flicked his head back like a snake but didn't move his feet.

The crowd booed Strunk and the umpire went out to the mound. We could hear the argument. As the umpire turned away Strunk told him to go to hell.

The second pitch was the same as the first. Leroy didn't move and the ball hit his cap bill.

The umpire wanted to put him on base.

Leroy shouted, "No, he didn't hit me. He's yellow. Let him pitch."

The crowd cheered Leroy again. Strunk delivered another duster and the ball went between Leroy's cap bill and his eyes. This time he didn't even flick his head.

Three balls . . . no strikes.

Two convicts dropped out of the stands and trotted across the infield to the mound. They meant business. When they talked Strunk listened and nodded his head. A signal passed around the infield.

The fourth pitch was right across Leroy's chest. It was Williams' ideal ball and it was the ball Leroy had been waiting for all season. He hit it clean and finished the Williams swing.

It was a clean single but the right fielder bobbled it and Leroy made the wide turn toward second. The throw into second was blocked and bobbled again and Leroy kept going. He ran in spurts, each spurt faster than the last. The throw to third got past the baseman and Leroy streaked for home, shouting.

He began sliding from twenty feet out. He slid so long he

stopped short. He had to get up and lunge for home plate with his hand. He made it as the ball whacked into the catcher's mitt and the crowd started coming out of the stands.

The guards tried to hold the crowd back and a warning siren sounded. But the convicts got to him and paraded around the field with Leroy on their backs. The game was called at this point and the reserve guards and trusties came out with billy clubs.

Later Coley and I learned from The Pen's manager that the committee had told Strunk they wanted Leroy to hit a home run. We never told the rest of the team or anybody else about that.

After we showered at The Pen we all went back to Doc Daniels' Drugstore. Everyone told everyone about it and when Doc Daniels heard it he came outside and personally led Leroy into the store with his spikes on.

"Leroy, from now on I want you to feel free to walk right in here anytime you feel like it."

Leroy smiled, and put his bat and his uniform bag up on the soda fountain. Doc bought Atlantic ales for everyone. Later, I bought a round and Coley bought a round.

And just as we were settling down in the booths with sandwiches, potato chips, and the jukebox going, Leroy picked up his glove and started spinning his ball off the ends of his fingers and said, "I'm getting a little stiff. Anyone feel like throwing me a few fast ones?"

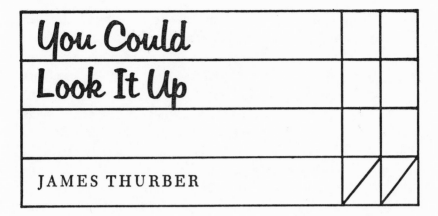

You Could Look It Up

JAMES THURBER

It all began when we dropped down to C'lumbus, Ohio, from Pittsburgh to play a exhibition game on our way out to St. Louis. It was gettin' on into September, and though we'd been leadin' the league by six, seven games most of the season, we was now in first place by a margin you could 'a' got it into the eye of a thimble, bein' only a half a game ahead of St. Louis. Our slump had given the boys the leapin' jumps, and they was like a bunch a old ladies at a lawn fete with a thunderstorm comin' up, runnin' around snarlin' at each other, eatin' bad and sleepin' worse, and battin' for a team average of maybe .186. Half the time nobody'd speak to nobody else, without it was to bawl 'em out.

Squawks Magrew was managin' the boys at the time, and he was darn near crazy. They called him "Squawks" 'cause when things was goin' bad he lost his voice, or perty near lost it, and squealed at you like a little girl you stepped on her doll or somethin'. He yelled at everybody and wouldn't listen to nobody, without maybe it was me. I'd been trainin' the boys for ten years, and he'd take more lip from me than from anybody else. He knowed I was smarter'n him, anyways, like you're goin' to hear.

This was thirty, thirty-one year ago; you could look it up, 'cause it was the same year C'lumbus decided to call itself the Arch City, on account of a lot of iron arches with electric-light bulbs into 'em which stretched acrost High Street. Thomas Albert Edison sent 'em a telegram, and they was speeches and maybe even President Taft opened the celebration by pushin' a button. It was a great week for the Buckeye capital, which was why they got us out there for this exhibition game.

Well, we just lose a double-header to Pittsburgh, 11 to 5 and 7 to 3, so we snarled all the way to C'lumbus where we put up at the Chittaden Hotel, still snarlin'. Everybody was tetchy, and when Billy Klinger took a sock at Whitey Cott at breakfast, Whitey throwed marmalade all over his face.

"Blind each other, whatta I care?" says Magrew. "You can't see nothin' anyways."

C'lumbus win the exhibition game, 3 to 2, whilst Magrew set in the dugout, mutterin' and cursin' like a fourteen-year-old Scotty. He bad-mouthed everybody on the ball club and he bad-mouthed everybody offa the ball club, includin' the Wright brothers, who, he claimed, had yet to build a airship big enough for any of our boys to hit it with a ball bat.

"I wisht I was dead," he says to me. "I wisht I was in heaven with the angels."

I told him to pull hisself together, 'cause he was drivin' the boys crazy, the way he was goin' on, sulkin' and bad-mouthin' and whinin'. I was older'n he was and smarter'n he was, and he knowed it. I was ten times smarter'n he was about this Pearl du Monville, first time I ever laid eyes on the little guy, which was one of the saddest days of my life.

Now, most people name of Pearl is girls, but this Pearl du Monville was a man, if you could call a fella a man who was only thirty-four, thirty-five inches high. Pearl du Monville was a midget. He was part French and part Hungarian, and maybe even part Bulgarian or somethin'. I can see him now, a sneer on his little pushed-in pan, swingin' a bamboo cane and smokin' a big cigar. He had a gray suit with a big black check into it, and he had a gray felt hat with one of them rainbow-colored hatbands onto it, like the young fellas wore in them days. He talked like he was talkin' into a tin can, but he didn't have no foreign accent. He might 'a' been fifteen or he might 'a' been a hundred, you couldn't tell. Pearl du Monville.

After the game with C'lumbus, Magrew headed straight for the Chittaden bar—the train for St. Louis wasn't goin' for three, four hours—and there he set, drinkin' rye and talkin' to this bartender.

"How I pity me, brother," Magrew was tellin' this bartender. "How I pity me." That was alwuz his favorite tune. So he was settin' there, tellin' this bartender how heartbreakin' it was to be manager of a bunch a blindfolded circus clowns, when up pops this Pearl du Monville outa nowheres.

It give Magrew the leapin' jumps. He thought at first maybe the D.T.'s had come back on him; he claimed he'd had 'em once, and little guys had popped up all around him, wearin' red, white and blue hats.

"Go on, now!" Magrew yells. "Get away from me!"

But the midget clumb up on a chair acrost the table from Magrew and says, "I seen that game today, Junior, and you ain't got no ball club. What you got there, Junior" he says, "is a side show."

"Whatta ya mean, 'Junior'?" says Magrew, touchin' the little guy to satisfy hisself he was real.

"Don't pay him no attention, mister," says the bartender. "Pearl calls everybody 'Junior,' 'cause it alwuz turns out he's a year older'n anybody else."

"Yeh?" says Magrew. "How old is he?"

"How old are you, Junior?" says the midget.

"Who, me? I'm fifty-three," says Magrew.

"Well, I'm fifty-four," says the midget.

Magrew grins and asts him what he'll have, and that was the beginnin' of their beautiful friendship, if you don't care what you say.

Pearl du Monville stood up on his chair and waved his cane around and pretended like he was ballyhooin' for a circus. "Right this way, folks!" he yells. "Come on in and see the greatest collection of freaks in the world! See the armless pitchers, see the eyeless batters, see the infielders with five thumbs!" and on and on like that, feedin' Magrew gall and handin' him a laugh at the same time, you might say.

You could hear him and Pearl du Monville hootin' and hollerin' and singin' way up to the fourth floor of the Chittaden, where the boys was packin' up. When it come time to go to the station, you can imagine how disgusted we was when we crowded into the doorway of that bar and seen them two singin' and goin' on.

"Well, well, well," says Magrew, lookin' up and spottin' us. "Look who's here. . . . Clowns, this is Pearl du Monville, a monseer of the old, old school. . . . Don't shake hands with 'em, Pearl, 'cause their fingers is made of chalk and would bust right off in your paws," he says, and he starts guffawin' and Pearl starts titterin' and we stand there givin' 'em the iron eye, it bein' the lowest ebb a ball-club manager'd got hisself down to since the national pastime was started.

Then the midget begun givin' us the ballyhoo. "Come on in!" he says, wavin' his cane. "See the legless base runners, see the outfielders with the butter fingers, see the southpaw with the arm of a little chee-ild!"

Then him and Magrew began to hoop and holler and nudge each other till you'd of thought this little guy was the funniest guy than even Charlie Chaplin. The fellas filed outa the bar without a word and went on up to the Union Depot, leavin' me to handle Magrew and his new-found crony.

Well, I got 'em outa there finely. I had to take the little guy along, 'cause Magrew had a holt onto him like a vise and I couldn't pry him loose.

"He's comin' along as masket," says Magrew, holdin' the midget in the crouch of his arm like a football. And come along he did, hollerin' and protestin' and beatin' at Magrew with his little fists.

"Cut it out, will ya, Junior?" the little guy kept whinin'. "Come on, leave a man loose, will ya, Junior?"

But Junior kept a holt onto him and began yellin', "See the guys with the glass arms, see the guys with the cast-iron brains, see the fielders with the feet on their wrists!"

So it goes, right through the whole Union Depot, with people starin' and catcallin', and he don't put the midget down till he gets him through the gates.

"How'm I goin' to go along without no toothbrush?" the midget asts. "What'm I goin' to do without no other suit?" he says.

"Doc here," says Magrew, meanin' me—"doc here will look after you like you was his own son, won't you, doc?"

I give him the iron eye, and he finely got on the train and prob'ly went to sleep with his clothes on.

This left me alone with the midget. "Lookit," I says to him. "Why don't you go on home now? Come mornin', Magrew'll forget all about you. He'll prob'ly think you was somethin' he seen in a nightmare maybe. And he ain't goin' to laugh so easy in the mornin', neither," I says. "So why don't you go on home?"

"Nix," he says to me. "Skiddoo," he says, "twenty-three for you," and he tosses his cane up into the vestibule of the coach and clam'ers on up after it like a cat. So that's the way Pearl du Monville come to go to St. Louis with the ball club.

I seen 'em first at breakfast the next day, settin' opposite each other; the midget playin' Turkey in the Straw on a harmonium and Magrew starin' at his eggs and bacon like they was a uncooked bird with its feathers still on.

"Remember where you found this?" I says, jerkin' my thumb at the midget. "Or maybe you think they come with breakfast on these trains," I says, bein' a good hand at turnin' a sharp remark in them days.

The midget puts down the harmonium and turns on me. "Sneeze," he says: "your brains is dusty." Then he snaps a couple drops of water at me from a tumbler. "Drown," he says, tryin' to make his voice deep.

Now, both them cracks is Civil War cracks, but you'd of thought they was brand new and the funniest than any crack Magrew'd ever heard in his whole life. He started hoopin' and hollerin' and the midget started hoopin' and hollerin', so I walked on away and set down with Bugs Courtney and Hank Metters, payin' no attention to this weak-minded Damon and Phidias acrost the aisle.

Well, sir, the first game with St. Louis was rained out, and there we was facin' a double-header next day. Like maybe I told you, we lose the last three double-headers we play, makin' maybe twenty-five errors in the six games, which is all right for the intimates of a school for the blind, but is disgraceful for the world's champions. It was too wet to go to the zoo, and Magrew wouldn't let us go to the movies, 'cause they flickered so bad in them days. So we just set around, stewin' and frettin'.

One of the newspaper boys come over to take a pitture of Billy Klinger and Whitey Cott shakin' hands—this reporter'd heard about the fight—and whilst they was standin' there, toe to toe, shakin' hands, Billy give a back lunge and a jerk, and throwed Whitey over his shoulder into a corner of the room, like a sack of salt. Whitey come back at him with a chair, and Bethlehem broke loose in that there room. The camera was tromped to pieces like a berry basket. When we finely got 'em pulled apart, I heard a laugh, and there was Magrew and the midget standin' in the doorway and givin' us the iron eye.

"Wrasslers," says Magrew, cold-like, "that's what I got for a ball club, Mr. Du Monville, wrasslers—and not very good wrasslers at that, you ast me."

"A man can't be good at everythin'," says Pearl, "but he oughta be good at somethin'."

This sets Magrew guffawin' again, and away they go, the midget taggin' along by his side like a hound dog and handin' him a fast line of so-called comic cracks.

When we went out to face that battlin' St. Louis club in a double-header the next afternoon, the boys was jumpy as tin toys with keys in their back. We lose the first game, 7 to 2, and are trailin', 4 to 0, when the second game ain't but ten minutes old. Magrew set there like a stone statue, speakin' to nobody. Then, in their half a the fourth, somebody singled to center and knocked in two more runs for St. Louis.

That made Magrew squawk. "I wisht one thing," he says. "I wisht I was manager of an old ladies' sewin' circus 'stead of a ball club."

"You are, Junior, you are," says a familyer and disagreeable voice.

It was that Pearl du Monville again, poppin' up outa nowheres, swingin' his bamboo cane and smokin' a cigar that's three sizes too big for his face. By this time we'd finely got the other side out, and Hank Metters slithered a bat acrost the ground, and the midget had to jump to keep both his ankles from bein' broke.

I thought Magrew'd bust a blood vessel. "You hurt Pearl and I'll break your neck!" he yelled.

Hank muttered somethin' and went on up to the plate and struck out.

We managed to get a couple runs acrost in our half a the sixth, but they come back with three more in their half a the seventh, and this was too much for Magrew.

"Come on, Pearl," he says. "We're gettin' outa here."

"Where you think you're goin?" I ast him.

To the lawyer's again," he says cryptly.

"I didn't know you'd been to the lawyer's once, yet," I says.

"Which that goes to show how much you don't know," he says.

With that, they was gone, and I didn't see 'em the rest of the day, nor know what they was up to, which was a God's blessin'. We lose the nightcap, 9 to 3, and that puts us into second place plenty, and as low in our mind as a ball club can get.

The next day was a horrible day, like anybody that lived through it can tell you. Practice was just over and the St. Louis club was takin' the field, when I hears this strange sound from the stands. It sounds like the nervous whickerin' a horse gives when he smells somethin' funny on the wind. It was the fans ketchin' sight of Pearl du Monville, like you have prob'ly guessed. The midget had popped up onto the field all dressed up in a minacher club uniform, sox, cap, little letters sewed onto his chest, and all. He was swingin' a kid's bat and the only thing kept him from lookin' like a real ballplayer seen through the wrong end of a microscope was this cigar he was smokin'.

Bugs Courtney reached over and jerked it outa his mouth and throwed it away. "You're wearin' that suit on the playin' field," he says to him, severe as a judge. "You go insultin' it and I'll take you out to the zoo and feed you to the bears."

Pearl just blowed some smoke at him which he still has in his mouth.

Whilst Whitey was foulin' off four or five prior to strikin' out, I went over to Magrew. "If I was as comic as you," I says, "I'd laugh myself to death," I says. "Is that any way to treat the uniform, makin' a mockery out of it?"

"It might surprise you to know I ain't makin' no mockery outa the uniform," says Magrew. "Pearl du Monville here has been made a bone-of-fida member of this so-called ball club. I fixed it up with the front office by long-distance phone."

"Yeh?" I says. "I can just hear Mr. Dillworth or Bart Jenkins agreein' to hire a midget for the ball club. I can just hear 'em." Mr. Dillworth was the owner of the club and Bart Jenkins was the secretary, and they never stood for no monkey business. "May I be so bold as to inquire," I says, "just what you told 'em?"

"I told 'em," he says, "I wanted to sign up a guy they ain't no pitcher in the league can strike him out."

"Uh-huh," I says, "and did you tell 'em what size of a man he is?"

"Never mind about that," he says. "I got papers on me, made out legal and proper, constitutin' one Pearl du Monville a bone-of-fida member of this former ball club. Maybe that'll shame them big babies into gettin' in there and swingin', knowin' I can replace any one of 'em with a midget, if I have a mind to. A St. Louis lawyer I seen twice tells me it's all legal and proper."

"A St. Louis lawyer would," I says, "seein' nothin' could make him happier than havin' you makin' a mockery outa this one-time baseball outfit," I says.

Well, sir, it'll all be there in the papers of thirty, thirty-one year ago, and you could look it up. The game went along without no scorin' for seven innings, and since they ain't nothin' much to watch but guys poppin' up or strikin' out, the fans pay most of their attention to the goin's-on of Pearl du Monville. He's out there in front a the dugout, turnin' handsprings, balancin' his bat on his chin, walkin' a imaginary line, and so on. The fans clapped and laughed at him, and he ate it up.

So it went up to the last a the eighth, nothin' to nothin', not more'n seven, eight hits all told, and no errors on neither side. Our pitcher gets the first two men out easy in the eighth. Then up come a fella name of Potter or Billings, or some such name, and he lammed one up against the tobacco sign for three bases. The next guy up slapped the first ball out into left for a base hit, and in come the fella from third for the only run of the ball game so far. The crowd yelled, the look a death come onto Magrew's face again, and even the midget quit his tomfoolin'. Their next man fouled out back a third, and we come up for our last bats like a bunch a schoolgirls steppin' into a pool of cold water. I was lower in my mind than I'd been since the day in Nineteen-four when Chesbro throwed the wild pitch in the ninth inning with a man on third and lost the pennant for the Highlanders. I knowed something just as bad was goin' to happen, which shows I'm a clairvoyun, or was then.

When Gordy Mills hit out to second, I just closed my eyes. I opened 'em up again to see Dutch Muller standin' on second, dustin' off his pants, him havin' got his first hit in maybe twenty times to the plate. Next up was Harry Loesing, battin' for our pitcher, and he got a base on balls, walkin' on a fourth one you could 'a' combed your hair with.

Then up come Whitey Cott, our lead-off man. He crotches down in what was prob'ly the most fearsome stanch in organized ball, but all he can do is pop out to short. That brung up Billy Klinger, with two down and a man on first and second. Billy took a cut at one you could 'a' knocked a plug hat offa this here Carnera with it, but then he gets sense enough to wait 'em out, and finely he walks, too, fillin' the bases.

Yes, sir, there you are; the tyin' run on third and the winnin' run on second, first a the ninth, two men down, and Hank Metters comin' to the bat. Hank was built like a Pope-Hartford and he couldn't run no faster'n President Taft, but he had five home runs to his credit for the season, and that wasn't bad in them days. Hank was still hittin' better'n anybody else on the ball club, and it was mighty heartenin', seein' him stridin' up towards the plate. But he never got there.

"Wait a minute!" yells Magrew, jumpin' to his feet. "I'm sendin' in a pinch hitter!" he yells.

You could 'a' heard a bomb drop. When a ball-club manager says he's sendin' in a pinch hitter for the best batter on the club, you know and I know and everybody knows he's lost his holt.

"They're goin' to be sendin' the funny wagon for you, if you don't watch out," I says, grabbin' a holt of his arm.

But he pulled away and run out towards the plate, yellin', "Du Monville battin' for Metters!"

All the fellas begun squawlin' at once, except Hank, and

he just stood there starin' at Magrew like he'd gone crazy and was claimin' to be Ty Cobb's grandma or somethin'. Their pitcher stood out there with his hands on his hips and a disagreeable look on his face, and the plate umpire told Magrew to go on and get a batter up. Magrew told him again Du Monville was battin' for Metters, and the St. Louis manager finely got the idea. It brung him outa his dugout, howlin' and bawlin' like he'd lost a female dog and her seven pups.

Magrew pushed the midget towards the plate and he says to him, he says, "Just stand up there and hold that bat on your shoulder. They ain't a man in the world can throw three strikes in there 'fore he throws four balls!" he says.

"I get it, Junior!" says the midget. "He'll walk me and force in the tyin' run!" And he starts on up to the plate as cocky as if he was Willie Keeler.

I don't need to tell you Bethlehem broke loose on that there ball field. The fans got onto their hind legs, yellin' and whistlin', and everybody on the field begun wavin' their arms and hollerin' and shovin'. The plate umpire stalked over to Magrew like a traffic cop, waggin' his jaw and pointin' his finger, and the St. Louis manager kept yellin' like his house was on fire. When Pearl got up to the plate and stood there, the pitcher slammed his glove down onto the ground and started stompin' on it, and they ain't nobody can blame him. He's just walked two normal-sized human bein's, and now here's a guy up to the plate they ain't more'n twenty inches between his knees and his shoulders.

The plate umpire called in the field umpire, and they talked a while, like a couple doctors seein' the bucolic plague or somethin' for the first time. Then the plate umpire come over to Magrew with his arms folded acrost his chest, and he told him to go on and get a batter up, or he'd forfeit the game to St. Louis. He pulled out his watch, but somebody batted it outa his hand in the scufflin', and I thought there'd be a free-for-all, with everybody yellin' and shovin' except Pearl du Monville, who stood up at the plate with his little bat on his shoulder, not movin' a muscle.

Then Magrew played his ace. I seen him pull some papers outa his pocket and show 'em to the plate umpire. The umpire begun lookin' at 'em like they was bills for somethin' he not only

never bought it, he never even heard of it. The other umpire
studied 'em like they was a death warren, and all this time the
St. Louis manager and the fans and the players is yellin' and
hollerin'.

Well, sir, they fought about him bein' a midget, and they
fought about him usin' a kid's bat, and they fought about where'd
he been all season. They was eight or nine rule books brung
out and everybody was thumbin' through 'em, tryin' to find out
what it says about midgets, but it don't say nothin' about midgets,
'cause this was somethin' never'd come up in the history of the
game before, and nobody'd ever dreamed about it, even when
they has nightmares. Maybe you can't send no midgets in to bat
nowadays, 'cause the old game's changed a lot, mostly for the
worst, but you could then, it turned out.

The plate umpire finely decided the contrack papers was
all legal and proper, like Magrew said, so he waved the St. Louis
players back to their places and he pointed his finger at their
manager and told him to quit hollerin' and get on back in the
dugout. The manager says the game is percedin' under protest,
and the umpire bawls, "Play Ball!" over 'n' above the yellin' and
booin', him havin' a voice like a hog-caller.

The St. Louis pitcher picked up his glove and beat at it
with his fist six or eight times, and then got set on the mound
and studied the situation. The fans realized he was really goin'
to pitch to the midget, and they went crazy, hoopin' and hollerin'
louder'n ever, and throwin' pop bottles and hats and cushions
down onto the field. It took five, ten minutes to get the fans
quieted down again, whilst our fellas that was on base set down
on the bags and waited. And Pearl du Monville kept standin' up
there with the bat on his shoulder, like he'd been told to.

So the pitcher starts studyin' the setup again, and you got
to admit it was the strangest setup in a ball game since the players cut off their beards and begun wearin' gloves. I wisht I could
call the pitcher's name—it wasn't old Barney Pelty nor Big Jack
Powell nor Harry Howell. He was a big right-hander, but I can't
call his name. You could look it up. Even in a crotchin' position, the ketcher towers over the midget like the Washington
Monument.

The plate umpire tries standin' on his tiptoes, then he tries crotchin' down, and he finely gets hisself into a stanch nobody'd ever seen on a baseball field before, kinda squattin' down on his hanches.

Well, the pitcher is sore as a old buggy horse in fly time. He slams in the first pitch, hard and wild, and maybe two feet higher'n the midget's head.

"Ball one!" hollers the umpire over 'n' above the racket, 'cause everybody is yellin' worsten ever.

The ketcher goes on out towards the mound and talks to the pitcher and hands him the ball. This time the big right-hander tries a undershoot, and it comes in a little closer, maybe no higher'n a foot, foot and a half above Pearl's head. It would 'a' been a strike with a human bein' in there, but the umpire's got to call it, and he does.

"Ball two!" he bellers.

The ketcher walks on out to the mound again, and the whole infield comes over and gives advice to the pitcher about what they'd do in a case like this, with two balls and no strikes on a batter that oughta be in a bottle of alcohol 'stead of up there at the plate in a big-league game between the teams that is fightin' for first place.

For the third pitch, the pitcher stands there flat-footed and tosses up the ball like he's playin' ketch with a little girl.

Pearl stands there motionless as a hitchin' post, and the ball comes in big and slow and high—high for Pearl, that is, it bein' about on a level with his eyes, or a little higher'n a grown man's knees.

They ain't nothin' else for the umpire to do, so he calls, "Ball three!"

Everybody is onto their feet, hoopin' and hollerin', as the pitcher sets to throw ball four. The St. Louis manager is makin' signs and faces like he was a contorturer, and the infield is givin' the pitcher some more advice about what to do this time. Our boys who was on base stick right onto the bag, runnin' no risk of bein' nipped for the last out.

Well, the pitcher decides to give him a toss again, seein' he come closer with that than with a fast ball. They ain't nobody ever seen a slower ball throwed. It come in big as a balloon and slower'n any ball ever throwed before in the major leagues.

It come right in over the plate in front of Pearl's chest, lookin' prob'ly big as full moon to Pearl. They ain't never been a minute like the minute that followed since the United States was founded by the Pilgrim grandfathers.

Pearl du Monville took a cut at that ball, and he hit it! Magrew give a groan like a poleaxed steer as the ball rolls out in front a the plate into fair territory.

"Fair ball!" yells the umpire, and the midget starts runnin' for first, still carryin' that little bat, and makin' maybe ninety foot an hour. Bethlehem breaks loose on that ball field and in them stands. They ain't never been nothin' like it since creation was begun.

The ball's rollin' slow, on down towards third, goin' maybe eight, ten foot. The infield comes in fast and our boys break from their bases like hares in a brush fire. Everybody is standin' up, yellin' and hollerin', and Magrew is tearin' his hair outa his head, and the midget is scamperin' for first with all the speed of one of them little dash-hounds carryin' a satchel in his mouth.

The ketcher gets to the ball first, but he boots it on out past the pitcher's box, the pitcher fallin' on his face tryin' to stop it, the shortstop sprawlin' after it full length and zaggin' it on over towards the second baseman, whilst Muller is scorin' with the tyin' run and Loesing is roundin' third with the winnin' run. Ty Cobb could 'a' made a three-bagger outa that bunt, with everybody fallin' over theirself tryin' to pick the ball up. But Pearl is still maybe fifteen, twenty feet from the bag, toddlin' like a baby and yeepin' like a trapped rabbit, when the second baseman finely gets a holt of that ball and slams it over to first. The first baseman ketches it and stomps on the bag, the base umpire waves Pearl out, and there goes your old ball game, the craziest ball game ever played in the history of the organized world.

Their players start runnin' in, and then I see Magrew. He starts after Pearl, runnin' faster'n any man ever run before. Pearl sees him comin' and runs behind the base umpire's legs and gets a holt onto 'em. Magrew comes up, pantin' and roarin', and him and the midget plays ring-around-a-rosy with the umpire, who keeps shovin' at Magrew with one hand and tryin' to slap the midget loose from his legs with the other.

Finely Magrew ketches the midget, who is still yeepin' like a stuck sheep. He gets holt of that little guy by both his ankles and starts whirlin' him round and round his head like Magrew was a hammer thrower and Pearl was the hammer. Nobody can stop him without gettin' their head knocked off, so everybody just stands there and yells. Then Magrew lets the midget fly. He flies on out towards second, high and fast, like a human home run, headed for the soap sign in center field.

Their shortstop tries to get to him, but he can't make it, and I knowed the little fella was goin' to bust to pieces like a dollar watch on a asphalt street when he hit the ground. But it so happens their center fielder is just crossin' second, and he starts runnin' back, tryin' to get under the midget, who had took to spiralin' like a football 'stead of turnin' head over foot, which give him more speed and more distance.

I know you never seen a midget ketched, and you prob'ly never even seen one throwed. To ketch a midget that's been throwed by a heavy-muscled man and is flyin' through the air, you got to run under him and with him and pull your hands and arms back and down when you ketch him, to break the compact of his body, or you'll bust him in two like a matchstick. I seen Bill Lange and Willie Keeler and Tris Speaker make some wonderful ketches in my day, but I never seen nothin' like that center fielder. He goes back and back and still further back and he pulls that midget down outa the air like he was liftin' a sleepin' baby from a cradle. They wasn't a bruise onto him, only his face was the color of cat's meat and he ain't got no air in his chest. In his excitement, the base umpire, who was runnin' back with the center fielder when he ketched Pearl, yells, "Out!" and that give hysteries to the Bethlehem which was ragin' like Niagry on that ball field.

Everybody was hoopin' and hollerin' and yellin' and runnin', with the fans swarmin' onto the field, and the cops tryin' to keep order, and some guys laughin' and some of the women fans cryin', and six or eight of us holdin' onto Magrew to keep him from gettin' at that midget and finishin' him off. Some of the fans picks up the St. Louis pitcher and the center fielder, and starts carryin' 'em around on their shoulders, and they was the craziest goin's-on knowed to the history of organized ball on this side of the 'Lantic Ocean.

I seen Pearl du Monville strugglin' in the arms of a lady
fan with a ample bosom, who was laughin' and cryin' at the same
time, and him beatin' at her with his little fists and bawlin' and
yellin'. He clawed his way loose finely and disappeared in the
forest of legs which made that ball field look like it was Coney
Island on a hot summer's day.

That was the last I ever seen of Pearl du Monville. I never
seen hide nor hair of him from that day to this, and neither did
nobody else. He just vanished into the thin of the air, as the fella
says. He was ketched for the final out of the ball game and that
was the end of him, just like it was the end of the ball game, you
might say, and also the end of our losin' streak, like I'm goin'
to tell you.

That night we piled onto a train for Chicago, but we wasn't
snarlin' and snappin' any more. No, sir, the ice was finely broke
and a new spirit come into that ball club. The old zip come back
with the disappearance of Pearl du Monville out back a second
base. We got to laughin' and talkin' and kiddin' together, and
'fore long Magrew was laughin' with us. He got a human look
onto his pan again, and he quit whinin' and complainin' and
wishtin' he was in heaven with the angels.

Well, sir, we wiped up that Chicago series, winnin' all four
games, and makin' seventeen hits in one of 'em. Funny thing
was, St. Louis was so shook up by that last game with us, they
never did hit their stride again. Their center fielder took to
misjudgin' everything that come his way, and the rest a the fellas
followed suit, the way a club'll do when one guy blows up.

'Fore we left Chicago, I and some of the fellas went out and
bought a pair of them little baby shoes, which we had 'em golded
over and give 'em to Magrew for a souvenir, and he took it all
in good spirit. Whitey Cott and Billy Klinger made up and was
fast friends again, and we hit our home lot like a ton of dynamite
and they was nothin' could stop us from then on.

I don't recollect things as clear as I did thirty, forty year
ago. I can't read no fine print no more, and the only person I got
to check with on the golden days of the national pastime, as the
fella says, is my friend, old Milt Kline, over in Springfield, and
his mind ain't as strong as it once was.

He gets Rube Waddell mixed up with Rube Marquard, for
one thing, and anybody does that oughta be put away where

he won't bother nobody. So I can't tell you the exact margin we win the pennant by. Maybe it was two and a half games, or maybe it was three and a half. But it'll all be there in the newspapers and record books of thirty, thirty-one year ago and, like I was sayin', you could look it up.

The Chosen

CHAIM POTOK

The Americanization of two fifteen-year-old yeshiva students. Danny Saunders and Reuven Malter, who later become best friends, meet for the first time as opponents on a baseball field. From the novel *The Chosen*.

Danny and I probably would never have met—or we would have met under altogether different circumstances—had it not been for America's entry into the Second World War and the desire this bred on the part of some English teachers in the Jewish parochial schools to show the gentile world that yeshiva students were as physically fit, despite their long hours of study, as any other American student. They went about proving this by organizing the Jewish parochial schools in and around our area into competitive leagues, and once every two weeks the schools would compete against one another in a variety of sports. I became a member of my school's varsity softball team.

On a Sunday afternoon in early June, the fifteen members of my team met with our gym instructor in the play yard of our school. It was a warm day, and the sun was bright on the asphalt floor of the yard. The gym instructor was a short, chunky man in his early thirties who taught in the mornings in a nearby public high school and supplemented his income by teaching in our yeshiva during the afternoons. He wore a white polo shirt, white pants, and white sweater, and from the awkward way the little black skullcap sat perched on his round, balding head, it was clearly apparent that he was not accustomed to wearing it with any sort of regularity. When he talked he frequently thumped his right fist into his left palm to emphasize a point. He walked on the balls of his feet, almost in imitation of a boxer's ring stance, and he was fanatically addicted to professional baseball. He had nursed our softball team along for two years, and by a mixture of patience, luck, shrewd manipulations during some tight ball games, and hard, fist-thumping harangues calculated to shove us into a patriotic awareness of the importance of athletics and physical fitness for the war effort, he was able to mold our original team of fifteen awkward fumblers into the top team of our league. His name was Mr. Galanter, and all of us wondered why he was not off somewhere fighting in the war.

During my two years with the team, I had become quite adept at second base and had also developed a swift underhand pitch that would tempt a batter into a swing but would drop into a curve at the last moment and slide just below the flaying bat for a strike. Mr. Galanter always began a ball game by putting me at second base and would use me as a pitcher only in very tight moments, because, as he put it once, "My baseball philosophy is grounded on the defensive solidarity of the infield."

That afternoon we were scheduled to play the winning team of another neighborhood league, a team with a reputation for wild, offensive slugging and poor fielding. Mr. Galanter said he was counting upon our infield to act as a solid defensive front. Throughout the warm-up period, with only our team in the yard, he kept thumping his right fist into his left palm and shouting at us to be a solid defensive front.

"No holes," he shouted from near home plate. "No holes, you hear? Goldberg, what kind of solid defensive front is that? Close in. A battleship could get between you and Malter. That's it. Schwartz, what are you doing, looking for paratroops? This is a ball game. The enemy's on the ground. That throw was wide, Goldberg. Throw it like a sharpshooter. Give him the ball

again. Throw it. Good. Like a sharpshooter. Very good. Keep
the infield solid. No defensive holes in this war."

We batted and threw the ball around, and it was warm and
sunny, and there was the smooth, happy feeling of the summer soon to come, and the tight excitement of the ball game.
We wanted very much to win, both for ourselves and, more
especially, for Mr. Galanter, for we had all come to like his
fist-thumping sincerity. To the rabbis who taught in the Jewish
parochial schools, baseball was an evil waste of time, a spawn
of the potentially assimilationist English portion of the yeshiva
day. But to the students of most of the parochial schools, an
inter-league baseball victory had come to take on only a shade
less significance than a top grade in Talmud, for it was an un-
questioned mark of one's Americanism, and to be counted a
loyal American had become increasingly important to us during
these last years of the war.

So Mr. Galanter stood near home plate, shouting instructions and words of encouragement, and we batted and tossed
the ball around. I walked off the field for a moment to set up
my eyeglasses for the game. I wore shell-rimmed glasses, and
before every game I would bend the earpieces in so the glasses
would stay tight on my head and not slip down the bridge of my
nose when I began to sweat. I always waited until just before a
game to bend down the earpieces, because, bent, they would
cut into the skin over my ears, and I did not want to feel the
pain a moment longer than I had to. The tops of my ears would
be sore for days after every game, but better that, I thought, than
the need to keep pushing my glasses up the bridge of my nose or
the possibility of having them fall off suddenly during an important play.

Davey Cantor, one of the boys who acted as a replacement
if a first-stringer had to leave the game, was standing near the
wire screen behind home plate. He was a short boy, with a
round face, dark hair, owlish glasses, and a very Semitic nose.
He watched me fix my glasses.

"You're looking good out there, Reuven," he told me.

"Thanks," I said.

"Everyone is looking real good."

"It'll be a good game."

He stared at me through his glasses. "You think so?" he asked.

"Sure, why not?"

"You ever see them play, Reuven?"

"No."

"They're murderers."

"Sure," I said.

"No, really. They're wild."

"You saw them play?"

"Twice. They're murderers."

"Everyone plays to win, Davey."

"They don't only play to win. They play like it's the first of the Ten Commandments."

I laughed. "That yeshiva?" I said. "Oh, come on, Davey."

"It's the truth."

"Sure," I said.

"Reb Saunders ordered them never to lose because it would shame their yeshiva or something. I don't know. You'll see."

"Hey, Malter!" Mr. Galanter shouted. "What are you doing, sitting this one out?"

"You'll see," Davey Cantor said.

"Sure." I grinned at him. "A holy war."

He looked at me.

"Are you playing?" I asked him.

"Mr. Galanter said I might take second base if you have to pitch."

"Well, good luck."

"Hey, Malter!" Mr. Galanter shouted. "There's a war on, remember?"

"Yes, sir!" I said, and ran back out to my position at second base.

We threw the ball around a few more minutes, and then I went up to home plate for some batting practice. I hit a long one out to left field, and then a fast one to the shortstop, who fielded it neatly and whipped it to first. I had the bat ready for another swing when someone said, "Here they are," and I rested the bat on my shoulder and saw the team we were going to play turn up our block and come into the yard. I saw Davey Cantor kick nervously at the wire screen behind home plate, then put his hands into the pockets of his dungarees. His eyes were wide and gloomy behind his owlish glasses.

I watched them come into the yard.

There were fifteen of them, and they were dressed alike in white shirts, dark pants, white sweaters, and small black skull-caps. In the fashion of the very Orthodox, their hair was closely cropped, except for the area near their ears from which mush-roomed the untouched hair that tumbled down into the long side curls. Some of them had the beginnings of beards, straggly tufts of hair that stood in isolated clumps on their chins, jaw-bones, and upper lips. They all wore the traditional under-garment beneath their shirts, and the tzitzit, the long fringes appended to the four corners of the garment, came out above their belts and swung against their pants as they walked. These were the very Orthodox, and they obeyed literally the Biblical commandment *And ye shall look upon it*, which pertains to the fringes.

In contrast, our team had no particular uniform, and each of us wore whatever he wished: dungarees, shorts, pants, polo shirts, sweat shirts, even undershirts. Some of us wore the garment, others did not. None of us wore the fringes outside his trousers. The only element of uniform that we had in common was the small, black skullcap which we, too, wore.

They came up to the first-base side of the wire screen behind home plate and stood there in a silent black-and-white mass, holding bats and balls and gloves in their hands. . . .

A man disentangled himself from the black-and-white mass of players and took a step forward. He looked to be in his late twenties and wore a black suit, black shoes, and a black hat. He had a black beard, and he carried a book under one arm. He was obviously a rabbi, and I marveled that the yeshiva had placed a rabbi instead of an athletic coach over its team.

Mr. Galanter came up to him and offered his hand.

"We are ready to play," the rabbi said in Yiddish, shaking Mr. Galanter's hand with obvious uninterest.

"Fine," Mr. Galanter said in English, smiling.

The rabbi looked out at the field. "You played already?" he asked.

"How's that?" Mr. Galanter said.

"You had practice?"

"Well, sure—"

"We want to practice."

"How's that?" Mr. Galanter said again, looking surprised.

"You practiced, now we practice."

"You didn't practice in your own yard?"

"We practiced."

"Well, then—"

"But we have never played in your yard before. We want a few minutes."

"Well, now," Mr. Galanter said, "there isn't much time. The rules are each team practices in its own yard."

"We want five minutes," the rabbi insisted.

"Well—" Mr. Galanter said. He was no longer smiling. He always liked to go right into a game when we played in our own yard. It kept us from cooling off, he said.

"Five minutes," the rabbi said. "Tell your people to leave the field."

"How's that?" Mr. Galanter said.

"We cannot practice with your people on the field. Tell them to leave the field."

"Well, now," Mr. Galanter said, then stopped. He thought for a long moment. The black-and-white mass of players behind the rabbi stood very still, waiting. I saw Davey Cantor kick at the asphalt of the yard. "Well, all right. Five minutes. Just five minutes, now."

"Tell your people to leave the field," the rabbi said.

Mr. Galanter stared gloomily out at the field, looking a little deflated. "Everybody off!" he shouted, not very loudly. "They want a five-minute warm-up. Hustle, hustle. Keep those arms going. Keep it hot. Toss some balls around behind home. Let's go!"

The players scrambled off the field.

The black-and-white mass near the wire screen remained intact. The young rabbi turned and faced his team.

He talked in Yiddish. "We have the field for five minutes," he said. "Remember why and for whom we play."

Then he stepped aside, and the black-and-white mass dissolved into fifteen individual players who came quickly onto the field. One of them, a tall boy with sand-colored hair and long arms and legs that seemed all bones and angles, stood at home plate and commenced hitting balls out to the players. He hit a few easy grounders and pop-ups, and the fielders shouted encouragement to one another in Yiddish. They handled themselves awkwardly, dropping easy grounders, throwing wild, fumbling fly balls. I looked over at the young rabbi. He had sat down on the bench near the wire screen and was reading his book.

Behind the wire screen was a wide area, and Mr. Galanter kept us busy there throwing balls around.

"Keep those balls going!" he fist-thumped at us. "No one sits out this fire fight! Never underestimate the enemy!"

But there was a broad smile on his face. Now that he was actually seeing the other team, he seemed not at all concerned about the outcome of the game. In the interim between throwing a ball and having it thrown back to me, I told myself that I liked Mr. Galanter, and I wondered about his constant use of war expressions and why he wasn't in the army.

Davey Cantor came past me, chasing a ball that had gone between his legs.

"Some murderers," I grinned at him.

"You'll see," he said as he bent to retrieve the ball.

"Sure," I said.

"Especially the one batting. You'll see."

The ball was coming back to me, and I caught it neatly and flipped it back.

"Who's the one batting?" I asked.

"Danny Saunders."

"Pardon my ignorance, but who is Danny Saunders?"

"Reb Saunders' son," Davey Cantor said, blinking his eyes.

"I'm impressed."

"You'll see," Davey Cantor said, and ran off with his ball.

My father, who had no love at all for Hasidic communities and their rabbinic overlords, had told me about Rabbi Isaac Saunders and the zealousness with which he ruled his people and settled questions of Jewish law.

I saw Mr. Galanter look at his wristwatch, then stare out at the team on the field. The five minutes were apparently over, but the players were making no move to abandon the field. Danny Saunders was now at first base, and I noticed that his long arms and legs were being used to good advantage, for by stretching and jumping he was able to catch most of the wild throws that came his way.

Mr. Galanter went over to the young rabbi who was still sitting on the bench and reading.

"It's five minutes," he said.

The rabbi looked up from his book. "Ah?" he said.

"The five minutes are up," Mr. Galanter said.

The rabbi stared out at the field. "Enough!" he shouted in Yiddish. "It's time to play!" Then he looked down at the book and resumed his reading.

The players threw the ball around for another minute or two, and then slowly came off the field. Danny Saunders walked past me, still wearing his first baseman's glove. He was a good deal taller than I, and in contrast to my somewhat ordinary but decently proportioned features and dark hair, his face seemed to have been cut from stone. His chin, jaw, and cheekbones were made up of jutting hard lines, his nose was straight and pointed, his lips full, rising to a steep angle from the center point beneath his nose and then slanting off to form a too-wide mouth. His eyes were deep blue, and the sparse tufts of hair on his chin, jawbones, and upper lip, the close-cropped hair on his head, and the flow of side curls along his ears were the color of sand. He moved in a loose-jointed, disheveled sort of way, all arms and legs, talking in Yiddish to one of his teammates and ignoring me completely as he passed by. I told myself that I did not like his Hasidic-bred sense of superiority and that it would be a great pleasure to defeat him and his team in this afternoon's game.

The umpire, a gym instructor from a parochial school two blocks away, called the teams together to determine who would bat first. I saw him throw a bat into the air. It was caught and almost dropped by a member of the other team.

During the brief hand-over-hand choosing, Davey Cantor came over and stood next to me.

"What do you think?" he asked.

"They're a snooty bunch," I told him.

"What do you think about their playing?"

"They're lousy."

"They're murderers."

"Oh, come on, Davey."

"You'll see," Davey Cantor said, looking at me gloomily.

"I just did see."

"You didn't see anything."

"Sure," I said. "Elijah the prophet comes in to pitch for them in tight spots."

"I'm not being funny," he said, looking hurt.

"Some murderers," I told him, and laughed. . . .

The umpire, who had taken up his position behind the pitcher, called for the ball and someone tossed it to him. He handed it to the pitcher and shouted, "Here we go! Play ball!" We settled into our positions.

Mr. Galanter shouted, "Goldberg, move in!" and Sidney Goldberg, our shortstop, took two steps forward and moved a little closer to third base. "Okay fine," Mr. Galanter said. "Keep that infield solid!"

A short, thin boy came up to the plate and stood there with his feet together, holding the bat awkwardly over his head. He wore steel-rimmed glasses that gave his face a pinched, old man's look. He swung wildly at the first pitch, and the force of the swing spun him completely around. His earlocks lifted off the sides of his head and followed him around in an almost horizontal circle. Then he steadied himself and resumed his position near the plate, short, thin, his feet together, holding his bat over his head in an awkward grip.

The umpire called the strike in a loud, clear voice, and I saw Sidney Goldberg look over at me and grin broadly.

"If he studies Talmud like that, he's dead," Sidney Goldberg said.

I grinned back at him.

"Keep that infield solid!" Mr. Galanter shouted from third base. "Malter, a little to your left! Good!"

The next pitch was too high, and the boy chopped at it, lost his bat and fell forward on his hands. Sidney Goldberg and I looked at each other again. Sidney was in my class. We were similar in build, thin and lithe, with somewhat spindly arms and legs. He was not a very good student, but he was an excellent shortstop. We lived on the same block and were good but not close friends. He was dressed in an undershirt and dungarees and was not wearing the four-cornered garment. I had on a light-blue shirt and dark-blue work pants, and I wore the four-cornered garment under the shirt.

The short, thin boy was back at the plate, standing with his feet together and holding the bat in his awkward grip. He let the next pitch go by, and the umpire called it a strike. I saw the young rabbi look up a moment from his book, then resume reading.

"Two more just like that!" I shouted encouragingly to the pitcher. "Two more, Schwartzie!" And I thought to myself, Some murderers.

I saw Danny Saunders go over to the boy who had just struck out and talk to him. The boy looked down and seemed to shrivel with hurt. He hung his head and walked away behind the wire screen. Another short, thin boy took his place at the plate. I looked around for Davey Cantor but could not see him.

The boy at bat swung wildly at the first two pitches and missed them both. He swung again at the third pitch, and I heard the loud *thwack* of the bat as it connected with the ball, and saw the ball move in a swift, straight line toward Sidney Goldberg, who caught it, bobbled it for a moment, and finally got it into his glove. He tossed the ball to me, and we threw it around. I saw him take off his glove and shake his left hand.

"That hurt," he said, grinning at me.

"Good catch," I told him.

"That hurt like hell," he said, and put his glove back on his hand.

The batter who stood now at the plate was broad-shouldered and built like a bear. He swung at the first pitch, missed, then swung again at the second pitch and sent the ball in a straight line over the head of the third baseman into left field. I scrambled to second, stood on the base, and shouted for the ball. I saw the left fielder pick it up on the second bounce and relay it to me. It was coming in a little high, and I had my glove raised for it. I felt more than saw the batter charging toward second, and as I was getting my glove on the ball he smashed into me like a truck. The ball went over my head, and I fell forward heavily onto the asphalt floor of the yard, and he passed me, going toward third, his fringes flying out behind him, holding his skullcap to his head with his right hand so it would not fall off. Abe Goodstein, our first baseman, retrieved the ball and whipped it home, and the batter stood at third, a wide grin on his face.

The yeshiva team exploded into wild cheers and shouted loud words of congratulations in Yiddish to the batter.

Sidney Goldberg helped me get to my feet.

"That momzer!" he said. "You weren't in his way!"

"Wow!" I said, taking a few deep breaths. I had scraped the palm of my right hand.

"What a momzer!" Sidney Goldberg said.

I saw Mr. Galanter come storming onto the field to talk to the umpire. "What kind of play was that?" he asked heatedly. "How are you going to rule that?"

"Safe at third," the umpire said. "Your boy was in the way."

Mr. Galanter's mouth fell open. "How's that again?"

"Safe at third," the umpire repeated.

Mr. Galanter looked ready to argue, thought better of it, then stared over at me. "Are you all right, Malter?"

"I'm okay," I said, taking another deep breath.

Mr. Galanter walked angrily off the field.

"Play ball!" the umpire shouted.

The yeshiva team quieted down. I saw that the young rabbi was now looking up from his book and smiling faintly.

A tall, thin player came up to the plate, set his feet in correct position, swung his bat a few times, then crouched into a waiting stance. I saw it was Danny Saunders. I opened and closed my right hand, which was still sore from the fall.

"Move back! Move back!" Mr. Galanter was shouting from alongside third base, and I took two steps back.

I crouched, waiting.

The first pitch was wild, and the yeshiva team burst into loud laughter. The young rabbi was sitting on the bench, watching Danny Saunders intently.

"Take it easy, Schwartzie!" I shouted encouragingly to the pitcher. "There's only one more to go!"

The next pitch was about a foot over Danny Saunders' head, and the yeshiva team howled with laughter. Sidney Goldberg and I looked at each other. I saw Mr. Galanter standing very still alongside third, staring at the pitcher. The rabbi was still watching Danny Saunders.

The next pitch left Schwartzie's hand in a long, slow line, and before it was halfway to the plate I knew Danny Saunders would try for it. I knew it from the way his left foot came forward and the bat snapped back and his long, thin body began its swift pivot. I tensed, waiting for the sound of the bat against the ball, and when it came it sounded like a gunshot. For a wild fraction of a second I lost sight of the ball. Then I saw Schwartzie dive to the ground, and there was the ball coming through the air where his head had been and I tried for it but it was moving too fast, and I barely had my glove raised before it was in center field. It was caught on a bounce and thrown to Sidney Goldberg, but by that time Danny Saunders was standing solidly on my base and the yeshiva team was screaming with joy.

Mr. Galanter called for time and walked over to talk to Schwartzie. Sidney Goldberg nodded to me, and the two of us went over to them.

"That ball could've killed me!" Schwartzie was saying. He was of medium size, with a long face and a bad case of acne. He wiped sweat from his face. "My God, did you see that ball?"

"I saw it," Mr. Galanter said grimly.

"That was too fast to stop, Mr. Galanter," I said in Schwartzie's defense.

"I heard about that Danny Saunders," Sidney Goldberg said. "He always hits to the pitcher."

"You could've told me," Schwartzie lamented. "I could've been ready."

"I only *heard* about it," Sidney Goldberg said. "You always believe everything you hear?"

"God, that ball could've killed me!" Schwartzie said again.

"You want to go on pitching?" Mr. Galanter said. A thin sheen of sweat covered his forehead, and he looked very grim.

"Sure, Mr. Galanter," Schwartzie said. "I'm okay."

"You're sure?"

"Sure I'm sure."

"No heroes in this war, now," Mr. Galanter said. "I want live soldiers, not dead heroes."

"I'm no hero," Schwartzie muttered lamely. "I can still get it over, Mr. Galanter. God, it's only the first inning."

"Okay, soldier," Mr. Galanter said, not very enthusiastically. "Just keep our side of this war fighting."

"I'm trying my best, Mr. Galanter," Schwartzie said.

Mr. Galanter nodded, still looking grim, and started off the field. I saw him take a handkerchief out of his pocket and wipe his forehead.

"Jesus Christ!" Schwartzie said, now that Mr. Galanter was gone. "That bastard aimed right for my head!"

"Oh, come on, Schwartzie," I said. "What is he, Babe Ruth?"

"You heard what Sidney said."

"Stop giving it to them on a silver platter and they won't hit it like that."

"Who's giving it to them on a silver platter?" Schwartzie lamented. "That was a great pitch."

"Sure," I said.

The umpire came over to us. "You boys planning to chat here all afternoon?" he asked. He was a squat man in his late forties, and he looked impatient.

"No, sir," I said very politely, and Sidney and I ran back to our places.

Danny Saunders was standing on my base. His white shirt was pasted to his arms and back with sweat.

"That was a nice shot," I offered.

He looked at me curiously and said nothing.

"You always hit it like that to the pitcher?" I asked.

He smiled faintly. "You're Reuven Malter," he said in perfect English. He had a low, nasal voice.

"That's right," I said, wondering where he had heard my name.

"Your father is David Malter, the one who writes articles on the Talmud?"

"Yes."

"I told my team we're going to kill you apikorsim this afternoon." He said it flatly, without a trace of expression in his voice.

I stared at him and hoped the sudden tight coldness I felt wasn't showing on my face. "Sure," I said. "Rub your tzitzit for good luck."

I walked away from him and took up my position near the base. I looked toward the wire screen and saw Davey Cantor standing there, staring out at the field, his hands in his pockets. I crouched down quickly, because Schwartzie was going into his pitch.

The batter swung wildly at the first two pitches and missed each time. The next one was low, and he let it go by, then hit a grounder to the first baseman, who dropped it, flailed about for it wildly, and recovered in time to see Danny Saunders cross the plate. The first baseman stood there for a moment, drenched in shame, then tossed the ball to Schwartzie. I saw Mr. Galanter standing near third base, wiping his forehead. The yeshiva team had gone wild again, and they were all trying to get to Danny Saunders and shake his hand. I saw the rabbi smile broadly, then look down at his book and resume reading.

Sidney Goldberg came over to me. "What did Saunders tell you?" he asked.

"He said they were going to kill us apikorsim this afternoon." . . .

The next batter hit a long fly ball to right field. It was caught on the run.

"Hooray for us," Sidney Goldberg said grimly as we headed off the field. "Any longer and they'd be asking us to join them for the Mincha Service."

"Not us," I said. "We're not holy enough."

"Where did they learn to hit like that?"

"Who knows?" I said.

We were standing near the wire screen, forming a tight circle around Mr. Galanter.

"Only two runs," Mr. Galanter said, smashing his right fist into his left hand. "And they hit us with all they had. Now we give them *our* heavy artillery. Now *we* barrage *them!*" His skullcap seemed pasted to his head with sweat. "Okay!" he said. "Fire away!"

The circle broke up, and Sidney Goldberg walked to the plate, carrying a bat. I saw the rabbi was still sitting on the bench, reading. I started to walk around behind him to see what book it was, when Davey Cantor came over, his hands in his pockets, his eyes still gloomy.

"Well?" he asked.

"Well what?" I said.

"I told you they could hit."

"So you told me. So what?" I was in no mood for his feelings of doom, and I let my voice show it.

He sensed my annoyance. "I wasn't bragging or anything," he said, looking hurt. "I just wanted to know what you thought."

"They can hit," I said.

"They're murderers," he said.

I watched Sidney Goldberg let a strike go by and said nothing.

"How's your hand?" Davey Cantor asked.

"I scraped it."

"He ran into you real hard."

"Who is he?"

"Dov Shlomowitz," Davey Cantor said. "Like his name, that's what he is," he added in Hebrew. "Dov" is the Hebrew word for bear.

"Was I blocking him?"

Davey Cantor shrugged. "You were and you weren't. The ump could've called it either way."

"He felt like a truck," I said, watching Sidney Goldberg step back from a close pitch.

"You should see his father. He's one of Reb Saunders' sha-mashim. Some bodyguard he makes."

"Reb Saunders has bodyguards?"

"Sure he has bodyguards," Davey Cantor said. "They protect him from his own popularity. Where've you been living all these years?"

"I don't have anything to do with them."

"You're not missing a thing, Reuven."

"How do you know so much about Reb Saunders?"

"My father gives him contributions."

"Well, good for your father," I said.

"He doesn't pray there or anything. He just gives him contributions."

"You're on the wrong team."

"No, I'm not, Reuven. Don't be like that." He was looking very hurt. "My father isn't a Hasid or anything. He just gives them some money a couple times a year."

"I was only kidding, Davey." I grinned at him. "Don't be so serious about everything."

I saw his face break into a happy smile, and just then Sidney Goldberg hit a fast, low grounder and raced off to first. The ball went right through the legs of the shortstop and into center field.

"Hold it at first!" Mr. Galanter screamed at him, and Sidney stopped at first and stood on the base.

The ball had been tossed quickly to second base. The second baseman looked over toward first, then threw the ball to the pitcher. The rabbi glanced up from the book for a moment, then went back to his reading.

"Malter, coach him at first!" Mr. Galanter shouted, and I ran up the base line.

"They can hit, but they can't field," Sidney Goldberg said, grinning at me as I came to a stop alongside the base.

"Davey Cantor says they're murderers," I said.

"Old gloom-and-doom Davey," Sidney Goldberg said, grinning.

Danny Saunders was standing away from the base, making a point of ignoring us both.

The next batter hit a high fly to the second baseman, who caught it, dropped it, retrieved it, and made a wild attempt at tagging Sidney Goldberg as he raced past him to second.

"Safe all around!" the umpire called, and our team burst out with shouts of joy. Mr. Galanter was smiling. The rabbi continued reading, and I saw he was now slowly moving the upper part of his body back and forth.

"Keep your eyes open, Sidney!" I shouted from alongside first base. I saw Danny Saunders look at me, then look away. Some murderers, I thought. Shleppers is more like it.

"If it's on the ground run like hell," I said to the batter who had just come onto first base, and he nodded at me. He was our third baseman, and he was about my size.

"If they keep fielding like that we'll be here till tomorrow," he said, and I grinned at him.

I saw Mr. Galanter talking to the next batter, who was nodding his head vigorously. He stepped to the plate, hit a hard grounder to the pitcher, who fumbled it for a moment then threw it to first. I saw Danny Saunders stretch for it and stop it.

"Out!" the umpire called. "Safe on second and third!"

As I ran up to the plate to bat, I almost laughed aloud at the pitcher's stupidity. He had thrown it to first rather than third, and now we had Sidney Goldberg on third, and a man on second. I hit a grounder to the shortstop and instead of throwing it to second he threw it to first, wildly, and again Danny Saunders stretched and stopped the ball. But I beat the throw and heard the umpire call out, "Safe all around! One in!" And everyone on our team was patting Sidney Goldberg on the back. Mr. Galanter smiled broadly.

"Hello again," I said to Danny Saunders, who was standing near me, guarding his base. "Been rubbing your tzitzit lately?"

He looked at me, then looked slowly away, his face expressionless.

Schwartzie was at the plate, swinging his bat.

"Keep your eyes open!" I shouted to the runner on third. He looked too eager to head for home. "It's only one out!"

He waved a hand at me.

Schwartzie took two balls and a strike, then I saw him begin to pivot on the fourth pitch. The runner on third started for home. He was almost halfway down the base line when the bat sent the ball in a hard line drive straight to the third baseman, the short, thin boy with the spectacles and the old man's face, who had stood hugging the base and who now caught the ball more with his stomach than with his glove, managed somehow to hold on to it, and stood there, looking bewildered and astonished.

I returned to first and saw our player who had been on third and who was now halfway to home plate turn sharply and start a panicky race back.

"Step on the base!" Danny Saunders screamed in Yiddish across the field, and more out of obedience than awareness the third baseman put a foot on the base.

The yeshiva team howled its happiness and raced off the
d. Danny Saunders looked at me, started to say something,
stopped, then walked quickly away.

I saw Mr. Galanter going back up the third-base line, his
face grim. The rabbi was looking up from his book and smiling.

I took up my position near second base, and Sidney Goldberg came over to me.

"Why'd he have to take off like that?" he asked.

I glared over at our third baseman, who was standing near
Mr. Galanter and looking very dejected.

"He was in a hurry to win the war," I said bitterly.

"What a jerk," Sidney Goldberg said.

"Goldberg, get over to your place!" Galanter called out.
There was an angry edge to his voice. "Let's keep that infield
solid!"

Sidney Goldberg went quickly to his position. I stood still
and waited.

It was hot, and I was sweating beneath my clothes. I felt
the earpieces of my glasses cutting into the skin over my ears,
and I took the glasses off for a moment and ran a finger over
the pinched ridges of skin, then put them back on quickly because Schwartzie was going into a windup. I crouched down,
waiting, remembering Danny Saunders' promise to his team
that they would kill us apikorsim. The word had meant, orig-
inally, a Jew educated in Judaism who denied basic tenets of
his faith, like the existence of God, the revelation, the resur-
rection of the dead. To people like Reb Saunders, it also meant
any educated Jew who might be reading, say, Darwin, and
who was not wearing side curls and fringes outside his trousers.
I was an apikoros to Danny Saunders, despite my belief in
God and Torah, because I did not have side curls and was
attending a parochial school where too many English subjects
were offered and where Jewish subjects were taught in Hebrew
instead of Yiddish, both unheard-of sins, the former because
it took time away from the study of Torah, the latter because
Hebrew was the Holy Tongue and to use it in ordinary class-
room discourse was a desecration of God's Name. I had never
really had any personal contact with this kind of Jew before.
My father had told me he didn't mind their beliefs. What annoyed him was their fanatic sense of righteousness, their ab-

solute certainty that they and they alone had God's ear, and every other Jew was wrong, totally wrong, a sinner, a hypocrite, an apikoros, and doomed, therefore, to burn in hell. I found myself wondering again how they had learned to hit a ball like that if time for the study of Torah was so precious to them and why they had sent a rabbi along to waste his time sitting on a bench during a ball game.

Standing on the field and watching the boy at the plate swing at a high ball and miss, I felt myself suddenly very angry, and it was at that point that for me the game stopped being merely a game and became a war. The fun and excitement were out of it now. Somehow the yeshiva team had translated this afternoon's baseball game into a conflict between what they regarded as their righteousness and our sinfulness. I found myself growing more and more angry, and I felt the anger begin to focus itself upon Danny Saunders, and suddenly it was not at all difficult for me to hate him.

Schwartzie let five of their men come up to the plate that half inning and let one of those five score. Sometime during that half inning, one of the members of the yeshiva team had shouted at us in Yiddish, "Burn in hell, you apikorsim!" and by the time that half inning was over and we were standing around Mr. Galanter near the wire screen, all of us knew that this was not just another ball game.

Mr. Galanter was sweating heavily, and his face was grim. All he said was, "We fight it careful from now on. No more mistakes." He said it very quietly, and we were all quiet, too, as the batter stepped up to the plate.

We proceeded to play a slow, careful game, bunting whenever we had to, sacrificing to move runners forward, obeying Mr. Galanter's instructions. I noticed that no matter where the runners were on the bases, the yeshiva team always threw to Danny Saunders, and I realized that they did this because he was the only infielder who could be relied upon to stop their wild throws. Sometime during the inning, I walked over behind the rabbi and looked over his shoulder at the book he was reading. I saw the words were Yiddish. I walked back to the wire screen. Davey Cantor came over and stood next to me, but he remained silent.

We scored only one run that inning, and we walked onto

the field for the first half of the third inning with a sense of doom.

Dov Shlomowitz came up to the plate. He stood there like a bear, the bat looking like a matchstick in his beefy hands. Schwartzie pitched, and he sliced one neatly over the head of the third baseman for a single. The yeshiva team howled, and again one of them called out to us in Yiddish. "Burn, you apikorsim!" and Sidney Goldberg and I looked at each other without saying a word.

Mr. Galanter was standing alongside third base, wiping his forehead. The rabbi was sitting quietly, reading his book.

I took off my glasses and rubbed the tops of my ears. I felt a sudden momentary sense of unreality, as if the play yard, with its black asphalt floor and its white base lines, were my entire world now, as if all the previous years of my life had led me somehow to this one ball game, and all the future years of my life would depend upon its outcome. I stood there for a moment, holding the glasses in my hand and feeling frightened. Then I took a deep breath, and the feeling passed. It's only a ball game, I told myself. What's a ball game?

Mr. Galanter was shouting at us to move back. I was standing a few feet to the left of second, and I took two steps back. I saw Danny Saunders walk up to the plate, swinging a bat. The yeshiva team was shouting at him in Yiddish to kill us apikorsim.

Schwartzie turned around to check the field. He looked nervous and was taking his time. Sidney Goldberg was standing up straight, waiting. We looked at each other, then looked away. Mr. Galanter stood very still alongside third base, looking at Schwartzie.

The first pitch was low, and Danny Saunders ignored it. The second one started to come in shoulder-high, and before it was two thirds of the way to the plate, I was already standing on second base. My glove was going up as the bat cracked against the ball, and I saw the ball move in a straight line directly over Schwartzie's head, high over his head, moving so fast he hadn't even had time to regain his balance from the pitch before it went past him. I saw Dov Shlomowitz heading toward me and Danny Saunders racing to first and I heard the yeshiva team shouting and Sidney Goldberg screaming and I jumped, pushing myself upward off the ground with all the strength I had in my legs and stretching my glove hand till I thought it would pull out of my shoulder. The ball hit the pocket of my glove with an impact that numbed my hand and went through me like an electric shock, and I felt the force pull me backward and throw me off balance, and I came down hard on my left hip and elbow. I saw Dov Shlomowitz whirl and start back to first, and I pushed myself up into a sitting position and threw the ball awkwardly to Sidney Goldberg, who caught it and whipped it to first. I heard the umpire scream "Out!" and Sidney Goldberg ran over to help me to my feet, a look of disbelief and ecstatic joy on his face. Mr. Galanter shouted "Time!" and came racing onto the field. Schwartzie was standing in his pitcher's position with his mouth open. Danny Saunders stood on the base line a few feet from first, where he had stopped after I had caught the ball, staring out at me, his face frozen to stone. The rabbi was staring at me, too, and the yeshiva team was deathly silent.

"That was a great catch, Reuven!" Sidney Goldberg said, thumping my back. "That was sensational!"

I saw the rest of our team had suddenly come back to life and was throwing the ball around and talking up the game.

Mr. Galanter came over. "You all right, Malter?" he asked. "Let me see that elbow."

I showed him the elbow. I had scraped it, but the skin had not been broken.

"That was a good play," Mr. Galanter said, beaming at me. I saw his face was still covered with sweat, but he was smiling broadly now.

"Thanks, Mr. Galanter."

"How's the hand?"

"It hurts a little."

"Let me see it."

I took off the glove, and Mr. Galanter poked and bent the wrist and fingers of the hand.

"Does that hurt?" he asked.

"No," I lied.

"You want to go on playing?"

"Sure, Mr. Galanter."

"Okay," he said, smiling at me and patting my back. "We'll put you in for a Purple Heart on that one, Malter."

I grinned at him.

"Okay," Mr. Galanter said. "Let's keep this infield solid!"

He walked away, smiling.

"I can't get over that catch," Sidney Goldberg said.

"You threw it real good to first," I told him.

"Yeah," he said. "While you were sitting on your tail."

We grinned at each other, and went to our positions.

Two more of the yeshiva team got to bat that inning. The first one hit a single, and the second one sent a high fly to short, which Sidney Goldberg caught without having to move a step. We scored two runs that inning and one run the next, and by the top half of the fifth inning we were leading five to three. Four of their men had stood up to bat during the top half of the fourth inning, and they had got only a single on an error to first. When we took to the field in the top half of the fifth inning, Mr. Galanter was walking back and forth alongside third on the balls of his feet, sweating, smiling, grinning, wiping his head nervously; the rabbi was no longer reading; the yeshiva team was silent as death. Davey Cantor was playing second, and I stood in the pitcher's position. Schwartzie had pleaded exhaustion, and since this was the final inning—our parochial school schedules only permitted us time for five-inning games—and the yeshiva team's last chance at bat, Mr. Galanter was taking no chances and told me to pitch. Davey Cantor was a poor fielder, but Mr. Galanter was counting on my pitching to finish off the game. My left hand was still sore from the catch, and the wrist hurt whenever I caught a ball, but the right hand was fine, and the pitches went in fast and dropped into the curve just when I wanted them to. Dov Shlomowitz stood at the plate, swung three times at what looked to him to be perfect pitches, and hit nothing but air. He stood there looking bewildered after the third swing, then slowly walked away. We threw the ball around the infield, and Danny Saunders came up to the plate.

The members of the yeshiva team stood near the wire fence, watching Danny Saunders. They were very quiet. The rabbi was sitting on the bench, his book closed. Mr. Galanter was shouting at everyone to move back. Danny Saunders swung his bat a few times, then fixed himself into position and looked out at me.

Here's a present from an apikoros, I thought, and let go the ball. It went in fast and straight, and I saw Danny Saunders' left foot move out and his bat go up and his body begin to pivot. He swung just as the ball slid into its curve, and the bat cut savagely through empty air, twisting him around and sending him off balance. His black skullcap fell off his head, and he regained his balance and bent quickly to retrieve it. He stood there for a moment, very still, staring out at me. Then he resumed his position at the plate. The ball came back to me from the catcher, and my wrist hurt as I caught it.

The yeshiva team was very quiet, and the rabbi had begun to chew his lip.

I lost control of the next pitch, and it was wide. On the third pitch, I went into a long, elaborate windup and sent him a slow, curving blooper, the kind a batter always wants to hit and always misses. He ignored it completely and the umpire called it a ball.

I felt my left wrist begin to throb as I caught the throw from the catcher. I was hot and sweaty, and the earpieces of my glasses were cutting deeply into the flesh above my ears as a result of the head movements that went with my pitching.

Danny Saunders stood very still at the plate, waiting.

Okay, I thought, hating him bitterly. Here's another present.

The ball went to the plate fast and straight, and dropped just below his swing. He checked himself with difficulty so as not to spin around, but he went off his balance again and took two or three staggering steps forward before he was able to stand up straight.

The catcher threw the ball back, and I winced at the pain in my wrist. I took the ball out of the glove, held it in my right hand, and turned around for a moment to look out at the field and let the pain in my wrist subside. When I turned back I saw that Danny Saunders hadn't moved. He was holding his bat in his left hand, standing very still and staring at me. His eyes were dark, and his lips were parted in a crazy, idiot grin. I heard the umpire yell "Play ball!" but Danny Saunders stood there, staring at me and grinning. I turned and looked out at the field again, and when I turned back he was still standing there, staring at me and grinning. I could see his teeth between his parted lips. I took a deep breath and felt myself wet with sweat. I wiped my right hand on my pants and saw Danny Saunders step slowly to the plate and set his legs in position. He was no longer grinning. He stood looking at me over his left shoulder, waiting.

I wanted to finish it quickly because of the pain in my wrist, and I sent in another fast ball. I watched it head straight for the plate. I saw him go into a sudden crouch, and in the fraction of a second before he hit the ball I realized that he had anticipated the curve and was deliberately swinging low. I was still a little off balance from the pitch, but I managed to bring my glove hand up in front of my face just as he hit the ball. I saw it coming at me, and there was nothing I could do. It hit the finger section of my glove, deflected off, smashed into the upper rim of the left lens of my glasses, glanced off my forehead, and knocked me down. I scrambled around for it wildly, but by the time I got my hand on it Danny Saunders was standing safely on first.

I heard Mr. Galanter call time, and everyone on the field came racing over to me. My glasses lay shattered on the asphalt floor, and I felt a sharp pain in my left eye when I blinked. My wrist throbbed, and I could feel the bump coming up on my forehead. I looked over at first, but without my glasses Danny Saunders was only a blur. I imagined I could still see him grinning.

I saw Mr. Galanter put his face next to mine. It was sweaty and full of concern. I wondered what all the fuss was about. I had only lost a pair of glasses, and we had at least two more good pitchers on the team.

"Are you all right, boy?" Mr. Galanter was saying. He looked at my face and forehead. "Somebody wet a handkerchief with cold water!" he shouted. I wondered why he was shouting. His voice hurt my head and rang in my ears. I saw Davey Cantor run off, looking frightened. I heard Sidney Goldberg say something, but I couldn't make out his words. Mr. Galanter put his arm around my shoulders and walked me off the field. He sat me down on the bench next to the rabbi. Without my glasses everything more than about ten feet away from me was blurred. I blinked and wondered about the pain in my left eye. I heard voices and shouts, and then Mr. Galanter was putting a wet handkerchief on my head.

"You feel dizzy, boy?" he said.

I shook my head.

"You're sure now?"

"I'm all right," I said, and wondered why my voice sounded husky and why talking hurt my head.

"You sit quiet now," Mr. Galanter said. "You begin to feel dizzy, you let me know right away."

"Yes, sir," I said.

He went away. I sat on the bench next to the rabbi, who looked at me once, then looked away. I heard shouts in Yiddish. The pain in my left eye was so intense I could feel it in the base of my spine. I sat on the bench a long time, long enough to see us lose the game by a score of eight to seven, long enough to hear the yeshiva team shout with joy, long enough to begin to cry at the pain in my left eye, long enough for Mr. Galanter to come over to me at the end of the game, take one look at my face, and go running out of the yard to call a cab.

The Cliché Expert Testifies on Baseball

FRANK SULLIVAN

Q—Mr. Arbuthnot, you state that your grandmother has passed away and you would like to have the afternoon off to go to her funeral.

A—That is correct.

Q—You are an expert in the clichés of baseball—right?

A—I pride myself on being well versed in the stereotypes of our national pastime.

Q—Well, we'll test you. Who plays baseball?

A—Big-league baseball is customarily played by brilliant outfielders, veteran hurlers, powerful sluggers, knuckle-ball artists, towering first basemen, key moundsmen, fleet base runners, ace southpaws, scrappy little shortstops, sensational war vets, ex-college stars, relief artists, rifle-armed twirlers, dependable mainstays, doughty right-handers, streamlined backstops, power-hitting batsmen, redoubtable infielders, erstwhile Dodgers, veteran sparkplugs, sterling moundsmen, aging twirlers, and rookie sensations.

Q—What other names are rookie sensations known by?

A—They are also known as aspiring rookies, sensational newcomers, promising freshmen, ex-sandlotters, highly touted striplings, and youngsters who will bear watching.

Q—What's the manager of a baseball team called?

A—A veteran pilot. Or youthful pilot. But he doesn't manage the team.

Q—No? What does he do?

A—He guides its destinies.

Q—How?

A—By the use of managerial strategy.

Q—Mr. Arbuthnot, please describe the average major-league-baseball athlete.

A—Well, he comes in three sizes, or types. The first type is tall, slim, lean, towering, rangy, huge, husky, big, strapping, sturdy, handsome, powerful, lanky, rawboned, and rugged.

Q—Quite a hunk of athlete.

A—Well, those are the adjectives usage requires for the description of the Type One, or Ted Williams, ballplayer.

Q—What is Type Two like?

A—He is chunky or stocky—that is to say, Yogi Berra.

Q—And the Third?

A—The third type is elongated and does not walk. He is Ol' Satchmo, or Satchel Paige.

Q—What do you mean Satchmo doesn't walk?

A—Not in the sports pages, he doesn't. He ambles.

Q—You mentioned a hurler, Mr. Arbuthnot. What is a hurler?

A—A hurler is a twirler.

Q—Well, what is a twirler?

A—A twirler is a flinger, a tosser. He's a moundsman.

Q—Moundsman?

A—Yes. He officiates on the mound. When the veteran pilot tells a hurler he is to twirl on a given day, that is a mound assignment, and the hurler who has been told to twirl is the mound nominee for that game.

Q—You mean he pitches?

A—That is right. You have cut the Gordian knot.

Q—What's the pitcher for the other team called?

A—He is the mound adversary, or mound opponent, of the mound nominee. That makes them rival hurlers, or twirlers. They face each other and have a mound duel, or pitchers' battle.

Q—Who wins?

A—The mound victor wins, and as a result he is a mound ace, or ace moundsman. He excels on the mound, or stars on it. He and the other moundsmen on his team are the mound corps.

Q—What happens to the mound nominee who loses the mound duel?

A—He is driven off the mound.

Q—What do you mean by that?

A—He's yanked. He's knocked out of the box.

Q—What's the box?

A—The box is the mound.

Q—I see. Why does the losing moundsman lose?

A—Because he issues, grants, yields, allows, or permits too many hits or walks, or both.

Q—A bit on the freehanded side, eh? Where does the mound victor go if he pitches the entire game?

A—He goes all the way.

Q—And how does the mound adversary who has been knocked out of the box explain his being driven off the mound?

A—He says, "I had trouble with my control," or "my curve wasn't working," or "I just didn't have anything today."

Q—What happens if a mound ace issues, grants, yields, allows, or permits too many hits and walks?

A—In that case, sooner or later, rumors are rife. Either that or they are rampant.

Q—Rife where?

A—In the front office.

Q—What's that?

A—That's the place where baseball's biggies—also known as baseball moguls—do their asking.

Q—What do they ask for?

A—Waivers on erratic southpaw.

Q—What are these baseball biggies further known as?

A—They are known as the Shrewd Mahatma or as Horace Stoneham, but if they wear their shirt open at the neck, they are known as Bill Veeck.

Q—What do baseball biggies do when they are not asking for waivers?

A—They count the gate receipts, buy promising rookies, sell aging twirlers, and stay loyally by Manager Durocher.

Q—And what does Manager Durocher do?

A—He guides the destinies of the Giants and precipitates arguments with the men in blue.

Q—What men in blue?

A—The umpires, or arbiters.

Q—What kind of arguments does Durocher precipitate?

A—Heated arguments.

Q—And the men in blue do what to him and other players who precipitate heated arguments?

A—They send, relegate, banish, or thumb them to the showers.

Q—Mr. Arbuthnot, how do you, as a cliché expert, refer to first base?

A—First base is the initial sack.

Q—And second base?

A—The keystone sack.

Q—What's third base called?

A—The hot corner. The first inning is the initial frame, and an inning without runs is a scoreless stanza.

Q—What is one run known as?

A—A lone run, but four runs are known as a quartet of tallies.

Q—What is a baseball?

A—The pill, the horsehide, the old apple, or the sphere.

Q—And what's a bat?

A—The bat is the willow, or the wagon tongue, or the piece of lumber. In the hands of a mighty batsman, it is the mighty bludgeon.

Q—What does a mighty batsman do?

A—He amasses runs. He connects with the old apple. He raps 'em out and he pounds 'em out. He belts 'em and he clouts 'em.

Q—Clouts what?

A—Circuit clouts.

Q—What are they?

A—Home runs. Know what the mighty batsman does to the mighty bludgeon?

Q—No. What?

A—He wields it. Know what kind of orgies he fancies?

Q—What kind?

A—Batting orgies. Slugfests. That's why his team pins.

Q—Pins what?

A—All its hopes on him.

Q—Mr. Arbuthnot, what is a runner guilty of when he steals home?

A—A plate theft.

Q—And how many kinds of baseball games are there?

A—Five main classifications: scheduled tussles, crucial contests, pivotal games, drab frays, and arc-light tussles.

Q—And what does the team that wins—

A—Sir, a baseball team never wins. It scores a victory, or gains one, or chalks one up, or it snatches.

Q—Snatches what?

A—Victory from the jaws of defeat.

Q—How?

A—By a ninth-inning rally.

Q—I see. Well, what do the teams that chalk up victories do to the teams that lose?

A—They nip, top, wallop, trounce, rout, down, subdue, smash, drub, paste, trip, crush, curb, whitewash, erase, bop, slam, batter, check, hammer, pop, wham, clout, and blank the visitors. Or they zero them.

Q—Gracious sakes! Now I know why ballplayers are old at thirty-five.

A—Oh, that isn't the half of it. They do other things to the visitors.

Q—Is it possible?

A—Certainly. They jolt them, or deal them a jolt. They also halt, sock, thump, larrup, vanquish, flatten, scalp, shellac, blast, slaughter, K.O., mow down, topple, whack, pound, rap, sink, baffle, thwart, foil, maul, and nick.

Q—Do the losers do anything at all to the victors?

A—Yes. They bow to the victors. And they taste.

Q—Taste what?

A—Defeat. They trail. They take a drubbing, pasting, or shellacking. They are in the cellar.

Q—What about the victors?

A—They loom as flag contenders. They're in the first division.

Q—Mr. Arbuthnot, what is the first sign of spring?

A—Well, a robin, of course.

Q—Yes, but I'm thinking of our subject here. How about when the ballplayers go south for spring training?

A—Ballplayers don't go south for spring training.

Q—Why, they do!

A—They do *not*. They wend their way southward.

Q—Oh, I see. Well, do all ballplayers wend their way southward?

A—No. One remains at home.

Q—Who is he?

A—The lone holdout.

Q—Why does the lone holdout remain at home?

A—He refuses to ink pact.

Q—What do you mean by that?

A—He won't affix his Hancock to his contract.

Q—Why not?

A—He demands a pay hike, or salary boost.

Q—From whom?

A—From baseball's biggies.

Q—And what do baseball's biggies do to the lone holdout?

A—They attempt to lure him back into the fold.

Q—How?

A—By offering him a new contract.

Q—What does lone holdout do then?

A—He weighs offer. If he doesn't like it, he balks at terms. If he does like it, he inks pact and gets pay hike.

Q—How much pay hike?

A—An undisclosed amount in excess of.

Q—That makes him what?

A—One of the highest-paid baseball stars in the annals of the game, barring Ruth.

Q—What if baseball's biggies won't give lone holdout pay hike?

A—In that case, lone holdout takes pay cut, old salary, or job in filling station in home town.

Q—Now, when baseball players reach the spring training camp and put on their uniforms—

A—May I correct you again, sir? Baseball players do not put on uniforms. They don them.

Q—I see. What for?

A—For a practice session or strenuous workout.

Q—And why must they have a strenuous workout?

A—Because they must shed the winter's accumulation of excess avoirdupois.

Q—You mean they must lose weight?

A—You put it in a nutshell. They must be streamlined, so they plunge.

Q—Plunge into what?

A—Into serious training.

Q—Can't get into serious training except by plunging, eh?

A—No. Protocol requires that they plunge. Training season gets under way in Grapefruit and Citrus Leagues. Casey Stengel bars night life.

Q—Mr. Arbuthnot, what is the opening game of the season called?

A—Let me see-e-e. It's on the tip of my tongue. Isn't that aggravating? Ah, I have it—the opener! At the opener, fifty-two thousand two hundred and ninety-three fans watch Giants bow to Dodgers.

Q—What do those fifty-two thousand two hundred and ninety-three fans constitute?

A—They constitute fandom.

Q—And how do they get into the ballpark?

A—They click through the turnstiles.

Q—Now, then, Mr. Arbuthnot, the climax of the baseball season is the World Series, is it not?

A—That's right.

Q—And what is the World Series called?

A—It's the fall classic, or crucial contest, also known as the fray, the epic struggle, and the Homeric struggle. It is part of the American scene, like ham and eggs or pumpkin pie. It's a colorful event.

Q—What is it packed with?

A—Thrills. Drama.

Q—What kind of drama?

A—Sheer or tense.

Q—Why does it have to be packed with thrills and drama?

A—Because if it isn't, it becomes drab fray.

Q—Where does the fall classic take place?

A—In a vast municipal stadium or huge ballpark.

Q—And the city in which the fall classic is held is what?

A—The city is baseball mad.

Q—And the hotels?

A—The hotels are jammed. Rooms are at a premium.

Q—Tickets also, I presume.

A—Ticket? If you mean the cards of admission to the fall classic, they are referred to as elusive series ducats, and they *are* at a premium, though I would prefer to say that they are scarcer than the proverbial hen's teeth.

Q—Who attends the series?

A—A milling throng, or great outpouring of fans.

Q—What does the great outpouring of fans do?

A—It storms the portals and, of course, clicks through the turnstiles.

Q—Causing what?

A—Causing attendance records to go by the board. Stands fill early.

Q—What else does the crowd do?

A—It yells itself hoarse. Pent-up emotions are released. It rides the men in blue.

Q—What makes a baseball biggie unhappy on the morning of a series tussle?

A—Leaden skies.

Q—Who is to blame for leaden skies?

A—A character known to the scribes as Jupiter Pluvius, or Jupe.

Q—What does rain dampen?

A—The ardor of the fans.

Q—If the weather clears, who gets credit for that?

A—Another character, known as Old Sol.

Q—Now, the team that wins the series—

A—Again, I'm sorry to correct you, sir. A team does not win a series. It wraps it up. It clinches it.

Q—Well, then what?

A—Then the newly crowned champions repair to their locker room.

Q—What reigns in that locker room?

A—Pandemonium, bedlam, and joy.

Q—Expressed how?

A—By lifting youthful pilot, or his equivalent, to the shoulders of his teammates.

Q—In the locker room of the losers, what is as thick as a day in—I mean so thick you could cut it with a knife?

A—Gloom. The losers are devoid.

Q—Devoid of what?

A—Animation.

Q—Why?

A—Because they came apart at the seams in the pivotal tussle.

Q—What happens to the newly crowned champions later?

A—They are hailed, acclaimed, and fêted. They receive mighty ovations, boisterous demonstrations, and thunderous welcomes.

Q—And when those are over?

A—They split the series purse and go hunting.

Q—Mr. Arbuthnot, if a powerful slugger or mighty batsman wields a mighty bludgeon to such effect that he piles up a record number of circuit clouts, what does that make him?

A—That is very apt to make him most valuable player of the year.

Q—And that?

A—That makes the kids of America look up to him as their hero.

Q—If most valuable player of the year continues the batting orgies that make the kids of America worship him, what then?

A—Then he becomes one of Baseball's Immortals. He is enshrined in Baseball's Hall of Fame.

Q—And after that?

A—Someday he retires and becomes veteran scout, or veteran pilot. Or sports broadcaster.

Q—And then?

A—Well, eventually a memorial plaque is unveiled to him at the opener.

Q—Thank you, Mr. Arbuthnot. You have been most helpful. I won't detain you any longer, and I hope your grandmother's funeral this afternoon is a tense drama packed with thrills.

A—Thanks a lot. Good-by now.

Q—Hold on a moment, Mr. Arbuthnot. Just for my own curiosity—couldn't you have said "thanks" and "good-by" and let it go at that, without adding that "lot" and "now" malarkey?

A—I could have, but it would have cost me my title as a cliché expert.

The Bingo Long Traveling All-Stars and Motor Kings

WILLIAM BRASHLER

Failing in his attempt for a disability settlement
for an injured player and higher wages for himself
and his teammates, home run slugger Bingo Long
breaks away from "Sallie Potter's Louisville Aces,
the World Champions of Colored Baseball," and
forms his own team. This was in the days before
Jackie Robinson broke baseball's color line, and an
ice age before the coming of million-dollar free
agents. From the novel *The Bingo Long Traveling
All-Stars and Motor Kings.*

Bingo and Leon were stooped under the hood of Bingo's Auburn
when Louis drove up in front of Chessie Joy's place in his 1938
Lincoln V-12 convertible. Bingo was fingering his spark plug
cables, making sure his man at the garage had put them in shape
for the road. Louis left his Lincoln idling and hopped out with
Mungo Redd, Splinter Tommy Washington, Isaac Nettles, and
Fat Sam Popper. Bingo had talked each one of them into jumping the Aces for his All-Stars. The only Ace infielder to balk at
the offer was Gerald Purvis, and he was into Sallie for a thousand
because of a new La Salle. If Gerald took off and left the La Salle
behind, Sallie would grab it and keep what Gerald had already
paid him. Gerald was the only player Sallie had comfortably
over the barrel. The others had grown wary of Sallie's financial
setups long ago. When Bingo approached them with his offer and
his sales pitch, they were easily persuaded. He had enough
money up front to turn their heads.

Since second-line pitcher Turkey Travis had agreed to come

along, Bingo needed only a center fielder and a first baseman to fill out his squad. He let Ezell Carter paint the team's name on the side of his Auburn with whitewash. Ezell messed up "Traveling" and "Motor Kings" pretty bad, but he got Bingo Long spelled right, so Bingo told him it was a good job. Louis had the initials "B.L.T.A.S.M.K. #2" painted on his Lincoln and he added a few five-point stars for class.

Louis was dressed in his custom blue pin-striped suit and vest. But the clothes couldn't begin to disguise that on all of Louis's five feet eleven inches hung only 140 pounds. His neck sprouted out of his collar into a wide, wet smile, giving him a look like he'd just finished his high school graduation. He cocked a skinny-visored touring cap on his head and, for the occasion, he sported a pair of snow white spats.

"Oh, there is a pretty partner!" Bingo howled when he laid eyes on him.

"Dressed up for the leaving," Louis said. He spun around and jerked his hips. "This town is seeing the last of this third baseman for a time."

"My, my, what a dandy," Leon said as he and the others looked Louis over. They were wearing suits as well; Bingo featured his usual carnation in the lapel.

"When you touring you got to do it in fashion," said Bingo. "The people got to know you in town."

Louis's Lincoln was long and spacious, and Bingo's Auburn could easily seat six, so the team had plenty of room for the small satchels they carried with them. Bingo put most of the equipment, the bats and balls he could scrape up, in his trunk. He and Leon drove together since most of the others preferred to go with Louis and sit in the open convertible.

Just before starting off, Isaac Nettles yelled at Bingo and walked over to talk with him. Isaac, who was thirty-eight and showing wisps of gray throughout his scalp, pinched the lines of his brow together as he talked. He was the darkest of all the Aces, with a dour, narrow face. His expression betrayed his age and the fact that he became more concerned about things than did most of the others.

"Hey, what you think about a suggestion I got to make the team complete?" Isaac said.

"Shoot," said Bingo. "I'm open for anything."

"Let's go to Raymond's and take him along. He could be manager or traveling secretary or something like that. Man, it would make it for him."

"Damn, I never thought about that. What you think, Leon?"

Leon looked up at the sky. "Foolish," he said.

"Why? Now just why?" objected Isaac.

"Money," said Leon. "Raymond's dead weight if he can't play. A traveling team can't afford no luxuries."

"Who says?" said Bingo.

Leon shook his head. "Damn, Bingo, common sense says it."

"Shit. Let's show Sallie how to take care of a top-rate ball player. Raymond can manage things like Isaac said, like counting up the take and all, until he gets his wheel back in shape."

"You a good man, Bingo," Isaac said. "Raymond will fly when we shows up."

Isaac ran back to Louis's car and the two autos started out. Leon hung his head off to the side of the seat. Bingo grinned at him. "You got to have understanding when you running a ball team, Leon. That's what it's about." He turned the car onto Raymond's street.

Bingo had not broken the final news of the team's formation to Sallie in person. He preferred instead to get his men together on that Friday morning and quietly leave for Pittsburgh. It was best not to get Sallie into another argument, for then Sallie would let loose with a bunch of threats in desperation just to keep his team. He would have to carry out the threats sooner or later or admit that he was licked. Lionel had told Bingo to break without that kind of fuss. It lacked style but the effect would be just as permanent. Sallie would have to cancel most of his league commitments unless he could assemble a ghost squad in time. Even then, he would lose his gate as soon as the people saw that Bingo, Leon, and most of the rest of the regulars were missing. The timing was also good, for Sallie was in hot water with the local politicians because of a craps operation he was running out of his restaurant. He wouldn't have a prayer in court if he tried to bring Bingo and the others in for breach of contract. He'd have to get back at Bingo on his own, and that gave Bingo the benefit of time. Bingo could have his team halfway across the country before Sallie could do anything to stop him, if he could stop him at all. The only thing Bingo knew for certain was that Sallie, sooner or later, would try.

Lionel Foster stood outside his Chop House eying the automobiles which had just parked in front of him. "So we have the Motor Kings, yes we do," he announced. A pair of his counter girls stepped out onto the sidewalk. They smiled at Bingo and Louis and rubbed the door of Louis's Lincoln as if it were too hot to touch.

"We is made for the open road," yelled Bingo. "Lionel, you ever dream we'd be looking this good?"

Louis got out of his car and clicked his heels. The girls stroked their thighs and purred at him.

"Now we only wonders if you can play some ball," Lionel said and ushered Bingo into the restaurant.

He set the team up with beers and steaks and then sat down at a table with Bingo and Leon.

"Glad to see the old man with you," Lionel said, nodding at Leon. "I thought you was a slave to Sallie's plantation for good, Leon. I did."

Leon looked at Lionel out of the corner of his eye but said nothing.

"I talk faster than Sallie, that's all," Bingo said.

"Or you got to say something different," said Lionel. He shook the ice in his whiskey. "But I'm glad to see you, Leon, because you is another reason why this might turn out to be some good money spent. Just so things don't get away from my man Bingo here. How about it, Bingo? Sallie fight you before you got away?"

"I did it like you said to, Lionel. We played Wednesday some boys from Ranolia and yesterday when we had off I did my packing and this morning we was gone. Sallie couldn't done it better hisself."

"He going to fight you every way. But if you got the odds, you can keep him off you until you rich enough to come back and do anything you want. Them papers ain't worth much to Sallie if he ain't got the boys to go with them. He can't do nothing because them courts is glad to see colored stumble around after themselves. Judge told me I was too rich for any nigger so he wasn't going to help me get more. That's what they going to tell Sallie when he try to get you."

"Funny talk coming from you," Leon said.

"Ain't it though?" Lionel agreed. "Here I is pulling for you boys like you was runaway slaves on the river." Lionel laughed out loud.

"Who says we ain't," said Leon.

"Ain't no slave ever run away with the money you got in your pocket, Leon. Remember that when you feeling like a slave sometime." Lionel finished his drink.

Bingo sawed at his steak. "I just brought Leon along to keep things laughing, Lionel. You know he ain't worth a nickel."

Lionel smiled once again and refilled his glass from the bottle on the table. He had always liked Bingo. Bingo never made trouble, never raised a fuss. He leaned over to him.

"You know what you got to do to make this thing move. You been on the road before so you know. The big cities is easy because the people know you and there is a lot of colored to come out. But when you get to those one-lump towns you is going to have to *sell* the product, you know that, Bingo. They ain't going to be putting out just to see their boys beat by the darkies so you got to show them something they ain't seen before and take your chances. You know you got to show first and win second before you going to take their money."

"Yeah, yeah, I know," said Bingo.

"Good. And watch out for the police because they can cut you when they wants to. There ain't no money sitting in the can."

"What our suits look like? You got them, Lionel?"

"The ladies is going on them. They some Elite suits with some fancy lettering. Don't worry about the outfits," he said.

"Okay, I won't," said Bingo.

Lionel gave Bingo Donus Youngs, a good fielding first baseman, and a kid outfielder by the name of Joe Calloway. Calloway had been a bat boy until he was old enough to try out for the Elite Giants. He was only eighteen, but Lionel thought he might be good enough to travel with Bingo and learn what he could from the Stars. Bingo named him Esquire Joe and told him not to let anything get by him in right field. Joe was tall and bony and Lionel said he had an arm like a rifle.

The uniforms were Elite Giant green and white, with pin stripes and five green stars running across the chest. Bingo had wanted "Bingo's All-Stars" over the numbers in back but Lionel said he didn't have the time for that. Bingo had to admit, though, that the uniforms were top rate, as sharp as any around. In Chicago he would pick up a set of two-tone caps, green bills and white crowns, to complete the outfit.

When they trotted out onto the field for the second game of the Elite Giants doubleheader, the Pittsburgh crowd gave them a loud welcome. Bingo led the team on with his lumbering walk and a smile from ear to ear. When he got to the infield he stopped and bowed to the people. His Stars circled him like elephants in the circus. They had used this entrance on other trips and the crowd loved it. When they stopped running they took out four balls and shuttled them from man to man, crisscross within the circle. They called it hotball because the ball never stopped changing hands and never touched the ground. Louis Keystone finally ended it by grabbing all four balls and putting them in his back pocket. But that did not stop the motions, and for a minute or so the Stars wildly pantomimed hotball with nothing but fresh air changing hands. The fans laughed and whistled, the kids in the crowd tried to figure out what was going on.

Louis, Mungo Redd, and Splinter Tommy Washington went through their routines in infield practice. As they moved, the three of them in their baggy whites and script letters looked identical even though Louis was twice as skinny and taller than the others and Mungo wore a pair of glasses that all but hid his eyes beneath the bill of his cap and Splinter, for all of his grace and casual nonchalance around the bag, sported a set of teeth so crooked they made him feel awkward and self-conscious off the field. But in the dust of the warm-up, Mungo and Tommy gobbled up double-play balls and skipped through the relay without a bobble. Tommy went across the bag and pivoted in the air with the toss to first. Louis at third took ground balls that skipped at him like stones on cement. After he gloved one, he flipped the ball backhand to a ball boy behind him and then waited for another. To finish up, the infield went through their routine without a ball, jumping and throwing and slapping their gloves in place of it. It was a smooth sight, even better than the hotball act, and the crowd applauded as if the Stars had just pulled one out in the ninth.

Yet there was nothing as sweet as watching Bingo take batting practice. He leaned into each pitch with his huge arms, whipping the bat around and cracking the ball. His usual blast was as high as it was far. At the peak of its ascent it hung in the sky like a dirigible about to burst, and then it lazily fell behind the fence. The kids in blue jeans and barebacks stood behind the backstop and winced each time Bingo smashed one. Some mimicked him, swinging an imaginary bat as he swung his, and then gazed off into the sky following the ball. They could feel the power, the icy connection stinging through them just as if they had swatted the ball like a fat bug and then circled the bases and heard the cheers. Bingo grinned at them, flexed the muscle in his right arm, and then fouled one straight back into the screen about head-high on the kids. It jolted the wires and sent them ducking and yelling.

Over on the sidelines Leon Carter was warming up. He was to pitch four innings and Turkey Travis would follow up. Louis Keystone was standing next to Leon, priming the crowd for a pregame contest. Four or five men leaned on the fence and listened to Louis's proposition.

"A little money against Mr. Leon's arm here. Can I interest a gambling man? Anyone among you all who can take a dollar away from me?"

He waved his hands in front of the men, pointing at Leon's arm as the pitcher warmed up with Sam Popper. Then Louis took out a few one-dollar bills from his back pocket and held them up.

"Right here now. A little money on Mr. Leon's arm. Take no chances, just bet against the man's skill. You win, I'll double your money. Two you take against my one."

Leon threw nonchalantly.

"Popper just holds his glove on a chewing gum wrapper, that's all," Louis said. "He don't move it a half inch, no sir. And old Leon throws the fastball over the wrapper. If he does I take your dollar, if he don't you take two from me. Ain't no man perfect, and that's the game. C'mon, gentlemen, you be the judge. Just a friendly gamble among us."

He flashed his bills up and fanned them. Three of the men held up a dollar. Fat Sam wadded up a wrapper and tossed it in front of him. Then he held his glove over it. Leon wound up and threw, and he missed the wrapper by a foot on the right.

"Oh, man, you is losing it and costing me money right off," Louis yelped.

He walked in front of the three men and peeled off two bucks for each. He then repeated the challenge. The same three and two more held up a buck. Leon wound and threw; Sam Popper never budged his mitt. The ball streaked into it like a beam of light. Louis hopped down the row of men and took their bills. All five put another in the air. Leon again reached back and threw and Fat Sam's mitt didn't move. Louis quickly grabbed his money. He held the bills up and called the bettors.

"Now it's a man's game, boys. You seen him do it and you seen him miss. Old Louis here is the fool because I plays every time and pays every time. Put your money against the man's arm. Show me what you got."

The first three men flashed bills again. Leon uncorked another fastball over the wrapper. Only two men followed with bills. Leon threw another down the center. Louis took their money. Four in a row. Louis didn't advertise anymore, but stared at Popper's mitt. Five was a good number; four men put their money up. Leon split the wrapper again. Louis hustled to collect. Only one man put up his dollar after that. But Leon hit home once more. Each ball had been thrown the same, like a machine had done it, and Sam never moved his mitt enough to raise a question about it. The man flashed another dollar. He glared at Leon, daring him to throw another strike. Leon threw, Louis took the dollar. Once more, Leon threw a submarine fastball, and Louis snatched the bill.

The man fanned his face with his hat. "You is worse than craps, Carter," he said. He waved Louis away. Louis stuffed the bills into his back pocket and trotted to the bench. Leon split the wrapper a few more times and put his warm-up jacket on. Then he walked to the bench to get his money from Louis.

The All-Stars met little resistance from the Elite Giants. It

was the Giants' second game of the day, an "appearance" game
as they called it, a game set up for the fans instead of the players.
They played nonchalantly, kidding the All-Stars about the routines Bingo made them go through. Leon glided through the
line-up with an assortment of experimental pitches, and Bingo's
men jumped on three Elite pitchers for nine runs. Only Esquire
Joe Calloway showed badly with three swinging strike-outs, but
he did bring in a long drive over his shoulder near the right-field
fence. Bingo liked him, he liked how the kid galloped along the
grass, he liked the kid's arm, and he liked Joe's big, level swing,
even though it didn't hit anything that afternoon. Most of all,
Bingo liked the way Esquire Joe seemed to enjoy himself while
he played. He held a loose, close-mouthed grin on his face as he
cradled long flies. There were few things Bingo liked better than
watching an outfielder outrun a high blast and then bring it home
like a soft peach off a tree.

"You boys doing good, real good," Lionel said to Bingo as
they walked from the field after the game. "You got class and
you got talent like nobody I seen around. You play it right,
Bingo, and you ain't going to be able to keep the people from
giving you their money."

Lionel had contacted some of the big promoters in the Mid-
west and set up a half dozen games in Cleveland, Toledo, and
Chicago. These were all league towns, so the All-Stars had to
work around schedules to get their games. After Chicago they
could hit Milwaukee and then head west across Wisconsin and
Iowa.

"You got to watch out for the other barnstormers like Max
Helverton's Hooley Speedballers and them white teams from
Michigan, them House of David boys with the beards," Lionel
told Bingo. "You can't follow them because you lose the edge
on the towns. You can play them but when you is done you
should go in the opposite direction. It ain't trouble; it's just good
business. And remember too, Bingo, that you got to hit those
towns when they ain't doing nothing big like harvesting or something because then you lose your crowd. Otherwise they going
to welcome you like you was a circus."

Bingo already knew most of what Lionel was telling him,
but he listened anyway because Lionel had run almost every

kind of traveling show around. Lionel helped him get up some paper for advertising and letters to send to town post offices announcing the All-Stars' arrival. The night before the team took off for Cleveland, Bingo sat down with Lionel and went over possible routines and antics to please the crowds. "Remember," Lionel said, "ain't nothing around pleases more than good ball playing. Better than folks has ever seen. They remember it because it *amazes* them. Yeah, it does."

Bingo called a meeting that night after the players had come in from the Chop House.

"I been doing some talking and some planning and I'm ready to present you with what we going to be doing on this tour. Now you all know how to play and how to look good like we did yesterday with the Giants. And when we be playing the big teams like the Detroit Cubans and the Velvets in Chicago and around in there we won't have no trouble either because they is our own people watching and we know what they likes. But some of you ain't been past Chicago and you don't know what happens out there. In them dog towns we got to play it with our nose. We got to please the people who works them farms. And if they want to see us clown then we clown them until they dead. But if they want to see us play straight then we do and take our chances against what they got. We just can't be looking bad or nonchalant or no good. Because then they be calling us a bunch of shuffles and they ain't going to be throwing their quarters in our socks. So they ain't much we can do until we see what the situation is but we got to be ready. We got to be polite and cheerful all the time even when we ain't feeling it. If we get trouble we just be leaving by the back way and getting on down the road with our hands in our pockets and whistling like we stole the lady's pie. Now that is something I thought I should say right off so you know where this team stands. Lionel say if we play it right we going to take their money. I think he's right because he been around. He takes some lumps too, yes he does. But that's what I got to say."

He stopped and wiped his mouth. Nobody said anything. Then he went on.

"We going to be playing a lot of white outfits too. Some of you ain't played much against white so you got to be prepared.

They take what they can out of you if you don't be on your guard. They going to slide into your leg and step on your foot if you leave it out there in plain sight. They going to be saying the same old things to rattle you and get you to forget how to play right. But they ain't nothing. They got to pitch to you when you up to the plate. I hit everything a white pitch can throw and they don't like it but they can't do much but run after it. So that's how we play them. You keep your heads turned behind your back all the time for something sneaking up on you. That's the way you play white."

Bingo stopped again and waited for a reaction. He could feel himself getting excited. The players sat and looked at him, blinking their eyes. Louis Keystone yawned.

"That was a nice speech, Bingo. Real nice," Leon finally said.

"Yeah, thanks, Leon," Bingo said, and he sat down and pulled out a Lucky.

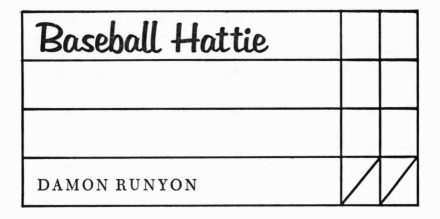

Baseball Hattie

DAMON RUNYON

It comes on springtime, and the little birdies are singing in the trees in Central Park, and the grass is green all around and about, and I am at the Polo Grounds on the opening day of the baseball season, when who do I behold but Baseball Hattie. I am somewhat surprised at this spectacle, as it is years since I see Baseball Hattie, and for all I know she long ago passes to a better and happier world.

But there she is, as large as life, and in fact twenty pounds larger, and when I call the attention of Armand Fibleman, the gambler, to her, he gets up and tears right out of the joint as if he sees a ghost, for if there is one thing Armand Fibleman loathes and despises, it is a ghost.

I can see that Baseball Hattie is greatly changed, and to tell the truth, I can see that she is getting to be nothing but an old bag. Her hair that is once as black as a yard up a stovepipe is gray, and she is wearing gold-rimmed cheaters, although she seems to be pretty well dressed and looks as if she may be in the money a little bit, at that.

But the greatest change in her is the way she sits there very quiet all afternoon, never once opening her yap, even when many of the customers around her are claiming that Umpire William Klem is Public Enemy No. 1 to 16 inclusive, because they think he calls a close one against the Giants. I am wondering if maybe Baseball Hattie is stricken dumb somewhere back down the years, because I can remember when she is usually making speeches in the grandstand in favor of hanging such characters as Umpire William Klem when they call close ones against the Giants. But Hattie just sits there as if she is in a church while the public clamor goes on about her, and she does not as much as cry out robber, or even you big bum at Umpire William Klem.

I see many a baseball bug in my time, male and female, but without doubt the worst bug of them all is Baseball Hattie, and you can say it again. She is most particularly a bug about the Giants, and she never misses a game they play at the Polo Grounds, and in fact she sometimes bobs up watching them play in other cities, which is always very embarrassing to the Giants, as they fear the customers in these cities may get the wrong impression of New York womanhood after listening to Baseball Hattie awhile.

The first time I ever see Baseball Hattie to pay any attention to her is in Philadelphia, a matter of twenty-odd years back, when the Giants are playing a series there, and many citizens of New York, including Armand Fibleman and myself, are present, because the Philadelphia customers are great hands for betting on baseball games in those days, and Armand Fibleman figures he may knock a few of them in the creek.

Armand Fibleman is a character who will bet on baseball games from who-laid-the-chunk, and in fact he will bet on anything whatever, because Armand Fibleman is a gambler by trade and has been such since infancy. Personally, I will not bet you four dollars on a baseball game, because in the first place I am not apt to have four dollars, and in the second place I consider horse races a much sounder investment, but I often go around and about with Armand Fibleman, as he is a friend of mine, and sometimes he gives me a little piece of one of his bets for nothing.

Well, what happens in Philadelphia but the umpire forfeits the game in the seventh inning to the Giants by a score of nine to nothing when the Phillies are really leading by five runs, and the reason the umpire takes this action is because he orders several of the Philadelphia players to leave the field for calling him a scoundrel and a rat and a snake in the grass, and also a baboon, and they refuse to take their departure, as they still have more names to call him.

Right away the Philadelphia customers become infuriated in a manner you will scarcely believe, for ordinarily a Philadelphia baseball customer is as quiet as a lamb, no matter what you do to him, and in fact in those days a Philadelphia baseball customer is only considered as somebody to do something to.

But these Philadelphia customers are so infuriated that they not only chase the umpire under the stand, but they wait in the street outside the baseball orchard until the Giants change into their street clothes and come out of the clubhouse. Then the Philadelphia customers begin pegging rocks, and one thing and another, at the Giants, and it is a most exciting and disgraceful scene that is spoken of for years afterwards.

Well, the Giants march along toward the North Philly station to catch a train for home, dodging the rocks and one thing and another the best they can, and wondering why the Philadelphia gendarmes do not come to the rescue, until somebody notices several gendarmes among the customers doing some of the throwing themselves, so the Giants realize that this is a most inhospitable community, to be sure.

Finally all of them get inside the North Philly station and are safe, except a big, tall, left-handed pitcher by the name of Haystack Duggeler, who just reports to the club the day before and who finds himself surrounded by quite a posse of these infuriated Philadelphia customers, and who is unable to make them understand that he is nothing but a rookie, because he has a Missouri accent, and besides, he is half paralyzed with fear.

One of the infuriated Philadelphia customers is armed with a brickbat and is just moving forward to maim Haystack Duggeler with this instrument, when who steps into the situation but Baseball Hattie, who is also on her way to the station to catch a train, and who is greatly horrified by the assault on the Giants.

She seizes the brickbat from the infuriated Philadelphia customer's grasp, and then tags the customer smack-dab between the eyes with his own weapon, knocking him so unconscious that I afterwards hear he does not recover for two weeks, and that he remains practically an imbecile the rest of his days.

Then Baseball Hattie cuts loose on the other infuriated Philadelphia customers with language that they never before hear in those parts, causing them to disperse without further ado, and after the last customer is beyond the sound of her voice, she takes Haystack Duggeler by the pitching arm and personally escorts him to the station.

Now out of this incident is born a wonderful romance between Baseball Hattie and Haystack Duggeler, and in fact it is no doubt love at first sight, and about this period Haystack Duggeler begins burning up the league with his pitching, and at the same time giving Manager Mac plenty of headaches, including the romance with Baseball Hattie, because anybody will tell you that a left-hander is tough enough on a manager without a romance, and especially a romance with Baseball Hattie.

It seems that the trouble with Hattie is she is in business up in Harlem, and this business consists of a boarding and rooming house where ladies and gentlemen board and room, and personally I never see anything out of line in the matter, but the rumor somehow gets around, as rumors will do, that in the first place, it is not a boarding and rooming house, and in the second place that the ladies and gentlemen who room and board there are by no means ladies and gentlemen, and especially ladies.

Well, this rumor becomes a terrible knock to Baseball Hattie's social reputation. Furthermore, I hear Manager Mac sends for her and requests her to kindly lay off his ballplayers, and especially off a character who can make a baseball sing high C like Haystack Duggeler. In fact, I hear Manager Mac gives her such a lecture on her civic duty to New York and to the Giants that Baseball Hattie sheds tears, and promises she will never give Haystack another tumble the rest of the season.

"You know me, Mac," Baseball Hattie says. "You know I will cut off my nose rather than do anything to hurt your club. I sometimes figure I am in love with this big bloke, but," she says, "maybe it is only gas pushing up around my heart. I will take something for it. To hell with him, Mac!" she says.

So she does not see Haystack Duggeler again, except at a distance, for a long time, and he goes on to win fourteen games in a row, pitching a no-hitter and four two-hitters among them, and hanging up a reputation as a great pitcher, and also as a hundred-percent heel.

Haystack Duggeler is maybe twenty-five at this time, and he comes to the big league with more bad habits than anybody in the history of the world is able to acquire in such a short time. He is especially a great rumpot, and after he gets going good in the league, he is just as apt to appear for a game all mulled up as not.

He is fond of all forms of gambling, such as playing cards and shooting craps, but after they catch him with a deck of readers in a poker game and a pair of tops in a crap game, none of the Giants will play with him any more, except of course when there is nobody else to play with.

He is ignorant about many little things, such as reading and writing and geography and mathematics, as Haystack Duggeler himself admits he never goes to school any more than he can help, but he is so wise when it comes to larceny that I always figure they must have great tutors back in Haystack's old home town of Booneville, Mo.

And no smarter jobbie ever breathes than Haystack when he is out there pitching. He has so much speed that he just naturally throws the ball past a batter before he can get the old musket off his shoulder, and along with his hard one, Haystack has a curve like the letter Q. With two ounces of brains, Haystack Duggeler will be the greatest pitcher that ever lives.

Well, as far as Baseball Hattie is concerned, she keeps her word about not seeing Haystack, although sometimes when he is mulled up he goes around to her boarding and rooming house, and tries to break down the door.

On days when Haystack Duggeler is pitching, she is always in her favorite seat back of third, and while she roots hard for the Giants no matter who is pitching, she puts on extra steam when Haystack is bending them over, and it is quite an experience to hear her crying lay them in there, Haystack, old boy, and strike this big tramp out, Haystack, and other exclamations of a similar nature, which please Haystack quite some, but annoy Baseball Hattie's neighbors back of third base, such as Armand Fibleman, if he happens to be betting on the other club.

A month before the close of his first season in the big league,

Haystack Duggeler gets so ornery that Manager Mac suspends him, hoping maybe it will cause Haystack to do a little thinking, but naturally Haystack is unable to do this, because he has nothing to think with. About a week later, Manager Mac gets to noticing how he can use a few ball games, so he starts looking for Haystack Duggeler, and he finds him tending bar on Eighth Avenue with his uniform hung up back of the bar as an advertisement.

The baseball writers speak of Haystack as eccentric, which is a polite way of saying he is a screwball, but they consider him a most unique character and are always writing humorous stories about him, though any one of them will lay you plenty of nine to five that Haystack winds up an umbay. The chances are they will raise their price a little, as the season closes and Haystack is again under suspension with cold weather coming on and not a dime in his pants pockets.

It is sometime along in the winter that Baseball Hattie hauls off and marries Haystack Duggeler, which is a great surprise to one and all, but not nearly as much of a surprise as when Hattie closes her boarding and rooming house and goes to live in a little apartment with Haystack Duggeler up on Washington Heights.

It seems that she finds Haystack one frosty night sleeping in a hallway, after being around slightly mulled up for several weeks, and she takes him to her home and gets him a bath and a shave and a clean shirt and two boiled eggs and some toast and coffee and a shot or two of rye whisky, all of which is greatly appreciated by Haystack, especially the rye whisky.

Then Haystack proposes marriage to her and takes a paralyzed oath that if she becomes his wife he will reform, so what with loving Haystack anyway, and with the fix commencing to request more dough off the boarding-and-rooming-house business than the business will stand, Hattie takes him at his word, and there you are.

The baseball writers are wondering what Manager Mac will say when he hears these tidings, but all Mac says is that Haystack cannot possibly be any worse married than he is single-o, and then Mac has the club office send the happy couple a little paper money to carry them over the winter.

Well, what happens but a great change comes over Haystack Duggeler. He stops bending his elbow and helps Hattie cook and wash the dishes, and holds her hand when they are in the movies, and speaks of his love for her several times a week, and Hattie is as happy as nine dollars' worth of lettuce. Manager Mac is so delighted at the change in Haystack that he has the club office send over more paper money, because Mac knows that with Haystack in shape he is sure of twenty-five games, and maybe the pennant.

In late February, Haystack reports to the training camp down South still as sober as some judges, and the other ball-players are so impressed by the change in him that they admit him to their poker game again. But of course it is too much to expect a man to alter his entire course of living all at once, and it is not long before Haystack discovers four nines in his hand on his own deal and breaks up the game.

He brings Baseball Hattie with him to the camp, and this is undoubtedly a slight mistake, as it seems the old rumor about her boarding-and-rooming-house business gets around among the ever-loving wives of the other players, and they put on a large chill for her. In fact, you will think Hattie has the smallpox.

Naturally, Baseball Hattie feels the frost, but she never lets on, as it seems she runs into many bigger and better frosts than this in her time. Then Haystack Duggeler notices it, and it seems that it makes him a little peevish toward Baseball Hattie, and in fact it is said that he gives her a slight pasting one night in their room, partly because she has no better social standing and partly because he is commencing to cop a few sneaks on the local corn now and then, and Hattie chides him for same.

Well, about this time it appears that Baseball Hattie discovers that she is going to have a baby, and as soon as she recovers from her astonishment, she decides that it is to be a boy who will be a great baseball player, maybe a pitcher, although Hattie admits she is willing to compromise on a good second baseman.

She also decides that his name is to be Derrill Duggeler, after his paw, as it seems Derrill is Haystack's real name, and he is only called Haystack because he claims he once makes a living stacking hay, although the general opinion is that all he ever stacks is cards.

It is really quite remarkable what a belt Hattie gets out
of the idea of having this baby, though Haystack is not excited
about the matter. He is not paying much attention to Baseball
Hattie by now, except to give her a slight pasting now and
then, but Hattie is so happy about the baby that she does not
mind these pastings.

Haystack Duggeler meets up with Armand Fibleman along
in midsummer. By this time, Haystack discovers horse racing
and is always making bets on the horses, and naturally he is
generally broke, and then I commence running into him in different spots with Armand Fibleman, who is now betting higher
than a cat's back on baseball games.

It is late August, and the Giants are fighting for the front
end of the league, and an important series with Brooklyn is coming up, and everybody knows that Haystack Duggeler will work
in anyway two games of the series, as Haystack can generally
beat Brooklyn just by throwing his glove on the mound. There
is no doubt but what he has the old Indian sign on Brooklyn,
and the night before the first game, which he is sure to work,
the gamblers along Broadway are making the Giants two-to-one
favorites to win the game.

This same night before the game, Baseball Hattie is home
in her little apartment on Washington Heights waiting for Haystack to come in and eat a delicious dinner of pigs' knuckles and
sauerkraut, which she personally prepares for him. In fact, she
hurries home right after the ball game to get this delicacy ready,
because Haystack tells her he will surely come home this particular night, although Hattie knows he is never better than even
money to keep his word about anything.

But sure enough, in he comes while the pigs' knuckles and
sauerkraut are still piping hot, and Baseball Hattie is surprised
to see Armand Fibleman with him, as she knows Armand back-
wards and forwards and does not care much for him, at that.
However, she can say the same thing about four million other
characters in this town, so she makes Armand welcome, and they
sit down and put on the pigs' knuckles and sauerkraut together,
and a pleasant time is enjoyed by one and all. In fact, Baseball
Hattie puts herself out to entertain Armand Fibleman, because
he is the first guest Haystack ever brings home.

Well, Armand Fibleman can be very pleasant when he wishes, and he speaks very nicely to Hattie. Naturally, he sees that Hattie is expecting, and in fact he will have to be blind not to see it, and he seems greatly interested in this matter and asks Hattie many questions, and Hattie is delighted to find somebody to talk to about what is coming off with her, as Haystack will never listen to any of her remarks on the subject.

So Armand Fibleman gets to hear all about Baseball Hattie's son, and how he is to be a great baseball player, and Armand says is that so, and how nice, and all this and that, until Haystack Duggeler speaks up as follows, and to wit:

"Oh, dag-gone her son!" Haystack says. "It is going to be a girl, anyway, so let us dismiss this topic and get down to business. Hat," he says, "you fan yourself into the kitchen and wash the dishes, while Armand and me talk."

So Hattie goes into the kitchen, leaving Haystack and Armand sitting there talking, and what are they talking about but a proposition for Haystack to let the Brooklyn club beat him the next day so Armand Fibleman can take the odds and clean up a nice little gob of money, which he is to split with Haystack.

Hattie can hear every word they say, as the kitchen is next door to the dining room where they are sitting, and at first she thinks they are joking, because at this time nobody ever even as much as thinks of skulduggery in baseball, or anyway, not much.

It seems that at first Haystack is not in favor of the idea, but Armand Fibleman keeps mentioning money that Haystack owes him for bets on the horse races, and he asks Haystack how he expects to continue betting on the races without fresh money, and Armand also speaks of the great injustice that is being done Haystack by the Giants in not paying him twice the salary he is getting, and how the loss of one or two games is by no means such a great calamity.

Well, finally Baseball Hattie hears Haystack say all right, but he wishes a thousand dollars then and there as a guarantee, and Armand Fibleman says this is fine, and they will go downtown and he will get the money at once, and now Hattie realizes that maybe they are in earnest, and she pops out of the kitchen and speaks as follows:

"Gentlemen," Hattie says, "you seem to be sober, but I

guess you are drunk. If you are not drunk, you must both be daffy to think of such a thing as phenagling around with a baseball game."

"Hattie," Haystack says, "kindly close your trap and go back in the kitchen, or I will give you a bust in the nose."

And with this he gets up and reaches for his hat, and Armand Fibleman gets up, too, and Hattie says like this:

"Why, Haystack," she says, "you are not really serious in this matter, are you?"

"Of course I am serious," Haystack says. "I am sick and tired of pitching for starvation wages, and besides, I will win a lot of games later on to make up for the one I lose tomorrow. Say," he says, "these Brooklyn bums may get lucky tomorrow and knock me loose from my pants, anyway, no matter what I do, so what difference does it make?"

"Haystack," Baseball Hattie says, "I know you are a liar and a drunkard and a cheat and no account generally, but nobody can tell me you will sink so low as to purposely toss off a ball game. Why, Haystack, baseball is always on the level. It is the most honest game in all this world. I guess you are just ribbing me, because you know how much I love it."

"Dry up!" Haystack says to Hattie. "Furthermore, do not expect me home again tonight. But anyway, dry up."

"Look, Haystack," Hattie says, "I am going to have a son. He is your son and my son, and he is going to be a great ballplayer when he grows up, maybe a greater pitcher than you are, though I hope and trust he is not left-handed. He will have your name. If they find out you toss off a game for money, they will throw you out of baseball and you will be disgraced. My son will be known as the son of a crook, and what chance will he have in baseball? Do you think I am going to allow you to do this to him, and to the game that keeps me from going nutty for marrying you?"

Naturally, Haystack Duggeler is greatly offended by Hattie's crack about her son being maybe a greater pitcher than he is, and he is about to take steps, when Armand Fibleman stops him. Armand Fibleman is commencing to be somewhat alarmed at Baseball Hattie's attitude, and he gets to thinking that he hears that people in her delicate condition are often irresponsible, and he fears that she may blow a whistle on this enterprise without realizing what she is doing. So he undertakes a few soothing remarks to her.

"Why, Hattie," Armand Fibleman says, "nobody can possibly find out about this little matter, and Haystack will have enough money to send your son to college, if his markers at the race track do not take it all. Maybe you better lie down and rest awhile," Armand says.

But Baseball Hattie does not as much as look at Armand, though she goes on talking to Haystack. "They always find out thievery, Haystack," she says, "especially when you are dealing with a fink like Fibleman. If you deal with him once, you will have to deal with him again and again, and he will be the first to holler copper on you, because he is a stool pigeon in his heart."

"Haystack," Armand Fibleman says, "I think we better be going."

"Haystack," Hattie says, "you can go out of here and stick up somebody or commit a robbery or a murder, and I will still welcome you back and stand by you. But if you are going out to steal my son's future, I advise you not to go."

"Dry up!" Haystack says. "I am going."

"All right, Haystack," Hattie says, very calm. "But just step into the kitchen with me and let me say one little word to you by yourself, and then I will say no more."

Well, Haystack Duggeler does not care for even just one little word more, but Armand Fibleman wishes to get this disagreeable scene over with, so he tells Haystack to let her have her word, and Haystack goes into the kitchen with Hattie, and Armand cannot hear what is said, as she speaks very low, but he hears Haystack laugh heartily and then Haystack comes out of the kitchen, still laughing, and tells Armand he is ready to go.

As they start for the door, Baseball Hattie outs with a long-nosed .38-caliber Colt's revolver, and goes root-a-toot-toot with it, and the next thing anybody knows, Haystack is on the floor yelling bloody murder, and Armand Fibleman is leaving the premises without bothering to open the door. In fact, the landlord afterwards talks some of suing Haystack Duggeler because of the damage Armand Fibleman does to the door. Armand himself afterwards admits that when he slows down for a breather a couple of miles down Broadway he finds splinters stuck all over him.

Well, the doctors come, and the gendarmes come, and there is great confusion, especially as Baseball Hattie is sobbing so she can scarcely make a statement, and Haystack Duggeler is so sure he is going to die that he cannot think of anything to say except oh-oh-oh, but finally the landlord remembers seeing Armand leave with his door, and everybody starts questioning Hattie about this until she confesses that Armand is there all right, and that he tries to bribe Haystack to toss off a ball game, and that she then suddenly finds herself with a revolver in her hand, and everything goes black before her eyes, and she can remember no more until somebody is sticking a bottle of smelling salts under her nose.

Naturally, the newspaper reporters put two and two together, and what they make of it is that Hattie tries to plug Armand Fibleman for his rascally offer, and that she misses Armand and gets Haystack, and right away Baseball Hattie is a great heroine, and Haystack is a great hero, though nobody thinks to ask Haystack how he stands on the bribe proposition, and he never brings it up himself.

And nobody will ever offer Haystack any more bribes, for after the doctors get through with him he is shy a left arm from the shoulder down, and he will never pitch a baseball again, unless he learns to pitch right-handed.

The newspapers make quite a lot of Baseball Hattie protecting the fair name of baseball. The National League plays a benefit game for Haystack Duggeler and presents him with a watch and a purse of twenty-five thousand dollars, which Baseball Hattie grabs away from him, saying it is for her son, while Armand Fibleman is in bad with one and all.

Baseball Hattie and Haystack Duggeler move to the Pacific Coast, and this is all there is to the story, except that one day some years ago, and not long before he passes away in Los Angeles, a respectable grocer, I run into Haystack when he is in New York on a business trip, and I say to him like this:

"Haystack," I say, "it is certainly a sin and a shame that Hattie misses Armand Fibleman that night and puts you on the shelf. The chances are that but for this little accident you will hang up one of the greatest pitching records in the history of baseball. Personally," I say, "I never see a better left-handed pitcher."

"Look," Haystack says. "Hattie does not miss Fibleman. It is a great newspaper story and saves my name, but the truth is she hits just where she aims. When she calls me into the kitchen before I start out with Fibleman, she shows me a revolver I never before know she has, and says to me, 'Haystack,' she says, 'if you leave with this weasel on the errand you mention, I am going to fix you so you will never make another wrong move with your pitching arm. I am going to shoot it off for you.'

"I laugh heartily," Haystack says. "I think she is kidding me, but I find out different. By the way," Haystack says, "I afterwards learn that long before I meet her, Hattie works for three years in a shooting gallery at Coney Island. She is really a remarkable broad," Haystack says.

I guess I forget to state that the day Baseball Hattie is at the Polo Grounds she is watching the new kid sensation of the big leagues, Derrill Duggeler, shut out Brooklyn with three hits.

He is a wonderful young left-hander.

The Great American Novel

PHILIP ROTH

Gil Gamesh is the greatest pitcher in the history of the Patriot League, a third major league whose history has been suppressed because of the scandalous incidents that caused its demise. War hero General Oakhart, the president of the ill-fated league, hopes his wise rule will make him a candidate in the 1936 election. And Mike Masterson is the league's greatest umpire. From the novel *The Great American Novel*.

Now as luck would have it—or so it seemed to the General at the outset—the very year he agreed to retire from the military to become President of the Patriot League, the nineteen-year-old Gil Gamesh came up to pitch for the Tycoons' crosstown rival, the Tri-City Greenbacks. Gamesh, throwing six shutouts in his first six starts, was an immediate sensation, and with his "I can beat anybody" motto, captured the country's heart as no player had since the Babe began swatting them out of the ball park in 1920. Only the previous year, in the middle of the most dismal summer of his life, the great Luke Gofannon had called it quits and retired to his farm in the Jersey flats, so that it had looked at the opening of the '33 season as though the Patriot League would be without an Olympian of the Ruth-Cobb variety. Then, from nowhere—or to be exact, from Babylonia, by way of his mother and father—came the youngster the General aptly labeled "the Talk of the World," and nothing Hubbell did over in the National League or Lefty Grove in the American was remotely comparable. The tall, slim, dark-haired left-hander was just what the doctor had ordered for a nation bewildered and frightened by a ruinous Depression—here was a kid who just would not lose, and he made no bones about it either. Nothing shy, nothing sweet, nothing humble about this young fellow. He could be ten runs on top in the bottom of the ninth, two men out, the bases empty, a count of 0 and 2 on the opposing team's weakest hitter, and if the umpire gave him a bad call he would be down off that mound breathing fire. "You blind robber—it's a strike!" However, if and when the *batter* should dare to put up a beef on a call, Gamesh would laugh like mad and call out to the ump, "Come on now, you can't tell anything by him—he never even seen it. He'd be the last guy in the *world* to know."

And the fans ate it up: nineteen years old and he had the courage and confidence of a Walter Johnson, and the competitive spirit of the Georgia Peach himself. The stronger the batter the better Gil liked it. Rubbing the ball around in those enormous paws that hung down practically to his knees, he would glare defiantly at the man striding up to the plate (some of them stars when he was still in the cradle) and announce out loud his own personal opinion of the fellow's abilities. "You couldn't lick a stamp. You couldn't beat a drum. Get your belly button in there, bud, you're what I call duck soup." Then, sneering away, he would lean way back, kick that right leg up sky-high like a chorus girl, and that long left arm would start coming around by way of Biloxi—and next thing you knew it was strike one. He would burn them in just as beautiful and nonchalant as that, three in a row, and then exactly like a barber, call out, "Next!" He did not waste a pitch, unless it was to throw a ball at a batter's head, and he did not consider that a waste. He knew a hundred ways to humiliate the opposition, such as late in the game deliberately walking the other pitcher, then setting the ball down on the ground to wave him from first on to second. "Go on, go on, you ain't gonna get there no other way, that's for sure." With the surprised base runner safely ensconced at second, Gil would kick the ball up into his glove with the instep of his shoe—"Okay, just stand there on the bag, bud," he would tell the opposing pitcher, "and watch these fellas try and hit me. You might learn somethin', though I doubt it."

Gamesh was seen to shed a tear only once in his career: when his seventh major league start was rained out. Some reports had it that he even took the Lord's name in vain, blaming Him of all people for the washout. Gil announced afterward that had he been able to work in his regular rotation that afternoon, he would have extended his shutout streak through those nine innings *and on to the very end of the season*. An outrageous claim, on the face of it, and yet there were those in the newsrooms, living rooms, and barrooms around this nation who believed him. As it was, even lacking his "fine edge," as he called it, he gave up only one run the next day, and never more than two in any game that year.

Around the league, at the start of that season, they would invariably begin to boo the headstrong nineteen-year-old when he stepped out of the Greenback dugout, but it did not appear to affect him any. "I never expect they are going to be very happy to see me heading out to the mound," he told reporters. "I wouldn't be, if I was them." Yet once the game was over, it invariably required a police escort to get Gamesh back to the hotel, for the crowd that had hated him nine innings earlier for being so cocksure of himself, was now in the streets calling his name—adults screaming right along with kids—as though it was the Savior about to emerge from the visiting team clubhouse in a spiffy yellow linen suit and two-toned perforated shoes.

It surely seemed to the General that he could not have turned up in the league president's box back of first at Greenback Stadium at a more felicitous moment. In 1933 just about everybody appeared to have become a Greenback fan, and the Patriot League pennant battle between the two Tri-City teams, the impeccably professional Tycoons, and the rough-and-tumble Greenbacks, made headlines East *and* West, and constituted just about the only news that didn't make you want to slit your throat over the barren dinner table. Men out of work—and there were fifteen million of them across the land, men sick and tired of defeat and dying for a taste of victory, rich men who had become paupers overnight—would somehow scrape two bits together to come out and watch from the bleachers as a big unbeatable boy named Gil Gamesh did his stuff on the mound. And to the little kids of America, whose dads were on the dole, whose uncles were on the booze, and whose older brothers were on the bum, he was a living, breathing example of that hero of American heroes, the he-man, a combination of Lindbergh, Tarzan, and (with his long, girlish lashes and brilliantined black hair) Rudolph Valentino: brave, brutish, and a lady-killer, and in possession of a sidearm fastball that according to Ripley's "Believe It or Not" could pass clear through a batter's chest, come out his back, and still be traveling at "major league speed."

What cooled the General's enthusiasm for the boy wonder was the feud that erupted in the second month of the season between young Gil and Mike Masterson, and that ended in tragedy on the last day of the season. The grand old man of umpiring had been assigned by General Oakhart to follow the Greenbacks around the country, after it became evident that Gamesh was just too much for the other officials in the circuit to handle. The boy could be rough when the call didn't go his way, and games had been held up for five and ten minutes at a time while Gamesh told the ump in question just what he thought of his probity, eyesight, physiognomy, parentage, and place of national origin. Because of the rookie's enormous popularity, because of the records he was breaking in game after game, because many in the crowd had laid out their last quarter to see Gamesh pitch (and because they were just plain intimidated), the umps tended to tolerate from Gamesh what would have been inexcusable in a more mature, or less spectacular, player. This of course was creating a most dangerous precedent vis-à-vis the Rules and the Regulations, and in order to prevent the situation from getting completely out of hand, General Oakhart turned to the finest judge of a fastball in the majors, in his estimate the toughest, fairest official who ever wore blue, the man whose booming voice had earned him the monicker "the Mouth."

"I have been umpiring in the Patriot League since Dewey took Manila," Mike the Mouth liked to tell them on the annual banquet circuit, after the World Series was over. "I have rendered more than a million and a half decisions in that time, and let me tell you, in all those years I have never called one wrong, at least not in my heart. In my apprentice days down in the minors I was bombarded with projectiles from the stands, I was threatened with switchblades by coaches, and once a misguided manager fired upon me with a gun. This three-inch scar here on my forehead was inflicted by the mask of a catcher who believed himself wronged by me, and on my shoulders and my back I bear sixty-four wounds inflicted during those 'years of trial' by bottles of soda pop. I have been mobbed by fans so perturbed that when I arrived in the dressing room I discovered all the buttons had been torn from my clothing, and rotten vegetables had been stuffed into my trousers and my shirt. But harassed and hounded as I have been, I am proud to say that I have never so much as changed the call on a close one out of fear of the consequences to my life, my limbs, or my loved ones."

This last was an allusion to the kidnapping and murder of Mike the Mouth's only child, back in 1898, his first year up with the P. League. The kidnappers had entered Mike's Wisconsin home as he was about to leave for the ball park to umpire a game between the Reapers and the visiting Rustlers, who were battling that season for the flag. Placing a gun to his little girl's blond curls, the intruders told the young umpire that if the Reapers lost that afternoon, Mary Jane would be back in her high chair for dinner, unharmed. If however the Reapers should win for any reason, then Masterson could hold himself responsible for his darling child's fate . . . Well, that game, as everyone knows, went on and on and on, before the Reapers put together two walks and a scratch hit in the bottom of the seventeenth to break the 3–3 tie and win by a run. In subsequent weeks, pieces of little Mary Jane Masterson were found in every park in the Patriot League.

It did not take but one pitch, of course, for Mike the Mouth to become the lifelong enemy of Gil Gamesh. Huge crowd, sunny day, flags snapping in the breeze, Gil winds up, kicks, and here comes that long left arm, America, around by way of the tropical Equator.

"That's a ball," thundered Mike, throwing his own left arm into the air (as if anybody in the ball park needed a sign when the Mouth was back of the plate).

"A ball!" cried Gamesh, hurling his glove twenty-five feet in the air. "Why, I couldn't put a strike more perfect across the plate! That was right in there, you blind robber!"

Mike raised one meaty hand to stop the game and stepped

out in front of the plate with his whisk broom. He swept the dust away meticulously, allowing the youth as much time as he required to remember where he was and whom he was talking to. Then he turned to the mound and said—in tones exceeding courteous—"Young fellow, it looks like you'll be in the league for quite a while. That sort of language will get you nothing. Why don't you give it up?" And he stepped back into position behind the catcher. "Play!" he roared.

On the second pitch, Mike's left arm shot up again. "That's two." And Gamesh was rushing him.

"You cheat! You crook! You thief! You overage, over-stuffed—"

"Son, don't say anymore."

"And what if I do, you pickpocket?"

"I will give you the thumb right now, and we will get on with the game of baseball that these people have paid good money to come out here today to see."

"They didn't come out to see no baseball game, you idiot—they come out to see me!"

"I will run you out of here just the same."

"Try it!" laughed Gil, waving toward the stands where the Greenback fans were already on their feet, whooping like a tribe of Red Indians for Mike the Mouth's scalp. And how could it be otherwise? The rookie had a record of fourteen wins and no losses, and it was not yet July. "Go ahead and try it," said Gil. "They'd mob you, Masterson. They'd pull you apart."

"I would as soon be killed on a baseball field," replied Mike the Mouth (who in the end got his wish), "as anywhere else. Now why don't you go out there and pitch. That's what they pay you to do."

Smiling, Gil said, "And why don't you go shit in your shoes."

Mike looked as though his best friend had died; sadly he shook his head. "No, son, no, that won't do, not in the Big Time." And up went the right thumb, an appendage about the size and shape of a nice pickle. Up it went and up it stayed, though for a moment it looked as though Gamesh, whose mouth had fallen open, was considering biting it off—it wasn't but an inch from his teeth.

"Leave the field, son. And leave it now."

"Oh sure," chuckled Gil, recovering his composure, "oh sure, leave the field in the middle of pitchin' to the first batter," and he started back out to the mound, loping nonchalantly like a big boy in an open meadow, while the crowd roared their love right into his face. "Oh sure," he said, laughing like mad.

"Son, either you go," Mike called after him, "or I forfeit this game to the other side."

"And ruin my perfect record?" he asked, his hands on his hips in disbelief. "Oh sure," he laughed. Then he got back to business: sanding down the ball in his big calloused palms, he called to the batsman on whom he had a two ball count, "Okay, get in there, bud, and let's see if you can get that gun off your shoulder."

But the batter had hardly done as Gil had told him to when he was lifted out of the box by Mike the Mouth. Seventy-one years old, and a lifetime of being banged around, and still he just picked him up and set him aside like a paperweight. Then, with his own feet dug in, one on either side of home plate, he made his startling announcement to the sixty thousand fans in Greenback Stadium—the voice of Enrico Caruso could not have carried any more clearly to the corners of the outfield bleachers.

"Because Greenback pitcher Gilbert Gamesh has failed to obey the order of the umpire-in-chief that he remove himself from the field of play, this game is deemed forfeited by a score of 9 to 0 to the opposing team, under rule 4.15 of the Official Baseball Rules that govern the playing of baseball games by the professional teams of the Patriot League of Professional Baseball Clubs."

And jaw raised, arms folded, and legs astride home plate —according to Smitty's column the next day, very like that Colossus at Rhodes—Mike the Mouth remained planted where he was, even as wave upon wave of wild men washed over the fences and onto the field.

And Gil Gamesh, his lips white with froth and his eagle eyes spinning in his skull, stood a mere sixty feet and six inches away, holding a lethal weapon in his hand.

The next morning. A black-and-white perforated shoe kicks open the door to General Oakhart's office and with a wad of newspapers in his notorious left hand, enter Gil Gamesh, shriek-

ing. "My record is not 14 and 1! It's 14 and 0! Only now, they
got me down here for a *loss!* Which is impossible! *And you two
done it!*"

"You 'done' it, young man," said General Oakhart, while
in a double-breasted blue suit the same deep shade as his umpire
togs, Mike the Mouth Masterson silently filled a chair by the
trophy cabinet.

"Youse!"

"You."

"Youse!"

"You."

"Stop saying 'you' when I say 'youse'—it *was* youse, and
the whole country knows it too! You and that thief! Sittin'
there free as a bird, when he oughtta be in Sing Sing!"

Now the General's decorations flashed into view as he
raised himself from behind the desk. Wearing the ribbons and
stars of a courageous lifetime, he was impressive as a ship's
figurehead—and of course he was still a powerfully built man,
with a chest on him that might have been hooped around like
a barrel. Indeed, the three men gathered together in the room
looked as though they could have held their own against a team
of horses, if they'd had to draw a brewery truck through the
streets of Tri-City. No wonder that the day before, the mob
that had pressed right up to his chin had fallen back from
Mike the Mouth as he stood astride home plate like the Eighth
Wonder of the World. Of course, ever since the murder of his
child, not even the biggest numbskull had dared to throw so
much as a peanut shell at him from the stands; but neither
did his bulk encourage a man to tread upon his toes.

"Gamesh," said the General, swelling with righteousness,
"no umpire in the history of this league has ever been found
guilty of a single act of dishonesty or corruption. Or even
charged with one. Remember that!"

"But—my perfect record! He ruined it—forever! Now I'll
go down in the history books as someone who once *lost!* And
I didn't! I couldn't! I can't!"

"And why can't you, may I ask?"

"Because I'm Gil Gamesh! I'm an immortal!"

"I don't care if you are Jesus Christ!" barked the General.

"There are Rules and Regulations in this world and you will follow them just like anybody else!"

"And who made the rules?" sneered Gamesh. "You? Or Scarface over there?"

"Neither of us, young man. *But we are here to see that they are carried out.*"

"And suppose I say the hell with you!"

"Then you will be what is known as an outlaw."

"And? So? Jesse James was an outlaw. And he's world-famous."

"True. But he did not pitch in the major leagues."

"He didn't want to," sneered the young star.

"But you do," replied General Oakhart, and, bewildered, Gamesh collapsed into a chair. It wasn't just *what* he wanted to, it was *all* he wanted to do. It was what he was *made* to do.

"But," he whimpered, "my perfect record."

"The umpire, in case it hasn't occurred to you, has a record too. A record," the General informed him, "that must remain untainted by charges of favoritism or falsification. Otherwise there would not even be major league baseball contests in which young men like yourself could excel."

"But there ain't no young men like myself," Gamesh whined. "There's me, and that's it."

"Gil . . ." It was Mike the Mouth speaking. Off the playing field he had a voice like a songbird's, so gentle and mellifluous that it could soothe a baby to sleep. And alas, it had, years and years ago . . . "Son, listen to me. I don't expect that you are going to love me. I don't expect that anybody in a ball park is going to care if I live or die. Why should they? I'm not the star. You are. The fans don't go out to the ball park to see the Rules and the Regulations upheld, they go out to see the home team win. The whole world loves a winner, you know that better than anybody, but when it comes to an umpire, there's not a soul in the ball park who's for him. He hasn't got a fan in the place. What's more, he cannot sit down, he cannot go to the bathroom, he cannot get a drink of water, unless he visits the dugout, and that is something that any umpire worth his salt does not ever want to do. He cannot have anything to do with the players. He cannot fool with them or kid with them, even though he may be a man who in his heart likes a little horseplay and a joke from time to time. If he so much as sees a ballplayer coming down the street, he will cross over or turn around and walk the other way, so it will not look to passersby that anything is up between them. In strange towns, when the visiting players all buddy up in a hotel lobby and go out together for a meal in a friendly restaurant, he finds a room in a boarding house and eats his evening pork chop in a diner all alone. Oh, it's a lonesome thing, being an umpire. There are men who won't talk to you for the rest of your life. Some will even stoop to vengeance. But that is not your lookout, my boy. Nobody is twisting Masterson's arm, saying, 'Mike, it's a dog's life, but you are stuck with it.' No, it's just this, Gil: somebody in this world has got to run the game. Otherwise, you see, it wouldn't be baseball, it would be chaos. We would be right back where we were in the Ice Ages."

"The Ice Ages?" said Gil, reflectively.

"Exactly," replied Mike the Mouth.

"Back when they was livin' in caves? Back when they carried clubs and ate raw flesh and didn't wear no clothes?"

"Correct!" said General Oakhart.

"Well," cried Gil, "maybe we'd be better off!" And kicking aside the newspapers with which he'd strewn the General's carpet, he made his exit. Whatever it was he said to the General's elderly spinster secretary out in the anteroom—instead of just saying "Good day"—caused her to keel over unconscious.

That very afternoon, refusing to heed the advice of his wise manager to take in a picture show, Gamesh turned up at Greenback Stadium just as the game was getting underway, and still buttoning up his uniform shirt, ran out and yanked the baseball from the hand of the Greenback pitcher who was preparing to pitch to the first Aceldama hitter of the day—and nobody tried to stop him. The regularly scheduled pitcher just walked off the field like a good fellow (cursing under his breath) and the Old Philosopher, as they called the Greenback manager of that era, pulled his tired old bones out of the dugout and ambled over to the umpire back of home plate. In his early years, the Old Philsopher had worn his seat out sliding up and down the bench, but after a lifetime of managing in the majors, he wasn't about to be riled by anything.

"Change the line-up, Mike. That big apple knocker out there on the mound is batting ninth now on my card."

To which Mike Masterson, master of scruple and decorum, replied, "Name?"

"Boy named Gamesh," he shouted, to make himself heard above the pandemonium rising from the stands.

"Spell it."

"Awww come on now, Michael."

"Spell it."

"G-a-m-e-s-h."

"First name?"

"Gil. G as in Gorgeous. I as in Illustrious. L as in Larger-than-life."

"Thank you, sir," said Mike the Mouth, and donning his mask, called, "Play!" . . .

The first Aceldama batsman stepped in. Without even taking the time to insult him, to mock him, to tease and to taunt him, without so much as half a snarl or the crooked smile, Gamesh pitched the ball, which was what they paid him to do.

"Strike-ah-one!" roared Mike.

The catcher returned the ball to Gamesh, and again, impersonal as a machine and noiseless as a snake, Gamesh did his chorus girl kick, and in no time at all the second pitch passed through what might have been a tunnel drilled for it by the first.

"Strike-ah-two!"

On the third pitch, the batter (who appeared to have no more idea where the ball might be than some fellow who wasn't even at the ball park) swung and wound up on his face in the dust. "Musta dropped," he told the worms.

"Strike-ah-three—you're out!"

"Next!" Gamesh called, and the second man in a Butcher uniform stepped up.

"Strike-ah-one!"

"Strike-ah-two!"

"Strike-ah-three—you're out!"

So life went—cruelly, but swiftly—for the Aceldama hitters for eight full innings. "Next!" called Gamesh, and gave each the fastest shave and haircut on record. Then with a man out on strikes in the top of the ninth, and 0 and 2 on the hitter—and the fans so delirious that after each Aceldama batter left the chair, they gave off an otherworldly, practically celestial sound, as though together they constituted a human harp that had just been plucked—Gamesh threw the ball too low. Or so said the umpire behind the plate, who supposedly was in a position to know.

"That's one!"

Yes, Gil Gamesh was alleged by Mike the Mouth Masterson to have thrown a ball—after seventy-seven consecutive strikes.

"Well," sighed the Old Philosopher, down in the Greenback dugout, "here comes the end of the world." He pulled out his pocket watch, seemingly taking some comfort in its precision. "Yep, at 2:59 P.M. on Wednesday, June 16, 1933. Right on time."

Out on the diamond, Gil Gamesh was fifteen feet forward from the rubber, still in the ape-like crouch with which he completed his big sidearm motion. In their seats the fans surged upwards as though in anticipation of Gil's bounding into the air and landing in one enormous leap on Mike the Mouth's blue back. Instead, he straightened up like a man—a million years of primate evolution passing instantaneously before their eyes—and there was that smile, that famous crooked smile. "Okay," he called down to his catcher, Pineapple Tawhaki, "throw it here."

"But—holy aloha!" cried Pineapple, who hailed from Honolulu, "he call ball, Gilly!"

Gamesh spat high and far and watched the tobacco juice raise the white dust on the first-base foul line. He could hit anything with anything, that boy. "Was a ball."

"Was?" Pineapple cried.

"Yep. Low by the hair off a little girl's slit, but low." And spat again, this time raising chalk along third. "Done it on purpose, Pineapple. Done it deliberate."

"Holy aloha!" the mystified catcher groaned—and fired the ball back to Gil. "How-why-ee?"

"So's to make sure," said Gil, his voice rising to a piercing pitch, "so's to make sure the old geezer standin' behind you hadn't fell asleep at the switch! JUST TO KEEP THE OLD SON OF A BITCH HONEST!"

"One and two," Mike roared. "Play!"

"JUST SO AS TO MAKE CLEAR ALL THE REST WAS EARNED!"

"Play!"

"BECAUSE I DON'T WANT NOTHIN' FOR NOTHIN' FROM YOUSE! I DON'T NEED IT! I'M GIL GAMESH! I'M AN IMMORTAL, WHETHER YOU LIKE IT OR NOT!"

"PLAY BAWWWWWWWWWW!"

Had he ever been more heroic? More gloriously contemptuous of the powers-that-be? Not to those fans of his he hadn't. They loved him even more for that bad pitch, deliberately thrown a fraction of an inch too low, than for the seventy-seven dazzling strikes that had preceded it. The wickedly accurate pitching machine wasn't a machine at all—no, he was a human being, made of piss and vinegar, like other human beings. The arm of a god, but the disposition of the Common Man: petty, grudging, vengeful, gloating, selfish, narrow, and mean. How could they *not* adore him?

His next pitch was smacked three hundred and sixty-five feet off the wall in left-center field for a double.

Much as he hated to move his rheumatism to and fro like this, the Old Philosopher figured it was in the interest of the United States of America, of which he had been a lifelong citizen, for him to trek out to the mound and offer his condolences to the boy.

"Those things happen, lad; settle down."

"That robber! That thief! That pickpocket!"

"Mike Masterson didn't hit it off you—you just dished up a fat pitch. It could happen to anyone."

"But not to me! It was on account of my rhythm bein' broke! On account of my fine edge bein' off!"

"That wasn't his doin' either, boy. Throwin' that low one was your own smart idea. See this fella comin' up? He can strong-back that pelota right outta here. I want for you to put him on."

"No!"

"Now do like I tell you, Gil. Put him on. It'll calm you down, for one, and set up the d.p. for two. Let's get out of this inning the smart way."

But when the Old Philosopher departed the mound, and

Pineapple stepped to the side of the plate to give Gamesh a target for the intentional pass, the rookie sensation growled, "Get back where you belong, you Hawaiian hick."

"But," warned the burly catcher, running halfway to the mound, "he say put him on, Gilly!"

"Don't you worry, Oahu, I'll put him on all right."

"*How?*"

Gil grinned.

The first pitch was a fastball aimed right at the batter's mandible. In the stands, a woman screamed—"He's a goner!" but down went the Aceldama player just in the nick of time.

"That's one!" roared Mike.

The second pitch was a second fastball aimed at the occipital. "My God," screamed the woman, "it killed him!" But miracle of miracles, the batter in the dust was seen to move.

"That's two!" roared Mike, and calling time, came around to do some tidying up around home plate. And to chat awhile. "Ball get away from you?" he asked Gamesh, while sweeping away with his broom.

Gamesh spat high in the air back over his shoulder, a wad that landed smack in the middle of second base, right between the feet of the Aceldama runner standing up on the bag. "Nope."

"Then, if you don't mind my asking, how do you explain nearly taking this man's head off two times in a row?"

"Ain't you never heard of the intentional pass?"

"Oh no. Oh no, not that way, son," said Mike the Mouth. "Not in the Big Time, I'm afraid."

"Play!" screeched Gamesh, mocking the umpire's foghorn, and motioned him back behind the plate where he belonged. "Ump, Masterson, that's what they pay you to do."

"Now listen to me, Gil," said Mike. "If you want to put this man on intentionally, then pitch out to him in the time-honored manner. But don't make him go down again. We're not barbarians in this league. We're men, trying to get along."

"Speak for yourself, Mouth. I'm me."

The crowd shrieked as at a horror movie when the third pitch left Gil's hand, earmarked for the zygomatic arch. And Mike the Mouth, even before making his call, rushed to kneel beside the man spread across the plate, to touch his wrist and see if he was still alive. Barely, barely.

"That's three!" Mike roared to the stands. And to Gamesh—
"And that's it!"

"*What's it?*" howled Gamesh. "He ducked, didn't he? He
got out of the way, didn't he? You can't give me the thumb—
I didn't even *nick* him!"

"Thanks to his own superhuman effort. His pulse is just
about beating. It's a wonder he isn't lying there dead."

"Well," answered Gamesh, with a grin, "that's his lookout."

"No, son, no, it is mine."

"Yeah—and what about line drives back at the pitcher!
More pitchers get hit in the head with liners than batters get
beaned in the noggin—and do you throw out the guy that hit
the line drive? No! Never! And the reason why is because they
ain't Gil Gamesh! Because they ain't me!"

"Son," asked Mike the Mouth, grimacing as though in pain,
"just what in the world do you think I have against you?"

"I'm too great, that's what!"

Donning his protective mask, Mike the Mouth replied,
"We are only human beings, Gamesh, trying to get along. That's
the last time I'll remind you."

"Boy, I sure hope so," muttered Gil, and then to the batter,
he called, "All right, bud, let's try to stay up on our feet this
time. All that fallin' down in there, people gonna think you're
pickled."

With such speed did that fourth pitch travel the sixty
feet and six inches to the plate that the batsman, had he been
Man o' War himself, could still not have moved from its path
in time. He never had a chance . . . Aimed, however, just
above the nasal bone, the fastball clipped the bill of his blue
and gray Aceldama cap and spun it completely around on his
head. Gamesh's idea of a joke, to see the smile he was sporting
way down there in that crouch.

"That's no good," thundered Mike, "take your base!"

"If he can," commented Gil, watching the shell-shocked
hitter trying to collect himself enough to figure out which way
to go, up the third- or the first-base line.

"And you," said Mike softly, "can take off too, son." And
here he hiked that gnarled pickle of a thumb into the air, and
announced, "You're out of the game!"

The pitcher's glove went skyward; as though Mike had hit his jackpot, the green eyes began spinning in Gil's head. "No!"

"Yes, or yes. Or I forfeit this one too. I'll give you to the letter C for Chastised, son. A. B. . . ."

"NO!" screamed Gil, but before Mike could bring down the guillotine, he was into the Greenback dugout, headed straight on to the showers, for that he should be credited with a *second* loss was more than the nineteen-year-old immortal could endure.

And thereafter, through that sizzling July and August, and down through the dog days of September, he behaved himself. No improvement in his disposition, of course, but it wasn't to turn him into Little Boy Blue that General Oakhart had put Mike the Mouth on his tail—it was to make him obedient to the Rules and the Regulations, and that Mike did. On his third outing with Mike behind the plate, Gamesh pitched a nineteen-inning three-hitter, and the only time he was anywhere near being ejected from the game, he restrained himself by sinking his prominent incisors into his glove, rather than into Mike's ear, which was actually closer at that moment to his teeth.

The General was in the stands that day, and immediately after the last out went around to the umpires' dressing room to congratulate his iron-willed arbiter. He found him teetering on a bench before his locker, his blue shirt so soaked with perspiration that it looked as though it would have to be removed from his massive torso by a surgeon. He seemed barely to have strength enough to suck his soda pop up through the straw in the bottle.

General Oakhart clapped him on the shoulder—and felt it give beneath him. "Congratulations, Mike. You have done it. You have civilized the boy. Baseball will be eternally grateful."

Mike blinked his eyes to bring the General's face into focus. "No. Not civilized. Never will be. Too great. He's right."

"Speak up, Mike, I can't hear you."

"I said—"

"Sip some soda, Mike. Your voice is a little gone."

He sipped, he sighed, he began to hiccup. "I oop said he's oop too great."

"Meaning what?"

"It's like looking in oop to a steel furnace. It's like being a tiny oop farm oop boy again, when the trans oop con oop tinental train oop goes by. It's like being trampled oop trampled oop under a herd of wild oop oop. Elephants. After an inning the ball doesn't even look like a oop anymore. Sometimes it seems to be coming in end oop over end oop. And thin as an ice oop pick. Or it comes in bent and ee oop long oop ated like a boomerang oop. Or it flattens out like an aspirin oop tab oop let. Even his oop change-up oop hisses. He throws with every muscle in his body, and yet at oop the end of nineteen oop nineteen oop innings like today, he is fresh oop as oop a daisy. General, if he gets any faster, I oop don't know if even the best eyes in the business will be able to determine the close oop ones. And close oop ones are all he throws oop."

"You sound tired, Mike."

"I'll oop survive," he said, closing his eyes and swaying.

But the General had to wonder. He might have been looking at a raw young ump up from the minors, worried sick about making a mistake his first game in the Big Time, instead of Mike the Mouth, on the way to his two millionth major league decision.

He had to rap Mike on the shoulder now to rouse him. "I have every confidence in you, Mike. I always have. I always will. I know you won't let the league down. You won't now, will you, Michael?"

"Oop."

"Good!"

What a year Gil went on to have (and Mike with him)! Coming into the last game of the year, the rookie had not only tied the record for the most wins in a single season (41), but had broken the record for the most strike-outs (349) set by Rube Waddell in 1904, the record for the most shutouts (16) set by Grover Alexander in 1916, and had only to give up less than six runs to come in below the earned run average of 1.01 set by Dutch Leonard the year he was born. As for Patriot League records, he had thrown more complete games than any other pitcher in the league's history, had allowed the fewest walks, the fewest hits, and gotten the most strike-outs per nine innings. Any wonder then, that after the rookie's late September no-hitter against Independence (his fortieth victory as against

the one 9–0 loss), Mike the Mouth fell into some sort of in-
sentient fit in the dressing room from which he could not be
roused for nearly twenty-four hours. He stared like a blind man,
he drooled like a fool. "Stunned," said the doctor, and threw
cold water at him. Following the second no-hitter—which came
four days after the first—Mike was able to make it just inside the
dressing room with his dignity intact, before he began the
howling that did not completely subside for the better part of
two days and two nights. He did not eat, sleep, or drink: just
raised his lips to the ceiling and hourly bayed to the other
wolves. "Something definitely the matter here," said the doctor.
"When the season's over, you better have him checked."

The Greenbacks went into the final day of the year only
half a game out in front of the Tycoons; whichever Tri-City
team should win the game, would win the flag. And Gamesh,
by winning his forty-second, would have won more games in a
season than any other pitcher in history. And of course there was
the chance that the nineteen-year-old kid would pitch his third
consecutive no-hitter . . .

Well, what happened was more incredible even than that.
The first twenty-six Tycoons he faced went down on strikes:
seventy-eight strikes in a row. There had not even been a foul
tip—either the strike was called, or in desperation they swung
at the ozone. Then, two out in the ninth and two strikes on the
batter (thus was it ever, with Gilbert Gamesh) the left-hander
fired into the catcher's mitt what seemed not only to the sixty-
two thousand three hundred and forty-two ecstatic fans packed
into Greenback Stadium, but to the helpless batter himself—who
turned from the plate without a whimper and started back to his
home in Wilkes-Barre, Pa.—the last pitch of the '33 Patriot
League season. Strike-out number twenty-seven. Victory number
forty-two. Consecutive no-hitter number three. The most perfect
game ever pitched in the major leagues, or conceived of by the
mind of man. The Greenbacks had won the pennant, and how!
Bring on the Senators and the Giants!

Or so it had seemed, until Mike the Mouth Masterson got
word through to the two managers that the final out did not
count, because at the moment of the pitch, *his back had been
turned to the plate.*

In order for the game to be resumed, tens of thousands of

spectators who had poured out onto the field when little Joe Iviri, the Tycoon hitter, had turned away in defeat, had now to be forced back up through the gates into the stands; wisely, General Oakhart had arranged beforehand for the Tri-City mounted constabulary to be at the ready, under the stands, in the event of just such an uprising as this, and so it was that a hundred whinnying horses, drawn up like a cavalry company and charging into the manswarm for a full fifteen minutes, drove the enraged fans from the field. But not even policemen with drawn pistols could force them to take their seats. With arms upraised they roared at Mike the Mouth as though he were their Fuehrer, only it was not devotion they were promising him.

General Oakhart himself took the microphone and attempted to address the raging mob. "This is General Douglas D. Oakhart, President of the Patriot League. Due to circumstances beyond his control, umpire-in-chief Mike Masterson was unable to make a call on the last pitch because his back was turned to the plate at that moment."

"KILL THE MOUTH! MURDER THE BUM!"

"According to rule 9.4, section e, of the Official—"

"BANISH THE BLIND BASTARD! CUT OFF HIS WHATSIS!"

"—game shall be resumed prior to that pitch. Thank you."

"BOOOOOOOOOOOOOOOOOOOOOOOOOOOOOO!"

In the end it was necessary for the General to step out onto the field of play (as once he had stepped onto the field of battle), followed behind by the Tri-City Symphony Orchestra; by his order, the musicians (more terrified than any army he had ever seen, French, British, American, or Hun) assembled for the second time that day in center field, and with two down in the ninth, and two strikes on the batter, proceeded to play the National Anthem again.

" 'O say can you see,' " sang the General.

Through his teeth, he addressed Mike Masterson, who stood beside him at home plate, with his cap over his chest protector. "What happened?"

Mike said, "I—I saw him."

Agitated as he was, he nonetheless remained at rigid attention, smartly saluting the broad stripes and bright stars.

"Who? When?"

"The one," said Mike.

"The one *what?*"

"Who I've been looking for. There! Headed for the exit back of the Tycoon dugout. I recognized him by his ears and the set of his chin," and a sob rose in his throat. "Him. The kidnapper. The masked man who killed my little girl."

"Mike!" snapped the General, "Mike, you were seeing things! You were imagining it!"

"It was *him!*"

"Mike, that was thirty-five years ago. You could not recognize a man after all that time, not by his ears, for God's sake!"

"Why not?" Mike wept. "I've seen him every night, in my sleep, since 12 September 1898."

" 'O say does that Star-Spangled Banner yet wave/O'er the land of the free, and the home—' "

"Play ball!" the fans were shouting. "Play the God damn game!"

It had worked. The General had turned sixty-two thousand savages back into baseball fans with the playing of the National Anthem! Now—if only he could step in behind the plate and call the last pitch! Or bring the field umpire in to take Mike's place on balls and strikes! But the first was beyond what he was empowered to do under the Rules and the Regulations; and the second would forever cast doubt upon the twenty-six strike-outs already recorded in the history books by Gamesh, and on the forty-one victories before that. Indeed, the field umpire had wisely pretended that he had not seen the last Gamesh pitch either, so as not to compromise the greatest umpire in the game by rendering the call himself. What could the General do then but depart the field?

On the pitcher's mound, Gil Gamesh had pulled his cap so low on his brow that he was in shadows to his chin. He had not even removed it for "The Star-Spangled Banner"—as thousands began to realize with a deepening sense of uneasiness and alarm. He had been there on the field since the last pitch thrown to Iviri—except for the ten minutes when he had been above it, bobbing on a sea of uplifted arms, rolling in the embrace of ten thousand fans. And when the last pack of celebrants had fled before the flying hooves, they had deposited him back on the mound, from whence they had plucked him—and run for their lives. And so there he stood, immobile, his eyes and mouth invisible to one and all. What was he thinking? What was going through Gil's mind?

Scrappy little Joe Iviri, a little pecking hitter, and the best lead-off man in the country at that time, came up out of the Tycoon dugout, sporting a little grin as though he had just been raised from the dead, and from the stands came an angry Vesuvian roar.

Down in the Greenback dugout, the Old Philosopher considered going out to the mound to peek under the boy's cap and see what was up. But what could he do about anything anyway? "Whatever happens," he philosophized, "it's going to happen anyway, especially with a prima donna like that one."

"Play!"

Iviri stepped in, twitching his little behind.

Gamesh pitched.

It was a curve that would have shamed a ten-year-old boy —or girl, for that matter. While it hung in the clear September light, deciding whether to break a little or not, there was time enough for the catcher to gasp, "Holy aloha!"

And then the baseball was ricocheting around in the tricky right-field corner, to which it had been dispatched at the same height at which it had been struck. A stand-up triple for Iviri.

From the silence in Greenback Stadium, you would have thought that winter had come and the field lay under three feet of snow. You would have thought that the ballplayers were all down home watching haircuts at the barber shop, or boasting over a beer to the boys in the local saloon. And all sixty-two thousand fans might have been in hibernation with the bears.

Pineapple Tawhaki moved in a daze out to the mound to hand a new ball to Gamesh. Immediately after the game, at the investigation conducted in General Oakhart's office, Tawhaki —weeping profusely—maintained that when he had come out to the mound after the triple was hit, Gamesh had hissed at him, "Stay down! Stay low! On you knees, Pineapple, if you know what's good for you!" "So," said Pineapple in his own defense, "I do what he say, sir. That all. I figger Gil want to throw drop-drop. Okay to me. Gil pitch, Pineapple catch. I stay down. Wait for drop-drop. That all, sir, that all in world!" Nonetheless, General Oakhart suspended the Hawaiian for two years—as an "accomplice" to the heinous crime—hoping that he might disappear for good in the interim. Which he did—only instead of heading home to pick pineapples, he wound up a derelict on Tattoo Street, the Skid Row of Tri-City. Well, better he destroy himself with drink, than by his presence on a Patriot League diamond keep alive in the nation's memory what came to be characterized by the General as "the second deplorable exception to the Patriot League's honorable record."

It was clear from the moment the ball left Gil's hand that it wasn't any drop-drop he'd had in mind to throw. Tawhaki stayed low—even as the pitch took off like something the Wright Brothers had invented. The batter testified at the hearing that it was still picking up speed when it passed him, and scientists interviewed by reporters later that day estimated that at the moment it struck Mike Masterson in the throat, Gamesh's rising fastball was probably traveling between one hundred and twenty and one hundred and thirty miles per hour. In his vain attempt to turn from the ball, Mike had caught it just between the face mask and the chest protector, a perfect pitch, if you believed, as the General did, that Masterson's blue bow tie was the bull's eye for which Gamesh had been aiming.

The calamity-sized black headline MOUTH DEAD; GIL BANISHED proved to be premature. To be sure, even before the sun went down, the Patriot League President, with the Commissioner's approval, had expelled the record-breaking rookie sensation from the game of baseball forever. But the indestructible ump rallied from his coma in the early hours of the morning; and though he did not live to tell the tale—he was a mute thereafter—at least he lived.

The fans never forgave the General for banishing their hero. To hear them tell it, a boy destined to be the greatest pitcher of all time had been expelled from the game just for throwing a wild pitch. Rattled by a senile old umpire who had been catching a few Zs back of home plate, the great rookie throws *one bad one,* and that's it, for life! Oh no, it ain't Oakhart's favorite ump who's to blame for standin' in the way of the damn thing—it's Gil!

Nor did the General's favorite ump forgive him either. The

very day they had unswathed the bandages and released him from the hospital, Mike Masterson was down at the league office, demanding what he called "justice." Despite the rule forbidding it, he was wearing his blue uniform off the field—in the big pockets once heavy with P. League baseballs, he carried an old rag and a box of chalk; and when he entered the office, there was a blackboard and an easel strapped to his back. Poor Mike had lost not only his voice. He wanted Gamesh to be indicted and tried by the Tri-City D.A.'s office for attempted murder.

"Mike, I must say that it comes as a profound shock to me that a man of your great wisdom should wish to take vengeance in that way."

STUFF MY WISDOM (wrote Mike the Mouth on the blackboard he had set before the General's desk) I WANT THAT BOY BEHIND BARS!

"But this is not like you at all. Besides, the boy has been punished plenty."

SAYS WHO?

"Now use your head, man. He is a brilliant young pitcher —and he will never pitch again."

AND I CAN'T TALK AGAIN! OR EVEN WHISPER! I CAN'T CALL A STRIKE! I CAN'T CALL A BALL! I HAVE BEEN SILENCED FOREVER AT SEVENTY-ONE!

"And will seeing him in jail give you your voice back, at seventy-one?"

NO! NOTHING WILL! IT WON'T BRING MY MARY JANE BACK EITHER! IT WON'T MAKE UP FOR THE SCAR ON MY FOREHEAD OR THE GLASS STILL FLOATING IN MY BACK! IT WON'T MAKE UP (here he had to stop to wipe the board clean with his rag, so that he would have room to proceed) FOR THE ABUSE I HAVE TAKEN DAY IN AND DAY OUT FOR FIFTY YEARS!

"Then what on earth is the use of it?"

JUSTICE!

"Mike, listen to reason—what kind of justice is it that will destroy the reputation of our league?"

STUFF OUR LEAGUE!

"Mike, it would blacken forever the name of baseball."

STUFF BASEBALL!

Here General Oakhart rose in anger—"It is a man who has lost his sense of values entirely, who could write those two words on a blackboard! Put that boy in jail, and, I promise you, you will have another Sacco and Vanzetti on your hands. You will make a martyr of Gamesh, and in the process ruin the very thing we all love."

HATE! wrote Mike HATE! And on and on, filling the board with the four-letter word, then rubbing it clean with his rag, then filling it to the edges, again and again.

On and on and on.

Fortunately the crazed Masterson got nowhere with the D.A.—General Oakhart saw to that, as did the owners of the Greenbacks and the Tycoons. All they needed was Gil Gamesh tried for attempted murder in Tri-City, for baseball to be killed for good in that town. Sooner or later, Gamesh would be forgotten, and the Patriot League would return to normal . . .

Wishful thinking. Gamesh, behind the wheel of his Packard, and still in his baseball togs, disappeared from sight only minutes after leaving the postgame investigation in the General's office. To the reporters who clung to the running board, begging him to make a statement about his banishment, about Oakhart, about baseball, about anything, he had but five words to say, one of which could not even be printed in the papers. "I'll be back, you ———!" and the Packard roared away. But the next morning, on a back road near Binghamton, New York, the car was found overturned and burned out—and no rookie sensation to be seen anywhere. Either the charred body had been snatched by ghoulish fans, or he had walked away from the wreck intact.

GIL KILLED? the headlines asked, even as the stories came in from people claiming to have seen Gamesh riding the rails in Indiana, selling apples in Oklahoma City, or waiting in a soup line in L.A. A sign appeared in a saloon in Orlando, Florida, that read GIL TENDING BAR HERE, and hanging beside it in the window was a white uniform with a green numeral, 19—purportedly Gil's very own baseball suit. For a day and a night the place did a bang-up business, and then the sallow, sullen, skinny boy who called himself Gil Gamesh took off with the contents of the register. Within the month, every bar in the South had one of those signs printed up and one of those uniforms, with

19 sewed on it, hanging up beside it in the window for a gag. Outside opera houses, kids scrawled GIL SINGING GRAND OPERA HERE TONIGHT. On trolley cars it was GIL TAKING TICKETS INSIDE. On barn doors, on school buildings, in rest rooms around the nation, the broken-hearted and the raffish wrote, I'LL BE BACK, G. G. His name, his initials, his number were everywhere.

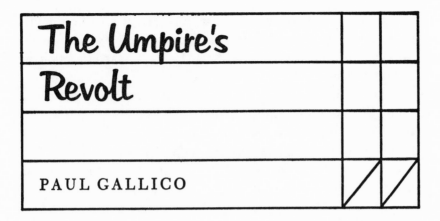

The Umpire's Revolt

PAUL GALLICO

Surely there will be none to whom our national pastime is meat and drink who will have forgotten Cassaday's Revolt, that near catastrophe that took place some years ago. It came close not only to costing the beloved Brooklyns the pennant and star pitcher Rafe Lustig his coveted $7500 bonus, but rocked organized baseball to its foundation.

The principal who gave his name and deed to the insurrection, Mr. Rowan (Concrete) Cassaday, uncorruptible, unbudgeable chief umpire of umpires of the National League, was supposed to have started it all. Actually, he didn't.

It is a fact that newspapers which focus the pitiless spotlight of publicity upon practically everyone connected with baseball, from magnate to bat boy, have a curiously blind side when it comes to umpires. They rarely seem to bother about what the sterling arbiters are up to, once the game is over.

Thus, at the beginning of this lamentable affair, no one had the slightest inkling that actually something had been invented capable of moving the immovable Concrete Cassaday, before whose glare the toughest player quailed and from whose infallible dictum there was no reprieve. That something was a woman, Miss Molly McGuire, queen of the lovely Canarsie section of Brooklyn, hard by fragrant Jamaica Bay.

The truth was, when umpire Cassaday went acourting Molly McGuire of a warm September night and sat with her on the stoop of the old brownstone house where she lived with her father, the retired boulevard besomer, Old Man McGuire, he was no longer concrete, but sludge. When the solid man looked up into the beautifully kept garden of Molly's face with its forget-me-not eyes, slipperflower nose, anemone mouth, and hair the gloss and color of the midnight pansy, you could have ladled him up with a spoon.

Old Man McGuire, ex-street-cleaning department, once he had ascertained that Cassaday could not further his yearning to become the possessor of a lifetime pass to Ebbets Field, such as are owned by politicians or bigwigs, left them to their wooing. However, he took his grief for assuaging—since he considered it something of a disgrace that his daughter should have taken up with that enemy of all mankind, and in particular the Brooklyns, an umpire—to the Old Heidelberg Tavern, presided over by handsome and capable Widow Katina Schultz.

This was in a sense patriotic as well as neighborly and practical, since everyone knew that blond widow Schultz was engaged to be married to Rafe Lustig, sensational Brooklyn right-hander. Rafe had been promised a bonus of $7500 if he won twenty-two games that season, which money he was intending to invest in Old Heidelberg to rescue it and his ladylove from the hands of the mortgage holders.

There was some division of opinion as to the manner in which Rowan Cassaday had acquired the nickname "Concrete." Ballplayers indicated that it referred unquestionably to the composition of his skull, but others said it was because of his square jaw, square shoulders, huge square head and square buttocks. Clad in his lumpy blue serge suit, pockets bulging with baseballs, masked and chest-protected, he resembled nothing so much as, in the words of a famous sports columnist, a concrete—ah—shelter.

Whatever, he was unbudgeable in his decisions, which were

rarely wrong, for he had a photographic eye imprinting an infallible record on his brain, which made him invaluable.

You would think it would have been sufficient for Molly, one hundred and three pounds of Irish enchantress, to have so solid and august a being helplessly in love with her. But it was also a fact that Molly was a woman, a creature who, even when most attractive and sure of herself, sometimes has to have a little tamper with fate or inaugurate a kind of test just to make certain. Molly's tamper, let it be said, was a beaut.

It was a sultry evening in mid-September, with the Dodgers a game or two away from grabbing the banner, and the Giants, Cards and Bucs all breathing down their necks. Molly perched on the top step of the stoop, with Concrete adoring her from three below. Old Man McGuire still sat in the window of the front parlor, collarless, with his feet on the open window ledge, reading *The Sporting News*.

Miss McGuire, who had attended the game that afternoon, looked down at her burly admirer and remarked casually, "Rowan, dear, do you know what? I've been thinking about the old blue serge suit you always wear on the ball field. It's most unbecoming to you."

"Eh?" Cassaday exclaimed, startled, for he had never given it so much as a thought. For years, the blue serge suit, belted at the back, with oversize patch pockets and the stiff-visored blue cap, had been as much a part of him as his skin.

"Uh-huh! It makes you look pounds heavier and yards broader, like the old car barns back of Ebbets Field. My girl friend who was with me at the game was saying what a pity, on account of you were such a fine figure of a man. Can't you wear something else for a change, Rowan, darling?"

A bewildered expression came into Cassaday's eyes and he stammered, "Wear s-something else? Molly, baby, you know there's nothing I wouldn't do for you, but the blue serge suit is the uniform and mark of me trade!"

"Oh, is it?" she asked, and stared down at him in a manner to cause icicles to form about his heart. "So you don't care about my being humiliated, sitting up there in the stands with my girl friend on Ladies' Day? And anyway, who said you had to wear it? Is there any rule about it?"

"Sure," replied Cassaday. "There must be—I mean there ought to—that is, I'd have to look it up." For he was suddenly assailed with the strangest doubt. If there was any man who was wholly conversant with the rules and regulations of baseball, it was he, and he could not recall at that moment ever having seen one that applied to his dress. "What did you have in mind, darling?"

"Why, just that it's a free country and you're entitled to wear something a little more suitable to your personality, a man with a fine build like yours."

"Do you really think so, then?"

"Of course I do. When you bend over to dust off the plate at the start of the game, every eye in the park is on you, and I won't have my friends passing remarks about your shape. Next Monday when the Jints come to Ebbets Field, I'll expect to see you dressed a little more classy."

Cassaday fluttered feebly once more, "It would be against all precedent, Molly. You wouldn't want ———"

"What I don't want is to see you in that awful suit again, either on or off the field," Molly concluded finally for him. "And I don't think I wish to talk about it any longer. But remember. I'll be at the game next Monday."

Concrete Cassaday, the terror of the National League, looked up at Molly McGuire and cooed, "Give us a kiss, Molly. I'm crazy about you."

"I don't know that I shall, naughty boy."

"Molly, baby, there's nothing I wouldn't do for you."

"I guess I'm crazy about you, too, honey."

With a pained expression on his wizened jockey's face, Old Man McGuire arose, descended the stoop and headed for Old Heidelberg, never dreaming at the moment the importance of what he had overheard.

I will refresh your memory as to some of the events of that awful Monday, when the Brooks trotted onto the cleanly out-lined Ebbets Field diamond against the hated Giants. Big Rafe Lustig, who had won twenty-one games, and had warmed up beautifully, took the mound to win his twenty-second game. This would clinch the $7500 bonus destined for the support of the tottering Old Heidelberg and just about put Brooklyn out of reach in the scamper for the rag down the homestretch.

Umpires Syme and Tarbolt had already taken up their stations at first and third. The head of the Giant batting order was aggressively swinging three war clubs. The batteries had been announced. Pregame tension was electric. Into this, marching stolidly from the dugout onto the field, looking neither right nor left, walked the apparition that was Concrete Cassaday.

He wore gray checked trousers, a horrid mustard-colored tweed coat with a plaid check overlay in red and green. His shirt was a gray-and-brown awning stripe worn with an orange necktie. From his pocket peered a dreadful Paisley handkerchief of red and yellow. On his head he wore a broad flat steamer cap of Kelly green with a white button in the center. Concrete Cassaday, at the behest of his lady love, and, no doubt, some long-dormant inner urge to express himself, had let himself go.

This sartorial catastrophe stalked to the plate, turned the ghastly cap around backward like a turn-of-the-century automobilist, and against a gasping roar that shook the girders of the field dedicated to Charlie Ebbets, called, "Play ball! Anybody makes any cracks is out of the game!"

Unfortunately, the storm of cheers and catcalls arising from the stands at the spectacle drowned out this fair warning, and Pat Coe, the manager, advancing on Cassaday with, "What the hell is this, Cassaday—Weber and Fields?" found himself thumbed from the premises before the words were out of his mouth.

Rafe Lustig, who had the misfortune to possess a sense of humor, fared even worse. With a whoop, he threw the ball over the top of the grandstand and, clutching at his eyes, ran around shouting, "I'm blind! I'm blind!" evoking roars of laughter until he fetched smack up against the object of his derision, who said, "Blind, are you, Rafe? Then ye can't pitch. And what's more, as long as I'm wearing this suit, you'll not pitch! Now beat it!"

Too late, Rafe sobered. "Aw, now, Concrete, have a ———"

"Git!"

Wardrobe or no wardrobe, when Cassaday said, "Git!" they got.

Slidey Simpson, the big, good-natured Negro first baseman, said, "Who-ee-ee, Mr. Cassaday! You sure enough dressed up like Harlem on Sunday night."

"March!" said Concrete.

Slidey marched with an expression of genuine grievance on his face, for he had really meant to be complimentary. Butts Barry, the heavy-hitting catcher, merely whinnied like a horse and found himself heading for his street clothes; Harry Stutz, the second baseman, was nailed making a rude gesture, and banished; Pads Franklin, the third baseman, went off the field for a look on his face; Allie Munson was caught by telepathy, apparently doing something derogatory all the way out in left field, and was waved off.

Sheltered by the dugout, the Giants somehow avoided the disaster that was engulfing the Brooklyn team. By the time Pat Coe managed to send word from the dressing room to lay off Cassaday and play ball, the Brooks fielded a heterogeneous mob of substitutes, utility infielders and bench-warmers including a deaf-and-dumb pitcher newly arrived from Hartford, whom the joyous and half-hysterical Giants proceeded to take apart.

Heinz Zimmer, the president of the club, had been thrown off the field by Cassaday for protesting, and was on the telephone to the office of the league president, who, advised of potential sabotage and riot at Ebbets Field, and the enormity of Cassaday's breach of everything sacred to the national sport, was frantically buzzing the office of the high commissioner of baseball.

Down on the diamond, the Giants were spattering hits against all walls and scoring runs in clusters; the fickle fans were hooting the hapless Dodger remnants. The press box was in an uproar. Photographers shot Cassaday from every angle, and even in color. All in all, it was an afternoon of the sheerest horror.

There was just one person in the park who was wholly and thoroughly pleased. This was Miss Molly McGuire.

You well remember the drama of the subsequent days, when the example set by Umpire Cassaday spread to other cities in both leagues, indicating that the revolt had struck a sympathetic chord in many umpirical hearts.

Indeed, there did not appear to be an arbiter in either circuit but seemed to be sick unto death of the blue serge suit. Ossa piled upon Pelion as reports came in from Detroit that Slats Owney had turned up in Navin Field in golf knickers and a plaid hunting cap; that in Cleveland, Iron Spine McGoorty had discarded his blue serge for fawn-colored slacks and a Harry Truman shirt, and that Mike O'Halloran had caused a near riot in the bleachers at St. Louis by appearing in white cricket flannels and shirt and an Old School tie.

As the climax to all this came the long-awaited ruling from the office of the high commissioner, a bureau noted from the days of Kenesaw Mountain Landis for incorruptible honesty. It was a bombshell to the effect that, after delving into files, clippings and yellowing documents dating back to the days of Abner Doubleday, there was no written rule of any kind with regard to the garb that shall be worn by a baseball umpire.

As far as regulations or possible penalties for infractions were concerned, an umpire might take the field in his pajamas, or wearing a ballet tutu, a pair of jodhpurs, a sarong or a set of hunting pinks complete with silk topper, and no one could penalize him or fine him a penny for it.

While the fans roared with laughter, the press fulminated and Rafe Lustig continued not to occupy the mound for Brooklyn; Concrete Cassaday, still hideously garbed, went on to render his impeccable decisions as the shattered Dodgers staggered under defeat after defeat, and no one knew just what to do.

A rule would undoubtedly have to be made up and incorporated, but the high commissioner was one who did not care to write rules while under fire. To force the maverick Cassaday back into his blue serge retroactively was not consonant with his ideas of good discipline and the best for the game. It was, as you recall, touch-and-go for a while. The revolt might burn itself out. And, on the other hand, it could, as it seemed to be doing, spread to the point where, by creating ridicule, it would do the grand old game an irreparable mischief.

That much you know because you remember the hoohaw. But you weren't around a joint in Canarsie known as The Old Heidelberg when a stricken old ex-asphalt polisher moaned audibly into his lager over the evil case to which his beloved Brooklyns had been brought because his wicked and headstrong daughter had seduced the chief of all the umpires into masquerading as a racehorse tout or the opening act at Loew's Flatbush Avenue Theater. And the sharp ears of a certain widow Katina Schultz, whose business was going out the window on the wings of Rafe Lustig's apparent permanent banishment from the chance to twirl bonus-winning No. 22, picked it up.

Miss Plevin, the secretary, entered the commissioner's office and said, "There's a Mrs. Schultz and a Mr. McGuire to see you, sir. They've been waiting all morning. Something to do with the Cassaday affair," she said.

"What?" cried the commissioner, now ready to grasp at any straw. "Why didn't you say so before? Send them in."

Mrs. Katina Schultz was a handsome blond woman in her thirties, with undoubted strength of character, not to mention of grip, for that was what she had on the arm of a small, unhappy-looking Irishman.

Holding firmly to him, Mrs. Schultz said, "Go on. Tell him what you told me down in the tavern last night."

With a surprising show of stubbornness, Old Man McGuire said, "I'll not! Oh, the shame of it will bring me to an early grave!"

"Oh, you are the most exasperating old man!" wailed Katina, and looked as though she were about to shake him. She turned to the commissioner and said, "My Rafe is losing his bonus, the Dodgers are blowing the pennant and he knows why Umpire Cassaday stopped wearing his blue suit. He says he wants a gold pass or something."

"Hah!" cried the commissioner. "If he knows any way to get Cassaday back into his blue serge suit, he can have a platinum pass studded with ———"

Old Man McGuire managed to look as cunning as a monkey, but in a way also as pathetic. "Just plain gold, yet honor," he said. "A lifetime pass to Ebbets Field. I'm an old man and not long for this world."

"O.K. It's yours. Now what's the story?"

"It's me daughter, Molly, as good as betrothed to Rowan Cassaday, the Evil One fly away with all umpires. She put him up to it." And he told of what he had overheard that evening on the stoop.

"Good grief!" the commissioner exploded. "A woman behind it. I didn't know that umpires ever ——— I beg your pardon. See here, Mr. McGuire. Do you think that if your daughter persuaded Umpire Cassaday into the revolting—ah—unusual outfit, she might likewise persuade him out of it and back into ———"

"With a nod of her head, he's that soft about her," Old Man McGuire replied. "But she won't."

"Why not?"

"She's a stubborn lass. Everybody in Canarsie is talking about her as the power behind Cassaday's Revolt. We've been at her, but she says Cassaday's within his rights and nobody but her can stop him. She's jealous over her influence with him, and it's gone to her head."

"H'm'm," mused the commissioner, "I see. And what is your interest in this affair, Mrs. Schultz?"

Katina explained the insoluble dilemma of the mortgage on Old Heidelberg, the $7500 bonus, the fading season and Cassaday's ultimatum to Rafe Lustig.

The commissioner nodded. "Cassaday is a valuable umpire, perhaps the most valuable we have, even though a little headstrong. I should not like to lose him. Still, if we can't make a rule now to order him back into his uniform, perhaps we ———" And here he paused as one suddenly riven with an idea.

Then he smiled quietly and said, "Go home, old man. Maybe you've earned your lifetime pass."

When they had left, he searched his drawer and gave Miss Plevin a telephone number to call. Electrical impulses surged through a copper wire, causing a bell to ring in a small office on Broadway in the Fifties with the legend SIME HOLTZMAN, PUBLICITY lettered on the grimy glass door.

"Sime, this is your old pal," said the commissioner, and told him what was on his mind.

At his end, Sime doodled a moment on a pad, chewing on a cigar, and then said, "Boy, you're in luck. I got just what you want. She's a real phony from Czechoslovakia and hasn't paid me for six months. Can she lay it on thick! She oozes that foreign charm that will drive any self-respecting American girl off her chump. You leave it to me, kid."

Thus it was that after the game the following afternoon, which the Bucs won from Brooklyn by the score thirteen runs to one, a flashy redhead, her age artfully concealed beneath six layers of make-up, sat in an even flashier sports roadster at the players' entrance to Ebbets Field, nursing a large bundle of roses, accompanied by Sime Holtzman and a considerable number of photographers.

When Umpire Cassaday, still in his rebel's outfit, mustard-colored coat, green cap and all, emerged, Sime blocked his path for the cameramen.

"Mr. Cassaday," Holtzman said, "allow me to present Miss Anya Bouquette of Prague, in Czechoslovakia. Miss Bouquette represents the Free Czechoslovakian Film Colony in the United States. They have chosen you the best-dressed umpire and she wishes to make the presentation ———"

At this point, Umpire Cassaday found himself with a bunch of roses in his arms and Miss Bouquette, a fragrant and not exactly repulsive bundle of femininity, draped about his neck, cooing in a thick Slavic accent, "Oooo! I am so hoppy because you are so beautifuls! I geev you wan kees, two kees, three kees ———

"I congratulates you, Mr. Cassaday!" she declaimed, accenting the second syllable. "In Czechoslovakia, thees costume would be the mos' best and would cotch all the girls for to marry. I am Czech. I love the United States and Freedom, and therefore I am loving you too. I geev you wan kees, two kees, three kees ———"

Thereafter, wherever Umpire Cassaday was, Mademoiselle Bouquette and the photographers were never far away. Holtzman worked out a regular schedule, duly noted in the press: Morning in the Brooklyn Museum, where she taught him European culture; lunch at Sardi's; dinner at 21 with the attaché of the Free Czechs, where Miss Bouquette announced that all men ought to dress like Mr. Cassaday; and so on.

In the meantime, word leaked from the commissioner's office that while no rule forcing umpires to wear blue serge was contemplated at the moment, so high was the esteem and regard in which Umpire Cassaday was held that consideration was being given to the idea of making his startling outfit the official uniform for all umpires.

The climax came the next afternoon at Ebbets Field, where the Pirates were playing their last game before the Giants returned for a short series, the last of the season, and the one that would decide the pennant.

In a box back of home plate, resplendent in a set of white fox furs purchased on credit restored by the new-found publicity and covered with orchids, sat Mademoiselle Anya Bouquette. This time she had a horseshoe of carnations and a huge parchment scroll, gold-embossed and dangling a red seal.

Umpire Cassaday had just emerged from the dugout, headed for home plate, when Sime Holtzman had a finger in his buttonhole and was hauling him toward the field box. Concrete had time only for one bewildered protest, "What, again?" smothered by Holtzman's "It's the Yugoslavs this time. They're crazy about your outfit. They've asked Miss Bouquette to present you with a scroll."

But upon this occasion the fans were ready. As Umpire Cassaday, with ears slightly reddened, stood with the floral horseshoe about his neck and Mademoiselle Bouquette arose with the parchment scroll unfurled, the united fanry of Flatbush, Jamaica Bay, Canarsie, Gowanus and other famous localities began to chant in unison, with a mighty handclap punctuating each digit.

"I geev you wan kees, two kees, three kees ———"

They had reached "eight kees," when a very small contretemps took place which was hardly noticed by anyone.

Four boxes away there sat a most exquisite-looking young lady, in a dark Irish way. Between the count of eight and nine kees, Miss Molly McGuire arose from her seat and marched from the premises. As I said, very few noticed this. One of those who did, out of the corner of his eye, was Umpire Rowan (Concrete) Cassaday.

This was the game, as I remember, in which Umpire Cassaday made one of the few palpable miscalls of his career. Pads Franklin, the Brooklyn lead-off hitter, looked at a ball that was so far over his head that the Buc catcher had to call for a ladder to pull it down. Concrete called him out on a third strike.

It was again a sultry September night. On the top of the stoop of the brownstone house in Canarsie sat Molly McGuire, fanning herself vigorously. Below her—many, many steps below her, almost at the bottom, in fact—crouched Rowan Concrete Cassaday, an unhappy and bewildered man, for he was up against the unsolvable.

"But, Molly, darling," he was protesting. "I only wanted to make you and your girl friend proud of me. Gosh, wasn't I voted the best-dressed umpire by the Free Czechoslovakian Film Players and awarded a certificate by Miss Anya Bouquette herself to prove ———"

Miss Molly McGuire's sniff echoed four blocks to the very edge of Jamaica Bay. "Rowan Cassaday! If you ever mention that woman's name in my presence again, our engagement is off!"

The square bulk of Umpire Cassaday edged upward one step. "But, Molly, baby, believe me. She doesn't mean a thing to me. I was only trying to please you, in the first place, by wearing something snappy. Why, the commissioner is even thinking of making it the regular ———"

Molly gave a little shudder at the prospect of Mademoiselle Bouquette forever buzzing around her too generous wildflower. "If you want to please me, Rowan Cassaday, you'll climb right back into your blue serge suit and cap again, and start looking like the chief of all the umpires ought to look!"

"But, Molly, baby, that's what I was doing in the first place, when you ———"

"Then do it for me, darling! Tomorrow!"

A glazed look came into the eyes of Rowan Cassaday, as it does into the eyes of all men when confronted by the awful, unanswerable, moonstruck logic of women. Nevertheless, he gained six steps without protest, and was able thus to arrive back where he had started from a hideous ten days ago—at the hem of her dainty skirt. And thus peace descended once more upon Flatbush.

Remember that wonderful day—a Thursday, I believe it was —when out from the dugout at game time marched that massive concrete figure once more impregnably armored, cap-a-pie, in shiny blue serge, the belted back spread to the load of league baseballs stuffed in the capacious pockets.

What a cheer greeted his appearance, and then what a roar went up as Rafe Lustig emerged from the dugout, swinging his glove and sweater. The historic exchange between the two will never be forgotten.

Rafe said, "Hi, Rowan."

Concrete replied, "Hi, Rafe."

What a day that was. How the long-silent bats of the Brooks pummeled the unhappy Jints. How the long-rested arm of Rafe Lustig, twirling out the $7500-bonus game and the everlasting rescue of Old Heidelberg, tamed the interlopers from Manhattan, disposing of them with no more than a single scratch hit. How the word spread like wildfire through the cities of the league that Cassaday's Revolt was over and blue serge once again was the order of the day.

Witness to all this was a happy Molly McGuire in a box back of home plate. Absent from the festivities was Mademoiselle Anya Bouquette, who, it seems, could not abide blue serge, for it reminded her of gloomy Sunday and an unhappy childhood in Prague, with people jumping off bridges.

And yet, if you looked closely, there was one difference to be observed, which, in a sense, gave notice who would wear the pants in the Cassaday household, came that day. For while indeed Concrete was poured back into the lumpy anonymity of the traditional garments—serge cap, coat, tie, breeches—yet from the breast pocket fluttered the tip of that awful red-and-yellow Paisley kerchief.

This was all that was left of Cassaday's Revolt. He had tasted individuality. He would never quite be the same again. But the object in his breast pocket remained unnoticed and unmentioned, except for the quiet smile of triumph reflected from the well-kept garden of the countenance of Miss Molly McGuire.

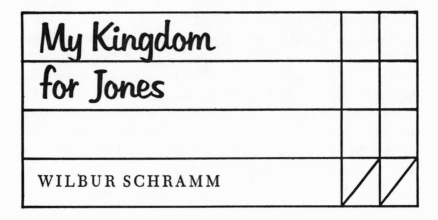

My Kingdom for Jones

WILBUR SCHRAMM

The first day Jones played third base for Brooklyn was like the day Galileo turned his telescope on the planets or Columbus sailed back to Spain. First, people said it couldn't be true; then they said things will never be the same.

Timothy McGuire, of the Brooklyn *Eagle*, told me how he felt the first time he saw Jones. He said that if a bird had stepped out of a cuckoo clock that day and asked him what time it was, he wouldn't have been surprised enough to blink an Irish eye. And still he knew that the whole future of baseball hung that day by a cotton thread.

Don't ask Judge Kenesaw Mountain Landis about this. He has never yet admitted publicly that Jones ever played for Brooklyn. He has good reason not to. But ask an old-time sports writer. Ask Tim McGuire.

It happened so long ago it was even before Mr. Roosevelt became President. It was a lazy Georgia spring afternoon, the first time McGuire and I saw Jones. There was a light-footed

little breeze and just enough haze to keep the sun from burning.
The air was full of fresh-cut grass and wistaria and fruit blos-
soms and the ping of baseballs on well-oiled mitts. Everyone in
Georgia knows that the only sensible thing to do on an afternoon
like that is sleep. If you can't do that, if you are a baseball writer
down from New York to cover Brooklyn's spring-training camp,
you can stretch out on the grass and raise yourself every hour
or so on one elbow to steal a glance at fielding practice. That
was what we were doing—meanwhile amusing ourselves half-
heartedly with a game involving small cubes and numbers—when
we first saw Jones.

The *Times* wasn't there. Even in those days they were keeping their sports staff at home to study for "Information Please."
But four of us were down from the New York papers—the *World,*
the *Herald,* Tim and I. I can even remember what we were
talking about.

I was asking the World, "How do they look to you?"

"Pitchers and no punch," the World said. "No big bats. No
great fielders. No Honus Wagner. No Hal Chase. No Ty Cobb."

"No Tinker to Evers to Chance," said the Herald. "Seven
come to Susy," he added soothingly, blowing on his hands.

"What's your angle today?" the World asked Tim.

Tim doesn't remember exactly how he answered that. To
the best of my knowledge, he merely said, "Ulk." It occurred to
me that the Brooklyn *Eagle* was usually more eloquent than that,
but the Southern weather must have slowed up my reaction.

The World said, "What?"

"There's a sorsh," Tim said in a weak, strangled sort of voice
—"a horse . . . on third . . . base."

"Why don't they chase it off?" said the Herald impatiently.
"Your dice."

"They don't . . . want to," Tim said in that funny voice.

I glanced up at Tim then. Now Tim, as you probably remember, was built from the same blueprints as a truck, with a magnificent red nose for a headlight. But when I looked at him, all
the color was draining out of that nose slowly, from top to
bottom, like turning off a gas mantle. I should estimate Tim was,
at the moment, the whitest McGuire in four generations.

Then I looked over my shoulder to see where Tim was

staring. He was the only one of us facing the ball diamond. I looked for some time. Then I tapped the World on the back.

"Pardon me," I asked politely, "do you notice anything unusual?"

"If you refer to my luck," said the World, "it's the same pitiful kind I've had since Christmas."

"Look at the infield," I suggested.

"Hey," said the Herald, "if you don't want the dice, give them to me."

"I know this can't be true," mused the World, "but I could swear I see a horse on third base."

The Herald climbed to his feet with some effort. He was built in the days when there was no shortage of materials.

"If the only way to get you guys to put your minds on this game is to chase that horse off the field," he said testily, "I'll do it myself."

He started toward the infield, rubbed his eyes and fainted dead away.

"I had the queerest dream," he said, when we revived him. "I dreamed there was a horse playing third base. My God!" he shouted, glancing toward the diamond. "I'm still asleep!"

That is, word for word, what happened the first day Jones played third base for Brooklyn. Ask McGuire.

When we felt able, we hunted up the Brooklyn manager, who was a chunky, red-haired individual with a whisper like a foghorn. A foghorn with a Brooklyn accent. His name was Pop O'Donnell.

"I see you've noticed," Pop boomed defensively.

"What do you mean," the Herald said severely, "by not notifying us you had a horse playing third base?"

"I didn't guess you'd believe it," Pop said.

Pop was still a little bewildered himself. He said the horse had wandered on the field that morning during practice. Someone tried to chase it off by hitting a baseball toward it. The horse calmly opened its mouth and caught the ball. Nothing could be neater.

While they were still marveling over that, the horse galloped thirty yards and took a ball almost out of the hands of an outfielder who was poised for the catch. They said Willie Keeler couldn't have done it better. So they spent an hour hitting fungo flies—or, as some wit called them, horse flies—to the horse. Short ones, long ones, high ones, grass cutters, line drives—it made no difference; the animal covered Dixie like the dew.

They tried the horse at second and short, but he was a little slow on the pivot when compared with men like Napoleon Lajoie. Then they tried him at third base, and knew that was the right, the inevitable place. He was a great wall of China. He was a flash of brown lightning. In fact, he covered half the short-stop's territory and two-thirds of left field, and even came behind the plate to help the catcher with foul tips. The catcher got pretty sore about it. He said that anybody who was going to steal his easy put-outs would have to wear an umpire's uniform like the other thieves.

"Can he hit?" asked the World.

"See for yourself," Pop O'Donnell invited.

The Superbas—they hadn't begun calling them the Dodgers yet—were just starting batting practice. Nap Rucker was tossing them in with that beautiful smooth motion of his, and the horse was at bat. He met the first ball on the nose and smashed it into left field. He laid down a bunt that waddled like a turtle along the base line. He sizzled a liner over second like a clothesline.

"What a story!" said the World.

"I wonder—" said the Herald—"I wonder how good it is."

We stared at him.

"I wouldn't say it is quite as good as the sinking of the *Maine*, if you mean that," said Tim.

"I wonder how many people are going to believe it," said the Herald.

"I'll race you to the phone," Tim said.

Tim won. He admits he had a long start. Twenty minutes later he came back, walking slowly.

"I wish to announce," he said, "that I have been insulted by my editor and am no longer connected with the Brooklyn *Eagle*. If I can prove that I am sober tomorrow, they may hire me back," he added.

"You see what I mean," said the Herald.

We all filed telegraph stories about the horse. We swore that every word was true. We said it was a turning point in baseball. Two of us mentioned Columbus; and one, Galileo. In return, we got advice.

THESE TROUBLED TIMES, NEWSPAPERS NO SPACE FOR FICTION, EXPENSE ACCOUNT NO PROVISION DRUNKEN LEVITY, the *Herald's* wire read. The *World* read, ACCURACY, ACCURACY, ACCURACY, followed by three exclamation points, and signed "Joseph Pulitzer." CHARGING YOUR TELEGRAM RE BROOKLYN HORSE TO YOUR SALARY, my wire said. THAT'S A HORSE ON YOU!

Have you ever thought what you would do with a purple cow if you had one? I know. You would paint it over. We had a horse that could play third base, and all we could do was sit in the middle of Georgia and cuss our editors. I blame the editors. It is their fault that for the last thirty years you have had to go to smoking rooms or Pullman cars to hear about Jones.

But I don't entirely blame them either. My first question would have been: How on earth can a horse possibly bat and throw? That's what the editors wondered. It's hard to explain. It's something you have to see to believe—like dogfish and political conventions.

And I've got to admit that the next morning we sat around and asked one another whether we really had seen a horse playing third base. Pop O'Donnell confessed that when he woke up he said to himself, *It must be shrimp that makes me dream about horses.* Then all of us went down to the park, not really knowing whether we would see a horse there or not.

We asked Pop was he going to use the horse in games.

"I don't know," he thundered musingly. "I wonder. There are many angles. I don't know," he said, pulling at his chin.

That afternoon the Cubs, the world champs, came for an exhibition game. A chap from Pennsylvania—I forget his name—played third base for Brooklyn, and the horse grazed quietly beside the dugout. Going into the eighth, the Cubs were ahead, 2–0, and Three-Finger Brown was tying Brooklyn in knots. A curve would come over, then a fast one inside, and then the drop, and the Superbas would beat the air or hit puny little rollers to the infield which Tinker or Evers would grab up and toss like a beanbag to Frank Chance. It was sickening. But in the eighth, Maloney got on base on an error, and Jordan walked. Then Lumley went down swinging, and Lewis watched three perfect ones sail past him. The horse still was grazing over by the Brooklyn dugout.

"Put in the horse!" Frank Chance yelled. The Cubs laughed themselves sick.

Pop O'Donnell looked at Chance, and then at the horse, and back at Chance, as though he had made up his mind about something. "Go in there, son, and get a hit," he said. "Watch out for the curve." "Coive," Pop said.

The horse picked up a bat and cantered out to the plate.

"Pinch-hitting for Batch," announced the umpire dreamily, "this horse." A second later he shook himself violently. "What am I saying?" he shouted.

On the Cubs' bench, every jaw had dropped somewhere around the owner's waist. Chance jumped to his feet, his face muscles worked like a coffee grinder, but nothing came out. It was the only time in baseball history, so far as I can find out, that Frank Chance was ever without words.

When he finally pulled himself together he argued, with a good deal of punctuation, that there was no rule saying you could play a horse in the big leagues. Pop roared quietly that there was no rule saying you couldn't, either. They stood there nose to nose, Pop firing methodically like a cannon, and Chance crackling like a machine gun. Chance gave up too easily. He was probably a little stunned. He said that he was used to seeing queer things in Brooklyn, anyway. Pop O'Donnell just smiled grimly.

Well, that was Jones's first game for Brooklyn. It could have been a reel out of a movie. There was that great infield—Steinfeldt, Tinker, Evers and Chance—so precise, so much a machine, that any ball hit on the ground was like an apple into a sorter. The infield was so famous that not many people remember Sheckard and Slagle and Schulte in the outfield, but the teams of that day knew them. Behind the plate was Johnny Kling, who could rifle a ball to second like an 88-mm. cannon. And on the mound stood Three-Finger Brown, whose drop faded away as though someone were pulling it back with a string.

Brown took a long time getting ready. His hand shook a

little, and the first one he threw was ten feet over Kling's head into the grandstand. Maloney and Jordan advanced to second and third. Brown threw the next one in the dirt. Then he calmed down, grooved one, and whistled a curve in around the withers.

"The glue works for you, Dobbin!" yelled Chance, feeling more like himself. Pop O'Donnell was mopping his forehead.

The next pitch came in fast, over the outside corner. The horse was waiting. He leaned into it. The ball whined all the way to the fence. Ted Williams was the only player I ever saw hit one like it. When Slagle finally got to the ball, the two runners had scored and the horse was on third. Brown's next pitch got away from Kling a few yards, and the horse stole home in a cloud of dust, all four feet flying. He got up, dusted himself off, looked at Chance and gave a horselaugh.

If this sounds queer, remember that queerer things happen in Brooklyn every day.

"How do we write this one up?" asked the Herald. "We can't put just 'a horse' in the box score."

That was when the horse got his name. We named him Jones, after Jones, the caretaker who had left the gate open so he could wander onto the field. We wrote about "Horse" Jones.

Next day we all chuckled at a banner headline in one of the Metropolitan papers. It read: JONES PUTS NEW KICK IN BROOKLYN.

Look in the old box scores. Jones got two hits off Rube Waddell, of Philadelphia, and three off Cy Young, of Boston. He pounded Eddie Plank and Iron Man McGinnity and Wild Bill Donovan. He robbed Honus Wagner of a hit that would have been a double against any other third baseman in the league. On the base paths he was a bullet.

Our papers began to wire us, WHERE DOES JONES COME FROM? SEND BACKGROUND, HUMAN INTEREST, INTERVIEW. That was a harder assignment than New York knew. We decided by a gentlemen's agreement that Jones must have come from Kentucky and got his first experience in a Blue Grass league. That sounded reasonable enough. We said he was long-faced, long-legged, dark, a vegetarian and a non-smoker. That was true. We said he was a horse for work, and ate like a horse. That was self-evident. Interviewing was a little harder.

Poor Pop O'Donnell for ten years had wanted a third baseman who could hit hard enough to dent a cream puff. Now
that he had one he wasn't quite sure what to do with it. Purple-
cow trouble. "Poiple," Pop would have said.

One of his first worries was paying for Jones. A strapping
big farmer appeared at the clubhouse, saying he wanted either
his horse or fifty thousand dollars.

Pop excused himself, checked the team's bank balance, then
came back.

"What color is your horse?" he asked.

The farmer thought a minute. "Dapple gray," he said.

"Good afternoon, my man," Pop boomed unctuously, holding
open the door. "That's a horse of another color." Jones was
brown.

There were some audience incidents too. Jonathan Daniels,
of Raleigh, North Carolina, told me that as a small boy that season he saw a whole row of elderly ladies bustle into their box
seats, take one look toward third base, look questioningly at one
another, twitter about the sun being hot, and walk out. Georgia
police records show that at least five citizens, cold sober, came to
the ball park and were afraid to drive their own cars home. The
American medical journals of that year discovered a new psycho-
neurosis which they said was doubtless caused by a feeling of
insecurity resulting from the replacement of the horse by the
horseless carriage. It usually took the form of hallucination—the
sensation of seeing a horse sitting on a baseball players' bench.
Perhaps that was the reason a famous pitcher, who shall here go
nameless, came to town with his team, took one incredulous look
at Brooklyn fielding practice, and went to his manager, offering
to pay a fine.

But the real trouble was over whether horses should be
allowed to play baseball. After the first shock, teams were generally amused at the idea of playing against a horse. But after
Jones had batted their star pitchers out of the box, they said the
Humane Society ought to protect the poor Brooklyn horse.

The storm that brewed in the South that spring was like
nothing except the storm that gathered in 1860. Every hotel
that housed baseball players housed a potential civil war. The
better orators argued that the right to play baseball should not
be separated from the right to vote or the responsibility of fight-

ing for one's country. The more practical ones said a few more horses like Jones and they wouldn't have any jobs left. Still others said that this was probably just another bureaucratic trick on the part of the Administration.

Even the Brooklyn players protested. A committee of them came to see old Pop O'Donnell. They said, wasn't baseball a game for human beings? Pop said he had always had doubts as to whether some major league players were human or not. They said touché, and this is all right so long as it is a one-horse business, so to speak. But if it goes on, before long won't a man have to grow two more legs and a tail before he can get in? They asked Pop how he would like to manage the Brooklyn Percherons, instead of the Brooklyn Superbas? They said, what would happen to baseball if it became a game for animals—say giraffes on one team, trained seals on a second and monkeys on a third? They pointed out that monkeys had already got a foot in the door by being used to dodge baseballs in carnivals. How would Pop like to manage a team of monkeys called the Brooklyn Dodgers, they asked.

Pop said heaven help anyone who has to manage a team called the Brooklyn Dodgers. Then he pointed out that Brooklyn hadn't lost an exhibition game, and that the horse was leading the league in batting with a solid .516. He asked whether they would rather have a World Series or a two-legged third baseman. They went on muttering.

But his chief worry was Jones himself.

"That horse hasn't got his mind on the game," he told us one night on the hotel veranda.

"Ah, Pop, it's just horseplay," said the World, winking.

"Nope, he hasn't got his heart in it," said Pop, his voice echoing lightly off the distant mountains. "He comes just in time for practice and runs the minute it's over. There's something on that horse's mind."

We laughed, but had to admit that Jones was about the saddest horse we had ever seen. His eyes were great brown pools of liquid sorrow. His ears drooped. And still he hit well over .500 and covered third base like a rug.

One day he missed the game entirely. It was the day the Giants were in town, and fifteen thousand people were there to watch Jones bat against the great Matty. Brooklyn lost the game, and Pop O'Donnell almost lost his hair at the hands of the disappointed crowd.

"Who would have thought," Pop mused, in the clubhouse after the game, "that that (here some words are omitted) horse would turn out to be a prima donna? It's all right for a major league ballplayer to act like a horse, but that horse is trying to act like a major league ballplayer."

It was almost by accident that Tim and I found out what was really bothering Jones. We followed him one day when he left the ball park. We followed him nearly two miles to a race track.

Jones stood beside the fence a long time, turning his head to watch the thoroughbreds gallop by on exercise runs and time trials. Then a little stable boy opened the gate for him.

"Po' ol' hoss," the boy said. "Yo' wants a little runnin'?"

"Happens every day," a groom explained to us. "This horse wanders up here from God knows where, and acts like he wants to run, and some boy rides him a while, bareback, pretending he's a race horse."

Jones was like a different horse out there on the track; not drooping any more—ears up, eyes bright, tail like a plume. It was pitiful how much he wanted to look like a race horse.

"That horse," Tim asked the groom, "is he any good for racing?"

"Not here, anyway," the groom said. "Might win a county-fair race or two."

He asked us whether we had any idea who owned the horse.

"Sir," said Tim, like Edwin M. Stanton, "that horse belongs to the ages."

"Well, mister," said the groom, "the ages had better get some different shoes on that horse. Why, you could hold a baseball in those shoes he has there."

"It's very clear," I said as we walked back, "what we have here is a badly frustrated horse."

"It's clear as beer," Tim said sadly.

That afternoon Jones hit a home run and absent-mindedly trotted around the bases. As soon as the game was over, he disappeared in the direction of the race track. Tim looked at me and shook his head. Pop O'Donnell held his chin in his hands.

"I'll be boiled in oil," he said. "Berled in erl," he said.

Nothing cheered up poor Pop until someone came in with a story about the absentee owner of a big-league baseball club who had inherited the club along with the family fortune. This individual had just fired the manager of his baseball farm system, because the farms had not turned out horses like Jones. "What are farms for if they don't raise horses?" the absentee owner had asked indignantly.

Jones was becoming a national problem second only to the Panama Canal and considerably more important than whether Mr. Taft got to be President.

There were rumors that the Highlanders—people were just beginning to call them the Yankees—would withdraw and form a new league if Jones was allowed to play. It was reported that a team of kangaroos from Australia was on its way to play a series of exhibition games in America, and President Ban Johnson, of the American League, was quoted as saying that he would never have kangaroos in the American League because they were too likely to jump their contracts. There was talk of a constitutional amendment concerning horses in baseball.

The thing that impressed me, down there in the South, was that all this was putting the cart before the horse, so to speak. Jones simply didn't want to play baseball. He wanted to be a race horse. I don't know why life is that way.

Jones made an unassisted triple play, and Ty Cobb accused Brooklyn of furnishing fire ladders to its infielders. He said that no third baseman could have caught the drive that started the play. At the end of the training season, Jones was batting .538, and fielding .997, had stolen twenty bases and hit seven home runs. He was the greatest third baseman in the history of baseball, and didn't want to be!

Joseph Pulitzer, William Randolph Hearst, Arthur Brisbane and the rest of the big shots got together and decided that if anyone didn't know by this time that Jones was a horse, the newspapers wouldn't tell him. He could find it out.

Folks seemed to find it out. People began gathering from all parts of the country to see Brooklyn open against the Giants— Matty against Jones. Even a tribe of Sioux Indians camped beside the Gowanus and had war dances on Flatbush Avenue, waiting for the park to open. And Pop O'Donnell kept his squad in the South as long as he could, laying plans to arrive in Brooklyn only on the morning of the opening game.

The wire said that night that 200,000 people had come to Brooklyn for the game, and 190,000 of them were in an ugly mood over the report that the league might not let Jones play. The governor of New York sent two regiments of the national guard. The Giants were said to be caucusing to decide whether they would play against Jones.

By game time, people were packed for six blocks, fighting to get into the park. The Sioux sent a young buck after their tomahawks, just in case. Telephone poles a quarter of a mile from the field were selling for a hundred dollars. Every baseball writer in the country was in the Brooklyn press box; the other teams played before cub reporters and society editors. Just before game time I managed to push into Pop O'Donnell's little office with the presidents of the two major leagues, the mayor of New York, a half dozen other reporters, and a delegation from the Giants.

"There's just one thing we want to know," the spokesman for the Giants was asking Pop. "Are you going to play Jones?"

"Gentlemen," said Pop in that soft-spoken, firm way of his that rattled the window blinds, "our duty is to give the public what it wants. And the public wants Jones."

Like an echo, a chant began to rise from the bleachers, "We want Jones!"

"There is one other little thing," said Pop. "Jones has disappeared."

There were about ten seconds of the awful silence that comes when your nerves are paralyzed, but your mind keeps on thrashing.

"He got out of his boxcar somewhere between Georgia and Brooklyn," Pop said. "We don't know where. We're looking."

A Western Union boy dashed in. "Hold on!" said Pop. "This may be news!"

He tore the envelope with a shaky hand. The message was from Norfolk, Virginia. HAVE FOUND ELEPHANT THAT CAN BALANCE MEDICINE BALL ON TRUNK, it read. WILL HE DO? If Pop had said what he said then into a telephone, it would have burned out all the insulators in New York.

Down at the field, the President of the United States himself was poised to throw out the first ball. "Is this Jones?" he asked. He was a little nearsighted.

"This is the mayor of New York," Pop said patiently. "Jones is gone. Run away."

The President's biographers disagree as to whether he said at that moment, "Oh, well, who would stay in Brooklyn if he could run?" or "I sympathize with you for having to change horses in midstream."

That was the saddest game ever covered by the entire press corps of the nation. Brooklyn was all thumbs in the field, all windmills at bat. There was no Jones to whistle hits into the outfield and make sensational stops at third. By the sixth inning, when they had to call the game with the score 18–1, the field was ankle-deep in pop bottles and the Sioux were waving their tomahawks and singing the scalp song.

You know the rest of the story. Brooklyn didn't win a game until the third week of the season, and no team ever tried a horse again, except a few dark horses every season. Pittsburgh, I believe, tried trained seals in the outfield. They were deadly at catching the ball, but couldn't cover enough ground. San Francisco has an entire team of Seals, but I have never seen them play. Boston tried an octopus at second base, but had to give him up. What happened to two rookies who disappeared trying to steal second base against Boston that spring is another subject baseball doesn't talk about.

There has been considerable speculation as to what happened to Jones. Most of us believed the report that the Brooklyn players had unfastened the latch on the door of his boxcar, until Pop O'Donnell's *Confidential Memoirs* came out, admitting that he himself had taken the hinges off the door because he couldn't face the blame for making baseball a game for horses. But I have been a little confused since Tim McGuire came to me once and said he might as well confess. He couldn't stand to think of that horse standing wistfully beside the track, waiting for someone to let him pretend he was a race horse. That haunted Tim. When he went down to the boxcar he found the door unlatched and the hinges off, so he gave the door a little push outward. He judged it was the will of the majority.

And that is why baseball is played by men today instead of by horses. But don't think that the shadow of Jones doesn't still lie heavy on the game. Have you ever noticed how retiring and silent and hangdog major league ballplayers are, how they cringe before the umpire? They never know when another Jones may break away from a beer wagon or a circus or a plow, wander through an unlocked gate, and begin batting .538 to their .290. The worry is terrible. You can see it in the crowds too. That is why Brooklyn fans are so aloof and disinterested, why they never raise their voices above a whisper at Ebbets Field. They know perfectly well that this is only minor league ball they are seeing, that horses could play it twice as well if they had a chance.

That is the secret we sports writers have kept all these years; that is why we have never written about Jones. And the Brooklyn fans still try to keep it a secret, but every once in a while the sorrow eats like lye into one of them until he can hold it back no longer, and then he sobs quietly and says, "Dem bums, if dey only had a little horse sense!"

Pride of the
Bimbos

JOHN SAYLES

Lewis Crawford, a twenty-year minor leaguer, plays out the string with the Brooklyn Bimbos Baseball Club, Inc., of Birmingham, Alabama. The Bimbos have a five-"man" club who perform in drag and tour the South playing local makeup teams at county fairs and carnivals. In this selection, Crawford's nine-year-old son, Denzel, the Bimbo's batboy, wanders into a boys' pickup game. From the novel *Pride of the Bimbos*.

Denzel wandered toward them with his glove under his arm. A few were in the outfield, crowding under liners and popups that a tall boy threw them. "I got it!" they called in unison, "Mine, mine!" Off to one side a dark, barrel-chested kid was playing pepper with a boy who had a bandage over his eye. The rest milled around, joking, tossing gloves and hats in the air, fighting over the remaining bat to take practice swings. They all seemed to know each other.

Denzel squatted next to a thin boy who sat on his glove at the fringe of the action, watching expectantly. He was the only one there smaller than Denzel.

"Gonna be a game?"

"Uh-huh." The thin boy looked up at him, surprised.

"They got regular teams?"

"Nope. They pick sides."

Denzel nodded.

"Hope I get to play," said the thin boy. "When the teams don't come out even I got to sit," he said, "every single time."

He waited for a word of support but Denzel just grunted and moved several feet away. *Might think we come together.*

The ones on what seemed to be the field hacked around a little longer until a movement to start a game began. "Let's go," someone said. "Get this show on the road."

"Somebody be captains."

"Somebody choose up."

Gradually they wandered in and formed a loose group around a piece of packing crate broken roughly in the shape of a home plate. They urged each other to get organized and shrugged their indifference over who would be the captains.

"C'mon, we don't have all day."

"Somebody just choose."

"Big kids against the little kids!" said a fat boy in glasses and they all laughed.

"Good guys against the bad guys!"

"Winners against the losers!"

"The men against the mice!"

"Okay," said the dark, barrel-chested kid, "Whynt we just have the same captains as yesterday?"

"Yeah, but not the same teams."

"Too lopsided."

"That was a slaughter."

"We got scobbed."

"Do it then," said the fat boy, "Bake and the Badger."

"Yeah, shoot for first pick."

"Let's go, choose up."

There was a sudden movement, everybody spreading in a semicircle around two of the boys, jostling not to be behind anyone, the thin boy hopping up and running to join them. Denzel got up slowly and walked to the rear of them. *No sense getting all hot and bothered. No big thing.* He drifted through hips and shoulders, quietly, till he stood in view of the captains.

They were shooting fingers, best four out of seven, like the World Series. The barrel-chested boy was one of the captains, the one they called the Badger, and the tall boy who had been throwing flies was the other.

Denzel slipped his glove on. It was an oversized Ted Kluszewski model his daddy had handed down to him. Each of the fingers seemed thick as his wrist and there was no web to speak of and no padding in the pocket. Orange and gunky.

The tall boy won on the last shoot and the Badger scowled. "Alley Oop!" Bake called without even looking.

"Haw-*raaat!*" A wiry kid with arms that hung to his knees trotted out from their midst and stood by Bake. "We got it now, can't lose. Can not *lose!*"

"Purdy!" The Badger barked it like an order and a solid-looking red-haired kid marched out and took his place.

The two first picks began to whisper and nudge at their captains.

"Vernon," whispered the wiry boy, "get Vernon."

"Vernon."

Vernon came to join them and he and Alley Oop slapped each other's backs at being together.

"Royce," whispered the big redhead. "They get Royce we've had it."

"Royce," said the Badger and Royce was welcomed into the fold.

"Psssst!" called the fat boy with the glasses to Alley Oop and Vernon. "Have him pick me. You guys need a third sacker."

"Ernie," they said, on their toes leaning over each of Bake's shoulders, "Ernierniernie!"

"Okay, Ernie," he said and Ernie waddled out with his glove perched on top of his head.

"Gahs looked like you needed some help," he told them. "Never fear, Ernie is here!"

The captains began to take more time in their picking. They considered and consulted and looked down the line before calling out a name. The Badger pounded quick, steady socks into the pocket of his glove while beside him Purdy slowly flapped the jaws of his first-baseman's mitt. Soon there were more that had been chosen than that hadn't. The ones who were picked frisked and giggled behind their captains while the ones who hadn't were statues on display. "You," the captains said now, still weighing abilities but unenthusiastic. Finally they just pointed. The Badger walked along the straggling line of left-overs like a general reviewing troops, stood in front of his next man and jerked his thumb back over his shoulder. When there was only one spot left for even teams Denzel and the thin boy were left standing. It was the Badger's pick.

Denzel stood at ease, eyes blank. It grew quiet. He felt the others checking him over and he smelled something. Topps bubble gum, the kind that came with baseball cards. He snuck a glance at the thin boy. His eyes were wide, fixed on the Badger, pleading. He had a round little puff of a catcher's mitt that looked like a red pincushion. There was no sign of a baseball ever having landed in it, no dent of a pocket.

Denzel felt the Badger considering him for a moment, eyes dipping to the thick-fingered old-timer's glove, but then he turned and gave a slight, exasperated nod to the thin boy. "We got him."

Before Denzel could get out of the way Bake's team streamed past him onto the field.

"First base!" they cried, "Dibs on shortstop!" Trotting around him as if he were a tree, looking through the space where he stood. "Bake?" they whined, "Lemme take left huh? I always get stuck at catcher or somethin." Denzel kept his face blank and tried to work the thing back down into his throat. They all knew each other, didn't know whether he was any good or not. No big thing.

He drifted off to the side, considered going back to the van, then sat beyond the third base line to watch. As if that was what he had come to do in the first place. Nice day to watch a ball game. He decided he would root for Bake's side.

"Me first," said the Badger, pointing with the bat handle, "you second, you third. Purdy you clean up. Fifth, sixth, semeightnon." They had full teams so Denzel couldn't offer to be all-time catcher and dive for foul tips. You didn't get to bat but it kept you busy and you could show them you could catch. Denzel kept his glove on.

He could tell he was better than a lot of them before they even started and some of the others when the end of the orders got up. The pitching was overhand but not fast. There was a rock that stuck out of the ground for first base and some cardboard that kept blowing so they had to put sod clumps on it for second and somebody's T-shirt for third. Bake played shortstop and was good and seemed a little older than the others.

The one called Purdy, the big red-headed one, fell to his knees after he struck out. Everybody had backed way up for him. Alley Oop made a nice one-handed catch in center. Whenever there was a close play at a base, Badger would run over and there would be a long argument and he would win. The thin boy had to be backed up at catcher by the batting team so it wouldn't take forever to chase the pitches that went through. The innings went a long time even when there weren't a lot of runs because the pitchers were trying tricky stuff and couldn't get it close. Denzel followed the action carefully, keeping track of the strikes and outs and runs scored, seeing who they backed up for and who they moved in for, who couldn't catch, who couldn't throw, keeping a book on them the way his daddy and Pogo had taught him he should. When fat Ernie did something funny he laughed a little along with the rest of them. Once somebody hit a grounder too far off to the left for the third baseman or left fielder to bother chasing. "Little help!" they called and Denzel scrambled after it. He backhanded it moving away, turned and whipped it hard into the pitcher. No one seemed to notice. He sat back down and the game started up again.

The Badger's side got ahead by three and stayed there, the two teams trading one or two runs each inning. They joked and argued with each other while waiting to bat. They practiced slides and catches in stop-action slow-motion and pretended to be TV commentators, holding imaginary microphones and interviewing themselves. They kept up a baseball chatter.

"*Hum*babe!" said the team in the field, "Chuckeratinthere-*iss*gahcantit*iss*gahcantit! *Hum*babe! *N*ostic*k*nostickchuckeratin-there—"

"*Lets*go!" said the team at bat, "*Biginninbiginninwe*gotta-team*we*gottateam*bang*itonoutthere! *Lets*golets go!"

Late in the fifth inning a mother's voice wailed over the babble from a distance.

"Jonathaaaan!"

There was a brief pause, the players looking at each other accusingly, seeing who would confess to being Jonathan.

"Jonathan Phelps you get in here!"

The thin boy with the catcher's mitt mumbled something,

looking for a moment as if he were going to cry, then ran off toward the camp.

Denzel squatted and slipped his glove on again. He wore it with his two middle fingers out, not for style but so he could make it flex a little. He waited.

The tall boy, Bake, walked in a circle at shortstop with his glove on his hip, looking around. "Hey kid!"

Who me? Denzel raised his eyebrows and looked to Bake.

"You play catcher for them."

Denzel began to rise but the Badger ran out onto the field. "Whoa na! No deal. I'm not takin him. Got enough easy outs awriddy. Will play thout a catcher, you gahs just back up the plate and will have to send somuddy in to cover if there's a play there."

Denzell squatted again and looked to Bake.

"Got to have even teams," he said. "I got easy outs too. If you only got eight that means your big hitters get up more."

"I'm not takin him, that's all there is to it." The Badger never looked to Denzel. "We don't need a catcher that bad. Not gonna get stuck with some little fairy."

Bake sighed. "Okay. He'll catch for us and you can have what's his name. Hewitt."

The Badger thought a minute, scowling, then agreed. Hewitt tossed his glove off and was congratulated on being traded to the winning side.

"Okay," said Bake, "you go catch. You're up ninth."

Denzel hustled behind the plate and the game started up. There was no catcher's gear, so though it was hardball he stood and one-hopped the pitches. He didn't let anything get by him to the kid who was backing him up. He threw the ball carefully to the pitcher. There were no foul tips. Badger got on and got to third with two out. Bake called time. He sent the right fielder in to cover the play at the plate and Denzel out to right.

The one called Royce was up. Denzel had booked him as strictly a pull-hitter. He played medium depth and shaded toward center. The first baseman turned and yelled at him.

"What you doing there? Move over. Get back. This gah can cream it!"

He did what the first baseman said but began to cheat in and over with the delivery.

The second pitch was in on the fists but Royce swung and blooped a high one toward short right. Denzel froze still.

"Drop it!" they screamed.

"Choke!"

"Yiyiyiyiyi!"

"I got it!" yelled somebody close just as Denzel reached up and took it stinging smack in the pocket using both hands the way his daddy had told him and then he was crashed over from the side.

He held on to the ball. Alley Oop helped him to his feet and mumbled that he was sorry, he didn't know that he really had it. The Badger stomped down on home plate so hard it split in half.

"Look what I found!" somebody called.

"Whudja step in, kid?"

"Beginner's luck."

Denzel's team trotted in for its at-bats. While they waited for the others to get in their positions Bake came up beside him.

"That mitt looks like you stole it out of a display window in the Hall of Fame," he said, and Denzel decided to smile. "Nice catch."

The first man up flied out to left and then Ernie stepped in. Ernie had made the last out of the inning before.

"Hold it! Hold it rat there!" Badger stormed in toward the plate. "Don't pull any of that stuff, who's up? Ninth man aint it? The new kid?"

"We changed the batting order," said Ernie. "You can do that when you make a substitution. The new kid bats in my spot and I bat where Hewitt was."

"Uhn-uh. No dice."

"That's the rules."

"Ernie," said Bake, stepping in and taking the bat from him, "let the kid have his ups. See what he can do."

Bake handed the bat to Denzel and the Badger stalked back into the field. It was a big, thick-handled bat, a Harmon Killebrew 34. Denzel liked the looks of the other one that was lying to the side but decided he'd stay with what he was given.

The Badger's team all moved in close to him. The center fielder was only a few yards behind second base.

"Tryn get a piece of it," said Ernie behind him, "just don't whiff, kid."

"Easyouteasyouteasyout!" came the chatter.

Denzel didn't choke up on the big bat. See what he can do.

The first four pitches were wide or too high. He let them pass.

"C'mon, let's go!"

"Wastin time."

"Swing at it."

"Let him hit," said the Badger. "Not goin anywheres."

The next one was way outside and he watched it.

"Come *awn!*" moaned the Badger, "s'rat *over!*"

"Whattaya want kid?"

"New batter, new batter!"

"Start calling strikes!"

"Egg in your beer?"

"See what he can do."

The pitcher shook his head impatiently and threw the next one high and inside. Denzel stepped back and tomahawked a shot down the line well over the left fielder's head.

"Attaboy! Go! Go!"

"Dig, baby, all the way!"

"Keep comin, bring it on!"

By the time the left fielder flagged it down and got it in Denzel was standing up with a triple.

"Way to hit! Way to hit, buddy."

"Sure you don't want him, Badger?"

"Foul ball," said the Badger. He was standing very still with his glove on his hip. "Take it over."

This time Bake and half his team ran out to argue. The Badger turned away and wouldn't listen to them.

"Get outa here," they said. "That was fair by a mile. You gotta be blind."

He wouldn't listen. "Foul ball."

"Get *off* it," they said, "you must be crazy."

Denzel sat on the base to wait it out. The third baseman sat on his glove beside him and said nice hit. The Badger began to argue, stomping around, his face turning red, finally throwing his glove down and saying he quit.

"Okay," said Bake, "have it your way."

"Nope." The Badger sulked off but not too far. "If you gonna cheat I don't want nothin to do with it."

"Don't *be* that way, Badger, dammit."

"Hell with you."

"Okay," said Bake, looking over to Denzel and shrugging for understanding, "we'll take it over."

Denzel lined the first pitch off the pitcher's knee and into right for a single. Three straight hits followed him and he crossed the plate with the tying run. The first baseman made an error and then the Badger let one through his legs and the game broke open.

Denzel sat back with the rest of the guys. They wrestled with each other and did knuckle-punches to the shoulder.

They compared talent with a professional eye.

"Royce is pretty fast."

"Not as fast as Alley Oop."

"Nobody's that fast."

"Alley Oop can *peel.*"

"But Royce is a better hitter."

"Maybe for distance but not for average."

"Nobody can hit it far as Purdy."

"If he connects."

"Yeah, he always tries to kill the ball. You got to just meet it."

"But if he ever connects that thing is gonna sail."

"Kiss it goodbye."

"Going, going, *gone!*"

Denzel sat back among them without talking, but following their talk closely, putting it all in his book. Alley Oop scored and asked Bake to figure his average for him and Bake drew the numbers in the dust with a stick till he came up with .625. That was some kind of average, everybody agreed. They batted through the order and Denzel got another single up the middle and died at second. It was getting late so they decided it would be last ups for Badger's team. The Badger was eight runs down and had given up.

Bake left Denzel in right for the last inning but nothing came his way. Purdy went down swinging for the last out and they split up. Bake and the Badger left together, laughing, but not before Bake asked Denzel his name and said see you tomorrow.

Denzel didn't tell him that he'd be gone tomorrow. That they'd have to go back to Jonathan Phelps.

St. Urbain's Horseman

MORDECAI RICHLER

A colony of American and Canadian show business plenipotentiaries, all burdened with their private agonies, are stationed in or near London. Unable to play cricket, they come together for their exclusive weekly ritual, a Sunday morning softball game at Hampstead Heath performed before a gallery that includes their former wives. From the novel *St. Urbain's Horseman*.

Summer.

Drifting through Soho in the early evening, Jake stopped at the Nosh Bar for a sustaining salt beef sandwich. He had only managed one squirting mouthful and a glance at the unit trust quotations in the *Standard* (S&P Capital was steady, but Pan Australian had dipped again) when he was distracted by a bulging-bellied American in a Dacron suit. The American's wife, unsuccessfully shoehorned into a mini-skirt, clutched a *London A to Z* to her bosom. The American opened a fat credit-card-filled wallet, briefly exposing an international medical passport which listed his blood type; he extracted a pound note and slapped it into the waiter's hand. "I suppose," he said, winking, "I get twenty-four shillings change for this?"

The waiter shot him a sour look.

"Tell your boss," the American continued, unperturbed, "that I'm a Gallicianer, just like him."

"Oh, Morty," his wife said, bubbling.

And the juicy salt beef sandwich turned to leather in Jake's mouth. It's here again, he realized, heart sinking, the season.

Come summer, American and Canadian show business plenipotentiaries domiciled in London had more than the usual hardships to contend with. The usual hardships being the income tax tangle, scheming and incompetent natives, uppity *au pairs* or nannies, wives overspending at the bazaar (Harrod's, Fortnum's, Asprey's), choosing suitable prep schools for the kids, doing without real pastrami and pickled tomatoes, fighting decorators and smog, and of course keeping warm. But come summer, tourist liners and jets began to disgorge demanding hordes of relatives and friends of friends, long (and best) forgotten schoolmates and army buddies, on London, thereby transmogrifying the telephone, charmingly inefficient all winter, into an instrument of terror. For there was not a stranger who phoned and did not exude warmth and expect help in procuring theater tickets and a night on the town ("What we're really dying for is a pub crawl. The swinging pubs. Waddiya say, old chap?") or an invitation to dinner at home. ("Well, Yankel, did you tell the Queen your Uncle Labish was coming? Did she bake a cake?")

The tourist season's dialogue, the observations, the complaints, was a recurring hazard to be endured. You agreed, oh how many times you agreed, the taxis were cute, the bobbies polite, and the pace slower than New York or, in Jake's case, Montreal. "People still know how to enjoy life here. I can see that." Yes. On the other hand, you've got to admit . . . the bowler hats are a scream, hotel service is lousy, there's nowhere you can get a suit pressed in a hurry, the British have snobby British accents and hate all Americans. Jealousy. "Look at it this way, it isn't home." Yes, a thousand times yes. All the same, everybody was glad to have made the trip, it was expensive but broadening, the world was getting smaller all the time, a global village, only next time they wouldn't try to squeeze so many countries into twenty-one days. "Mind you, the American Express was very, very nice everywhere. No complaints in that department."

Summer was charged with menace, with schnorrers and greenhorns from the New Country. So how glorious, how utterly delightful, it was for the hard-core show biz expatriates (those who weren't in Juan-les-Pins or Dubrovnik) to come together on a Sunday morning for a sweet and soothing game of softball, just as the Raj of another dynasty had used to meet on the cricket pitch in Malabar.

Sunday morning softball on Hampstead in summer was unquestionably the fun thing to do. It was a ritual.

Manny Gordon tooled in all the way from Richmond, stowing a fielder's mitt and a thermos of martinis in the boot, clapping a sporty tweed cap over his bald head and trapping himself and his starlet of the night before into his Aston-Martin at nine A.M. C. Bernard Farber started out from Ham Common, picking up Al Levine, Bob Cohen, Jimmy Grief and Myer Gross outside Mary Quant's on the King's Road. Moey Hanover had once startled the staff at the Connaught by tripping down the stairs on a Sunday morning, wearing a peak cap and T-shirt and blue jeans, carrying his personal Babe Ruth bat in one hand and a softball in the other. Another Sunday Ziggy Alter had flown in from Rome, just for the sake of a restorative nine innings.

Frankie Demaine drove in from Marlow-on-Thames in his Maserati. Lou Caplan, Morty Calman, and Cy Levi usually brought their wives and children. Monty Talman, ever mindful of his latest twenty-one-year-old girlfriend, always cycled to the Heath from St. John's Wood. Wearing a maroon track suit, he usually lapped the field eight or nine times before anyone else turned up.

Jake generally strolled to the Heath, his tattered fielder's mitt and three enervating bagels filled with smoked salmon concealed under the *Observer* in his shopping bag. Some Sundays, like this one, possibly his last for a while, Nancy brought the kids along to watch.

The starting line-up on Sunday, June 28, 1963 was:

AL LEVINE'S TEAM	LOU CAPLAN'S BUNCH
Manny Gordon, ss.	Bob Cohen, 3b.
C. Bernard Farber, 2b.	Myer Gross, ss.
Jimmy Grief, 3b.	Frankie Demaine, lf.
Al Levine, cf.	Morty Calman, rf.
Monty Talman, 1b.	Cy Levi, 2b.

Ziggy Alter, lf.	Moey Hanover, c.
Jack Monroe, rf.	Johnny Roper, cf.
Sean Fielding, c.	Jason Storm, 1b.
Alfie Roberts, p.	Lou Caplan, p.

Jake, like five or six others who had arrived late and hung over (or who were unusually inept players), was a sub. A utility fielder, Jake sat on the bench with Lou Caplan's Bunch. It was a fine, all but cloudless, morning but looking around Jake felt there were too many wives, children, and kibitzers about. Even more ominous, the Filmmakers' First Wives Club or, as Ziggy Alter put it, the Alimony Gallery, was forming, seemingly relaxed but actually fulminating, on the grass behind home plate.

First Al Levine's Team and then Lou Caplan's Bunch, both sides made up mostly of men in their forties, trotted out, sunken bellies quaking, discs suddenly tender, hemorrhoids smarting, to take a turn at fielding and batting practice.

Nate Sugarman, once a classy shortstop, but since his coronary the regular umpire, bit into a digitalis pill, strode onto the field, and called, "Play ball!"

"Let's go, boychick."

"We need a hit," Monty Talman, the producer, hollered.

"*You* certainly do," Bob Cohen, who only yesterday had winced through a rough cut of Talman's latest fiasco, shouted back snidely from the opposite bench.

Manny, hunched over the plate cat-like, trying to look menacing, was knotted with more than his usual fill of anxiety. If he struck out, his own team would not be too upset because it was early in the game, but Lou Caplan, pitching for the first time since his Mexican divorce, would be grateful, and flattering Lou was a good idea because he was rumored to be ready to go with a three-picture deal for Twentieth; and Manny had not been asked to direct a big-budget film since *Chase. Ball one, inside.* If, Manny thought, I hit a single I will be obliged to pass the time of day with that stomach-turning queen Jason Storm, 1b., who was in London to make a TV pilot film for Ziggy Alter. *Strike one, called.* He had never hit a homer, so that was out, but if come a miracle he connected for a triple, what then? He would be stuck on third sack with Bob Cohen, strictly second featuresville, a born loser, and Manny didn't want to be seen with Bob, even for an inning, especially with so many producers and agents about. K-NACK! *Goddammit, it's a hit! A double, for Chrissake!*

As the players on Al Levine's bench rose to a man, shouting encouragement—

"Go, man. Go."

"Shake the lead out, Manny. Run!"

—Manny, conscious only of Lou Caplan glaring at him ("It's not my fault, Lou."), scampered past first base and took myopic, round-shouldered aim on second, wondering should he say something shitty to Cy Levi, 2b., who he suspected was responsible for getting his name on the blacklist years ago.

Next man up to the plate, C. Bernie Farber, who had signed to write Lou Caplan's first picture for Twentieth, struck out gracefully, which brought up Jimmy Grief. Jimmy swung on the first pitch, lifting it high and foul, and Moey Hanover, c., called for it, feeling guilty because next Saturday Jimmy was flying to Rome and Moey had already arranged to have lunch with Jimmy's wife on Sunday. Moey made the catch, which brought up Al Levine, who homered, bringing in Manny Gordon ahead of him. Monty Talman grounded out to Gross, ss., retiring the side.

Al Levine's Team, first inning: two hits, no errors, two runs.

Leading off for Lou Caplan's Bunch, Bob Cohen smashed a burner to center for a single and Myer Gross fanned, bringing up Frankie Demaine and sending all the outfielders back, back, back. Frankie whacked the third pitch long and high, an easy fly had Al Levine been playing him deep left instead of inside right, where he was able to flirt hopefully with Manny Gordon's starlet, who was sprawled on the grass there in the shortest of possible Pucci prints. Al Levine was the only man on either team who always played wearing shorts—shorts revealing an elastic bandage which began at his left kneecap and ran almost as low as the ankle.

"Oh, you poor darling," the starlet said, making a face at Levine's knee.

Levine, sucking in his stomach, replied, "Spain," as if he were tossing the girl a rare coin.

"Don't tell me," she squealed. "The beach at Torremolinos. Ugh!"

"No, no," Levine protested. "The civil war, for Chrissake. Shrapnel. Defense of Madrid."

Demaine's fly fell for a homer, driving in a panting Bob Cohen.

Lou Caplan's Bunch, first inning: one hit, one error, two runs.

Neither side scored in the next two innings, which were noteworthy only because Moey Hanover's game began to slip badly. In the second Moey muffed an easy pop fly and actually let C. Bernie Farber, still weak on his legs after a cleansing, all but foodless, week at Forest Mere Hydro, steal a base on him. The problem was clearly Sean Fielding, the young RADA graduate whom Columbia had put under contract because, in profile, he looked like Peter O'Toole. The game had only just started when Moey Hanover's wife, Lilian, had ambled over to Al Levine's bench and stretched herself out on the grass, an offering, beside Fielding, and the two of them had been giggling together and nudging each other ever since, which was making Moey nervy. Moey, however, had not spent his young manhood at a yeshiva to no avail. Not only had he plundered the Old Testament for most of his winning *Rawhide* and *Bonanza* plots, but now that his Lilian was obviously in heat again, his hard-bought Jewish education, which his father had always assured him was priceless, served him splendidly once more. Moey remembered his *David ha'Melech: And it came to pass in the morning, that David wrote a letter to Joab, and sent it by the hand of Uriah. And he wrote in the letter, saying, Set Uriah in the forefront of the hottest battle, and retire ye from him, that he may be smitten, and die.*

Amen.

Lou Caplan yielded two successive hits in the third and Moey Hanover took off his catcher's mask, called for time, and strode to the mound, rubbing the ball in his hands.

"I'm all right," Lou said. "Don't worry. I'm going to settle down now."

"It's not that. Listen, when do you start shooting in Rome?"

"Three weeks tomorrow. You heard something bad?"

"No."

"You're a friend now, remember. No secrets."

"No. It's just that I've had second thoughts about Sean Fielding. I think he's very exciting. He's got lots of appeal. He'd be a natural to play Domingo."

As the two men began to whisper together, players on Al Levine's bench hollered, "Let's go, gang."

"Come on. Break it up, Moey."

Moey returned to the plate, satisfied that Fielding was as good as in Rome already. May he do his own stunts, he thought.

"Play ball," Nate Sugarman called.

Alfie Roberts, the director, ordinarily expected soft pitches from Lou, as he did the same for him, but today he wasn't so sure, because on Wednesday his agent had sent him one of Lou's properties to read and—Lou's first pitch made Alfie hit the dirt. That settles it, he thought, my agent already told him it doesn't grab me. Alfie struck out as quickly as he could. Better be put down for a rally-stopper than suffer a head fracture.

Which brought up Manny Gordon again, with one out and runners on first and third. Manny dribbled into a double play, retiring the side.

Multi-colored kites bounced in the skies over the Heath. Lovers strolled on the tow paths and locked together on the grass. Old people sat on benches, sucking in the sun. Nannies passed, wheeling toddlers with titles. The odd baffled Englishman stopped to watch the Americans at play.

"Are they air force chaps?"

"Filmmakers, actually. It's their version of rounders."

"Whatever is that enormous thing that woman is slicing?"

"Salami."

"*On the Heath?*"

"Afraid so. One Sunday they actually set up a bloody folding table, right over there, with cold cuts and herrings and mounds of black bread and a whole bloody side of smoked salmon. *Scotch. Ten and six a quarter, don't you know?*"

"On the Heath?"

"Champagne *in paper cups.* Mumm's. One of them had won some sort of award."

Going into the bottom of the fifth, Al Levine's Team led 6–3, and Tom Hunt came in to play second base for Lou Caplan's Bunch. Hunt, a Negro actor, was in town shooting *Othello X* for Bob Cohen.

Moey Hanover lifted a lazy fly into left field, which Ziggy Alter trapped rolling over and over on the grass until—just before getting up—he was well placed to look up Natalie Calman's skirt. Something he saw there so unnerved him that he dropped the ball, turning pale and allowing Hanover to pull up safely at second.

Johnny Roper walked. Which brought up Jason Storm, to the delight of a pride of British fairies who stood with their dogs on the first base line, squealing and jumping. Jason poked a bouncer through the infield and floated to second, obliging the fairies and their dogs to move up a base.

With two out and the score tied 7–7 in the bottom half of the sixth, Alfie Roberts was unwillingly retired and a new pitcher came in for Al Levine's Team. It was Gordie Kaufman, a writer blacklisted for years, who now divided his time between Madrid and Rome, asking a hundred thousand dollars a spectacular. Gordie came in to pitch with the go-ahead run on third and Tom Hunt stepping up to the plate for the first time. Big black Tom Hunt, who had once played semi-pro ball in Florida, was a militant. If he homered, Hunt felt he would be put down for another buck nigger, good at games, but if he struck out, which would call for rather more acting skill than was required of him on the set of *Othello X*, what then? He would enable a bunch of fat, foxy, sexually worried Jews to feel big, goysy. Screw them, Hunt thought.

Gordie Kaufman had his problems too. His stunning villa on Mallorca was run by Spanish servants, his two boys were boarding at a reputable British public school, and Gordie himself was president, sole stockholder, and the only employee of a company that was a plaque in Liechtenstein. And yet—and yet —Gordie still subscribed to the *Nation;* he filled his Roman slaves with anti-apartheid dialogue and sagacious Talmudic sayings; and whenever the left-wing *pushke* was passed around he came through with a nice check. I must bear down on Hunt, Gordie thought, because if he touches me for even a scratch single I'll come off a patronizing ofay. If he homers, God forbid, I'm a shitty liberal. And so with the count 3 and 2, and a walk, the typical social-democrat's compromise, seemingly the easiest way out for both men, Gordie gritted his teeth, his proud Trotskyite past getting the best of him, and threw a fast ball right at Hunt, bouncing it off his head. Hunt threw away his bat and started for the mound, fist clenched, but not so fast that players from both sides couldn't rush in to separate the two men, both of whom felt vindicated, proud, because they had triumphed over impersonal racial prejudice to hit each other as individuals on a fun Sunday on Hampstead Heath.

Come the crucial seventh, the Filmmakers' First Wives Club grew restive, no longer content to belittle their former husbands from afar, and moved in on the baselines and benches, undermining confidence with their heckling. When Myer Gross, for instance, came to bat with two men on base and his teammates shouted, "Go, man. Go," one familiar grating voice floated out over the others. "Hit, Myer. Make your son proud of you, *just this once.*"

What a reproach the first wives were. How steadfast! How unchanging! Still Waiting For Lefty after all these years. Today maybe hair had grayed and chins doubled, necks had gone pruney, breasts drooped and stomachs dropped, but let no man say these crones had aged in spirit. Where once they had petitioned for the Scotsboro Boys, broken with their families over mixed marriages, sent their boy friends off to defend Madrid, split with old comrades over the Stalin-Hitler Pact, fought for Henry Wallace, demonstrated for the Rosenbergs, and never, never yielded to McCarthy . . . today they clapped hands at China Friendship Clubs, petitioned for others to keep hands off Cuba and Vietnam, and made their sons chopped liver sandwiches and sent them off to march to Aldermaston.

The wives, alimonied but abandoned, had known the early struggling years with their husbands, the self-doubts, the humiliations, the rejections, the cold-water flats, and the blacklist, but they had always remained loyal. They hadn't altered, their husbands had.

Each marriage had shattered in the eye of its own self-made hurricane, but essentially the men felt, as Ziggy Alter had once put it so succinctly at the poker table, "Right, wrong, don't be silly, it's really a question of who wants to grow old with Anna Pauker when there are so many juicy little things we can now afford."

So there they were, out on the grass chasing fly balls on a Sunday morning, short men, overpaid and unprincipled, all well within the coronary and lung cancer belt, allowing themselves to look ridiculous in the hope of pleasing their new young wives and girlfriends. There was Ziggy Alter, who had once written a play "with content" for the Group Theater. Here was Al Levine, who had used to throw marbles under horses' legs at demonstrations and now raced two horses of his own at Epsom. On the pitcher's mound stood Gordie Kaufman, who had once carried a banner that read *No Pasarán* through the streets of Manhattan and now employed a man especially to keep Spaniards off the beach at his villa on Mallorca. And sweating under a catcher's mask there was Moey Hanover, who had studied at a yeshiva, stood up to the committee, and was now on a sabbatical from Desilu.

Usually the husbands were able to avoid their used-up wives. They didn't see them in the gaming rooms at the White Elephant or in the Mirabelle or Les Ambassadeurs. But come Brecht to Shaftesbury Avenue and without looking up from the second row center they could feel them squatting in their cotton bloomers in the second balcony, burning holes in their necks.

And count on them to turn up on a Sunday morning in summer on Hampstead Heath just to ruin a game of fun baseball. Even homering, as Al Levine did, was no answer to the drones.

"It's nice for him, I suppose," a voice behind Levine on the bench observed, "that on the playing field, with an audience, if you know what I mean, he actually appears virile."

The game dragged on. In the eighth inning Jack Monroe had to retire to his Mercedes-Benz for his insulin injection and

Jake Hersh, until now an embarrassed sub, finally trotted on to the field. Hersh, thirty-three, one-time relief pitcher for Room 41, Fletcher's Field High (2–7), moved into right field, mindful of his disc condition and hoping he would not be called on to make a tricksy catch. He assumed a loose-limbed stance on the grass, waving at his wife, grinning at his children, when without warning a sizzling line drive came right at him. Jake, startled, did the only sensible thing: he ducked. Outraged shouts and moans from the bench reminded Jake where he was, in a softball game, and he started after the ball.

"Fishfingers."

"*Putz!*"

Runners on first and third started for home as Jake, breathless, finally caught up with the ball. It had rolled to a stop under a bench where a nanny sat watching over an elegant perambulator.

"Excuse me," Jake said.

"Americans," the nurse said.

"I'm a Canadian," Jake protested automatically, fishing the ball out from under the bench.

Three runs scored. Jake caught a glimpse of Nancy, unable to contain her laughter. The children looked ashamed of him.

In the ninth inning with the score tied again, 11–11, Sol Peters, another sub, stepped cautiously to the plate for Lou Caplan's Bunch. The go-ahead run was on second and there was only one out. Gordie Kaufman, trying to prevent a bunt, threw right at him and Sol, forgetting he was wearing his contact lenses, held the bat in front of him to protect his glasses. The ball hit the bat and rebounded for a perfectly laid down bunt.

"Run, you shmuck."

"Go, man."

Sol, terrified, ran, carrying the bat with him.

Monty Talman phoned home.

"Who won?" his wife asked.

"We did. 13–12. But that's not the point. We had lots of fun."

"How many you bringing back for lunch?"

"Eight."

"*Eight?*"

"I couldn't get out of inviting Johnny Roper. He knows Jack Monroe is coming."

"I see."

"A little warning. Don't, for Chrissake, ask Cy how Marsha is. They're separating. And I'm afraid Manny Gordon is coming with a girl. I want you to be nice to her."

"*Anything else?*"

"If Gershon phones from Rome while the guys are there please remember I'm taking the call upstairs. And please don't start collecting glasses and emptying ashtrays at four o'clock. It's embarrassing. Bloody Jake Hersh is coming and it's just the sort of incident he'd pick on and joke about for months."

"I never coll—"

"All right, all right. Oh, shit, something else. Tom Hunt is coming."

"The actor?"

"Yeah. Now listen, he's very touchy, so will you please put away Sheila's doll."

"Sheila's doll?"

"If she comes in carrying that bloody golliwog I'll die. Hide it. Burn it. Hunt gets script approval these days, you know."

"All right, dear."

"See you soon."

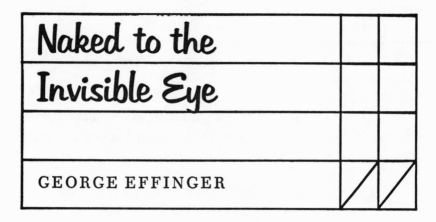

Naked to the Invisible Eye

GEORGE EFFINGER

The Bear shortstop looked out toward the kid on the mound before settling himself in the batter's box. The pitcher's name was Rudy Ramirez, he was only nineteen and from somewhere in Venezuela. That was all anybody knew about him; this was his first appearance in a professional ball game. The Bear shortstop took a deep breath and stepped in.

That kid Ramirez looked pretty fast during his warmups, he thought. The shortstop damned the fate that made him the focus of attention against a complete unknown. The waters surged; his thoughts shuffled and died.

The Venezuelan kid looked in for his sign. The shortstop looked down to the third-base coach, who flashed the *take* signal; that was all right with him. *I'm only batting .219, I want to see this kid throw one before . . .*

Ramirez went into his stretch, glanced at the runner on first . . .

With that kid Barger coming off the disabled list I might not be able to . . .

Ramirez' right leg kicked, his left arm flung back . . .

The shortstop's shrieking flood of thought stilled, his mind was as quiet as the surface of a pond stagnating. The umpire called the pitch a ball.

Along the coaching lines at third Sorenson was relaying the *hit-and-run* sign from the dugout. *All right,* thought the shortstop, *just make contact, get a good ground ball, maybe a hit, move the man into scoring position* . . .

Ramirez nodded to his catcher, stretched, checked the runner . . .

My luck, I'll get an easy double-play ball to the right side . . .

Ramirez kicked, snapped, and pitched . . .

The shortstop's mind was silent, ice-cold, dead, watching the runner vainly flying toward second, the catcher's throw beating him there by fifteen feet. Two out. One ball and one strike.

Sorenson called time. He met the shortstop halfway down the line.

"You damn brainless idiot!" said the coach. "You saw the sign, you *acknowledged* the sign, you stood there with your thumb in your ear looking at a perfect strike! You got an awful short memory?"

"Look, I don't know—"

"I'll tell you what I *do* know," said Sorenson. "I know that'll cost you twenty dollars. Maybe your spot in the lineup."

The shortstop walked to the on-deck circle, wiped his bat again with the pine-tar. His head was filled with anger and frustration. Back in the batter's box he stared toward the pitcher in desperation.

On the rubber Ramirez worked out of a full windup with the bases empty. His high kick hid his delivery until the last moment. The ball floated toward the plate, a fat balloon belt-high, a curve that didn't break . . .

The hitter's mind was like a desert, his mind was like an empty glass, a blank sheet of paper, his mind was totally at rest . . .

The ball nicked the outside corner for a called strike two. The Bear shortstop choked up another couple of inches on the handle. *He'll feed me another curve, and then the fast ball* . . .

Ramirez took the sign and went into his motion. The wrist flicked, the ball spun, broke . . . The shortstop watched, unawed, very still, like a hollow thing, as the curve broke sharply, down the heart of the plate, strike three, side retired.

The Tigers managed to score an insurance run in the top half of the ninth, and Rudy Ramirez went back to the mound with a five-to-three lead to protect. The first batter he was scheduled to face was the Bear pitcher, who was replaced in the order by pinch-hitter Frank Asterino.

A sense of determination, confidence made Asterino's mind orderly. It was a brightly lit mind, with none of the shifting doubts of the other. Rudy felt the will, he weighed the desire, he discovered the man's dedication and respected it. He stood off the rubber, rubbing the shine from the new ball. He reached for the rosin bag, then dropped it. He peered in at Johnston, his catcher. The sign: the fast ball.

Asterino guarded the plate closely. Johnston's mitt was targeted on the inside—start off with the high hard one, loosen the batter up. Rudy rocked back, kicked that leg high, and threw. The ball did not go for the catcher's mark, sailing out just a little. A not-overpowering pitch right down the pipe—a true gopher ball.

Rudy thought as the ball left his hand. He found that will of Asterino's, and he held it gently back. *Be still. Do not move; yes, be still.* And Asterino watched the strike intently as it passed.

Asterino watched two more, both curves that hung tantalizing but untouched. Ramirez grasped the batter's desire with his own, and blotted up all the fierce resolution there was in him. Asterino returned to the bench amid the boos of the fans, disappointed but unbewildered. He had struck out but, after all, that was not so unusual.

The top of the batting order was up, and Rudy touched their disparate minds. He hid their judgment behind the glare of his own will, and they struck out; the first batter needed five pitches and the second four. They observed balls with as much passive interest as strikes, and their bats never left their shoulders. No runs, no hits, no errors, nothing across for the Bears in the ninth. The game was over; Rudy earned a save for striking out the four batters he faced in his first pro assignment.

Afterward, local reporters were met by the angry manager of the Bears. When asked for his impression of the young Tiger pitcher he said, "I didn't think he looked *that* sharp. How you supposed to win managing a damn bunch of zombies?" In the visitors' clubhouse Tiger manager Fred Marenholtz was in a more expansive mood.

"Where did Ramirez come from?" asked one reporter.

"I don't really know," he said. "Charlie Cardona checks out Detroit's prospects down there. All I know is the telegram said that he was signed, and then here he is. Charlie's dug up some good kids for us."

"Did he impress you tonight?"

Marenholtz settled his wire-rim glasses on his long nose and nodded. "He looked real cool for his first game. I'm going to start him in the series with the Reds this weekend. We'll have a better idea then, of course, but I have a feeling he won't be playing Class B ball long."

After the game with the Bears, the Tigers showered quickly and boarded their bus. They had a game the next night against the Selene Comets. It was a home game for the Tigers, and they were all glad to be returning to Cordele, but the bus ride from the Bears' stadium would be four or five hours. They would get in just before dawn, sleep until noon, have time for a couple of unpleasant hamburgers, and get to the park in time for practice.

The Tigers won that game, and the game the next night, also. The Comets left town and were replaced by the Rockhill Reds, in for a Saturday afternoon game and a Sunday doubleheader. This late in the summer the pitching staffs were nearly exhausted. Manager Marenholtz of the Tigers kept his promise to the newspapermen; after the Saturday loss to the Reds he went to Chico Guerra, his first-string catcher, and told him to get Rudy Ramirez ready for the second game the next day.

Ramirez was eager, of course, and confident. Marenholtz was sitting in his office when Rudy came into the locker room before the Sunday doubleheader, a full half hour before practice began. Marenholtz smiled, remembering his own first game.

He had been an outfielder; in the seventh inning he had run into the left-field wall chasing a long fly. He dropped the ball, cracked his head, and spent the next three weeks on the disabled list. Marenholtz wished Ramirez better luck.

The Tigers' second-string catcher, Maurie Johnston, played the first game, and Guerra sat next to Ramirez in the dugout, pointing out the strengths and weaknesses of the opposing batters. Ramirez said little, just nodding and smiling. Marenholtz walked by them near the end of the first game. "Chico," he said, "ask him if he's nervous."

The catcher translated the question into Spanish. Ramirez grinned and answered. "He say no," said Guerra. "He jus' wan' show you what he can do."

The manager grunted a reply and went back to his seat, thinking about cocky rookies. The Tigers lost the first game, making two in a row dropped to the last-place Reds. The fans didn't seem to mind; there were only twenty games left until the end of the season, and there was no way possible for the Tigers to fall from first place short of losing all of them. It was obvious that Marenholtz was trying out new kids, resting his regulars for the Hanson Cup playoffs. The fans would let him get away with a lot, as long as he won the cup.

Between games there was a high school band marching in the outfield, and the local Kiwanis Club presented a plaque to the Tigers' center fielder, who was leading the league with forty-two home runs. Ramirez loosened up his arm during all this; he stood along the right-field foul-line and tossed some easy pitches to Guerra. After a while the managers brought out their lineup cards to the umpires and the grounds crew finished grooming the infield. Ramirez and Guerra took their positions on the field, and the rest of the team joined them, to the cheers of the Tigers' fans.

Skip Stackpole, the Reds' shortstop and leadoff batter, was settling himself in the batter's box. Rudy bent over and stared toward Guerra for the sign. An inside curve. Rudy nodded.

As he started into his windup he explored Stackpole's mind. It was a relaxed mind, concentrating only because Stackpole enjoyed playing baseball; for him, and for the last-place Reds, the game was meaningless. Rudy would have little difficulty.

Wait, thought Rudy wordlessly, forcing his will directly into Stackpole's intellect. *Not this one. Wait.* And Stackpole waited. The ball broke sharply, over the heart of the plate, for the first strike. There was a ripple of applause from the Tiger fans.

Guerra wanted a fast ball. Rudy nodded, kicked high, and threw. *Quiet,* he thought, *do not move.* Right down the pipe, strike two.

This much ahead of the hitter, Guerra should have called for a couple of pitches on the outside, to tease the batter into swinging at a bad pitch. But the catcher thought Stackpole was off balance. The Reds had never seen Ramirez pitch before. Guerra called for another fast ball. Rudy nodded and went into his windup. He kept Stackpole from swinging. The Reds' first hitter was called out on strikes; the Tiger fans cheered loudly as Guerra stood and threw the ball down to third base. Ramirez could hear his infielders chattering and encouraging him in a language that he didn't understand. He got the ball back and looked at the Reds' second man.

The new batter would be more of a challenge. He was hitting .312, battling with two others for the last place in the league's top ten. He was more determined than anyone Ramirez had yet faced. When Rudy pitched the ball, he needed more mental effort to keep the man from swinging at it. The pitch was too high. Ramirez leaned forward; Guerra wanted a low curve. The pitch broke just above the batter's knees, over the outside corner of the plate. One ball, one strike. The next pitch was a fast ball, high and inside. Ball two. Another fast ball, over the plate. *Wait,* thought Rudy, *wait.* The batter waited, and the count was two and two. Rudy tried another curve, and forced the batter to watch it helplessly. Strike three, two out.

Ramirez felt good, now. The stadium full of noisy people didn't make him nervous. The experienced athletes on the other team posed no threat at all. Rudy knew he could win today; he knew that there wasn't a batter in the world who could beat him. The third hitter was no problem for Rudy's unusual talent. He struck out on four pitches. Rudy received a loud cheer from the fans as he walked back to the dugout. He smiled and waved, and took a seat next to the water cooler with Guerra.

The Tigers scored no runs in their part of the first inning, and Rudy went back to the mound and threw his allotment of warmups. He stood rubbing up the ball while the Reds' cleanup hitter settled himself at the plate. Rudy disposed of the Reds' best power hitter with three pitches, insolently tossing three fast straight balls straight down the heart of the plate. Rudy got the other two outs just as quickly. The fans gave him another cheer as he walked from the mound.

The Tigers got a hit but no runs in the second, and Ramirez struck out the side again in the top of the third. In the bottom of the third Doug Davies, the Tiger second baseman, led off with a sharp single down the left-field line. Rudy was scheduled to bat next; he took off his jacket and chose a light bat. He had never faced an opposing pitcher before. He had never even taken batting practice in the time he had been with the Tigers. He walked to the plate and took his place awkwardly.

He swung at two and watched two before he connected. He hit the ball weakly, on the handle of the bat, and it dribbled slowly down the first-base line. He passed it on his way to first base, and he saw the Reds' pitcher running over to field it. Rudy knew that he'd be an easy out. *Wait*, he thought at the pitcher, *stop. Don't throw it*. The pitcher held the ball, staring ahead dazedly. It looked to the fans as if the pitcher couldn't decide whether to throw to first, or try for the lead runner going into second. Both runners were safe before Rudy released him.

Rudy took a short lead toward second base. He watched the coaches for signs. On the next pitch Davies broke for third. Rudy ran for second base. The Reds' catcher got the ball and jumped up. *Quiet*, thought Rudy. *Be still*. The catcher watched both Davies and Rudy slide in safely.

Eventually, the Tigers' lead-off man struck out. The next batter popped up in the infield. The third batter in the lineup, Chico Guerra, hit a long fly to right field, an easy enough chance for the fielder. But Rudy found the man's judgment and blocked it with his will. *Not yet*, he thought, *wait*. The outfielder hesitated, seeming as if he had lost the ball in the setting sun. By the time he ran after it, it was too late. The ball fell in and rolled to the wall. Two runs scored and Guerra lumbered into third base.

"Now we win!" yelled Rudy in Spanish. Guerra grinned and yelled back.

The inning ended with the Tigers ahead, three to nothing. Rudy was joking with Guerra as he walked back on the field. His manner was easy and supremely confident. He directed loud comments to the umpire and the opposing batters, but his Spanish went uninterpreted by his catcher. The top of the Reds' batting order was up again in the fourth inning, and Rudy treated them with total disregard, shaking off all of Guerra's signs except for the fast ball, straight down the middle. Stackpole, the leadoff batter, struck out again on four pitches. The second batter needed only three, and the third hitter used four. No one yet had swung at a pitch. Perhaps the fans were beginning to notice, because the cheer was more subdued as the Tigers came back to the bench. The Reds' manager was standing up in the dugout, angrily condemning his players, who went out to their positions with perplexed expressions.

The game proceeded, with the fans growing quieter and quieter in the stands, the Reds' manager getting louder in his damnations, the Tiger players becoming increasingly uneasy about the Reds' lack of interest. Rudy didn't care; he kept pitching them in to Guerra, and the Rockhill batters kept walking back to their dugout, shrugging their shoulders and saying nothing. Not a single Rockhill Red had reached first base. The ninth inning began in total silence. Rudy faced three pinch-hitters and, of course, struck them out in order. He had not only pitched a no-hit game, not only pitched a *perfect* game, but he had struck out twenty-seven consecutive batters. Not once during the entire game did a Rockhill player even swing at one of his pitches.

Marenholtz was waiting in the dugout. "Take a shower and see me in my office," he said, indicating both Guerra and Ramirez.

Marenholtz was a tall, thin man with sharp, birdlike features. He was sitting at his desk, smoking a cigar. He smoked cigars only when he was very angry, very worried, or very happy. Tonight, while he waited for Guerra and the new kid, he was very worried. Baseball, aged and crippled, didn't need this kind of notoriety.

There were half a dozen local newspapermen trying to force their way into the clubhouse. He had given orders that there would be no interviews until he had a chance to talk to Ramirez himself. He had phone calls from newscasters, scouts, fans, gamblers, politicians, and relatives. There was a stack of congratulatory telegrams. There was a very worried telegram from the team's general manager, and a very worried telegram from the front office of the Tigers' major league affiliate.

There was a soft knock on the door. "Guerra?" Marenholtz called out.

"*Si.*"

"Come on in, but don't let anybody else come in with you except Ramirez."

Guerra opened the door and the two men entered. Behind them was a noisy, confused crowd of Tiger players. Marenholtz sighed; he would have to find out what happened, and then deal with his team. Then he had to come up with an explanation for the public.

Ramirez was grinning, evidently not sharing Marenholtz and Guerra's apprehension. He said something to Guerra. The catcher frowned and translated for Marenholtz. "He say, don' he do a good job?"

"That's what *I* want to know!" said Marenholtz. "What *did* he do? You know it looks a little strange that not one guy on that team took swing number one."

Guerra looked very uncomfortable. "*Si,* maybe he just *good.*"

Marenholtz grunted. "Chico, did he look *that* good?"

Guerra shook his head. Ramirez was still smiling. Marenholtz stood up and paced behind his desk. "I don't *mind* him pitching a perfect game," he said. "It's a memorable achievement. But I think his effort would be better appreciated if one of those batters had tried *hitting.* At least *one.* I want you to tell me why they didn't. If you can't, I want you to ask *him.*"

Guerra shrugged and turned to Ramirez. They conversed for a few seconds, and then the catcher spoke to Marenholtz. "He say he don' want them to."

Marenholtz slammed his fist on his desk. "That's going to

make a great headline in *The Sporting News*. Look, if somehow he paid off the Reds to throw the game, even *they* wouldn't be so stupid as to do it that way." He paused, catching his breath, trying to control his exasperation. "All right, I'll give him a chance. Maybe he *is* the greatest pitcher the world has ever known. Though I doubt it." He reached for his phone and dialed a number. "Hello, Thompson? Look, I need a favor from you. Have you turned off the field lights yet? O.K., leave 'em on for a while, all right? I don't care. I'll talk to Mr. Kaemmer in the morning. And hang around for another half hour, O.K.? Well, screw the union. We're having a little crisis here. Yeah, Ramirez. Understand? Thanks, Thompson." Marenholtz hung up and nodded to Guerra. "You and your battery mate here are going to get some extra practice. Tell him I want to hit some off him, right now. Don't bother getting dressed again. Just put on your mask and get out on the field." Guerra nodded unhappily and led Rudy away.

The stadium was deserted. Marenholtz walked through the dugout and onto the field. He felt strangely alone, cold and worried; the lights made odd, vague shadows that had never bothered him before. He went to the batter's box. The white lines had been all but erased during the course of the game. He leaned on the bat that he had brought with him and waited for the two men.

Guerra came out first, wearing his chest protector and carrying his mask and mitt. Behind him walked Ramirez, silently, without his usual grin. He was dressed in street clothes, with his baseball spikes instead of dress shoes. Rudy took his place on the mound. He tossed a ball from his hand to his glove. Guerra positioned himself and Marenholtz waved to Rudy. No one had said a word.

Rudy wound up and pitched, a medium fast ball down the middle. Marenholtz swung and hit a low line drive down the right-field line that bounced once and went into the stands. Rudy threw another and Marenholtz hit it far into right center field. The next three pitches he sent to distant, shadowed parts of the ball park. Marenholtz stepped back for a moment. "He was throwing harder during the game, wasn't he?" he asked.

"I think so," said Guerra.

"Tell him to pitch me as hard as he did then. And throw some good curves, too." Guerra translated, and Ramirez nodded. He leaned back and pitched. Marenholtz swung, connected, and watched the ball sail in a huge arc, to land in the seats three hundred and fifty feet away in right field.

Rudy turned to watch the ball. He said nothing. Marenholtz tossed him another from a box on the ground. "I want a curve, now," he said.

The pitch came, breaking lazily on the outside part of the plate. Marenholtz timed it well and sent it on a clothesline into center field, not two feet over Ramirez' head. "All right," said the manager, "tell him to come here." Guerra waved, and Rudy trotted to join them. "One thing," said Marenholtz sourly. "I want him to explain why the Reds didn't hit him like that."

"I wanna know, too," said Guerra. He spoke with Ramirez, at last turning back to Marenholtz with a bewildered expression. "He say he don' wan' *them* to hit. He say you wan' hit, he *let* you hit."

"Oh, hell," said Marenholtz. "I'm not stupid."

Rudy looked confused. He said something to Guerra. "He say he don' know why you wan' hit *now*, but he do what you say."

The manager turned away in anger. He spit toward the dugout, thinking. He turned back to Guerra. "We got a couple of balls left," he said. "I want him to pitch me just like he did to the Reds, understand? I don't want him to *let* me hit. Have him try to weave his magic spell on me, too."

Rudy took a ball and went back to the mound. Marenholtz stood up to the plate, waving the bat over his shoulder in a slow circle. Ramirez wound up, kicked, and threw. His fastest pitch, cutting the heart of the plate.

Quiet, thought Rudy, working to restrain his manager's furious mind. *Easy, now. Don't swing. Quiet.*

Marenholtz' mind was suddenly peaceful, composed, thoughtless. The pitch cracked into Guerra's mitt. The manager hadn't swung at it.

Rudy threw ten more pitches, and Marenholtz didn't offer at any of them. Finally he raised his hand. Rudy left the mound again. Marenholtz stood waiting, shaking his head. "Why didn't

I swing? Those pitches weren't any harder than the others."
Marenholtz said.

"He just say he don' want you to swing. In his head he tell
you. Then you don' swing. He say it's easy."

"I don't believe it," said the manager nervously. "Yeah,
O.K., he can do it. He *did* do it. I don't like it." Guerra shook his
head. The three stood on the empty field for several seconds in
uneasy silence. "Can he do that with anybody?" asked Marenholtz.

"He say, *si.*"

"Can he do it any time? *Every* time?"

"He say, *si.*"

"We're in trouble, Chico." Guerra looked into Marenholtz'
frightened face and nodded slowly. "I don't mean just us. I
mean *baseball.* This kid can throw a perfect game, every time.
What do you think'll happen if he makes it to the majors? The
game'll be dead. Poor kid. He scares me. Those people in the
stands aren't going to like it any better."

"What you gonna do, Mr. Marenholtz?" asked Guerra.

"I don't know, Chico. It's going to be hard keeping a bunch
of perfect games secret. Especially when none of the hitters
ever takes the bat off his shoulder."

The following Thursday the Tigers had a night game at
home against the Kings. Rudy came prepared to be the starting
pitcher, after three days' rest. But when Marenholtz announced
the starting lineup, he had the Tigers' long relief man on the
mound. Rudy was disappointed, and complained to Guerra.
The catcher told him Marenholtz was probably saving him for
the next night, when the Kings' ace left-hander was scheduled
to pitch.

On Friday Ramirez was passed over again. He sat in the
dugout, sweating in his warmup jacket, irritated at the manager.
Guerra told him to have patience. Rudy couldn't understand
why Marenholtz wouldn't pitch him, after the great game
Ramirez had thrown in his first chance. Guerra just shrugged
and told Rudy to study the hitters.

Rudy didn't play Saturday, or in either of the Sunday
doubleheader's games. He didn't know that the newspapermen
were as mystified as he. Marenholtz made up excuses, saying

Rudy had pulled a back muscle in practice. The manager refused to make any comments about Ramirez' strange perfect
game, and as the days passed the clamor died down.

The next week Rudy spent on the bench, becoming angrier
and more frustrated. He confronted Marenholtz several times,
with Guerra as unwilling interpreter, and each time the manager
just said he didn't feel that Ramirez was "ready." The season
was coming to its close, with only six games left, and Rudy was
determined to play. As the games came and went, however, it
became obvious that he wasn't going to get the chance.

On the day of the last game, Marenholtz announced that
Irv Tappan, his number-one right-hander, would start. Rudy
stormed out of the dugout in a rage. He went back to the
locker room and started to change clothes. Marenholtz signaled
to Guerra, and they followed Ramirez.

"All right, Ramirez, what're you doing?" asked the manager.

"He say he goin' home," said Guerra, translating Rudy's
shouted reply.

"If he leaves before the game is over, he's liable to be fined.
Does he know that?"

"He say he don' care."

"Tell him he's acting like a kid," said Marenholtz, feeling
relieved.

"He say you can go to hell."

Marenholtz took a deep breath. "O.K., Chico. Tell him
we've enjoyed knowing him, and respect his talent, and would
like to invite him to try out for the team again next spring."

"He say go to hell."

"He's going home?" asked Marenholtz.

"He say you 'mericanos jealous, and waste his time. He
say he can do other things."

"Well, tell him we're sorry, and wish him luck."

"He say go to hell. He say you don' know your *ano* from
a hole in the groun'."

Marenholtz smiled coldly. "Chico, I want you to do me a
favor. Do yourself a favor too; there's enough here for the two
of us. You let him finish clearing out of here, and you go with
him. I don't know where he's going this time of day. Probably
back to the hotel where he stays. Keep with him. Talk to him.

Don't let him get away, don't let him get drunk, don't let him talk to anybody else."

Guerra shrugged and nodded. Ramirez was turning to leave the clubhouse. Marenholtz grabbed Guerra's arm and pushed him toward the furious boy. "Go on," said the manager, "keep him in sight. I'll call the hotel in about three or four hours. We got a good thing here, Chico, my boy." The catcher frowned and hurried after Rudy.

Marenholtz walked across the dressing room, stopping by his office. He opened the door and stared into the darkened room for a few seconds. He wanted desperately to sit at his desk and write the letters and make the phone calls, but he still had a game to play. The job seemed so empty to him now. He *knew* this would be the last regular game he'd see in the minor leagues. Next spring he and Ramirez would be shocking them all at the Florida training camps. Next summer he and Ramirez would own the world of major league baseball.

First, though, there was still the game with the Bears. Marenholtz closed the door to the office and locked it. Then he went up the tunnel to the field. All that he could think of was going back to the Big Time.

After the game, Fred Marenholtz hurried to his office. The other players grabbed at him, swatting at his back to congratulate him on the end of the season. The Tigers were celebrating in the clubhouse. Cans of beer were popping open, and sandwiches had been supplied by the front office. The manager ignored them all. He locked the door to the office behind him. He called Ramirez' hotel and asked for his room.

Guerra answered, and reported that Ramirez was there, taking a nap. The catcher was instructed to tell Rudy that together they were all going to win their way to the major leagues. Guerra was doubtful, but Marenholtz wouldn't listen to the catcher's puzzled questions. The manager hung up. He pulled out a battered address book from his desk drawer, and found the telephone number of an old friend, a contract lawyer in St. Louis. He called the number, tapping a pencil nervously on the desk top while the phone rang.

"Hello, Marty?" he said when the call was finally answered.

"Yes. Who's this calling please?"

"Hi. You won't remember me, but this is Fred Marenholtz."

"Freddie! How are you? Lord, it's been fifteen years. Are you in town?"

Marenholtz smiled. Things were going to be all right. They chatted for a few minutes, and then Marenholtz told his old friend that he was calling on business.

"Sure, Freddie," said the lawyer. "For Frantic Fred Marenholtz, anything. Is it legal?" Marenholtz laughed.

The photographs on the office wall looked painfully old to Marenholtz. They were of an era too long dead, filled with people who themselves had long since passed away. Baseball itself had withered, had lost the lifeblood of interest that had infused the millions of fans each spring. It had been too many years since Fred Marenholtz had claimed his share of glory. He had never been treated to his part of the financial rewards of baseball, and after his brief league career it was time to make his bid.

Marenholtz instructed the lawyer in detail. Old contracts were to be broken, new ones drawn up. The lawyer wrote himself in for five percent as payment. The manager hung up the phone again. He slammed his desk drawer closed in sheer exuberance. Then he got up and left his office. He had to thank his players for their cooperation during the past season.

"Tell him he's not going to get anything but investigated if he doesn't go with us." It was late now, past midnight. Ramirez' tiny hotel room was stifling. Rudy rested on the bed. Guerra sat in a chair by the single window. Marenholtz paced around, his coat thrown on the bed, his shirt soaked with perspiration.

"He say he don' like the way you run the club. He don' think you run him better," said Guerra wearily.

"All right. Explain to him that we're not going to cost him anything. The only way *we* can make any money is by making sure *he* does O.K. We'll take a percentage of what he makes. That's his insurance."

"He wan' know why you wan' him now, you wouldn't play him before."

"Because he's a damn fool, is why! Doesn't he know what would happen if he pitched his kind of game, week after week?"

"He think he make a lot of money."

Marenholtz stopped pacing and stared. "Stupid Spanish idiot!" he said. Guerra, from a farming village in Panama, glared resentfully. "I'm sorry, Chico. Explain it to him." The catcher went to the edge of the bed and sat down. He talked with Rudy for a long while, then turned back to the manager.

"O.K., Mr. Marenholtz. He didn' think anybody noticed."

"Fine," said Marenholtz, taking Guerra's vacated chair. "Now let's talk. Chico, what were you planning to do this winter?"

Guerra looked puzzled again. "I don' know. Go home."

"No. You're coming with me. We're taking young Mr. Ramirez here and turn him into a pitcher. If not that, at least into an intelligent thrower. We got a job, my friend."

They had six months, and they could have used more. They worked hard, giving Rudy little time to relax. He spent weeks just throwing baseballs through a circle of wire on a stand. Guerra and Marenholtz helped him learn the most efficient way to pitch, so that he wouldn't tire after half a game; he studied films of his motions, to see where they might be improved, to fool the hitters and conserve his own energy. Guerra coached him on the fundamentals: fielding his position, developing a deceptive throw to first base, making certain that his windup was the same for every different pitch.

After a couple of months Ramirez' control was sharp enough to put a ball into Guerra's mitt wherever the catcher might ask. Marenholtz watched with growing excitement—they were going to bring it off. Rudy was as good as any mediocre pitcher in the majors. Marenholtz was teaching him to save his special talent for the tight situations, the emergencies where less attention would be focused on the pitcher. Rudy was made to realize he had eight skilled teammates behind him; if he threw the ball where the catcher wanted it, the danger of long hits was minimized. A succession of pop-ups and weak grounders would look infinitely better than twenty-seven passive strikeouts.

Before the spring training session began, Rudy had developed a much better curve that he could throw with reasonable control, a passable change-up, a poor slider, and a slightly off-speed fast ball. He relied on Guerra and Marenholtz for instructions, and they schooled him in all the possible situations until he was fed up.

"Freddie Marenholtz! Damn, you look like you could still get out there and play nine hard ones yourself. Got that phenom of yours?"

"Yeah, you want him to get dressed?" Marenholtz stood by a batting cage in the training camp of the Nashville Cats, a team welcomed into the American League during the expansion draft three years previously. The Florida sun was already fierce enough in March to make Marenholtz uncomfortable, and he shielded his eyes with one hand as he talked to Jim Billy Westfahl, the Cats' manager.

"All right," said Westfahl. "You said you brought this kid Ramirez and a catcher, right? What's his name?"

"Guerra. Only guy Ramirez ever pitched to."

"Yeah, well, you know we got two good catchers in Portobenez and Staefler. If Guerra's going to stick, he's going to have to beat them out."

Marenholtz frowned. Guerra was *not* going to beat them out of their jobs. But he had to keep the man around, both because he could soothe Ramirez' irrational temper and because Guerra presented a danger to the plan. But the aging catcher might have to get used to watching the games from the boxes. He collected three and a half percent of Rudy's income, and Marenholtz couldn't see that Guerra had reason to complain.

Rudy came out of the locker room and walked to the batting cage. Guerra followed, looking uneasy among the major league talents. Ramirez turned to Westfahl and said something in Spanish. Guerra translated. "He say he wan' show you what he can do."

"O.K., I'm game. *Somebody's* going to have to replace McAnion. It may as well be your kid. Let's see what he looks like."

Rudy pitched to Guerra, and Westfahl made a few noncommittal remarks. Later in the day Rudy faced some of the Cats' regulars, and the B squad of rookies. He held some of them back, pitched to some of them, and looked no less sharp than any of the other regular pitchers after a winter's inactivity. In the next few weeks Marenholtz and Guerra guided Rudy well, letting him use his invisible talent sparingly, without attracting undue notice, and Ramirez seemed sure to go north with the team when the season began. Guerra didn't have the same luck. A week before spring training came to an end he was optioned to the Cats' Double A farm club. Guerra pretended to be upset, and refused to report.

By this time Marenholtz had promoted a large amount of money. The newly appointed president of *RR Star Enterprises* had spent the spring signing contracts while his protégé worked to impress the public. Permissions and royalty fees were deposited from trading card companies, clothing manufacturers, grooming product endorsements (Rudy was hired to look into a camera and say, "I like it. It makes my hair neat without looking greasy." He was finally coached to say, "I like it" and the rest of the line was given to a sexy female model), fruit juice advertisements, and sporting goods dealers.

The regular season began at home for the Cats. Rudy Ramirez was scheduled to pitch the third game. Rudy felt little excitement before the game; what he did feel was in no way different in kind or quantity from his nervousness before his first appearance with the Cordele Tigers. The slightly hostile major league crowd didn't awe him: he was prepared to awe the four thousand spectators who had come to watch the unknown rookie.

Fred Marenholtz had briefed Rudy thoroughly; before the game they had decided that an impressive but nonetheless credible effort would be a four- or five-hit shutout. For an added touch of realism, Rudy might get tired in the eighth inning, and leave for a relief pitcher. Marenholtz and Guerra sat in field boxes along the first-base side, near the dugout. Ramirez could hear their shouts from the mound. He waved to them as he took his place before the National Anthem was sung.

Rudy's pitches were not particularly overpowering. His fast ball was hittable; only the experience of the Cats' catcher prevented it from sailing time after time over the short left field fence. Ramirez' weeks of practice saved him: his pitches crossed the plate just above the batter's knees, or handcuffed him close around the fists, or nicked the outside edge of the plate. Rudy's curve was just good enough to keep the hitters guessing. The first batter hit a sharp ground ball to short, fielded easily for the first out. The second batter lofted a fly to right field for the second out. Rudy threw three pitches to the third batter, and then threw his first mistake, a fast ball belt-high, down the middle. Rudy knew what would happen—a healthy swing, and then a quick one-run lead for the White Sox. Urgently, desperately, he sought the batter's will and grasped it in time. The man stood stupidly, staring at the most perfect pitch he would see in a long while. It went by for a called strike three, and Rudy had his first official major league strikeout.

Marenholtz stood and applauded when Rudy trotted back to the dugout. Guerra shouted something in Spanish. Ramirez' teammates slapped his back, and he smiled and nodded and took his place on the bench. He allowed a double down the line in the second inning, set the White Sox down in order in the third and fourth, gave up a single and a walk in the fifth, a single in the sixth, no hits in the seventh, two singles in the eighth, and two to the first two batters in the ninth. Rudy had pitched wisely, combining his inferior skill with judicious use of his mental talent. Sometimes he held back a batter for just a fraction of a second, so that the hitter would swing late. Other times he would prevent a batter from running for a moment, to insure his being thrown out at first. He caused the opposition's defense to commit errors so that the Cats could score the runs to guarantee victory.

The manager of the Cats came out to the mound to talk with Ramirez in the ninth. Carmen Velillo, the Cats' third baseman, joined the conference to translate for Rudy. Ramirez insisted he was strong enough to finish, but the manager brought in a relief pitcher. Rudy received a loud cheer from the fans as he went off the field. The Cats' new man put down the rally, and Ramirez had a shutout victory. After Rudy and Velillo had answered the excited questions of the newsmen, Marenholtz and Guerra met him for a celebration.

Marenholtz held interviews with reporters from national magazines or local weeklies. Coverage of Ramirez' remarkable success grew more detailed; as the season progressed Rudy saw his picture on the front of such varied periodicals as *Sports Illustrated* and *Esquire*. By June Rudy had won eleven games and lost none. His picture appeared on the cover of *Time*. A small article in *Playboy* announced that he was the greatest natural talent since Grover Cleveland Alexander. He appeared briefly on late-night television programs. He was hired to attend supermarket openings in the Nashville area. He loved winning ball games, and Marenholtz, too, gloried in returning a success to the major leagues that had treated him so shabbily in his youth.

The evening before Ramirez was to start his twelfth ball game, he was having dinner with Marenholtz and Guerra. The older man was talking about his own short playing career, and how baseball had deteriorated since then. Guerra nodded and said little. Ramirez stared quietly at his plate, toying with his food and not eating. Suddenly he spoke up, interrupting Marenholtz' flow of memories. He spoke in rapid Spanish; Marenholtz gaped in surprise. "What's he saying?" he asked.

Guerra coughed nervously. "He wan' know why he need us," he said. "He say he do pretty good by himself."

Marenholtz put his cigar down and stared angrily at Ramirez. "I was wondering how long it would take him to think he could cut us out. Tell him if it hadn't been for us he'd either be in trouble, or in Venezuela. If it hadn't been for us he wouldn't have that solid bank account and his poor gray mama wouldn't have the only color television south of the border. And if that doesn't work, tell him maybe he *doesn't* need us, but he signed the contracts."

Guerra said a few words, and Rudy answered. "What's he say now?" asked Marenholtz.

"Nothing," said Guerra, staring down at his own plate. "He jus' say he thank you, but he wan' do it by himself."

"Oh, hell. Tell him to forget that and pitch a good game tomorrow. *I'll* do the worrying. That's what I'm for."

"He say he do that. He say he pitch you a good game."

"Well, thank you, Tom, and good afternoon, baseball fans everywhere. In just a few moments we'll bring you live coverage of the third contest of this weekend series, a game between the Nashville Cats, leaders in the American League Midlands division, and the Denver Athletics. It looks to be a pitchers' duel today, with young Rudy Ramirez, Nashville's astonishing rookie, going against the A's veteran right-hander, Morgan Stepitz."

"Right, Chuck, and I think a lot of the spectators in the park today have come to see whether Ramirez can keep his streak alive. He's won eleven, now, and he hasn't been beaten so far in his professional career. Each game must be more of an ordeal than the last for the youngster. The strain will be starting to take its toll."

"Nevertheless, Tom, I have to admit it's been a very long time since I've seen anyone with the poise of that young man. He hasn't let his success make him overconfident. I'm sure that defeat, when it comes, will be a hard blow, but I'm just as certain that Rudy Ramirez will recover and go on to have a truly amazing season."

"A lot of fans have written in to ask what the record is for most consecutive games won. Well, Ramirez has quite a way to go. The major league record is nineteen, set in 1912 by Rube Marquard. But even if Ramirez doesn't go on to break that one, he's still got the start on a great season. He's leading both leagues with an Earned Run Average of 1.54, and has an excellent shot at thirty wins."

Rudy looked around at the stadium. The Nashville park was new, built five years ago in hopes of attracting a major league franchise. It was huge, well-designed, and, generally filled with noisy fans. The sudden success of the usually hapless Cats was easily traced: Rudy Ramirez. He was to pitch again today, and his enthusiastic rooters crowded the spacious park. Bedsheet banners hung over railings, wishing him luck and proclaiming Ramirez to be the best-loved individual on the continent. Rudy, still innocent of English, did not know what they said.

He could see Marenholtz and Guerra sitting behind the dugout. Rudy touched the visor of his cap in salute. Then he turned to face the first of the Athletics' hitters.

"O.K., the first batter for the A's is the second baseman, number 12, Jerry Kleiner. Kleiner's batting .262 this season. He's a switch-hitter, and he's batting right-handed against the south-paw, Ramirez.

"Ramirez takes his sign from Staefler, winds up, and de-livers. Kleiner takes the pitch for a called strike one. Ramirez has faced the A's only once before this season, shutting them out on four hits.

"Kleiner steps out to glance down at the third-base coach for the signal. He steps back in. Ramirez goes into his motion. Kleiner lets it go by again. No balls and two strikes."

"Ramirez is really piping them in today, Tom."

"That's right, Chuck. I noticed during his warmups his fast ball seemed to be moving exceptionally well. It will tend to tail in toward a right-handed batter. Here comes the pitch—strike three! Kleiner goes down looking."

"Before the game we talked with Cats' catcher Bo Staefler, who told us that Ramirez' slider is improving as the season gets older. That can only be bad news for the hitters in the American League. It may be a while before they can solve his style."

"Stepping in now is the A's right fielder, number 24, Ricky Gonzalvo. Gonzalvo's having trouble with his old knee injury this year, and his average is down to .244. He crowds the plate a little on Ramirez. The first pitch is inside, knocking Gonzalvo down. Ball one.

"Ramirez gets the ball back, leans forward for his sign. And the pitch . . . in there for a called strike. The count is even at one and one."

"He seems to have excellent control today, wouldn't you say, Tom?"

"Exactly. Manager Westfahl of the Cats suggested last week that the pinpoint accuracy of his control is sometimes enough to rattle a batter into becoming an easy out."

"There must be *some* explanation, even if it's magic."

"Ramirez deals another breaking pitch, in there for a called strike two. I wouldn't say it's all magic, Chuck. It looked to me as though Gonzalvo was crossed up on that one, obviously ex-pecting the fast ball again."

"Staefler gives him the sign. Ramirez nods, and throws. Fast ball, caught Gonzalvo napping. Called strike three; two away now in the top of the first.

"Batting in the number three position is the big first baseman, Howie Bass. Bass' brother, Eddie, who plays for the Orioles, has the only home run hit off Ramirez this season. Here comes Ramirez' pitch . . . Bass takes it for strike one."

"It seems to me that the batters are starting out behind Ramirez, a little overcautious. That's the effect that a winning streak like his can have. Ramirez has the benefit of a psychological edge working for him, as well as his great pitching."

"Right, Tom. That pitch while you were talking was a called strike two, a good slider that seemed to have Bass completely baffled."

"Staefler gives the sign, but Ramirez shakes his head. Ramirez shakes off another sign. Now he nods, goes into his windup, and throws. A fast ball, straight down the middle, strike three. Bass turns to argue with the umpire, but that'll do him no good. Three up and three down for the A's, no runs, no hits, nothing across."

The Cats' fans jumped to their feet, but Fred Marenholtz listened angrily to their applause. He caught Rudy's eye just as the pitcher was about to enter the dugout. Before Marenholtz could say anything, Rudy grinned and disappeared inside. Marenholtz was worried that the sophisticated major league audience would be less likely to accept the spectacle of batter after batter going down without swinging at Ramirez' pitches. The older man turned to Guerra. "What's he trying to do?" he asked.

Guerra shook his head. "I don' know. Maybe he wan' strike out some."

"Maybe," said Marenholtz dubiously, "but I didn't think he'd be that dumb."

The Cats got a runner to second base in their part of the first inning, but he died there when the cleanup hitter sent a line drive over the head of the A's first baseman, who leaped high to save a run. Rudy walked out to the mound confidently, and threw his warmups.

"All right," said Marenholtz, "let's see him stop that nonsense now. This game's being televised all over the country." He watched Ramirez go into his motion. The first pitch was a curve that didn't break; a slow pitch coming toward the plate as fat as a basketball. The A's batter watched it for a called strike. Marenholtz swore softly.

Rudy threw two more pitches, each of them over the plate for strikes. The hitter never moved his bat. Marenholtz' face was red with anger. Rudy struck out the next batter in three pitches. Guerra coughed nervously and said something in Spanish. Already the fans around them were remarking on how strange it was to see the A's being called out on strikes without making an effort to guard the plate. The A's sixth batter took his place in the batter's box, and three pitches later he, too, walked back to the bench, a bewildered expression on his face.

Marenholtz stood and hollered to Ramirez. "What the hell you doing?" he said, forgetting that the pitcher couldn't understand him. Rudy walked nonchalantly to the dugout, taking no notice of Marenholtz.

Guerra rose and edged past Marenholtz to the aisle. "You going for a couple of beers?" asked Marenholtz.

"No," said Guerra. "I think I just *goin'*."

"Well, Tom, it's the top of the third, score tied at nothing to nothing. I want to say we're getting that pitchers' battle we promised. We're witnessing one heck of a good ball game so far. The Cats have had only one hit, and rookie Rudy Ramirez hasn't let an Athletic reach first base."

"There's an old baseball superstition about jinxing a pitcher in a situation like this, but I might mention that Ramirez has struck out the first six men to face him. The record for consecutive strikeouts is eleven, held by Gaylord Perry of the old Cleveland Indians. That mark was set the last year the Indians played in Cleveland, before their move to New Orleans."

"This sort of game isn't a new thing for Ramirez, either, Tom. His blurb in the Cats' pressbook mentions that in his one start in the minor leagues, he threw a perfect game and set a Triangle League record for most strikeouts in a nine-inning game."

"O.K., Chuck. Ramirez has finished his warmups here in the top of the third. He'll face the bottom of the A's order. Batting in the seventh position is the catcher, number 16, Tolly Knecht. Knecht's been in a long slump, but he's always been something of a spoiler. He'd love to break out of it with a hit against Ramirez here. Here's the pitch . . . Knecht was taking all the way, a called strike one."

"Maybe the folks at home would like to see Ramirez' form here on the slow-motion replay. You can see how the extra-high kick tends to hide the ball from the batter until the very last moment. He's getting the full force of his body behind the pitch, throwing from the shoulder with a last, powerful snap of the wrist. He ends up here perfectly balanced for a sudden defensive move. From the plate the white ball must be disguised by the uniform. A marvelous athlete and a terrific competitor."

"Right, Chuck. That last pitch was a good breaking ball; Knecht watched it for strike two. I think one of the reasons the hitters seem to be so confused is the excellent arsenal of pitches that Ramirez has. He throws his fast ball intelligently, saving it for the tight spots. He throws an overhand curve and a side-arm curve, each at two different speeds. His slider is showing up more and more as his confidence increases."

"Ramirez nods to Staefler, the catcher. He winds up, and throws. Strike three! That's seven, now. Knecht throws his bat away in frustration. The fans aren't too happy, either. Even the Cats' loyal crowd is beginning to boo. I don't think I've ever seen a team as completely stymied as the A's are today."

"I tell you, I almost wish I could go down there myself. Some of Ramirez' pitches look just too good. It makes me want to grab a bat and take a poke at one. His slow curves seem to hang there, inviting a good healthy cut. But, of course, from our vantage point we can't see what the batters are seeing. Ramirez must have tremendous stuff today. Not one Athletic hitter has taken a swing at his pitches."

When the eighth Athletic batter struck out, the fans stood and jeered. Marenholtz felt his stomach tightening. His mouth was dry and his ears buzzed. After the ninth batter fanned, staring at a mild, belt-high pitch, the stadium was filled with boos. Marenholtz couldn't be sure that they were all directed at the unlucky hitters.

Maybe I ought to hurry after Guerra, thought Marenholtz. *Maybe it's time to talk about that bowling alley deal again. This game is rotten at its roots already. It's not like when I was out there. We cared. The fans cared. Now they got guys like Grobert playing, they're nearly gangsters. Sometimes the games look like they're produced from a script. And Ramirez is going to topple it all. The kid's special, but that won't save us. Good God, I feel sorry for him. He can't see it coming. He won't see it coming. He's out there having a ball. And he's going to make the loudest boom when it all falls down. Then what's he going to do? What's he going to do?*

Rudy walked jauntily off the field. The spectators around Marenholtz screamed at him. Rudy only smiled. He waved to Marenholtz, and pointed to Guerra's empty seat. Marenholtz shrugged. Ramirez ducked into the dugout, leaving Marenholtz to fret in the stands.

After the Cats were retired in the third, Rudy went out to pitch his half of the fourth. A policeman called his name, and Rudy turned. The officer stood in the boxes, at the edge of the dugout, stationed to prevent overeager fans from storming the playing field. He held his hand out to Rudy and spoke to him in English. Rudy shook his head, not understanding. He took the papers from the policeman and studied them for a moment. They were contracts that he had signed with Marenholtz. They were torn in half. Ramirez grinned; he looked up toward Marenholtz' seat behind the dugout. The man had followed Guerra, had left the stadium before he could be implicated in the tarnished proceedings.

For the first time since he had come to the United States, Rudy Ramirez felt free. He handed the contracts back to the mystified police officer and walked to the mound. He took a few warmups and waited for Kleiner, the A's leadoff batter. Ramirez took his sign and pitched. Kleiner swung and hit a shot past the mound. Rudy entered Kleiner's mind and kept him motionless beside the plate for a part of a second. The Cats' shortstop went far to his left, grabbed the ball and threw on the dead run; the runner was out by a full step. There were mixed groans and cheers from the spectators, but Rudy didn't hear. He was watching Gonzalvo take his place in the batter's box. Maybe Rudy would let him get a hit.

The Rookie

ELIOT ASINOF

The Rookie walked into the batter's circle behind home plate
and listened to the roar of the tremendous crowd. He swung
the two big bats over his head, stretching the muscles in his
powerful arms, and recorded the deafening noises for his memory. Dropping to one knee, he stroked his favorite piece of shiny
ash, and wiped the dirt from the tapered white barrel. He
could not resist looking up toward the towering, triple-tiered
stadium around him. For the fourth time today he waited there
for his turn at bat; each time he would wallow in the exultation
that ran through him, repeating under his breath for his senses
to enjoy: "You're in the big-time, Mike. . . . At last, you're in
the big-time!"

At last . . . after sixteen grueling, sweltering summers in
squalid, Southern towns. At last . . . after sixteen years, the
whole span of a ball-player's life. For a moment, he reveled in
the thrill that beat against his insides and almost made him
weep. At last . . . he was a Major Leaguer.

But now a hot wave of savage noise rose from the stands, jarring him rudely from his reverie, and brought him back to the sticky climate of this crucial September ball game. He turned to watch Red Schalk fidgeting in the batter's box, then the pitch twisting half-speed to the plate. He saw the hitter's badly timed stride and the ball curve elusively by him, the bat remaining ineptly on his shoulder. The Rookie heard the umpire's callous cry:

"Steee-rike one!"

Mike braced himself for the new roar of the crowd, multiplying the tension in this ninth-inning climax, and considered the crisis in the game. There were two men out, and the tying and winning runs danced helplessly off second and first, itching to hit pay dirt. The game was going down to the wire; it was clearly up to Red Schalk to take it there.

The Rookie added to the bellowing mob behind him, and roared aloud his desperate hopes:

"Keep alive, Red! Keep alive!"

But within him, he knew he meant something else: keep it alive for me . . . for ME! Get on base and leave those runners sitting out there. Selfishly, Mike felt himself begging for the hero's job—to hit that long blow and bust up the game. He transferred his body into Red's, his hands on Red's bat, his power, timing, co-ordination, and most of all, his will into Red's. To The Rookie, this day was a personal climax, far more important to him than the goddam game. It had to be his day; for after sixteen struggling years to get here, he knew damn well he had it coming to him.

"Mike!" he heard. "The resin. Gimme the resin."

He looked up to see Red walking toward him from the plate. He picked up the resin bag and went to meet him.

"Sonovabitch!" Red muttered under his breath.

"Take it easy, Red," Mike said, trying to steady him; the "veteran" was having it rough. "Get loose."

Red rubbed the resin over his sweaty hands.

"Can't get 'em dry enough. . . ."

Scare sweat, The Rookie thought. The guy is scared up there. A chance to be a hero and the guy is scared.

"Take your time, Red. . . ."

"Sonovabitch, Mike . . . can't get loose."

"Take it easy . . ." and he noticed now the guy was shaking. Mike went back to the batter's circle and spat his contempt. He'd give half his pay to be in this guy's spot right now, but the Redhead didn't know whether to piss or go blind. And this was a "bonus baby"—Red Schalk, the new-type ball-player. They had handed him twenty grand for being a high school hero, for hitting .400 against the patsy pitchers, and playing with babies. Twenty G's for merely signing his lousy name. When Mike signed to play pro ball, they gave him a nickel cigar . . . and he didn't even smoke. He thought back . . . he was just a raw kid out in a Pennsylvania mining town, hating the black mines that threatened to swallow his future. Instead, he had practically lived on the sandlots, driving his natural baseball skills to perfection, hoping to spend the rest of his life with a bat, not a pick, and wear a cap without a flashlight over the peak.

He grunted at his memories, and spat a portion of rich brown tobacco juice skillfully down the length of his extra bat.

"Com'mon, Red!" he hollered, fighting back his bitterness. "Get on that sack!"

Mike watched the pitcher lean into the shadows to pick up the catcher's sign, his intense concentration hidden under the lowered peak. The pitch spun in, an exact facsimile of the previous strike . . . and it tied the Redhead in the exact same knot. Mike groaned helplessly and bit harshly at his lip as the umpire roared again:

"Steerike two!"

Fooled him twice . . . the lousy Redhead . . . fooled the big-time Major Leaguer, over anxious in the clutch like a stinking high school kid. Red had never even waved his stick. Christ . . . you'd think a guy three years in the big-time would at least know how to get set.

He shivered as an icy wind passed through him, frantic now that everything vital to him seemed so far beyond his control.

He heard Red calling him again.

"Mike. . . ." The voice was low and charged with fear. "Mike. . . ." and he spluttered his confession like a frightened, guilty child: "I . . . I don't wanna hit!"

"What!" Mike snarled, hardly believing, only conscious of something rotten happening. "What! You don't wanna hit?" Then it occurred to him that he had come across this before. The kid had found himself in a crucial spot and hated it. Some punks just weren't cut out for it; they were great only when it didn't count. The hitters with crap in their blood.

Mike looked into the quivering face, amazed at its pallor. He guessed the kid had given up on himself.

"I don't feel good, Mike," Red was saying. "I can't stand up there. . . ."

The Rookie thought of all the drunks he had sobered up; this looked like a tougher job.

"Don't tell that to the Skipper, Red," he said. "I gotta feeling he won't appreciate it."

So now the bottom was falling out; this was supposed to be the hitter who would give him a crack at the big one. Mike felt himself sinking in the field of quicksand . . . down, down he went . . . the towering steel that enclosed it seemed to loom higher, much higher. . . .

"Com'mon, Red," the umpire growled at them. "Let's get the game moving."

Mike grabbed the hitter roughly by the arm. What the hell could he say? "Get back in there and hit or you'll never hit again. Not in this League, anyway." His voice was harsh with anger. "Be tough," he added. "Be tough up there!" And he turned away, spitting the taste of his words. Maybe he oughta pray, too.

Oh you crud, you mighty crud! he muttered under his breath, and he let his memory flash back four wasted years to a city in the Texas League. For there he had first come across Red Schalk, a pink-cheeked, 19-year-old bonus-baby out of Georgia. He remembered how they babied him, trying to justify the ridiculous twenty grand investment. He was some big-shot scout's fair-haired boy, the big prospect. Mike had watched them coddle Red all season, letting him nurse his .302 batting average to make it look good. A year later, they moved Red Schalk up to the big-time.

Mike had burned up at the move. Hadn't he outhit Red by a dozen points, and wasn't he a dozen times the glove man?

Where were the rewards for his years of consistently good ball-playing? What about the promises they'd made to him . . . year after year? Why doesn't he go up? he demanded to know. Why not him?

Sure, Mike, the Scout had told him; you're a fine ball-player. But up in the Big Leagues they're after the younger kids. By all rights, you should be up there . . . and if it hadn't been for the war and those years you lost, you would be. Sorry, Mike . . . you know how it is . . . a kid of 19 has a much longer ride ahead of him. . . .

The plain and simple truth had been made apparent to him; they just didn't want him anymore. He was over thirty by then, and they considered him a secondary piece of property.

Now he was thirty-five, an old man of thirty-five . . . a rookie of thirty-five, playing his first day in the Majors. It did not escape him that he was here by a fluke. The mother club had been riddled with injuries down the stretch, and they decided to use Mike in this crucial September series rather than some green kid. At the last minute, they called him in Texas and flew him up during the night. As he got off the plane in the morning, they hurriedly signed him to a big league contract. He never even got a chance to get some sleep.

Sixteen years he had plugged his heart out for a crack at the big leagues; when they finally needed him, they threw it in his face.

In the locker room before the game, the Skipper came over to meet him. "You're in the line-up today, Kutner," he said tersely. "Show me something." And he walked away.

The players watched The Rookie smile sourly at this. Those who knew him saw his determination and understood it. To them, it was a matter of winning a pennant, and a few extra thousand bucks to show for it. Oh, that was something, all right. But to this man, it was much more . . . it was a test of a lifetime struggle. They all knew Mike was good, as good as almost any of them—and if the ball had bounced differently, he might have been up there all these years instead of them. But now, at thirty-five, he could be called old. Those who did not know him looked curiously across the room at the signs of his age: his partially bald head, the dark, leathery skin in back of his neck, his heavy, uneven walk . . . and they wondered how many years they had left for themselves. Respectfully, they left him alone while he dressed.

He had waited until they were all out to finish. He laced his shoes tightly and put on his new cap. His uniform was clean and he liked its fresh-sterile smell. With tremendous pride he walked over to the big mirror by the shower room and stood solidly before it. He looked at himself for a long moment, allowing the glow to penetrate his senses. A lush tingling tickled the back of his neck, bringing goose bumps to his skin. He had never felt so wonderful.

"You're here, Mike," he had said out loud. "You finally made it!" Then he clenched his fists as the tears came to his eyes. "You're here, goddamit . . . and you're not going back!"

The umpire's voice brought him out of his reverie.

"Play ball!" he hollered.

The Rookie raised his eyes to Schalk at the plate and watched him feebly wave his bat through the air like he was flagging a train. Red was now an empty shell of a man, a skeleton of bones in a big league uniform, faking through the motions of being a hitter. Look at him, Mike thought. Look at what they picked instead of me! Suddenly, he felt the years of resentment boiling inside him, for here was the sickening symbol of his frustrations. His anger rose furiously to his throat, almost choking him, and he exploded at the Redhead with consummate violence:

'Stand up there like a pro, you goddam yellow punk!" he hollered. "Get on that goddam base!"

At once, he was conscious of what he had done. A ballplayer doesn't blow up that way. That's what you don't do. Instinctively, his mind, his bright, quick baseball mind went back to work for him. He looked out to the pitcher's mound, thinking how much he'd like to be the chucker for this one pitch. If that mug knew the insides of Schalk's guts he'd be laughing out loud. But the pitcher was fingering his own resin bag, and Mike smiled despite himself; the jerk was probably scared too. The Rookie felt like the only veteran in the ball park.

The pitcher looked for a sign, a studied smile on his face.

He'll curve him again, Mike thought. Any decent curve'll get him. Red can't even see anymore . . . just little colored spots in front of his eyes. Count him out, ump . . . Red Schalk, K.O.

The curve spun rapidly in. Red went through the motions, stepping like he knew what he was doing, as if to take his cut. The ball curved from the inside to cut the corner of the plate, but it never got there. It bounded painfully off Red's leg.

"Take yer base!" the umpire bellowed.

Red lay moaning in the dust, rubbing his thigh.

Well, kiss my butt, Mike thought as he went to him, guessing the breaking pitch might have been a good one.

"You O.K., Red?" he asked. Maybe the guy did pray at that.

"Yeah, yeah. I'm O.K." he said. "It's funny, Mike . . . I never saw it." And he got up, loosening his leg on the way to first.

Mike grinned. It's good you didn't, he thought . . . it's goddam good you didn't. And he turned his concentration quickly to the job before him.

Behind him, the crowd rose to a frenzy at the bases-loaded climax. The Rookie swung the two bats like a windmill and listened to the wild stampede.

It's all yours now; there's nothing left to the day but you. Go back sixteen years, Rookie, and maybe ten thousand turns at bat. None of them matter . . . none of them. Just this one, Mike; just this one, beautiful moment. . . .

He heard the Skipper's voice from the bench, an anti-climax to his mood:

"It's up to you, Kutner. Show me something!"

I'll show you something, you dumb bastard, Mike thought. He tossed away the extra stick and started to dig a foothold in the batter's box. It's all up to you . . . this game, maybe even the big pennant. This is the turn that counted. The other three meant nothing . . . the neat sacrifice bunt, the base on balls, and that long, well-hit fly ball the center-fielder dragged down. They were all routine. This is the spot, Rookie. Blast one and bust up the game!

They were really down to the wire now. All around him there was a tremendous din, a wild persistent yelling that racked his ears. He looked up through the bubbling joy in his heart to face the pitcher. He saw the three runners dance anxiously off their bases. From the bench they were hollering at him: "Com'mon, Mike. Clobber one!"

The pitcher was getting his sign, this time without a smile.

Here we go, Rookie. Tag one and you're a Major Leaguer for the rest of your natural-born life! To Mike, there were no doubts; as sure as he was alive he knew he was going to. He couldn't keep the smile off his face; this was the spot he had waited sixteen years for.

Mike watched the pitcher take a full, slow windup. He cocked his bat menacingly over his shoulder and waited for the throw. It came half-speed, spinning toward the outside corner. He stepped toward the pitch and lashed viciously at the ball with full power. As he finished his pivot, he knew he had gotten only a slice of it. The ball skidded off into the upper grandstand behind him.

"Steee-rike one!" he heard the umpire cry.

He leaned over to pick up dirt, muttering profanities at himself. He was set. He saw it all the way. Yet he hadn't met it squarely. Was it because he was tired? Or too eager? . . . But then he realized this had happened to him too many times over this past year. His memory flashed him pictures of powerful smashes of just such a pitch, years ago. But now he didn't always get around in time. There was something missing; the thin edge of timing and co-ordination that made the difference had dulled over the years. He swiped viciously at the dirt and sprayed it over the ground in anger, and remembered what the scout had told him in Texas, four years ago. His age was catching up with him; he was thirty-five and past his prime.

He heard the cries from the other bench now, beamed directly to him over the stamping and screaming of the crowd.

"*Hey, Pop . . . how'd you break in here?*"

He took a moment to adjust his cap and looked squarely into their dugout. They were all on the front step, nervously bellowing at him.

"*Hey, Baldy . . . where's your cane?*"

He stepped back in the box and dug in again. He would like that pitch once more, just to prove he could clobber it. But he knew damn well he wouldn't get it now.

"*Hey, Rookie. Let's see that fine head of skin again!*"

Be set, Mike, and stay loose. This punk has nothing he can throw by you. The ducks are on the pond, Mike, and yours to knock in. It's a picnic, man, a picnic!

He watched the arm swing up and around, the big stride toward the plate, and the little ball spun bullet-speed toward him. It came high and tight, and Mike ducked carefully away from it.

"Steee-rike two!" the ump called.

Mike turned on him in a sudden ferocious rage that raced through him like an electric shock.

"What!" he roared. "It knocked me down! It was a waste pitch!"

"It was in there, buddy. Quit yer crying and get back in there and hit!"

The Rookie slammed the end of his bat against the ground like a sledge hammer, close to the umpire's feet. He was livid.

"No . . . goddamit . . . it knocked me down!"

In a second, the Manager and coaches were there, crowding around the ump, hammering away at him in unsuppressed rage. Not a nice word was spoken.

When the dust had cleared, Mike stood anxiously to the side, trying to collect himself. It was a terrible call, that strike, and it came at a terrible time. It put him way behind the pitcher, making it real tough for him to cut loose. He had to guard that plate now, instead of making the pitcher come in there with it. He couldn't pick out the throw he liked. Mike thought it was the kind of call an ump would never make on a star. But on a rookie. . . .

"Play ball!" the ump shouted, masking his face, trying to recover his prestige.

Mike turned, his anger still drumming in his gut.

"Take it easy, ump. I got a little something riding on this pitch . . . so take it easy."

The ump lifted his mask and leaned toward him.

"You're pretty sassy for a rookie, buddy."

Sure, Mike thought. There it was.

"Yeah . . ." he said, as sour as he could make it.

"Get up there and hit!"

Behind him he heard the Skipper again.

"To hell with him, Kutner. You got the big one left."

Sure . . . nothing to it. Sorry you had to swallow a call like that, but you still gotta produce. The sacks are loaded and only you can pull out this ball game. That's what you'll get paid for, buddy, and nothing else matters. The stinkin' ump could call another zombie against you, and you're out, just as if you whiffed one, and the game is gone. An hour later, it don't matter anymore that it wasn't your fault. You didn't produce . . . that's what mattered. It's just a big, round K.O. in the papers tomorrow. And because you're thirty-five, you're back in the bush leagues on the first train out.

Then he heard the jockeys from the other bench again.

"*Grampa . . . hey, Grampa! Who does yer grandson play for?*"

"*Get out the rockin' chair . . . here comes Papa Kutner!*"

Mike reached down again to finger some dirt at his feet. He rubbed his hands dry and gripped tightly the narrow handle of his bat. Back in the batter's box, he dug his spikes in position. He faced the pitcher and started thinking baseball again.

Get set, he told himself. Be ready for anything. It's still up to you, Mike. He can't get it by you . . . he can't get it by. . . .

"*Ba-a-a-l-d-e-e-eeeeee!*"

The arm swung around again, and Mike's keen eyes followed the movement of the pitcher's hand. His sharp baseball sense picked up a tiny quirk in the pitcher's delivery that clearly indicated curve ball. Mike set himself and moved his body toward the pitch. The ball spun down the inside and started curving late. He pivoted with all his power and met the pitch out front with the fat part of the bat. The sharp crack rang out, beautiful and clear as a bell, and everyone in the park knew that ball was really tagged.

Mike started to first, watching it sail up and up, into the sky, way above the stadium roof, soaring deep toward the left field bleachers. He heard the tremendous, ear-splitting roar of the 50,000 who were a part of it, and the happiness beat glowingly against his ribs. It was the big one! You've done it, Mike . . . you blasted one in the clutch, with the sacks loaded! He rounded first base with tears in his eyes, for he knew, at last, that the world was all his.

As he made his turn, he looked up again to follow the end flight of the ball, wanting to feast on the sight of it disappearing into the seats out there. Suddenly his throat constricted in an agonizing gasp. The ball . . . it wasn't falling right. The wind above the roof had caught it and was pulling it toward the foul line. He followed it down now, sinking deep into the bleachers, but at an angle he could not guess. He saw the foul pole, the tall white shaft; an icy tremor ran through him as the ball fell out of sight into a scramble of spectators.

He never heard the umpire's call. Short of second base, he stopped and turned slowly back to home plate. From some place deep within him, his instincts had called the play: foul ball.

He was right.

It took him a long time to walk back to the plate. He needed all the time he could get now. A sense of doom came over him and he couldn't shake it off. For a moment he thought he'd been feeling it all day, a feeling that luck was down on him, just like always . . . the real luck, luck when you really needed it. Then he realized what he was doing to himself and he cursed his momentary weakness. Just like the Skipper said: Mike, you still got the big one left!

But the thought of trying again somehow depressed him, almost as if he were suddenly very tired. He wondered how much drive he had left in him. For sixteen years he had pushed his body and his spirit, trying with all his heart to get up this far. Now, it seemed to him, his entire effort was to be packed into one brief moment of time. One more pitch, maybe. It must be now . . . there's no more time . . . no more time.

Maybe it was too much to ask of a man.

At the plate, the bat-boy was holding his bat, waiting for him.

"Straighten it out, Mike," he said.

Sure, sure. . . . Stop the wind and straighten it out.

He ran his hand fondly along the end of the bat, subconsciously feeling for the dent. He wished he had more time.

"All right, Kutner," the ump called him. "Batter up!"

Mike played with his belt, trying to stall. His mind was cluttered with doubts and he wanted to shake them loose. Hitting is a state of mind, as important to co-ordination, timing, and power as a good pair of eyes. He was thinking of too many things now to be a hitter.

The jockeys found it timely to get back on him.

"*Com'mon Pop. Better get back up there before they dig you under!*"

"*Too bad, Baldy. . . . You shot yer wad on a foul ball!*"

Somehow or other he was thinking of all the winter jobs he held over the years. He hated them all . . . gas station attendant, special delivery postman, road gangs . . . they amounted to nothing. Just wasting the winter to get to the spring. After all these years, the whole deal seemed like such a stupid waste.

"*Back to the mines, Pop!*" The jockeys again.

He was about to step in, and it backed him away. "Back to the mines." The words rattled around in his head like loose marbles. It made his head spin as he thought how close he was to it.

"Let's go, Kutner . . . play ball!" The ump was insistent.

Com'mon, Mike. You gotta get up there. You gotta get up there and hit. Suddenly, he leaned over and picked up a tiny pebble. He told himself that unless he put it in his pocket he wouldn't hit. For a moment, he stood there, studying the pebble, debating with himself. It was a foolish superstition and he always rejected them. If you let yourself go, a million little things will deflect you, threaten you, strip you of your will to hit. He had seen guys who became slaves to their petty superstitions. Yet, something almost made him change. Compulsively, he threw the pebble away and stepped up to the plate.

They were ready for him:

"*Yo, Pop. I heard you were in the war . . . which one?*"

He moved his big bat around, trying to loosen the clothing on his shoulders. It didn't seem to set properly. He dug and redug his back foot in the corner of the box. He felt something about his position was different . . . some minute arrangement of his feet, or the balance of his body as he set himself. He watched the pitcher get his sign and his mind began an agonizing conjecture. Would he curve him again . . . half-speed? Would he waste one, or make him cut at something bad? Would he try to throw a hard one by him, under his chin . . . or low outside? It was hard not to guess. Don't guess, he told himself. That's suicide. You're still the hitter. Just be ready . . . be ready.

"*They got a ball club back at the mines, Pop?*"

He cocked his bat over his shoulder and was conscious of the wet pull of his shirt against him. He made a quick movement of his body to release it. It disturbed him, and he thought of stepping out of the box again. Then he remembered the pebble and wondered about superstitions: he regretted not saving it.

"When ya leave here, turn yer bat in for a pickax!"

Mike watched the pitcher nod and smile to the catcher. The windup was calm and kept him waiting. It seemed like an endless moment of time.

O.K., Mike . . . guard that dish, he told himself. No fear . . . guard that dish. The ball spun lightly off the chucker's fingers and fluttered toward the plate. He saw it start to break, a slow curve breaking toward the outside corner. It didn't look good to him . . . but it might be. In a split second he had to decide, his own judgment shaken by his fear of the umpire. The delicate instrument of timing was shattered, and the balance of his power upset. He stepped toward the pitch and started his swing, lashing at the ball with half a will, half a prayer.

He didn't come near it . . . and the game was over.

For a moment he just stood there, wondering how sick he must have looked. He even tried to guess how far outside the plate the ball had passed.

Then the final thunderous roar of the crowd rose from the stands like a tidal wave, blasting into his ears the consequences of his failure. It was too much for him to take.

"No!" he screamed. "Goddamit . . . NO!" And he beat the plate brutally with his bat, refusing to accept this.

He turned to face the pitcher's mound, swinging his bat like he was ready to hit again, demanding that the game go on.

"Throw the goddam ball!" he hollered savagely. "Throw the goddam ball!"

But their entire team had gathered around the pitcher, slapping his back, clutching and tearing at his triumph. They lifted him to their shoulders to cart him off the field. Mike watched them, letting their spirited laughter bite into him, as if it were aimed at him. He hated them now, the lucky sonovabitchin' pitcher, the lousy jockeys. . . . He stared at them, trying to smear them with his hatred, hoping to provoke one more derisive cat-call from them that might unleash his rage and goad him to attack them all. But they never saw him, nor even acknowledged his presence there, and he finally turned away from the plate for the long walk in.

He moved toward the bedlam of the stands now, and saw the screaming faces. A moment ago they were all yours . . . all yours, Mike. They were yelling for you. He looked into the dejection of his dugout and his naked failure came home to him. In a rage, he pulled his bat back, ready to fling it into the crowd, to scatter them and shut them up. He swallowed the top of his anger and held on.

In the stands behind the dugout, they were waiting for him, the harsh faces of the sadistic punks who wallowed in the luxury of a few last kicks at the guy who was down.

"Kutner . . . you stink!"

"You're a bum. . . ."

"Oooooooohh . . . what a bum!"

He bristled at their hoots and sneering laughter and wondered how he could get through that gantlet. He gripped his bat tightly as he approached them, trying not to hurry his walk.

"Whatta star! . . . Where'd they pick you up?"

"Back to the Minors, Kutner. . . ."

He felt their stale-beer-spittle spray into his hot face, and he choked on his bubbling rage. A sloppy hand reached over and stole his cap from his head.

"You won't need this no more. . . ."

"Naaah . . . back to the bush leagues!"

He stopped on the bottom step and looked up at them. They taunted him, waving his cap at him, just out of reach. Inside him, suddenly the dam burst, and he flung himself toward the cap, over the dugout and into the stands. In a second he caught the terrified heckler and wrenched the cap from him. With his other hand he started smashing at him in a wild fury, bellowing hoarsely at the top of his lungs.

At once the crowd dispersed, scrambling over each other like scared chickens, and watched in their own terror. The ushers and cops came for him, four of them pulling him off, trying to hold him still, for his rage was only part spent.

They carried him down the steps again, into the dim corridors below the stands, and stood him hard against the wall, just outside the locker room.

"Take it easy, rookie . . ." a cop said, his hands tight on Mike's wrist.

Mike breathed heavily, and looked through the door at the ball-players inside. He saw them, glum and silent on their benches, unlacing their shoes, quietly passing around smokes and cold beer. As he felt the heavy restraint of the cops, he saw Red Schalk among them, close to the door, and their eyes met. His arms were pinned to his side and he tried to wriggle loose.

"Easy, rookie . . . easy . . ." he heard again. "That ain't the way for a Major Leaguer to act. . . ."

The words knifed into him, twisting into his thoughts, and he lowered his eyes from the Redhead's. He wondered how in hell he'd ever be able to go through that door into the locker room again.

Voices of a Summer Day

IRWIN SHAW

Benjamin Federov, fifty, once again circles the bases as he watches his teen-age son play center field in the sunshine of a summer day, a scene that awakens his memory of the "distant, mortal innings of boyhood and youth." But Mr. Federov does have one request: eliminate the traditional chant of "Kill the umpire." From the novel *Voices of a Summer Day*.

The red flag was up when he drove up to the house. He went in. The house was silent. "Peggy," he called. "Peggy!" There was no answer. His wife was not there nor either of his children.

He went out and looked at the ocean. The waves were ten feet high and there was about eight hundred yards of foam ripping between the tide line, marked by seaweed, and the whitecaps of the open Atlantic. The beach was deserted except for a tall girl in a black bathing suit, who was walking along the water's edge with two Siamese cats pacing beside her. The girl had long blond hair that hung down her back and blew in the wind. Her legs and arms were pollen-colored against the sea, and the cats made a small pale jungle at her ankles. The girl was too far away for him to tell whether she was pretty or not and she didn't look in his direction, but he wished he knew her. He wished he knew her well enough to call out and see her smile and wait for him to join her so that they could walk along the beach together, attended by toy tigers, the noise of the surf beating at them as she told him why a girl like that walked alone on an empty beach on a bright summer afternoon.

He watched her grow smaller and smaller in the distance, the cats, the color of the desert, almost disappearing against the sand. She was outlined for a last moment against the dazzle of the waves and then the beach was empty again.

It was no afternoon for swimming, and the girl was gone, and he didn't feel like hanging around the house alone so he went in and changed his clothes and got into the car and drove into town. On the high school field, there was a pickup game of baseball in progress, boys and young men and several elderly athletes who by Sunday morning would regret having slid into second base on Saturday afternoon.

He saw his son playing center field. He stopped the car and got out and lay back in the sun on the hot planks of the benches along the third-base line, a tall, easy-moving man with a powerful, graying head. He was dressed in slacks and a short-sleeved blue cotton shirt, the costume of a man consciously on holiday. On the long irregular face there were the not unexpected signs of drink and overwork. He was no longer young, and, although at a distance his slimness and way of moving gave a deceptive appearance of youth, close-up age was there, experience was there, above all around the eyes, which were deep black, almost without reflections, hooded by heavy lids and a dark line of thick lashes that suggested secret Mediterranean mourning against the olive tint of the skin stretched tight over jutting cheek bones. He greeted several of the players and spectators, and the impression of melancholy was erased momentarily by the good humor and open friendliness of his voice. The combination of voice and features was that of a man who might be resigned and often cynical, but rarely suspicious. He was a man who permitted himself to be cheated in small matters. Taxi drivers, employees, children, and women took advantage of him. He knew this, each time it happened, and promptly forgot it.

On the field, the batter was crouching and trying to work the pitcher for a walk. The batter was fifteen years old and small for his age. The pitcher was six feet three inches tall and had played for Columbia in 1947.

The third baseman, a boy of eighteen named Andy Roberts, called out, "Do you want to take my place, Mr. Federov? I promised I'd be home by four."

"Thanks, no, Andy," Federov said. "I batted .072 last season and I've hung up my spikes."

The boy laughed. "Maybe you'd have a better season this year if you tried."

"I doubt it," Federov said. "It's very rare that your average goes up after fifty."

The batter got his walk, and while he was throwing his bat away and trotting down to first base Federov waved to his son out in center field. His son waved back. "Andy," Federov said, "how's Mike doing?"

"Good field, no hit," Andy said.

"Runs in the family," said Federov. "My father never hit a curve ball in his life either."

The next batter sent a line drive out toward right center, and Michael made a nice running catch over his shoulder and pivoted and threw hard and accurately to first base, making the runner scramble back hurriedly to get there before the throw. Michael was left-handed and moved with that peculiar grace that left-handers always seemed to Federov to have in all sports. There had never been a left-hander before in Federov's family, nor in his wife's family that he knew of, and Federov sometimes wondered at this genetic variance and took it as a mark of distinction, a puzzling designation, though whether for good or ill he could not say. Michael's sister, eleven years old and too smart for her age, as Federov sometimes told her, teased Michael about it. "Sinister, sinister," she chanted when she disagreed with her brother's opinions, "Old Pope Sinister the First."

Old Pope Sinister the First popped up to shortstop his next time at bat and then came over to sit beside his father. "Hi, Dad." He touched his father lightly but affectionately on the shoulder. "How're things in the dirty city?"

"Dirty," Federov said. He and his brother ran a building and contracting business together, and while there was a lot of work unfinished on both their desks, the real reason the brothers had stayed in New York on a hot Saturday morning was to try to arrange a settlement with Louis's third wife, whom he wanted to divorce to marry a fourth wife, and who was all for a vengeful and scandalous action in court. Louis was the architect of the firm, and this connection with the arts, plus his quiet good looks, made him a prey for women and a permanent subsidy for the legal profession.

"Where's your mother?" Federov asked his son. "The house was empty when I got in."

"Bridge, hairdresser's, I don't know," Michael said carelessly. "You know—dames. She'll turn up for dinner."

"I'm quite sure she will," Federov said.

Michael's side was retired, and he picked up his glove and started toward his position in the field. "Mike," Federov said, "you swung at a high ball, you know."

"I know," Michael said. "I'm a confirmed sinner."

He was thirteen years old but, like his sister, was a ransacker of libraries and often sounded it.

Five minutes later there was a dispute about a close call at first base, and two or three boys shouted, good-naturedly, "Oh, you bum!" and "Kill the umpire!"

"Stop that!" Federov said sharply. Then he was as surprised as the boys themselves by the harshness of his tone. They kept quiet after that, although they eyed him curiously. Ostentatiously, Federov looked away from them. He had heard the cry thousands of times before, just as the boys had, and he didn't want to have to explain what was behind his sudden explosion of temper. Ever since the President had been shot, Federov, sometimes consciously, sometimes unconsciously, had refrained from using words like "kill" or "murder" or "shoot" or "gun," and had skipped them, when he could, in the things he read, and moved away from conversations in which the words were likely to come up. He had heard about the mocking black-bordered advertisement in the Dallas newspaper that had greeted the President on his arrival in the city, and he had read about the minister who said that schoolchildren in the city had cheered upon being told of the President's death, and he had heard from a lineman friend of his on the New York Giants football team that, after the game they had played in Dallas ten days after the President was killed, an open car full of high school boys and girls had followed the Giants' bus through downtown Dallas, chanting, "Kennedy gawn, Johnson next, Kennedy gawn, Johnson next."

"Kids," the lineman had said wonderingly, "just kids, like anybody else's kids. You couldn't believe it. And nobody tried to stop them."

Kids, just kids. Like the boys on the field in front of him. Like his own son. In the same blue jeans, going to the same kind of schools, listening to the same awful music on radio and television, playing the same traditional games, loved by their parents as he loved his son and daughter. Kids shouting a tribal chant of hatred for a dead man who had been better than any of them could ever hope to be.

The hell with it, he thought. You can't keep thinking about it forever.

With an effort of will he made himself fall back into lazy afternoon thoughtlessness. Soon, lulled by the slow familiar rhythm of the game, he was watching the field through half-dozing, sun-warmed eyes, lying back and not keeping track of what was happening as boys ran from base to base, stopped grounders, changed sides. He saw his son make two good plays and one mediocre one without pride or anxiety. Michael was tall for his age, and broad, and Federov took what he realized was a normal fatherly pleasure in watching his son's movements as, loose-limbed and browned by the sun, he performed in the wide green spaces of the outfield.

Dozing, almost alone on the rows of benches, one game slid into other games, other generations were at play many years before . . . in Harrison, New Jersey, where he had grown up; on college campuses, where he had never been quite good enough to make the varsity, despite his fleetness of foot and sure-handedness in the field. The sounds were the same through the years—the American sounds of summer, the tap of bat against ball, the cries of the infielders, the wooden plump of the ball into catchers' mitts, the umpires calling "Strike three and you're out." The generations circled the bases, the dust rose for forty years as runners slid from third, dead boys hit doubles, famous men made errors at shortstop, forgotten friends tapped the clay from their spikes with their bats as they stepped into the batter's box, coaches' voices warned, across the decades, "Tag up, tag up!" on fly balls. The distant, mortal innings of boyhood and youth . . .

It Happens Every Spring

VALENTINE DAVIES

College professor Vernon Simpson discovers a
miracle repellent: when applied to a baseball, the
ball avoids contact with wood. Under an assumed
name, Simpson turns pro and pitches St. Louis to
a pennant, but his identity has been revealed by
the time the World Series is about to begin. From
the novel *It Happens Every Spring*.

World Series fever hit St. Louis in a big way. Hotels were
crowded and theatres were jammed. Mr. Stone could have sold
every seat in his ball park many times over. A pair of bleacher
seats and a brand-new Cadillac were considered about an even
exchange. All normal activities came to a standstill during the
afternoon of the game. Nor was the campus immune to all this
excitement. There were few faculty members who had not smug-
gled radios into their offices to listen to the Series broadcast,
play by play. The fall semester had just begun, and students
crowded every radio, public and private—in cars; in drugstores;
in fraternity houses—everywhere—tense, silent groups of under-
graduates clustered about a loud-speaker or a television screen.

The lucky ones, who were able to wangle seats—professors,
instructors and students alike—shamelessly cut classes to attend
the game. Mixed in with the typical crowd of baseball fans, who
jammed the stadium, were a surprising number of staid professors who had not witnessed a baseball game since the turn of

the century. And many an elderly dean was astonished to find himself rooting and shouting with the best of them in a most undignified manner.

For King Kelly was the hero of the Series, and by this time there were few people connected with the University who did not know that he was Teaching Fellow Vernon Simpson.

Having enjoyed a four-day rest, Vernon pitched the opening game and won it handily. But New York came back the next day with a vengeance and blasted poor Hooper for six runs in one explosive inning. St. Louis was clearly out of the running for the rest of the afternoon.

With the score tied at one game each, the Series moved to New York. Debbie and her mother spent anxious hours each afternoon huddled over the radio in the living room, hanging on every word.

Before a record crowd, in the vast New York stadium, Vernon stifled the big-city sluggers and won the third game, giving St. Louis a 2 to 1 lead. But next day the New Yorkers staged another seventh-inning uprising, this time at the expense of Erickson, and pulled up even again at two games all. With only one day off, Kelly was forced to pitch the fifth game. The strain was beginning to show, and he wasn't having an easy time of it. In fact, he came up to the last half of the ninth with a very shaky one-run lead. Vernon walked the first man up and allowed the second to fly out to Bevan in deep right field. Bearing down now, he struck out the next batter, but not before a wild pitch had put the tying run on third. With two out, Vernon worked the count on Rudnik to three and two.

Listening to the broadcast, Debbie and Mrs. Greenleaf sat petrified, holding their breath.

"Here comes the pitch!" The sportscaster's voice was hoarse with tension. "It's got to be good this time! . . . It is! Rudnik swings—and he misses! . . . And that's the game, folks, Kelly's done it again!"

Debbie jumped up cheering and hugging her mother in wild excitement. Then suddenly she stopped and switched off the radio as her father entered the room. But Mrs. Greenleaf was too excited to think.

"Hurray!" she shouted, happily, "Vernon won again!"

Debbie's gasp was followed by a deathly silence. Mrs. Greenleaf's hand went up to her mouth; she looked at Debbie, horrified. Debbie turned to her father.

"Yes, it's true, Dad," she said calmly. "You may not believe it but—Vernon is King Kelly."

Dr. Greenleaf looked from one to the other in surprise. "Have you just found that out?" he said.

"No, Dad," said Debbie, lamely, "but we didn't think you knew . . ."

"Why didn't you say something, Alfred?" his wife demanded indignantly.

"Because there didn't appear to be anything to say. If Debbie wants to marry a baseball player, that's her affair . . ."

"But he's not just a baseball player, Dad," said Debbie. "He's Vernon . . . !"

Her father shook his head slowly. "He's just a baseball player now," he said.

St. Louis returned home with a 3 to 2 lead in games. All they needed was one more victory to win the Series. But now Jimmy Dolan had to do some fateful master-minding. The obvious move was to put Kelly in to pitch the next game and end the Series then and there. But King Kelly had pitched three out of the five long, hard-fought games, and he had been none too steady in the last one. If he should pitch the next game and drop it, Jimmy would lose his ace-in-the-hole, and the Series would be as good as over. On the other hand, if he sent Hooper in, the worst that could happen, if he lost, was that the Series would be tied again and he would have Kelly, refreshed and ready after a two-day rest, to pitch the final and deciding game. After many long powwows with Mr. Stone and others, Dolan decided to take a chance on Hooper and save Kelly for the final game.

And Hooper almost made it, too. Rising to unprecedented heights, he held the explosive gang from Gotham in check for eight tight, tingling innings. But then in the ninth, with two men on, he made the fatal error of trying to slip a slow ball past block-buster Billy Marx. There was a sharp resounding crack, a roar from the crowd, a scuffle in the right-field bleachers, and three New York runners went trotting merrily around the diamond.

Sitting in the dugout, Monk and Vernon looked at each other glumly.

"There goes the old ball game," Monk said.

He slapped Vernon gently on the knee. "You better get a good night's rest, kid," he told him, "you're gonna have a busy day tomorrow."

Vernon slept long and peacefully, and awoke next morning, refreshed and eager. The fact that he was to pitch the deciding game of the World Series did not disturb him unduly. It would no doubt be a somewhat strenuous and exciting afternoon, but Vernon felt that he had plenty of justification for his calm, unruffled confidence. Monk was still snoring gently in the next bed, as Vernon tiptoed into the bathroom to take a shower, and was still blissfully sleeping when Vernon had finished dressing. Taking advantage of the privacy, Vernon took his little sponge in its pliofilm bag into the bathroom to fill it for the last time. He opened the medicine cabinet and took out the bottle which contained his precious "hair tonic." To his surprise, the bottle was almost empty. He was quite certain that it had been more than half full the day before. It didn't matter, of course; he still had one full bottle left in his suitcase. Nevertheless, it seemed odd. He couldn't understand it.

He emptied what little liquid there was onto the sponge and returned to the bedroom to get the other bottle. As he did so, he glanced at his watch. It was high time Monk was up, too.

He crossed to Monk's bed and reached out his hand to shake him. But instead, he stopped and stared incredulously. Monk had rolled over in his sleep so that the shiny bald center of his cranium was less than half an inch from the wooden headboard of the bed. The wiry wreath of hair surrounding his bald spot was shiny with grease. With each breath, his head moved closer to the wood, and as it did so, his stiff crown of hair flattened and rose again in gently rhythmic waves. Vernon watched the strange undulations with a mixture of anxiety and amusement. That explained what had happened to the rest of the "hair tonic" in the bottle.

Vernon went to his suitcase to get the other bottle. He couldn't find it. He searched through the suitcase feverishly, scrambling its contents and scattering them all over the floor. He had seen the bottle there when he had packed to leave the train. But now it was gone!

He turned and grabbed Monk's shoulder and shook him violently.

"Monk . . . ! Monk . . . !" he said.

Lanigan rolled over and opened one eye.

"Monk, did you take a bottle out of my suitcase?"

"Huh?" said Monk. "Bottle? Bottle of what?"

"Hair tonic," said Vernon, tensely. "Did you take the bottle out of my suitcase?"

"Oh . . . the hair tonic . . . yeah," said Monk sitting up sleepily. "I meant to tell you. I seen it in there yesterday. I didn't think you'd mind."

He yawned and stretched elaborately.

"But it's my last bottle," said Vernon. "What did you do with it?"

"Why I gave it to Jimmy. He's gettin' pretty thin on top, too." He rubbed his bald spot. "It done me a lot of good, kid— look, I'm growin' a whole new . . ."

But Vernon had gone, slamming the door behind him. Monk looked after him, shaking his head.

"Jumpin' Jupiter," he said, "what a character!"

Vernon tore down the hall to Dolan's room at a dead run. He knocked at the door. There was no answer. He knocked again—louder. Still no answer. He tried the door; it was unlocked. He opened it cautiously and entered the room. Through the open bathroom door he saw Jimmy at the washstand. The water was running full force and Jimmy was splashing generous handfuls onto his face. Vernon crossed the room and stood in the doorway.

"Jimmy," he said, "I'm sorry to bother you . . ."

Dolan went on splashing away.

"Jimmy . . . !" Vernon shouted.

But the roar of the faucet drowned him out. He entered the bathroom and awkwardly tapped Dolan on the shoulder. Jimmy turned with a start and squinted at Vernon, his hands and face dripping with water.

"Oh," he said, "it's you, Kelly . . ."

"Er—I wanted to talk to you," said Vernon.

"What did you say?" said Dolan.

"I want to talk to you!" Vernon shouted.

"Okay," said Jimmy, "what's on your mind?"

"It's about the hair tonic," said Vernon, loudly.

"About what?"

"The hair tonic!" Vernon bellowed. "Monk said he gave you a bottle of my hair tonic."

"Oh, yeah," said Jimmy, returning to his ablutions. "Monk said it'll grow hair on a billiard ball. Kind of an insult."

"It's a very rare solution. It can't be duplicated."

"Okay," said Dolan. "I'm willing to pay for it. How much do you . . . ?"

"No, no!" Vernon shouted anxiously. "It's not that. It's my last bottle, Jimmy—I need it!"

Dolan turned and looked at Vernon.

"*You* need it? What for? You want to play for the House of David?"

Vernon could think of no plausible explanation. He cursed his own stupidity. Why had he ever said it was hair tonic? He could have told Monk it was any one of a dozen other things—a special medicine, for instance—anything but hair tonic.

"It's just a peculiarity—a superstition," he said. "And especially today."

Dolan shook his head. "I've heard of rabbits' feet and elks' teeth—but lucky hair tonic—that's a new one!"

"Please," said Vernon desperately. "Have you got it, Jimmy?"

"Yeah, yeah," said Jimmy. "If that's going to make you happy."

He opened the medicine cabinet with his wet hands and looked inside, blinking.

"Where did I put it?" he said. "Oh, yeah, there it is."

He reached up and grabbed the bottle. A larger one started to topple off the crowded shelf and he juggled the two bottles with his slippery wet hands. Vernon watched in agonized horror, involuntarily reaching out. But it was too late. The little bottle slipped from Dolan's hand and fell into the basin with a crash. Vernon stood there, dumb and helpless, watching the World Series running down the drain.

The eyes and ears of the nation were on Vernon as he walked out to the mound to start the game. Newsreel and television cameras were focused on him. Sportscasters described every move to a nation-wide network. The stands were packed to overflowing with a tense, excited crowd. Monk had been faithful to the last, and Debbie sat between her mother and Mr. Forsythe in a safe location in the upper stand.

Vernon's calm, almost leisurely appearance gave no indication of what was going on inside him. The sponge in his pocket held less than half the amount of the magic solution he needed for a full nine-inning game. Vernon was facing almost certain disaster and he knew it. But he was not entirely without resources. He had worked out a plan of campaign. He knew that by now he had a tremendous psychological advantage over the batters, and he planned to make the utmost use of it. He would start by anointing the ball for at least the first two innings before hazarding any pitching on his own. From then on he would use the liquid as sparingly as possible, rubbing the ball into his glove only in the pinches, and he would hope and pray for the breaks.

The first three innings went surprisingly well. Even after he had stopped using the solution, he was able to hold the New York batters scoreless while St. Louis built up a two-run lead.

It wasn't until the middle of the fourth that Hammond stunned the crowd by connecting for a solid two-base hit off Kelly. Such a thing was practically unheard of and it shook Vernon quite as badly as it did the fans. In fact, he was so disturbed that he hit the next man, Sterling, on the sleeve, with an inside pitch, and walked Brown, the New York catcher after that. With the bases full and one out, he used a little of the fluid to strike the next man out. He decided to take his chances against Creston, the New York pitcher who came up next, but Creston rapped out an unexpected single which brought in one run, and now he faced Arizola, the head of the New York list. Vernon took no more chances. He pounded the ball into his glove and Arizola went down swinging.

Neither team got anywhere in the fifth, but in the first half of the sixth Vernon was in serious trouble again. His sponge was almost dry now, and what little liquid he had left he could use only in dire emergency. The bitter lesson of the two hits in the fourth had made him very leery of putting any straight clean pitches over the plate, and in trying to cut the corners he had walked three men. The bases were full, and now he was facing

Lefty Hiller, one of the most consistent sluggers in either league. To put it straight over was an obvious form of suicide, and to walk him meant a run. Mustering all the control he had, Vernon managed to work the count to three and two. Lefty took a determined stand and swung his big bat ominously. Vernon threw one for the inside corner.

"Bawl Four!" roared Brannick, the umpire behind the plate.

Lanigan was beside himself as Hiller and the other New York runners happily trotted ahead a base. He tore off his mask and started bellowing at the umpire. The stands were in an uproar as the tying run came in.

The calm and jovial Mr. Forsythe jumped to his feet.

"Kill the ump!" he roared.

Debbie frantically pulled at his sleeve. "Sit down, sit down before Vernon sees you!"

Still fuming and grumbling, Forsythe sat.

At the plate, Monk was stamping and raging and waving his arms, describing Brannick's optical deficiencies in no uncertain terms. Nor was Brannick suffering this abuse in silence. He was shouting and threatening and waving his finger under Lanigan's nose as Vernon walked calmly in from the mound.

"Take it easy, Monk," he said. "I'm sorry, but Brannick's right. I missed the corner by six inches."

Monk was too flabbergasted to reply. He stood there with his mouth open, staring incredulously at Vernon. But to Brannick, such calm agreement was unheard of. He turned on Vernon suspiciously.

"Say, what's the matter with you?" he said.

Some good luck, good fielding and a double play pulled Vernon through the first half of the seventh. And in the last half, St. Louis went on a hitting spree which knocked Creston and Jacobs out of the box and gave them a two-run lead. With two men on and none out, it looked as if the game would be sewed up right there. But Harry Bevan hit into a double play and Manning, the next St. Louis batter, had been hitting badly all afternoon.

Sitting in the dugout next to Vernon, Monk looked very unhappy. "Judas, that's tough," he said. "I thought we was gonna put it on ice right now."

He took off his cap and scratched his head. Vernon looked

over at Monk's circle of greasy hair. His face lit up. He reached out his right hand and rubbed his fingers through the thick grease. Lanigan turned and looked at Vernon, startled.

"Hey, Kelly, what's eatin' you?"

Vernon looked at his hand. His fingers were shining. Perhaps he could get enough for one or two pitches.

"I just did it for luck, Monk," he said, and rubbed Lanigan's head again.

Monk gave him a worried look and quickly put on his cap.

Manning had popped out, and Vernon followed Monk from the dugout carefully guarding his right hand as he walked across to the mound. He refused any warm-up pitches and beckoned Granite, the first New York batter, into the box. Before he wound up, he rubbed his greasy fingers on the ball.

It worked. Granite swung at two beauties and missed them clean. But Vernon made the mistake of trying to stretch it for a third, and Granite connected for a two-base Texas Leaguer.

The next man up was Hammond. The same Hammond who had caused Vernon all the trouble in the fourth. Whatever else happened, he was not going to let him have two long hits in a row. He used the last bit of his solution and struck Hammond out.

It was then that the mayhem really began. Sterling got a double, and Brown and Wheeler a single each. The score was tied again.

Debbie turned and looked at Mr. Forsythe, bewildered. "I don't understand it," she said. "They've never done this to Vernon before."

"Nonsense," said Forsythe, indignantly. "They've used three pitchers against him, and Vernon's holding his own against all three of them."

He heard a sharp crack and turned his head to see the ball sailing over the shortstop's head as another runner crossed the plate.

Mrs. Greenleaf glanced at the scoreboard. New York had five runs; St. Louis—four.

"I'm afraid he's not holding his own any more," she said.

Monk rubbed up a new ball and walked slowly out toward the mound and handed it to Kelly.

"Where's that old hop, kid?" he said.

Vernon shook his head grimly. "I haven't got it any more
. . . It's gone," he said.

"Okay, kid, just relax. Let 'em connect. You got seven men
behind you. They'll handle 'em. They're a great ball team." He
turned and walked back to the plate.

They'd better be, thought Vernon, as he returned to the
mound. There was nothing he could do to help them any more.
He looked over toward the bull pen, hopefully. But Dolan hadn't
even sent another pitcher out to warm up. After all these months,
not even Dolan could believe what was happening to Kelly.

Vernon steeled himself, and pitched. The batter swung
sharply, and the ball came bounding across the infield toward
third. With lightning precision, Whitey Davis came in on it,
scooped up the ball and whipped it across to Baker at second.
Baker shot it on to first for a dazzling double play.

As Vernon slowly crossed the infield toward the dugout, he
was lost in thought. The beautiful precision of that double play
had made him realize the truth of what Lanigan had said. They
were a great ball team—all of them. They were real ball players. He felt a wave of gratitude and affection for his teammates,
and an added sense of responsibility. He put on his jacket and
sat unhappily in a corner of the dugout.

"What did I tell you, Kelly?" said Monk, gleefully, as he sat
down next to Vernon. "Quit worryin' out there. This game ain't
over yet!"

"I wish it were," said Vernon.

"You gotta keep your chin up, kid. You gotta go out there
lookin' cocky. You gotta keep bluffin', see?"

"I'm afraid they've called my bluff," said Vernon.

But Monk didn't hear him. He was on his feet cheering.
Whitey Davis had wrapped out a whistling single.

Dolan was pacing back and forth in front of the dugout,
changing his strategy to meet each new development of the
game. Now he sent Rogers in to pinch-hit for Bailey, and he sent
Hooper and Erickson out to the bull pen to warm up. Rogers
completed his mission perfectly, laying down a delicate sacrifice
bunt which sent Whitey to second. And then Bronco Turner
rocked the ball park with a home run high into the left-field
stands. The next two batters went out in rapid succession, but

nobody cared. St. Louis was ahead again, 6 to 5, and if they could only manage to hold the fighting, slugging invaders scoreless for just this one more inning, the game, the Series and the world would all be theirs.

As his teammates leapt out of the dugout and scattered to their positions, Vernon rose and looked at Dolan uncertainly. Jimmy nodded and gave him a slap on the back.

"I'm leaving you in there, Kelly," he said. "It's your game to win or lose."

Vernon stood there. He started to say something and then he stopped. He slipped off his jacket and Dolan took it from him. Vernon turned and walked grimly toward the mound. He would have to face New York's heaviest hitters, one right after the other. He knew what was going to happen. He knew it was hopeless. But all his emotions were frozen inside him now; he was beyond despair or terror. He was numb and dazed. He couldn't feel— he could only think in a strange, detached and logical sort of way.

Winters, the first man up, hit the first ball Vernon pitched for a ringing single which he nearly stretched into a two-bagger. This was the beginning, thought Vernon. And it was going to end in a debacle. It was merely a question of how long Dolan would leave him in.

Vernon braced himself and went on pitching with grim, automaton-like persistence. While Winters danced tormentingly back and forth off first, Vernon laboriously worked out his string on Pike to three and two. Monk called for an inside pitch and Vernon tried his best. But Brannick called a ball and sent Pike trotting happily down to first.

Vernon caught Monk's return and stood poised in the pitcher's box. His face was a white mask. The winning run was on first—one good long hit and the Series would be over. The next three batters were Hiller, Granite and Hammond. All three of them had been socking him unmercifully. What was the use? He might just as well quit right now.

But something within him refused to accept this verdict; some crazy, illogical spark insisted that he keep on trying.

He gave a quick glance toward first and pitched. Hiller took a swift cut at the ball and sent it shooting straight up into the sky. When it came down, Monk was under it and there was one out.

Well, that was an unexpected piece of luck, thought Vernon, but it didn't alter the situation. There was still Granite and Hammond. And Granite was already in the batter's box, brandishing his war club menacingly and grinning at Kelly confidently.

Vernon took a deep breath and pitched. He saw Granite swing and connect and he saw the ball go sailing in a high rising arc. He turned in the box and followed it with his eyes. This was it. This was the end. Far away in right field he saw Bevan leap high into the air, his glove flat against the concrete wall. He saw him miraculously spear the ball and come tumbling to the ground with a jarring, bruising thud, and then he saw him jump up, still clinging to the ball.

As the crowd roared its appreciation, Vernon felt another sharp wave of gratitude. Once more he had been saved by the skill of his teammates.

And now he faced Hammond, the power-house. In each of his last two trips to the plate he had smashed out a two-bagger.

Mr. Forsythe turned to Debbie.

"Two out and Hammond up," he said. "This is the game right here."

There was a deathly silence in the stands as Vernon pitched. The ball was high and wide and Hammond let it go. How long could this ordeal last? It seemed to Vernon that he had been out there on that pitcher's box for hours. He wiped the cold sweat from his forehead and set himself to pitch again. He tried to keep it low and close, but the ball came across the plate just the way Hammond liked it. He hit it squarely on the nose. With a sinking, hopeless feeling of disaster, Vernon saw the ball coming straight toward him, high above his head. Reaching up, he made a blind, desperate leap into the air. Then he felt a sharp, stinging blow that sent him reeling backward off his feet. He landed sprawling on his back with a violent jolt that knocked his wind out. He lay there for an instant, stunned. Then he looked up. His hand felt numb and dead, but the ball remained stuck in his glove.

Still lying there, he frowned as he tried to collect himself. He was aware of a mighty roar, and the air seemed to be filled with flying cushions and paper and score cards. He craned his neck and looked about. His teammates were rushing towards him from all sides. He slowly began to pick himself up, and it was only then that it dawned on him that his ordeal was over; that the reason for all the roaring and the excitement was that he had won the game.

Voo and Doo

HOKE NORRIS

I am a utility outfielder named Bill Bailey who I have got to admit all my baseball life I have been hanging on everywhere, always afraid I was going to be traded or sent down, and usually right. I was always the second or third or fourth man thrown in on trades to balance the swap, or "the player to be decided later," or even once the player that went for the $1 unconditional waiver price. If there is anything worse than being offered and taken for $1, it is being offered and not taken.

I have hung on, I say in all modesty, because I have got the will to win and I like the game and do not know how to do anything else. With a little luck I would be up there with Maris and Mantle and the other "greats of the game," and may still be there, if things work out, because I am part of a scheme now and I am frightened a little but excited because they can not send me down again. I will explain later.

I have a lifetime batting average of .189 and my best year in the majors was with the Cubs in 1961 when I batted .219 in

48 games—32 times as a pinch-hitter and the rest of them after
the left fielder got lost in the vines at Wrigley Field. I have got
a pretty good throwing arm but it is so lonesome out there in
left field. I never felt so lonesome in my life, especially in the
long innings, of which there were several of them. But better
than the bench. I remember once with the Cubs I sat on the
bench through a doubleheader in Philadelphia that they won
13 to 12 the first game, and we won 11 to 10 the second game,
both games going 12 innings and using 16 pitchers. I sat there
on the bench for eight hours of baseball.

I have played for both of the Chicago teams, and Philadelphia, the old St. Louis Browns where I broke in, and Washington
and Kansas City, switching leagues sometimes, and in the bushes
for Salt Lake City, Wilson, San Diego, Toronto, Elmira, El Paso,
Spokane, Oil City, but never on a team that won the pennant
or even finished second. I have a wife (ex) living somewhere
around San Diego that was a waitress in a bar near Phoenix
called Three Strikes that I met when I was with the Cubs and
spring training in Mesa, and she is married now to a bartender
who used to be a lefthanded pitcher for Kansas City.

But I am at bat now, the wind is blowing out, the fences are
close, the pitcher is frightened, and I am going to knock the "old
sphere" out of the park. My only problem is that I am frightened,
too. Voo plus Doo spells Voodoo, which is something I will have
to explain later.

I will explain now why I am writing this. Some day—a day
now postponed by my recent luck—I am going to retire from
baseball and not knowing anything else, I plan to become a
writer. So I start this account of my latest travels between places
you would not think you could get there between, or anywhere
else, and am trying to remember the advice that a friend gave
me when I told him that I had "literary aspirations." He is a
sports writer in Oil City named Marv Engles. He advised me to
read a lot, especially the sports pages and learn the languages.
Avoid the old cliches like "pill" or "horsehide" for baseball and
"circuit clout" or "four-bagger" for home run, and learn the new
cliches. I like the old ones best myself. They are almost like a
song sometimes. But Marv is the expert and I am trying to take
his advice and remember how he would write—such things as

"two men aboard" instead of two men on base, and "speedballing southpaw" instead of lefthanded fast ball pitcher. Marv also said to listen to the broadcasts because the announcers know all the new cliches, and he is right. I got "doubledip" for "double header" just yeterday from Milo Allen Bakhaus the veteran famed pro TV man here. And I got from him also at the same time "absorbed his seventh setback in ten decisions" for a pitcher that loses seven "tilts" on ten "outings." We lost a doubleheader (doubledip) to the Mets yesterday, and it was tough "going down in defeat" before the "permanent cellar dwellers" and "proverbial last-place New Yorkers," but it was more like a "split" for me because it "boosted" my "literary lore" or resources. Marv says keep your prose lively. Always mix your pitches. Do not let them get ahead of you. I am going to try to retire the side on nine pitches, like Mark Twain and Gen. Lew Wallace and Zane Grey and all the other great "literary hurlers" of "antiquity." Besides, I want to put down what I have been through recently.

What I have been through started on July 16 of last year when Voo and Doo showed up in Oil City. They are twins and their real names are Herman and Sherman Fowler though which is Herman and which is Sherman I still can not tell them apart unless they strip and I can see the mole on the back of Sherman's left leg. Or is it Herman's left leg? You see how it is with Herman and Sherman Fowler. We call them Voo and Doo because of something that happened in the fall after the season ended but that is something else I will have to explain later. Somehow in writing you always have to postpone the game and have a doubleheader later. I mean "doubledip." I can say now just that we are not sure which is Voo and which is Doo, calling them what first comes to mind, except that they claim that Voo is Herman and is the pitcher and Doo is Sherman and is the catcher and has the mole.

They got to Oil City just in time. In July the losing managers always begin complaining about the decisions of the umpires and the spitballs the opposing pitchers are throwing and other imaginary things to take their minds off losing, and the minds of the fans and the owners, too. Our manager Coy Becker was going through the routine. We were in sixth place in a six-team league and had just lost a couple of players also: One of the starting pitchers, Phil Combs, had got himself beaned by a fist that belonged to a batter that he had beaned, and our first-string catcher named Dusty Ways chipped his ankle bone knocking the dirt out of his spikes at the plate. Dusty always did have a mighty hefty swing. And we were all in a bad humor and next to winning a few games we needed most somebody or something to take it out on, and who could find better goats than a couple of hill billy twins showing up in camp asking for a tryout?

Our manager Coy Becker brought them to us and left them standing there next to the batting cage. At our mercy, you might say. The fellows looked them up and down, with side-long glances, and began making wise cracks without looking at them. Then Dusty with his left ankle in a cast hobbled up to them and said, "Do you boys want to play baseball?" They nodded. "Well," said Dusty, "there is something wrong here. We can not start batting practice because the pitcher's box is locked. You fellows go get the key from Mister Becker. And while you are there ask him for some base lines, too. Ours are worn out. Then we will let you play ball with us."

Our beaned pitcher Phil Combs was standing there with his jaws sewed together with wire, grinning like a skeleton.

"Dusty," I said, "lay off of them."

I still do not know why I tried to spoil his fun for him but with those five words I made two friends, and a new career for myself. They were grateful, and hill billies never forget. Maybe they frightened me a little. They were sandy-haired and freckle-faced, and as lean as a flagpole and looking about as hard, and about five feet ten each. They had blue eyes and thin lips, and when they narrowed and hardened something in my mind said, "Look out." One of their looks is like getting your throat cut with a switchblade knife. I do not like violence or wrongdoing either for that matter. They both make me sort of sick to my stomach and maybe standing there in the heat and the grinning players I knew that somebody would get hurt if they went off for the key to the pitchers box and some base lines.

"Give them a chance," I said.

Dusty's mouth fell open and Phil's would have too if it had not been wired shut. In all the storied legends and history of baseball nobody had ever spoiled a joke on a hill billy tryout, and in baseball next to winning it is tradition that counts most. Never run the bases in the wrong direction, or even change the throwing pattern after a strike out with nobody "aboard." Hill billies and other rookies are always fair game.

Dusty cursed and Phil made what sounds he could.

"We knew they were kidding," one of the twins said to me, and the other one said, "We knew, but thank you." I still do not know if they knew, but their lips and eyes had narrowed and maybe that had been enough for me. I had felt a little chill at my backbone and an empty, stirring motion in my stomach that I am still trying to understand. Dusty and Phil retired to the shade of the dugout, and Coy Becker came out and said, "We need a pitcher and we need a catcher," with dirty looks toward the dugout, "and these boys say that they are a pitcher and a catcher, and can hit, and we need hitters, too," with a dirty look at me, "and so we are going to give them a tryout. Take away the batting cage. We will stimulate a playing situation."

Coy sent me down to second to take throws from the catcher, put a fast runner on first and told some of the best batters to get ready. He was being cute too but I could not interfere when the manager gave an order. The twins got their spiked shoes out of their old leather satchel and put them on, and the catcher put on a mask, chest protector and shinguards and mitt. They were wearing faded, wrinkled khaki pants and faded checkered sports shirts with the tails out; they looked like they belonged in the police lineup at a hick police station after a raid on the local pool hall, and I could not help feeling sorry for them. We were "hitless wonders" but even "hitless wonders" can hit hill billy tryout pitchers and sometimes the old pros smashed line drives back at them that shattered kneecaps and caved in ribs and castrated them and generally incapacitated and de-ambitioned the "young hopefuls." And from second base I could see something. The pitcher was standing there bareheaded in the sun and heat—they had not bothered to give them caps—and I could see his knees trembling. They quivered the faded khaki pants legs like wind at a windowshade. O God, I said to myself, dreading what was to come. The first batter stepped up, grinning, ready to take out on the twin what he could not take out on opposing "twirlers." "Are you not going to let him warm up?" I shouted, but nobody heeded. The pitcher threw, and the man on first ran to second. The catcher stood there with his arm cocked. The team yelled instructions, each in his own humorous way. Coy waved the base stealer back to first. In the shouting and merriment nobody seemed to notice what I noticed: The pitcher had thrown a perfect strike, and furthermore a fast ball that was the fastest ball I had even seen. The batter had not taken his bat off his shoulder. I began not feeling sorry for the twins.

The batter let the second pitch also pass without moving. The runner broke for second. The catcher threw me a ball that could have gone down the barrel of a cannon without touching the walls. I was waiting with the ball for the runner still eight steps away, and he just skidded and stopped, and walked back to first without looking at Coy. This time the batters shouted at *him*, adding laughter. Again nobody seemed to notice that the pitcher had thrown a strike, though the batter was standing a little thoughtful at the plate. The next time, he swung, and from second base it seemed to me that he missed the ball by three feet. I doubt if he saw it. The runner was also a little thoughtful, standing there with both feet on first base. The pitcher's knees were not trembling now. I began to feel a sort of joy. History might be "in the making" here in Oil City.

The second batter hit a dribbler foul down the third base line; the third, a topped roller back to the pitcher; the fourth, nothing, the fifth, nothing . . . in dead silence. When a baseball team is dead silent, it is either dead or overwhelmed. Ours was not quite dead. To make a short story even shorter, we had us a new pitcher and a new catcher. Coy Becker's only worry became: Would the big boys take them away from us? He knew they would eventually, but he was going to get the most out of the twins possible before they went to the great beyond. He pitched the pitcher every third day, and then every second day, and he didn't lose a game. He pitched shut-outs and one-runners, he pitched two no-hit games, and one perfect game. And the catcher batted around .325, and nobody ever stole second on him. And eventually we noticed about the pitcher that he was also batting .325 which is a rare thing in a game that they do not even bother usually to announce the pitchers' batting averages they're always so low and nobody expects a "twirler" to hit any-way. And all of this in Southern heat, too, and in parks where the badgers had to be chased out of and their holes filled in (if they were at all) before game time, and where the pitcher's mound was always either too high or too low or too close or too far away from home plate, where uniforms were laundered once a week and you spent more time on the bus than in bed and the food was either all fried or half raw, and the coaching was what you might get in the little league in Lakamazoo, South Dakota.

But we were great—all of us, even the hitless wonders picked up, with such "inspiration"—and the twins were unbeatable. I wish that I could report that we won the pennant but the early won-lost record was too much to overcome, and not even Coy Becker would pitch the twin *every* day. We did finish second, which as Marv Engles wrote in the Oil City *Enterpriser* it was "a triumph of no mean proportions." We had, to quote him again, "burned up the league" and "set the bushes afire" and "put Oil City on the sports map." Sometimes I wonder while reading Marv why he himself never made it to the majors, in Chicago or New York or Philadelphia. Maybe he could, if I told him what I know—how the twins operated, how they made those "eye-popping records" and "rewrote the record books." It would be a big "scoop" for him and maybe could get him a big time job but it will have to wait, if I ever do tell him. I am just writing this for practice, and to get it out of my system. Maybe "confess" is the word. If you ever see it, you will know that somebody stole it from me.

I want this to be complete and so I must now before going on report an event that happened on the last day of the season. We were just playing out the string, all the standings were frozen because no win or loss would change them now and "the pressure was off." But the twin pitched like it was the seventh game of the world series, and he had a shut-out going through the sixth inning. He was at bat in our half of the sixth and took a strike, and then hit the dirt to get out of the way of a brush-back. The next pitch caught him on the shin and down he went, hugging the "injured member." You take your knocks in baseball. You do not rub the "injured member" or otherwise display pain or anger. You do not want to give the opposition the pleasure of

joy in your agony. It is a matter of pride. The "twirler" twin was
still young and he got up rubbing his leg and glaring out at the
mound. The "receiver" twin ran out and they whispered to each
other. Coy went out too and talked to them and finally the
pitcher trotted on down to first. He was "erased" in a double
play that ended the inning, and Coy thought it best to put in
another pitcher. The twin pitcher sat by himself in a corner of
the dugout, not talking, a sort of steam coming off of him. The
relief pitcher allowed three earned runs and one unearned run
that lost the game that the twin could have added to his win
column. When the "receiver" twin came to the dugout next
between innings he and his brother sat together and whispered.
Their lips and eyes were thin and cold, and again something
said to me "Look out!" The catcher twin was up third and took
a ball, then a strike, then he swung and the ball fell in for a base
hit and the bat flew out at the pitcher and hit him on the right
kneecap. All the way to the dugout I could hear the crack and
crunch of meat and bone. The pitcher fell and the twin catcher
ran to first, looking over his shoulder out at the mound. On the
bench his brother sat there smiling and nodding. The opposing
pitcher was a pretty good young prospect just starting out. I do
not remember his name or know where he is today. He will not
go far, and I will never hear his name again. I report this event
for what it is worth. What it was worth to me was a feeling of
pain and sickness to my stomach. They were wrong, those boys,
if they did what I think they did.

But anyway I accepted when they invited me to go home
with them for a few days. I did not have anywhere else to go
that anybody was waiting there for me, and the twins seemed
friendly. I had helped them on their first day. And Marv Engles
had put their name in the paper, and in the big headlines too. It
was the first time they had ever had their name in any paper, I
guess, and they were grateful to him too. So he came along. We
all went in the 1958 Oldsmobile sedan that the boys had driven
to the park on their first day. Its seats were spilling their guts and
its windows were cracked but it got us there. We drove all day
across the plains and then up into the hills, with the air cooling
and the green of the trees darkening and thickening. We went
up and up into the mountains, off the main highway on to a

narrow paved road, then on to a dirt road that was more up and down and around than flat and straight, and I would have got seasick if it had been water. The closer we got the more relaxed and loud became the twins. They had been tense and quiet with the team—like "strung bows," Marv said, or tight drums, or a lighted fuse, you always expected them to snap or fire or blow up though they never did. Now you would not have known they were the same boys. They were home again. "Home to the hills," Marv said.

Home was a big log house that had never been painted that sat on about a 45 degree slope that ended out of sight 300 feet below in a creek. I wondered at first where the Fowlers grew their crops or otherwise earned their feed and keep, but found out soon enough. The yard was full of kids that were bashful and hung back, and Herm and Sherm went laughing and shouting from one to the other, giving out gifts that I did not know they had bought. The kids said "Thank ye," one after the other, and Marv said "Listen to the Elizabethan in their voices. These people are English and have been isolated so long they have never learned to talk American." I did not know what language Elizabethan was and I could not understand much that was said. Ma and Pa came out and spoke it too, with a lot of grinning and laughing. They were "grizzled mountaineers," as Marv said to me, aside. "They are telling the twins that their oldest brother got a year and a day in Atlanta for moonshining." So I knew how they made their living.

They took us in and one of the twins said we were all thirsty. Pa went to a corner cupboard and poured some clear liquid into tumblers, filling them, and returned to us with them. "What is it?" I inquired, and the twins laughed and one of them said, "Water. Real mountain dew."

I was thirsty and so turned up the tumbler and took a big drink and tried to swallow but somebody had lit a match in my mouth and my throat caught fire. I coughed and choked and they pounded me on the back, laughing. Marv tossed his off easy, and so did the twins, and then settled down to drinking. I contented myself with sips but even so got higher than the mountain, and do not remember much of the night. I remember being frightened. We drank and talked, with me not understanding much that was said. Then we walked and went to visit some relatives of the twins. Their cabin had a TV aerial a mile high and one of the twins said, "This is where we watched baseball. We saw you pinch-hit once for the Cubs." The other twin said, "You struck out," and they and Marv laughed. So did I.

The relatives turned out to be two old women—"crones," said Marv, "old women of the mountain." They had no teeth and wore black. They drank the fire water too with us and built up a fire under a pot, no other light out there in the yard before the shack, and it was all ghostly, with the shadows close under the trees, and the wind from the mountain whistling like the sound the fans make when a foul ball rolls down the screen. The old women stirred with a long stick in the black pot, and whatever it was, it bubbled and steamed up in their faces, and Marv recited, "Double double toil and trouble fire burn and cauldron bubble." I could not decide what was toil and trouble about doubles—doubles were great in any league—but Marv seemed pleased by his apt words. "This is voodoo," he said to the twins, "and so I dub thee knights of the bat Sir Voo and Sir Doo." So you see where they got their names. Marv wrote to a friend of his later and the friend put it in the *Sports Illustrated*.

Marv also mentioned two characters named Faust and Mephistopheles that he said played in a fast league a couple of centuries ago. I looked them up later to get the spelling. Faust sold his soul to the devil Mephistopheles, and I understood what Marv meant: The twins had sold their souls. "I would too, for the future those kids have got," Marv said. "In fact," he said, his voice a little thick, and his eyes shining, "I would sell my mother, for enough money. You did not know that about me, did you, Bill Bailey?" I did not know that about him then, and do not know it now. Marv is a gentleman. But I think he was right, that night, about the twins. The "old women of the mountain" and the fire under the pot and the twins there with their long thin faces and thin lips—I could believe in the devil that night, and maybe still can.

But it turned out that all the old women were cooking was something they called Brunswick stew, a sort of thick soup with everything in it—"filet of fenny snake," Marv said, "eye of newt and toe of frog, wool of bat and tongue of dog, adder's leg and howlet's wing, tooth of wolf, witches mummy, maw and gulf of raven shark," Marv said, with great pride and oratory like an actor. But the stuff was tasty, if I remember right, and I think I do, because I am a pretty good trencherman, which has given me a weight problem ever since I have been in baseball. The stuff was hot as pepper, and I must have eaten a lot of it, and drunk a lot too. I woke up in the night with my belly and throat in flames, and my head beating like a worn-out drum. I walked out across the yard, climbing, and went to the top of the hill behind the house. There I saw a sort of flat valley—a pasture, I guess it was—and four flares set up. In the light Herman and Sherman Fowler were throwing and catching. They had a diamond set up, with bases and a pitchers mound. So this was where they learned to play, I thought. They were silent. They threw and caught all alone. Nothing else existed for them. Then I saw a funny thing: They exchanged mitts and places, and the catcher became the pitcher, and vice versa. The game went on, silent throwing and catching, the twins as solemn as a couple of mourners. Just a joke, I thought; taking turns, like boys at play. I started to call to them, but decided not to, for some reason. I would have spoiled something, if I had. I watched for a while, and went back to the house, and to sleep.

In the late winter—I at Key West, a deck hand on a tourist fishing boat—I got a letter from the twins that is self-explanatory:

> We guess you have heared by now. We are going home to mother and you are going with us. What we mean is They are sending us up in the spring and we told them that we wood not go up without you going too. So to make us happy they said they would take you. You are part of the bargain. We are joking ha ha. We told them that you was a good man. Do not think we are doing you a favor. You deserve it. See you in Sorrysota in March.

And so I did, underpaid and overweight as usual but happy to be with a big league club again. We went through spring training and the "grapefruit league" exhibition games with no "untoward incident," and the twin never losing a game and the both averaging about .280 at bat (even the best hitters drop when they go from the minors to the majors). I was still "utility" but happy. I would extend myself in the record books, which is where baseball players get all the immortality that they expect. It is better than none at all.

We opened the season against the Cubs in Chicago. It was cold and misty, as always in Chicago in April, and the regular left fielder "developed a virus" and ran a fever, and I found myself in there again with my back to the vines on the Wrigley wall. The vines were still dead now and the crowd was small and the wind blew off the lake, but this time I did not mind the loneliness. I was not only on the roster. I was in the lineup. The manager Cleve ("Andy") Anderson started Herman ("Voo") Fowler "on the mound," with Sherman ("Doo") Fowler "behind the plate." So said "Andy" Anderson. So said the scorer and the field announcer and the box scores. I do not know which one of them was the starting pitcher and which one of them was the starting catcher. More about that little matter in a moment.

Both pitchers started out "rough," as Milo Allen Bakhaus of "TV fame" would say. Nobody got on base the first two innings. I batted eighth, and so came to bat second in the third inning, with one out. I just stood there and the "opposing hurler" walked me on four pitches. He also walked the next two—Pitcher Fowler and First Baseman Clether—and for the first time since August 8, 1962, I found myself standing on third base in a major league ball park. The Cubs changed pitchers. The "reliefer" was getting in his warm up throws when some jackass in the boxes behind the Cubs' dugout began braying in a loud voice, "Won't you come home Bill Bailey," from the famous song with the same name as mine. I thought he would fracture a tonsil soon, and shut up, so did not pay much attention to him. "Why won't you come home Bill Bailey," he bellowed, standing and pointing out at me so nobody would miss the joke, and the Cubs in the dugout took it up, singing along with him, and then the crowd, and soon there was a regular community sing going. The relief pitcher had meanwhile struck out the next batter. It was two out, with that recital blasting away at full voice. I began to be pleased and to listen and look over into the stands and grin. I hadn't had so much attention before in all my life. So it was not my fault what happened. I strayed a little from the base, listening to "Won't

you come home Bill Bailey," and felt something brush my arm.
I turned and there stood the Cub third baseman with the ball
in his hand, grinning, and the third base umpire bellowing "Out!"
and our third base coach calling me names. The side had been
retired. A day late and a dollar short.

I trotted to the dugout for my glove. "Andy" Anderson had
his back turned to me. I never did care for him. He has got shifty
eyes. In left field I heard the song change to "Why didn't you
go home Bill Bailey, why didn't you go home." Over the rest of
the play I will "draw a merciful curtain," until the end of the
fifth with the score still "knotted" at nothing all, and the singing
dying down in the stands. In the fifth I escaped—that is the word
—for a little while in the clubroom beneath the stands. To get
there you walk up a long dark tunnel, on boards cut and frayed
by cleats, and turn left and there it is. I walked in and found two
players there ahead of me. "In a trice" I identified them. The
twins. I was about to speak but then realized that they both had
off their jackets. The pitcher's number was 7 and the catcher's
number was 11—I could see the numbers on the backs of their
jackets and watched, "in shocked silence," while they passed in
the swap from one player to the other. They put them on, fast,
and started buttoning up. They were tucking in the tails when
they saw me. The stopped "in mid gesture," and just stared,
with their mouths and eyes wide open. Then those mouths and
eyes thinned and chilled, and my throat and mouth got dry and
my stomach restless. They walked to me, and stood one at each
side, and slightly in front of me.

"Fellows," I said, trying to be calm and pleasant, "but fellows, this is not right."

They seemed to draw closer to me, without moving. They
were a sort of presence there, and I remembered the fire beneath
the pot, and the two witches, and how the twins had looked in
the light, their faces long and thin, like twin devils.

"Mr. Anderson knows," said the new pitcher, and the new
catcher said, "And if it is all right with him, it is all right with
everybody."

"But tell me," I said, swallowing, curious though frightened,
"have you two been swapping, changing the battery, in every
game?"

They nodded, together, grinning a little thin grin, watching me with those eyes of ice.

"But why?" I said.

"We are really both pitchers," said the new pitcher, and the new catcher said, "We could not decide which one of us would be the pitcher."

"Why not both of you?"

"We would have a better chance if only one of us was the pitcher."

"And you could win more games, one of you coming in in the middle of the game."

"It did not start that way. It started because we could not agree and we had a fight. It just worked out that way. Now you are going to keep quiet about it."

I did not want to keep quiet about it. This was wrong—it was against all the rules of fair play and baseball. But I could remember all the years in the bushes, and all the years on the bench, and the catchers who did not take off their gear, and the song they had just sung in the stands and caused me to get picked off third base. I did not want the bench again, I did not want the bushes again. I wanted what I had.

I decided—I suppose that Marv Engles would say that I sold my soul to the devil. "Let us go and talk to Mr. Anderson," I said.

We went out together, a twin on each side of me, like a convoy. Mr. Anderson was shouting at his third base coach who turned his back now and returned to his post. Mr. Anderson sat down, his face red and his breath coming hard. He saw us together in the door and got up and walked slowly to us. He looked into our faces, licked his lips and went from red to white.

"Mr. Anderson," said the new pitcher, "he knows."

"Mr. Anderson," said the new catcher, "he knows, and has promised to behave if you will not trade him or send him down again."

"Mr. Anderson," I said, "I have promised to behave if you will play me every day."

Mr. Anderson went through the expected sputters and oaths, and nodded and went back to his seat and held his head in his hands. He seemed to have suddenly lost weight. I went back to left field, and the new pitcher won the game. I am still in left field, and a little overweight, and batting .199, but will come on strong later, and feel better now that I have got it all down, out of my system and on to paper. They sing "Bill Bailey" for me regularly now, but I can take it, and Milo Allen Bakhaus of "TV fame" refers to my "budding hitting streak" when I get a hit and I let him talk without protest. Yet one thing is incomplete. I want to show this to somebody. What is a "confession" that nobody hears? You might as well strike at the wind. So I am sending it down to Marv Engles, confidential, strictly, for his eyes and his information only. I hope that he will like it and give me encouragement in my "literary efforts," and understand. I know that he will not betray me. Marv is "a gentleman and a scholar."

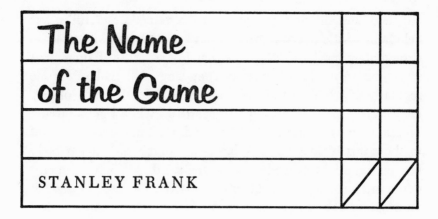

The Name of the Game

STANLEY FRANK

Messlin was in the clubhouse the day they found the Big Guy's World Series watch in Gaban's spare glove. Pinning the rap on Gaban as the sneak thief who had been raiding the team's lockers since spring training should have been a relief to Messlin. He was a new man, a rookie punk like Gaban; the nervous finger of suspicion had brushed him before it transfixed Gaban. But Messlin, who derived a sense of personal dignity from baseball, flinched in an agony of embarrassment when the Big Guy slashed Gaban's mouth with the back of his hand.

The blow sent Gaban reeling across the room like a cornered rat and the rasp of his spikes was harsh in the clubhouse. The Big Guy, emboldened by the righteous indignation of the team and conscious that he represented it, advanced upon Gaban to scramble his unhandsome features. Gaban was a rat, all right, but he did not cringe. He lashed out and punched the Big Guy's pulpy nose into his face. They always said Gaban had the guts of a burglar.

Gaban had a wonderful pair of hands and he knew how to use them. He might have cut the Big Guy down to his inconsiderable size in a formal fight, but this was a pleasure fight and the Big Guy weighed two hundred and twenty pounds, and not all of it was blubber.

He grabbed the collar of Gaban's uniform, twisted it in his huge paw and brought up his free arm under Gaban's chin. The smack of Gaban's skull against the wall was loud and distinct above their muffled explosions of breathing. The Big Guy, lusting with purposeful pleasure, was about to let Gaban have it again when the Old Man, the manager, rescued the locker-room thief and flung him away as if he were an obscene thing.

"Get out of here!" the Old Man snarled. "Don't stop to take a shower! You've polluted the place enough already!"

Gaban went back to the minors that night and Messlin was among the half dozen rookies who went with him. Madden, the team secretary, phoned the boys and gave them their marching orders.

"The Old Man would've told you this himself," Madden said, "but he's pretty cut up by what happened this afternoon. That dirty bum, that Gaban! It's not the first time. You'll be back, kid. You're young. By the way, keep that rumpus in the clubhouse under your hat. You understand?"

Messlin said he understood. He was young and he had pride of ambition, but he understood a phony could not be tolerated in baseball. Sure, they had to release him, and a few others at the same time to make a splash story and not make it too pointed that a ballplayer was a crook. For the game's sake, not for Gaban's.

Anyway, Messlin figured, he would have been sent back to the minors three weeks later, in the middle of May, when the rosters were cut. He needed work on his curve ball, and his change of pace was no bargain. Going out three weeks earlier meant a difference of only a couple of hundred bucks in salary. It was a small sacrifice for Messlin when he was twenty to keep the shame of baseball that was Gaban under his hat.

It was different with Gaban, though. Gaban was a fine ballplayer with possibilities of greatness; he was ready for the big league. The team needed him, couldn't win the pennant without him. Fesler, the veteran second baseman, was a cinch to fold up when the sun baked the diamond and the heat drained a man's vitality and his willingness to punish himself.

The Old Man had planned to break in Gaban gradually at second base, then make him the full-time regular when Fesler wilted, but the Old Man unhesitantly kissed off the pennant when Gaban turned out to be a wrong guy. The private assurance that baseball was clean sustained Messlin through the disappointment and drudgery of the minor leagues, served as a cushion against disillusion when the boys spoke, as ballplayers will, of the Black Sox and the soulless baseball corporations.

Messlin knew he was strictly a sucker for baseball and Gaban alone disturbed the illusion he kept deep within himself. Gaban was back in the majors a year later—the other league, but still the big league. Gaban presently had a World Series watch he could show in public, and two years later he had another memento to go with it, a diamond ring in proof of his membership on the best ball club in America. Gaban was a great star, a hero.

Sometimes, when he thought of it, Messlin liked to believe Gaban was a reformed character, but he guessed from behind-the-hand whispers he heard in the dugouts that Gaban still was a poolroom bum at heart. Messlin felt someone had pulled a bad boner somewhere along the line.

And now Messlin and Gaban were on the same ball club. Gaban's ball club. Gaban was manager of the Drakes, the team that was bringing Messlin back to the big leagues after twelve years of semi-anonymity in the minors. Twelve years of pretty good pitching had gone for Sweeney because a few men wanted to forget they had been in the clubhouse the day the Big Guy's watch was found in Gaban's glove and all the others remembered that he had failed once. They weren't kidding Messlin. They didn't have to tell him he was getting another shot at the big leagues because the war suddenly invested old-timers, who knew the racket and were unlikely to be drafted, with a brief measure of value.

Now they were asking him to win games for the one man in baseball he despised. His boss was the one guy in the business who resented him as a man resents the reminder of a half-forgotten indiscretion more than the stigma itself. The Old Man was dead; the Big Guy was living on his annuities; only two or three of those who had been in the clubhouse that day still were in baseball, and they were in the other league.

There were four hundred major leaguers and they picked the one wrong guy Messlin had ever known to be a manager. Messlin guessed what Gaban was thinking: *Five thousand bush leaguers in America and I drew the one jerk who knows where the body is buried.* Messlin, a simple man who had neither the talent nor the temperament for philosophy, laughed out of the wrong side of his mouth and tried to forget the one day neither cared to remember.

Messlin made a good try the first time he saw Gaban in training camp. He gave the boss a big hello and said, "Hi, Froggy, you look ready." That was bad; that was a mistake.

Unconsciously, automatically, Messlin used the nickname by which Gaban had been known when he was breaking in. They called him Froggy in the old days for his funny half hop in pouncing on ground balls, for the green and garish, they're-off-and-running clothes he affected, and for his grating, irritating voice, which he used incessantly. The nickname struck a clamorous gong across the years, vibrating memories both preferred to forget.

Messlin should have known the hop had gone out of Gaban's legs and he should have seen that Gaban now dressed like the successful, publicity-hungry actors and businessmen who fawned upon him. Gaban's voice had not changed, though. It still was a penetrating, brassy bellow and it had inspired the nickname which he now was called with affection by ten million fans. Gaban had put the nickname and the affection to work by talking himself into the managership of the Drakes, and it was no surprise to Messlin. Anyone, he reflected, who could talk himself off the commissioner's blacklist and out of jail was a cinch to talk himself into a job.

The man they called Gabby gave Messlin a furtive once-over. He studiously ignored Messlin's proffered hand and pulled his five-buck tie deeper into the billowing collar of his silk initialed shirt. Gaban looked sharp, like money in the bank. His snappy sport jacket and doeskin slacks made Messlin uncomfortably conscious of his own wrinkled, dark gray suit. His other suit.

"You look older than the pictures make you out," Gaban was saying. The inference was plain and Messlin got it on the first bounce. Gaban didn't want him, wouldn't have had him if he had not been bought before the Drakes appointed a new manager.

"Maybe you can pitch. I'll find out soon enough. The draft hasn't taken all the good ballplayers yet. Hey, Dog Face!" Gaban raised his voice to greet the hotel golf pro and startled three aged ladies in a far corner of the lobby. "I'll buy you a drink! A Mickey."

Gaban went off and left Messlin feeling as unnecessary as another neck. The brush-off told him another guy remembered a certain day in a certain clubhouse. The knowledge that he had Gaban on the hip gave Messlin a fleeting surge of superiority, but it didn't stay with him long. He could take refuge in his virtue and his morality, but he would be taking it in the minors while Gaban would be taking the bows and the big money in the majors.

It could have been worse though. During the first weeks of training, Messlin perceived that Gaban was vain enough to want the pennant more than he wanted an undisturbed conscience. Gaban would keep him on the ball club as long as he pitched and kept his mouth shut. It was a running gag among the Drakes that Gaban would haul his mother out of bed and give her a shot in the arm if he thought she could steal a base and win a ball game for him.

Pitching for the Drakes and winning games for Gaban gave Messlin no lift of stimulation, even after the squad was cut to twenty-five men and he was safe for the season. Messlin had thought it would be different. When he learned the Drakes were bringing him back to the big league, he dusted off the shining hope locked in a pigeonhole of his brain for twelve years and he thrilled privately to the prospect of playing on a proud pennant winner.

But the Drakes were all arrogance and no pride. Playing with the Drakes was a degrading experience for Messlin, because the Drakes had to debase themselves to play Gaban's way. Taking their cue from the manager, they were vicious and ruthless and overbearing. They argued excessively with the umpires, they antagonized unduly the other clubs and, goaded by Gaban, they made unnecessary muscles.

In Messlin's book, they were a shrill neighborhood gang imitating the local loafer and trying to be very tough indeed about the whole thing. He was ashamed to find himself hoping they, his own club, would get their ears knocked off.

It could have been different. The Drakes were a good club and they were winning ball games. Messlin might have been animated by the discovery that he was a better pitcher in the big league than he was in the minors. His infield cut off and turned into double plays ground balls which sifted through the humpty-dumpties in the minors for base hits. Wild-swinging kids in the bushes took a cut at everything they could reach and hit stuff that was supposed to fool them, but the big leaguers tried to guess with the pitcher, and Messlin, who knew the racket, did all right in the strategy department.

In midseason it was obvious that the Drakes had only the Kings, the co-favorites, to beat for the pennant, and Messlin was forced to admit Gaban might do it. By dint of great hammering, one becomes a blacksmith. Gaban told them they could win, and his voice, a raucous needle playing a cracked record, pounded at the players until the idea obsessed them and drove them wild. Every ball game was a crusade, and Messlin, who could distinguish between spirit and hysteria, wondered how long it would be before the relentless pressure Gaban was piling on them blew the team apart at the seams.

Gaban, always a great ballplayer, was playing the game of his life and the inspirational impact on the team was making him a winning manager. That was the hell of it for Messlin.

One Gaban in baseball was bad enough; a team of Gabans was infinitely worse. All the players were aping Gaban's bombastic mannerisms and his selfish, cynical attitude toward the game. Messlin really didn't blame the other guys. Gaban was the big noise, the most magnetic personality of the year. His success and his recklessness were contagious. Messlin could even see himself falling in line with the others, except for the superimposed picture which gave him perspective and depth every time he looked at Gaban.

Messlin was an alien in his own clubhouse, and that's how

he wanted it to be when Clemons, the rookie catcher, was victimized by Gaban's maniacal greed for victory. They were playing the Phillies, and Gaban, maneuvering the staff to have his regular starters ready for a series with the Kings opening the next day, tried to get away with a second-string pitcher. The Drakes powdered the ball and had the game safely in the bag until the Phillies put on a storm in the eighth. Gaban called Messlin from the bullpen to put out the fire. Clemons, who had been in the game all the way to rest Payne, the No. 1 catcher, gave him the old pep-and-vinegar chatter, and Messlin, after a few warm-up throws, went to work.

A couple of outfield flies scored a run for the Phils, but the Drakes still were three to the good. Messlin, pitching carefully, operated on the batter who represented the third out. With the count three and two, Messlin tried to break off his big jug, the slow curve. The batter expected a fast ball and was fooled by the pitch, but he got a small piece of the ball and lifted a high foul which climbed lazily toward the stands between first and home.

Clemons ripped off his mask and chased the ball. Messlin relaxed when he saw the foul would drop into the stands, but Clemons kept going with his head up, digging furiously.

"No! No!" Messlin yelled. "Can't get it! No, Clem! No!"

Messlin hollered as loudly as he could, but he might have been whispering for all the good it did. Gaban opened his wonderful set of pipes and his voice drowned Messlin's, rose above the crowd's roar.

"Lots of room!" Gaban bawled. "Yah, go get it! Lots of room!"

Clemons heard Gaban and he kept going. Now the ball was dropping swiftly and Messlin, going tight with fear, saw it would fall three or four rows behind the low railing separating the field from the stands. Messlin recoiled violently when Clemons, still listening to Gaban and going all out, collided heavily with the stand.

He hung grotesquely over the railing for a moment, like a sack of flour, then slumped back on the field. The ball bounced crazily on the concrete and the fans chased it, but Clemons lay where he fell.

Messlin was the first to reach Clemons. The kid wasn't out, but he was pretty woozy and he moaned softly while he was coming out of the ether. They carried him off, and Messlin, seeing his jaws twitch spasmodically, guessed it hurt like hell.

There were one strike and one inning to go. Payne climbed into his harness and caught the third strike Messlin threw past the batter in a cold rage. Messlin got rid of the Phillies in the ninth just in time to get the team back to the clubhouse as Clemons was going out on a stretcher.

The kid tried to whip up a smile when Messlin squeezed his arm, but it was a feeble effort. Gaban looked at him casually, almost impersonally. His interest in ballplayers ceased at that precise instant when they no longer were able to help him win games.

The intern from the ambulance waited for the Great Man to ask him the obvious question. He finally tapped Gaban on the shoulder. "I suppose you want to know about this man."

"Yeh, what goes, doc?" Gaban was as offhand as if he were asking the clubhouse boy to get his shoes shined.

"He has a cracked rib, for one thing."

Gaban snorted. "Gehrig won pennants for the Yankees with busted bones sticking out through his skin. We'll strap him up and he'll be catching in three weeks."

"Maybe," the intern said wryly, "but you can't fix that torn cartilage in his knee with a strip of adhesive. He'll be lucky if he's walking in three months. It may be longer if he needs an operation."

Gaban sailed his glove across the room and hitched up his pants. He sensed the sobering thought which suddenly tempered the team's exhilaration: *It could have been me. So the club wins the pennant and I wind up in the hospital with a stiff leg. Where do I come off?* Gaban was fast on the upbeat. His face was flushed and his eyes were bright with invention.

"You got to take it to win in this league!" he screamed at the players. "You don't win by waving how-do-you-do to the tough ones and playing 'em safe! They don't give that World Series dough to the nice, careful guys! Yah, you got to knock yourself out trying or you'll get knocked off! You, Payne! Tear up them dames' phone numbers! You got to catch every day from here in!"

Payne, a swaggering youth who was wearing out the seat of his pants sitting in Gaban's lap, went into his hardboiled act.

"That World Series dough won't be as hard to take as the work," he sneered, blowing hard on his cigarette. "I'll make new gates in the stands surroundin' those fouls."

The clubhouse was a babble of bravado. The Drakes assured one another they would murder the Kings, and a piece of Messlin's heart went dead inside him.

He was shocked by the brutality and he was outraged by the stupidity which had cost them a valuable player for the sake of an out in a game they were in no danger of losing. Ballplayers had to stick together and protect themselves from the wolves waiting to stick them. Gaban was willing to sacrifice the entire career of Clemons, a good kid, for one lousy ball game, and nobody cried out in protest.

Messlin had to get out of there before the band constricting his throat choked him. Walking under the deserted, clammy stands toward the exit, Messlin abruptly decided to get good and stiff for the first time in three years. He went out on the street, and he was heading for a little joint where a ballplayer could get a load without everybody in the world knowing about it when he heard his name called from a cab parked at the curb. He looked and saw Harren, the King coach, waving.

Messlin knew all about the rule against fraternizing with opposing ballplayers. He also knew Harren from way back, and he said nuts to the rule. Harren was his catcher in the minors eight years ago and had taught him everything he knew about pitching. Harren was a good guy, his kind of guy. He appreciated the worth of a ballplayer and he prized his self-respect above a pennant. Messlin got into the cab.

Harren gave the driver the address of a restaurant downtown, but he didn't know it was around the corner from Gaban's apartment. Messlin knew, but he didn't care. Harren started to say he had taken advantage of an off day to scout the Drakes, but Messlin was in no mood to make small talk and they drove to the restaurant in silence. Harren ordered a beer, and Messlin said he wanted Bourbon, straight. Harren started to say something when he heard the order, but he glanced at Messlin's face and shrugged.

"How's the kid?" Harren asked after they had taken a belt from their drinks. "It looked like he gave himself a bad jolt."

"He's out for the season," Messlin said grimly. "Gaban ran him into the hospital."

Harren cursed Gaban, softly, savagely and fluently. He called him seventeen different species of low, no-good animal life, and Messlin punctuated each blast against his manager with short nods.

"You go into the game for the money," Harren raved, "but it doesn't last long. Then you play for peanuts and you have no home life, but you want to hang on because you get a bang just being part of the game. Then you see a dirty, contemptible skunk like Gaban hit the jack pot. It's enough to make you cut your throat. There'll be no living with that cheap phony if he wins, but he won't make it."

"Why not?" Messlin demanded. After all, the pennant meant five or six grand to him and you can't eat illusions.

"Everybody in the league hates Gaban's guts and they'll break a leg to stop him. It's not enough that he beats you. He must humiliate you and rub it in. You guys have the best team, but you won't win, because the percentages must catch up with Gaban."

Harren said he wanted another drink, and Messlin had more of the same. The drinks cooled the hot anger gnawing at them and they began, as ballplayers will, to trade stories of people they knew and things they had seen. Harren told of the time Lefty Gomez delayed a World Series game to stare at a plane overhead, and then Messlin told the one about the bush-league umpire who was quick to pull a watch on the boys when the peace was disturbed. The umpire got into a jam one day, and he tried to work the watch gag when the boys began to push him around. In the confusion, though, somebody lifted his watch, and the umpire almost went out of his mind when a dog ran up to the plate with the watch in its mouth.

To illustrate the story, Messlin took out his own watch and held it aloft. He was coming to the punch line when the chuckle died in his throat and his grin froze into a grimace.

Gaban was standing at the bar glaring at him, too far to hear what he was saying, too close to the guilty suspicion lurking in his mind to escape the significance of the watch. Gaban's eyes shifted to the eager anticipation on Harren's face, darted back to Messlin and singed him with hatred before he walked out.

"Uh-uh," Harren breathed. "There goes trouble. We better get out of here. No, that's no good. He may be hanging around outside, and it'll look worse if we leave together. I'll go first, and if I see him I'll try to square you. Sorry this happened kid. See you."

Messlin settled down to do some serious drinking. He figured he might as well be stiff as the way he was. Gaban could fine him a couple of hundred for giving hard liquor a play, and Messlin decided to get his money's worth. He sat there belting the stuff until the bartender, who was wise in these things, took the money out of his wallet, replaced it with a note to that effect, and gave a reliable cabbie two bucks to take him to the hotel.

Messlin was not a drinking man and he could not persuade the cat to crawl out of his mouth until noon. He looked terrible and he felt worse, and it was only by strenuous exercise of his will power that he got to the ball park no more than a half hour late. He pulled himself together a little when he found Gaban was late himself. Gaban, in fact, did not show up until it was almost time to go out for batting practice.

The Great Man was not quite himself, and it was a vast improvement. He went over the Kings' batting order quietly and methodically, telling his pitchers what he wanted them to throw, but he warmed up as he went along. At the end he was screaming and slobbering, and the Drakes broke down the door in their zeal to beat the Kings' brains out, in keeping with their manager's parting exhortation.

The mob was large and devoted in its allegiance to the home team, and the Drakes, already full of fire and fury, reacted splendidly. They put on a show for the people. They peppered the customers in the cheap seats with line drives, and even Messlin, shagging flies in the outfield, began to get the fever.

A swelling chorus of catcalls greeted the Kings as they struggled on the field, and the faithful told them, with virtuosity and vehemence, to take a flying jump for themselves. Messlin presently sensed something was cooking. The Kings were not tossing the ball around or taking prodigious swipes at the atmosphere with their bats. They were lined up in silence along the steps of their dugout, as though they were waiting for something to happen.

It happened when Gaban went up for his last round of batting practice. The Kings suddenly came to life. They began to yell at Gaban, and Messlin, in the outfield, could tell by the volume and intensity of their voices that this was an extra-special dose the jockeys were giving Gaban. And then Messlin's ear, trained to pick up only what he wanted to hear, began to distinguish the taunting words, and his knees sagged under him.

"Hey, Gabby, what time is it?" the Kings roared in unison. "Pardon me, sir! Have you got a watch?" they shrieked in a shrill falsetto. "Who stole the watch, Gabby? Is that number on your uniform from the program or the warden's office? Who stole the watch? Where are your stripes, Gabby? Who stole the watch?"

Gaban turned livid, then white. He tried to foul off the ball into the Kings' dugout, and when that failed, he let his bat fly when he swung at a pitch, and he scattered his tormenters on the bench. The Kings poured it to him and Gaban went crazy.

Someone had blown the whistle on the secret a handful of men had kept for twelve years. Messlin wondered wildly who it could be. And then another thought hit him between the eyes and staggered him.

He remembered the silly story he had told Harren the night before in the bar. Again he saw Gaban's contorted face and his own dangling watch turning back time in the archives of Gaban's memory.

Gaban had seen him laughing and showing the watch to Harren. Harren was a King coach. The Kings were jabbing him with the bones of an exhumed skeleton. Messlin knew that was how it had to add up for Gaban. Messlin wanted to drop into a hole in the ground and pull the lid over him.

The umpires tried to pipe down the rumpus when the game started, but the Kings had too much on Gaban to let him get away and, besides, the umpires never counted Gaban among their favorite people. Gaban had Hovey, his ace pitcher, dust off the King hitters, but they got up screaming vile abuse, and their spikes reflected the sunlight when they slid into second base.

Gaban, who had the guts of a burglar, challenged the Kings

to meet him under the stands after the game, then stepped up to the plate and knocked in two runs with a double. The Kings got a run back when Krindle, the league's leading hitter, teed off and belted one out of sight and mind. It was a ball game and Gaban was winning it with his double and the small miracles he was working in the field with the wonderful pair of hands which had been known to dip into teammates' pockets.

The eighth, with the meat of the Kings' batting order coming up, figured to be Hovey's tough inning and it was launched with the promise of a storm when the lead-off man singled. Krindle, who could hit a ball farther than it could be shot from a gun, strode toward the plate hefting three pieces of lumber. Hovey dusted his hands on the resin bag and nodded when Gaban raised both hands and brought them down with a sweeping motion. It was no secret; everybody in the ball park knew Krindle was going to be knocked down by the next pitch.

Hovey wound up and let the thing go. Krindle stood there motionless and Messlin, sitting on the bench, stopped breathing. He had seen it happen before and it was going to happen again. Krindle was frozen at the plate. He couldn't duck the pitch. He didn't.

Krindle swayed slightly, then collapsed in sections. The King bench erupted in a stream of players going for Gaban and Hovey, and the Drakes went out to meet them, but the umpires and the cops were on the alert and they broke it up. A doctor ran on the field, pushed back Krindle's eyelids and told them to call an ambulance. A concussion.

The field was cleared and King runners perched on first and second with none out. Hovey went back to the mound, but Hovey, who really wasn't a bad guy, was through. The beaning had unnerved him completely and his first two pitches sent Payne diving into the dirt.

Gaban called time, looked at the men in the bullpen, then wheeled and barked at the bench, "Messlin! Get on your horse! Come on! Yah, you! Messlin!"

The men on the bench were accustomed to Gaban's giddy hunches, but this one floored them. Messlin had worked the day before; he wasn't warmed up. A helluva situation to throw a guy into, cold.

But Messlin knew the score. He knew Gaban was putting him on the spot deliberately. If they lost the game, the rap would be on him. The customers had no truck with technical explanations.

Gaban took charge of the infield conference while Messlin was trying to get the hinges out of his arm.

"Two balls and no strikes on this bum," he snapped. "We can't afford to work on him. He wants to bunt. Lay it in there for him. The rest play it tight. Throw to first, I'll cover."

They squared away and Messlin bowled a good bunting ball, low and outside, down the alley. The guy laid it down nicely and Messlin bounced off the rubber fast to intercept the ball. He slapped it to the ground with his glove, wheeled and threw a strike to first.

It was a perfect throw, Gaban could have caught it in his teeth. But Gaban's teeth were buried in the dirt. Gaban had taken off in a desperate dive and the ball sailed over his head into right field. Before it was returned to Messlin, the Kings had two runs, the batter was on second base and the park was clamorous with despair.

For an agonized moment, Messlin thought Gaban had fallen in hustling to cover the bag. He actually felt sorry for the guy, lying there and beating the ground with his fists in a paroxysm of impotent rage. It was a tough break, a rotten way to blow a big ball game. But Gaban's act for the crowd was too exaggerated. He betrayed himself to Messlin, and the pitcher went limp when the shock of realization broke over him.

Gaban got up and tossed his glove in the air in a gesture of disgust. He waved to the bullpen and Messlin felt a wordless cry coming up from his belly. Gaban had been slow in covering the bag and now he was telling the people the fault wasn't his. He was telling them the throw had been wild, that Messlin had choked in the clutch and lost the game.

The people rose on their hind legs and booed Messlin out of the ball park. A lemon thrown from the upper tier bounced against his leg. Messlin went to the clubhouse, heaved a chair through the glass door of Gaban's office and went home. He heard the score over the radio and he saw the Kings win the next two games to sweep the series and go away in first place.

The Drakes were licked. There was a month to go, but the Drakes were cooked because the hypodermic of confidence Gaban had been giving them all season no longer was taking. The Kings had stripped them of their arrogance and Gaban never had fortified it with the essential core of pride.

They lost three more in a row before they came out of the swoon, and the Kings, smelling the World Series money, went on winning. Gaban raged at them, but his needles had been blunted by the Kings and they quit cold on him.

Only Gaban refused to give up. Gaban was thirty-five years old and he was playing on his nerve, but his nerve was such that he was playing the best second base in the business. Gaban picked them up and carried them on his back, and presently, when their slump scraped bottom, the Drakes got off and pulled their own weight.

Their wheels meshed again, and then the Kings started to come back to them. The hopped-up youth who had replaced Krindle in the King line-up developed a blind spot which was thoroughly exploited by the pitchers, and the teams wheeled into the stretch locked in a head-to-head struggle all over again.

They came down to the pay-off, a four-game series, with the Kings leading by two games and needing only an even break in their own park for the clincher. The Drakes had to win three out of four to keep alive, and Hovey won the first in the grand manner, with a shutout. Gaban wrapped up the second game with three base hits, but the manager of the Kings also knew the tricks of rabble-rousing and his ballplayers did not have tin ears. The Kings wore their hitting clothes in the third game and the pennant was on the line for either team to take.

Gaban had no choice for the big blowoff. He sent Hovey back to the trenches with one day of rest, and Hovey, a dead-game guy, frustrated the Kings for seven innings by sheer power of will. He had a two-run lead going into the eighth and he came out of it with only one. Nobody in the crowded bullpen had to tell Messlin to heat up for the ninth. Hovey was dying on his feet.

Hovey was brave and tenacious, but he died and Messlin went in there with score tied, one out and a man on second base. Messlin held the hopes of twenty-five men in his right-hand, and he lifted them by getting the batter on a ground ball to Gaban.

The runner moved to third, but Messlin felt good. He slapped the ball into his glove impatiently when the next batter, who could be the third out, walked back to the dugout.

The round little man who was the announcer waddled out of the King dugout and picked up the microphone of the p.a. system. A big, familiar figure got off the bench and stooped over the bat rack. Krindle, the best hitter in the league, was going to be the pinch hitter. Krindle found his stick, dug his holes at the plate and the crowd tore down the joint.

Gaban called for time and Payne went out to meet him on the mound.

"Down he goes," Gaban said tersely. "This guy hasn't seen a pitch since Hovey skulled him. Throw one at his head and he'll faint. He'll be a setup for that big jug outside. You got it? Throw it down his throat, but good, with the first one."

Messlin nodded and took his stretch. He drew a bead on Krindle's ear, his target. He went into his motion and then his arm was locked in a vise.

He saw a high-speed mental movie of Krindle freezing at the plate and falling to the ground. He saw Krindle, a good ball-player, ruined for a pennant, and Messlin knew he couldn't throw at the man's head. He had gone into his pitching motion and it was too late to change his grip on the ball for the big jug. He had to go through with the fast ball no thirty-three-year-old pitcher could throw past Krindle.

He let it go and Krindle whipped his bat. There was a one-two crack, like two pistol shots, and the second exploded against Messlin's knee. Messlin's reflexes were sharper, more urgent, than the pain which surged through him. He saw two white blurs, the man from third running home with the winning run and the ball rolling away.

Messlin started for the ball, but he had no legs to support him. He fell on his face. He crawled on his belly for the little white ball and he was reaching and grabbing the air when the other white blur roared across the plate. He still was reaching when two men helped him to his feet. Messlin didn't know the men, but their gray uniforms and brass buttons were vaguely familiar.

The park cops left him at the door of the clubhouse and

Messlin went into the sullen silence broken by Gaban's choked cursing. Messlin hobbled to the nearest bench and, although his leg was sending messages of misery to his brain, Messlin laughed. His laughter soared above Gaban's raving and they looked at him in shocked disbelief.

"You're through with this club!" Gaban shouted, and his voice cracked. "You gutless, double-crossing bum! What are you laughing at?"

"Froggy, I'm laughing at you," Messlin said, but he no longer was laughing. "Imagine a louse like you winning the pennant."

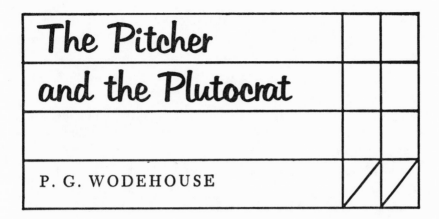

The Pitcher and the Plutocrat

P. G. WODEHOUSE

The main difficulty in writing a story is to convey to the reader clearly yet tersely the natures and dispositions of one's leading characters. Brevity, brevity—that is the cry. Perhaps, after all, the playbill style is the best. In this drama of love, baseball, frenzied finance, and tainted millions, then, the principals are as follows, in their order of entry:

Isabel Rackstraw (a peach).

Clarence Van Puyster (a Greek god).

Old Man Van Puyster (a proud old aristocrat).

Old Man Rackstraw (a tainted millionaire).

More about Clarence later. For the moment let him go as a Greek god. There were other sides, too, to Old Man Rackstraw's character; but for the moment let him go as a Tainted Millionaire. Not that it is satisfactory. It is too mild. He was *the* Tainted Millionaire. The Tainted Millions of other Tainted Millionaires were as attar of roses compared with the Tainted Millions of Tainted Millionaire Rackstraw. He preferred his millions tainted.

His attitude toward an untainted million was that of the sportsman toward the sitting bird. These things are purely a matter of taste. Some people like Limburger cheese.

It was at a charity bazaar that Isabel and Clarence first met. Isabel was presiding over the Billiken, Teddy Bear, and Fancy Goods stall. There she stood, that slim, radiant girl, buncoing the Younger Set out of its father's hard-earned with a smile that alone was nearly worth the money, when she observed, approaching, the handsomest man she had ever seen. It was—this is not one of those mystery stories—it was Clarence Van Puyster. Over the heads of the bevy of gilded youths who clustered round the stall their eyes met. A thrill ran through Isabel. She dropped her eyes. The next moment Clarence had bucked center; the Younger Set had shredded away like a mist; and he was leaning toward her, opening negotiations for the purchase of a yellow Teddy Bear at sixteen times its face value.

He returned at intervals during the afternoon. Over the second Teddy Bear they became friendly; over the third, intimate. He proposed as she was wrapping up the fourth Golliwog, and she gave him her heart and the parcel simultaneously. At six o'clock, carrying four Teddy Bears, seven photograph frames, five Golliwogs, and a Billiken, Clarence went home to tell the news to his father.

Clarence, when not at college, lived with his only surviving parent in an old red-brick house at the north end of Washington Square. The original Van Puyster had come over in Governor Stuyvesant's time in one of the then fashionable ninety-four-day boats. Those were the stirring days when they were giving away chunks of Manhattan Island in exchange for trading-stamps; for the bright brain which conceived the idea that the city might possibly at some remote date extend above Liberty Street had not come into existence. The original Van Puyster had acquired a square mile or so in the heart of things for ten dollars cash and a quarter interest in a peddler's outfit. The *Columbus Echo and Vespucci Intelligencer* gave him a column and a half under the heading: "Reckless Speculator. Prominent Citizen's Gamble in Land." On the proceeds of that deal his descendants had led quiet, peaceful lives ever since. If any of them ever did a day's work, the family records are silent on the point. Blood was their

long suit, not Energy. They were plain, homely folk, with a re-
fined distaste for wealth and vulgar hustle. They lived simply,
without envy of their richer fellow citizens, on their three hundred thousand dollars a year. They asked no more. It enabled
them to entertain on a modest scale; the boys could go to college,
the girls buy an occasional new frock. They were satisfied.

Having dressed for dinner, Clarence proceeded to the library, where he found his father slowly pacing the room. Silver-
haired old Vansuyther Van Puyster seemed wrapped in thought.
And this was unusual, for he was not given to thinking. To be
absolutely frank, the old man had just about enough brain to
make a jay-bird fly crooked, and no more.

"Ah, my boy," he said, looking up as Clarence entered. "Let
us go in to dinner. I have been awaiting you for some little time
now. I was about to inquire as to your whereabouts. Let us be
going."

Mr. Van Puyster always spoke like that. This was due to
Blood.

Until the servants had left them to their coffee and cigarettes,
the conversation was desultory and commonplace. But when the
door had closed, Mr. Van Puyster leaned forward.

"My boy," he said quietly, "we are ruined."

Clarence looked at him inquiringly.

"Ruined much?" he asked.

"Paupers," said his father. "I doubt if when all is over, I shall
have much more than a bare fifty or sixty thousand dollars a
year."

A lesser man would have betrayed agitation, but Clarence
was a Van Puyster. He lit a cigarette.

"Ah," he said calmly. "How's that?"

Mr. Van Puyster toyed with his coffee-spoon.

"I was induced to speculate—rashly, I fear—on the advice of
a man I chanced to meet at a public dinner, in the shares of a
certain mine. I did not thoroughly understand the matter, but my
acquaintance appeared to be well versed in such operations, so I
allowed him to—and, well, in fact, to cut a long story short, I am
ruined."

"Who was the fellow?"

"A man of the name of Rackstraw. Daniel Rackstraw."

"Daniel Rackstraw!"

Not even Clarence's training and traditions could prevent a slight start as he heard the name.

"Daniel Rackstraw," repeated his father. "A man, I fear, not entirely honest. In fact, it seems that he has made a very large fortune by similar transactions. Friends of mine, acquainted with these matters, tell me his behavior toward me amounted practically to theft. However, for myself I care little. We can rough it, we of the old Van Puyster stock. If there is but fifty thousand a year left, well—I must make it serve. It is for your sake that I am troubled, my poor boy. I shall be compelled to stop your allowance. I fear you will be obliged to adopt some profession." He hesitated for a moment. "In fact, work," he added.

Clarence drew at his cigarette.

"Work?" he echoed thoughtfully. "Well, of course, mind you, fellows *do* work. I met a man at the club only yesterday who knew a fellow who had met a man whose cousin worked."

He reflected for a while.

"I shall pitch," he said suddenly.

"Pitch, my boy?"

"Sign on as a professional ballplayer."

His father's fine old eyebrows rose a little.

"But, my boy, er—The—ah—family name. Our—shall I say *noblesse oblige?* Can a Van Puyster pitch and not be defiled?"

"I shall take a new name," said Clarence. "I will call myself Brown." He lit another cigarette. "I can get signed on in a minute. McGraw will jump at me."

This was no idle boast. Clarence had had a good college education, and was now an exceedingly fine pitcher. It was a pleasing sight to see him, poised on one foot in the attitude of a Salome dancer, with one eye on the batter, the other gazing coldly at the man who was trying to steal third, uncurl abruptly like the mainspring of a watch and sneak over a swift one. Under Clarence's guidance a ball could do practically everything except talk. It could fly like a shot from a gun, hesitate, take the first turning to the left, go up two blocks, take the second to the right, bound in mid-air like a jack rabbit, and end by dropping as the gentle dew from heaven upon the plate beneath. Briefly, there was class to Clarence. He was the goods.

Scarcely had he uttered these momentous words when the butler entered with the announcement that he was wanted by a lady at the telephone.

It was Isabel.

Isabel was disturbed.

"Oh, Clarence," she cried, "my precious angel wonder-child, I don't know how to begin."

"Begin just like that," said Clarence approvingly. "It's fine. You can't beat it."

"Clarence, a terrible thing has happened. I told Papa of our engagement, and he wouldn't hear of it. He was furious. He c-called you a b-b-b—"

"A what?"

"A p-p-p—"

"That's a new one on me," said Clarence, wondering.

"A b-beggarly p-pauper. I knew you weren't well off, but I thought you had two or three millions. I told him so. But he said no, your father had lost all his money."

"It is too true, dearest," said Clarence. "I am a pauper. But I'm going to work. Something tells me I shall be rather good at work. I am going to work with all the accumulated energy of generations of ancestors who have never done a hand's turn. And some day when I—"

"Good-by," said Isabel hastily, "I hear Papa coming."

The season during which Clarence Van Puyster pitched for the Giants is destined to live long in the memory of followers of baseball. Probably never in the history of the game has there been such persistent and widespread mortality among the more distant relatives of office-boys and junior clerks. Statisticians have estimated that if all the grandmothers alone who perished between the months of April and October that year could have been placed end to end they would have reached considerably further than Minneapolis. And it was Clarence who was responsible for this holocaust. Previous to the opening of the season skeptics had shaken their heads over the Giants' chances for the pennant. It had been assumed that as little new blood would be forthcoming as in other years, and that the fate of Our City would rest, as usual, on the shoulders of the white-haired veterans who were boys with Lafayette.

And then, like a meteor, Clarence Van Puyster had flashed upon the world of fans, bugs, chewing gum, and nuts (pea and human). In the opening game he had done horrid things to nine men from Boston; and from then onward, except for an occasional check, the Giants had never looked back.

Among the spectators who thronged the bleachers to watch Clarence perform there appeared week after week a little, gray, dried-up man, insignificant except for a certain happy choice of language in moments of emotion and an enthusiasm far surpassing that of the ordinary spectator. To the trained eye there is a subtle but well marked difference between the fan, the bug, and —the last phase—the nut of the baseball world. This man was an undoubted nut. It was writ clear across his brow.

Fate had made Daniel Rackstraw—for it was he—a Tainted Millionaire, but at heart he was a baseball spectator. He never missed a game. His library of baseball literature was the finest in the country. His baseball museum had but one equal, that of Mr. Jacob Dodson of Detroit. Between them the two had cornered, at enormous expense, the curio market of the game. It was Rackstraw who had secured the glove worn by Neal Ball, the Cleveland shortstop, when he made the only unassisted triple play in the history of the game; but it was Dodson who possessed the bat which Hans Wagner used as a boy. The two men were friends, as far as rival connoisseurs can be friends; and Mr. Dodson, when at leisure, would frequently pay a visit to Mr. Rackstraw's country home, where he would spend hours gazing wistfully at the Neal Ball glove buoyed up only by the thought of the Wagner bat at home.

Isabel saw little of Clarence during the summer months, except from a distance. She contented herself with clipping photographs of him from the evening papers. Each was a little more unlike him than the last, and this lent variety to the collection. Her father marked her new-born enthusiasm for the national game with approval. It had been secretly a great grief to the old buccaneer that his only child did not know the difference between a bunt and a swat, and, more, did not seem to care to know. He felt himself drawn closer to her. An understanding, as pleasant as it was new and strange, began to spring up between parent and child.

As for Clarence, how easy it would be to cut loose to practically an unlimited extent on the subject of his emotions at this time. One can figure him, after the game is over and the gay throng has dispersed, creeping moodily—but what's the use? Brevity. That is the cry. Brevity. Let us on.

The months sped by. August came and went, and September; and soon it was plain to even the casual follower of the game that, unless something untoward should happen, the Giants must secure the National League pennant. Those were delirious days for Daniel Rackstraw. Long before the beginning of October his voice had dwindled to a husky whisper. Deep lines appeared on his forehead; for it is an awful thing for a baseball nut to be compelled to root, in the very crisis of the season, purely by means of facial expression. In this time of affliction he found Isabel an ever-increasing comfort to him. Side by side they would sit at the Polo Grounds, and the old man's face would lose its drawn look, and light up, as her clear young soprano pealed out above the din, urging this player to slide for second, that to knock the stitching off the ball; or describing the umpire in no uncertain voice as a reincarnation of the late Mr. Jesse James.

Meanwhile, in the American League, Detroit had been heading the list with equal pertinacity; and in far-off Michigan Mr. Jacob Dodson's enthusiasm had been every whit as great as Mr. Rackstraw's in New York. It was universally admitted that when the championship series came to be played, there would certainly be something doing.

But, alas! How truly does Epictetus observe: "We know not what awaiteth us around the corner, and the hand that counteth its chickens ere they be hatched ofttimes graspeth but a lemon." The prophets who anticipated a struggle closer than any on record were destined to be proved false.

It was not that their judgment of form was at fault. By every law of averages the Giants and the Tigers should have been the two most evenly matched nines in the history of the game. In fielding there was nothing to choose between them. At hitting the Tigers held a slight superiority; but this was balanced by the inspired pitching of Clarence Van Puyster. Even the keenest supporters of either side were not confident. They argued at length, figuring out the odds with the aid of stubs of pencils and the backs of envelopes, but they were not confident. Out of all those frenzied millions two men alone had no doubts. Mr. Daniel Rackstraw said that he did not desire to be unfair to Detroit. He wished it to be clearly understood that in their own class the Tigers might quite possibly show to considerable advantage. In some rural league down South, for instance, he did not deny that they might sweep all before them. But when it came to competing with the Giants—here words failed Mr. Rackstraw, and he had to rush to Wall Street and collect several tainted millions before he could recover his composure.

Mr. Jacob Dodson, interviewed by the Detroit *Weekly Rooter*, stated that his decision, arrived at after a close and careful study of the work of both teams, was that the Giants had rather less chance in the forthcoming tourney than a lone gumdrop at an Eskimo tea-party. It was his carefully considered opinion that in a contest with the Avenue B Juniors the Giants might, with an effort, scrape home. But when it was a question of meeting a live team like Detroit—here Mr. Dodson, shrugging his shoulders despairingly, sank back in his chair, and watchful secretaries brought him round with oxygen.

Throughout the whole country nothing but the approaching series was discussed. Wherever civilization reigned, and in Jersey City, one question alone was on every lip: Who would win? Octogenarians mumbled it. Infants lisped it. Tired businessmen, trampled underfoot in the rush for the West Farms express, asked it of the ambulance attendants who carried them to hospital.

And then, one bright, clear morning, when all Nature seemed to smile, Clarence Van Puyster developed mumps.

New York was in a ferment. I could have wished to go into details, to describe in crisp, burning sentences the panic that swept like a tornado through a million homes. A little encouragement, the slightest softening of the editorial austerity, and the thing would have been done. But no. Brevity. That was the cry. Brevity. Let us on.

The Tigers met the Giants at the Polo Grounds, and for five days the sweat of agony trickled unceasingly down the corrugated foreheads of the patriots who sat on the bleachers. The men from Detroit, freed from the fear of Clarence, smiled grim smiles and proceeded to knock holes through the fence. It was in vain

that the home fielders skimmed like swallows around the diamond. They could not keep the score down. From start to finish
the Giants were a beaten side.

Broadway during that black week was a desert. Gloom
gripped Lobster Square. In distant Harlem red-eyed wives faced
silently scowling husbands at the evening meal, and the children
were sent early to bed. Newsboys called the extras in a whisper.

Few took the tragedy more nearly to heart than Daniel
Rackstraw. Each afternoon found him more deeply plunged in
sorrow. On the last day, leaving the ground with the air of a
father mourning over some prodigal son, he encountered Mr.
Jacob Dodson of Detroit.

Now, Mr. Dodson was perhaps the slightest bit shy on the
finer feelings. He should have respected the grief of a fallen foe.
He should have abstained from exulting. But he was in too ex-
hilarated a condition to be magnanimous. Sighting Mr. Rackstraw, he addressed himself joyously to the task of rubbing the
thing in. Mr. Rackstraw listened in silent anguish.

"If we had had Brown—" he said at length.

"That's what they all say," whooped Mr. Dodson. "Brown!
Who's Brown?"

"If we had had Brown, we should have—" He paused. An
idea had flashed upon his overwrought mind. "Dodson," he said,
"listen here. Wait till Brown is well again, and let us play this
thing off again for anything you like a side in my private park."

Mr. Dodson reflected.

"You're on," he said. "What side bet? A million? Two million? Three?"

Mr. Rackstraw shook his head scornfully.

"A million? Who wants a million? I'll put up my Neal Ball
glove against your Hans Wagner bat. The best of three games.
Does that go?"

"I should say it did," said Mr. Dodson joyfully. "I've been
wanting that glove for years. It's like finding it in one's Christmas
stocking."

"Very well," said Mr. Rackstraw. "Then let's get it fixed up."

Honestly, it is but a dog's life, that of the short-story writer.
I particularly wished at this point to introduce a description of
Mr. Rackstraw's country home and estate, featuring the private

ball park with its fringe of noble trees. It would have served a double purpose, not only charming the lover of nature, but acting as a fine stimulus to the youth of the country, showing them the sort of home they would be able to buy some day if they worked hard and saved their money. But no. You shall have three guesses as to what was the cry. You give it up? It was "Brevity! Brevity!" Let us on.

The two teams arrived at the Rackstraw house in time for lunch. Clarence, his features once more reduced to their customary finely chiseled proportions, alighted from the automobile with a swelling heart. He could see nothing of Isabel, but that did not disturb him. Letters had passed between the two. Clarence had warned her not to embrace him in public, as McGraw would not like it; and Isabel accordingly had arranged a tryst among the noble trees which fringed the ball park.

I will pass lightly over the meeting of the two lovers. I will not describe the dewy softness of their eyes, the catching of their breath, their murmured endearments. I could, mind you. It is at just such descriptions that I am particularly happy. But I have grown discouraged. My spirit is broken. It is enough to say that Clarence had reached a level of emotional eloquence rarely met with among pitchers of the National League, when Isabel broke from him with a startled exclamation, and vanished behind a tree; and, looking over his shoulder, Clarence observed Mr. Daniel Rackstraw moving toward him.

It was evident from the millionaire's demeanor that he had seen nothing. The look on his face was anxious, but not wrathful. He sighted Clarence, and hurried up to him.

"Say, Brown," he said, "I've been looking for you. I want a word with you."

"A thousand, if you wish it," said Clarence courteously.

"Now, see here," said Mr. Rackstraw. "I want to explain to you just what this ball game means to me. Don't run away with the idea I've had you fellows down to play an exhibition game just to keep me merry and bright. If the Giants win today, it means that I shall be able to hold up my head again and look my fellow man in the face, instead of crawling around on my stomach and feeling like thirty cents. Do you get that?"

"I am hep," replied Clarence with simple dignity.

"And not only that," went on the millionaire. "There's more to it. I have put up my Neal Ball glove against Mr. Dodson's Wagner bat as a side bet. You understand what that means? It means that either you win or my life is soured for keeps. See?"

"I have got you," said Clarence.

"Good. Then what I wanted to say was this. Today is your day for pitching as you've never pitched before. Everything depends on whether you make good or not. With you pitching like mother used to make it, the Giants are some nine. Otherwise they are Nature's citrons. It's one thing or the other. It's all up to you. Win, and there's twenty thousand dollars waiting for you above what you share with the others."

Clarence waved his hand deprecatingly.

"Mr. Rackstraw," he said, "keep your dough. I care nothing for money."

"You don't?" cried the millionaire. "Then you ought to exhibit yourself in a dime museum."

"All I ask of you," proceeded Clarence, "is your consent to my engagement to your daughter."

Mr. Rackstraw looked sharply at him.

"Repeat that," he said. "I don't think I quite got it."

"All I ask is your consent to my engagement to your daughter."

"Young man," said Mr. Rackstraw, not without a touch of admiration, "you have gall."

"My friends have sometimes said so," said Clarence.

"And I admire gall. But there is a limit. That limit you have passed so far that you'd need to look for it with a telescope."

"You refuse your consent."

"I never said you weren't a clever guesser."

"Why?"

Mr. Rackstraw laughed. One of those nasty, sharp, metallic laughs that hit you like a bullet.

"How would you support my daughter?"

"I was thinking that you would help to some extent."

"You were, were you?"

"I was."

"Oh?"

Mr. Rackstraw emitted another of those laughs.

"Well," he said, "it's off. You can take that as coming from an authoritative source. No wedding bells for you."

Clarence drew himself up, fire flashing from his eyes and a bitter smile curving his expressive lips.

"And no Wagner bat for you!" he cried.

Mr. Rackstraw started as if some strong hand had plunged an auger into him.

"What!" he shouted.

Clarence shrugged his superbly modeled shoulders in silence.

"Say," said Mr. Rackstraw, "you wouldn't let a little private difference like that influence you any in a really important thing like this ball game, would you?"

"I would."

"You would hold up the father of the girl you love?"

"Every time."

"Her white-haired old father?"

"The color of his hair would not affect me."

"Nothing would move you?"

"Nothing."

"Then, by George, you're just the son-in-law I want. You shall marry Isabel; and I'll take you into partnership this very day. I've been looking for a good, husky bandit like you for years. You make Dick Turpin look like a preliminary three-round bout. My boy, we'll be the greatest team, you and I, that ever hit Wall Street."

"Papa!" cried Isabel, bounding happily from behind her tree.

Mr. Rackstraw joined their hands, deeply moved, and spoke in low, vibrant tones:

"Play ball!"

Little remains to be said, but I am going to say it, if it snows. I am at my best in these tender scenes of idyllic domesticity.

Four years have passed. Once more we are in the Rackstraw home. A lady is coming down the stairs, leading by the hand her little son. It is Isabel. The years have dealt lightly with her. She is still the same stately, beautiful creature whom I would have described in detail long ago if I had been given half a chance. At the foot of the stairs the child stops and points at a small, wooden object in a glass case.

"Wah?" he says.

"That?" says Isabel. "That is the bat Mr. Wagner used to use when he was a little boy."

She looks at a door on the left of the hall, and puts a finger to her lip.

"Hush!" she says. "We must be quiet. Daddy and Grandpa are busy in there cornering wheat."

And softly mother and child go out into the sunlit garden.

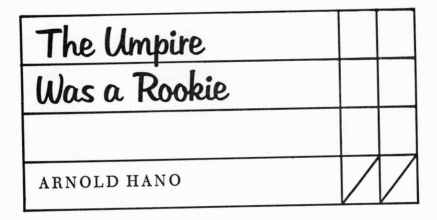

The Umpire Was a Rookie

ARNOLD HANO

His name was Bill Needy, a man of up-and-down lines and high shoulders, not broad and tapering like the ballplayers who had trudged up the same iron stairway. So the fans clustered below did not ask him for autographs, even though he carried the same sort of black bag in his right hand.

He heard a hoarse voice say, "Must be a new trainer or some-thin'," and then he was out of the chilly mid-April sunshine, moving quickly through the white-tile corridor to the door marked Umpires' Dressing Room.

The three other men were already in their dark uniforms, and their eyes swung to him as he threw his bag onto a long wooden bench and began swiftly to undress.

The biggest of the three, a red-faced, white-haired man with a jaw that unhinged like a swinging lantern, put down the ball-and-strike indicator he was playing with, and walked over.

Needy knew him, of course. He was McQuinn, the senior umpire in the league. McQuinn, whom he had watched on his living-room screen during last year's World Series, a man with a bellowing voice and a quietly domineering manner.

"You Needy?" McQuinn said, and Needy was amused at how soft-spoken McQuinn really was, off the diamond.

Needy stood up. He was shirtless now, white-skinned compared with the others, thin and bony-chested. He sensed the difference between himself and them, and he hoped that it went no further than the tans they had acquired during spring training down South.

"Yes," he said, "I'm Needy." He was annoyed at the squeak in his voice. "You're Mr. McQuinn."

McQuinn laughed, and Needy heard the bellow, "You hear that? Mr. McQuinn. I hope you two bums learn something from that."

The tallest one, a turkey-necked, red-headed man, walked over, and even in those three steps, Needy saw the boy from the plow who had become one of the finest pitchers the league had seen in the last quarter century. He drawled, "I'm Carlson," and Needy wanted to say, "Yes, I've seen you pitch." Carlson had been with the Cubs for fourteen years until his fast ball deserted him. Five years ago he had returned to the major leagues as an umpire.

But Needy couldn't say that, because he had never seen Carlson pitch. He had never, in fact, been inside a major-league park before this day.

He nodded and took the tall man's hand and felt all the pressure that was at the same time warm and crushing.

The third man, short and thick through the waist, bowlegged and bald, waddled over to Needy. "If you mister me," he said, "I'll fall down dead. All I ever hear is insults. I'm Jankowicz."

"Needy," he said again, clearing his throat, and he stood there, wondering whether he would ever match up to them or even come close.

They eyed him with a frank curiosity. He was the new man in the league, called up just yesterday to replace Jake Mandell, the umpire who had broken his leg getting off a plane at Idlewild, flying in from an exhibition in Cleveland. The doctors said Mandell would be staring up at the ceiling for nearly two months.

Wiley, the league president, had wired the three top minor-league heads for their recommendations. They all had different choices, but Needy's league president had called the commissioner of all baseball on his private phone and talked for a half hour. The commissioner spoke to Wiley. Wiley picked Needy.

So the three other umpires stood a few yards off and watched Needy. And Needy felt the perspiration trickle down his ribs.

McQuinn broke the silence finally. He said, "I suppose you've boned up on the ground rules?"

Needy nodded. "Your league has pretty much the same rules we had back in the Association. That makes it easier."

McQuinn nodded his great head. "It does," he said, "but this is a tough park."

Needy frowned. He had shown his new league badge to the park attendant earlier that day and walked all over Robin Field, studying the angles and the shadows, the high fence in right field where balls sometimes stuck in the chicken wire, the sharp corner in left where the play got out of sight unless the third-base umpire was swift in getting back. Needy was not to umpire at third, and he guessed that was why. He was to be at second base, where the plays were often tough and dusty and bruising, but where they fell into a pattern: double play, hit-and-run, steal, force-out, pick-off.

In a way, Needy was glad he was going to be at second. It might force a quick showdown. Tad Roush was the Robin manager. He also was the Robin shortstop. Needy knew Roush firsthand. The two had tangled in the Association five years ago.

Then Carlson broke in. "Not the playing field, son," he said, and Needy smiled thinly. They must have been within five years of the same age. "He means the park. The fans."

And Needy understood. The fans were different here, so Needy had heard, men and women who had become a legend, just as their borough on the wrong side of the muddy river had become a legend. They were fans who came early and started howling long before the first pitch—and Needy could hear them even now through the thick white-tile walls—fifty-two thousand of them, the most vociferous, partisan fans in the world.

Jankowicz said, "They're tough out here, all right." He shook his head and grinned. "I've had my share of beer in my day, but I hate to have it thrown at me."

"With soft tomatoes as a side dish," McQuinn added.

"I've been through it," Needy said quietly.

"Good," McQuinn said. "When you've been through it, you either go one way or the other. You must have gone the right way, boy, or you wouldn't be here today. They don't take chickens or lilies in this league. Now, the other league ——" He snorted in contempt.

The other two laughed. Needy knew how each big league thought it was the only league. But Needy wasn't laughing. McQuinn didn't know the real trouble. Needy had seen fans litter the field with vile epithets and pulpy fruit. It had never bothered him much. The real trouble was himself and Roush. McQuinn didn't know about that. Needy doubted that anybody knew about it or remembered. Maybe Roush hadn't remembered. After all, it was an unimportant game, five years back, and Roush had gone a long way since then.

A bell rang softly in the dressing room and the three other men seemed to stiffen a bit, their smiles fading. "Come on," McQuinn said, taking Needy's arm; "let's go meet them." And the four umpires moved swiftly through the door and onto the gravel path, through the exit door next to the Robins' dugout.

They stepped to the plate while the fans called down their stereotyped insults, and Needy grinned. They weren't so tough. And then a raucous voice from the stands yelled, "All right, McQuinn, don't call 'em like you did when the Phils were in last time, you blind bum!" And a snicker filtered from the stands.

Needy stiffened. Lord, he thought, they remembered from one season to the next. They were riding McQuinn for a call he'd made no more recently than last September, at least seven months ago.

Needy stood at the plate, watching the opposing pitchers wheel in their last practice throws, while the ground crew motored its rollers over the moist, sweet-smelling infield dirt, and from the stands came a rising murmur as the new season rushed up.

And Roush came out of the Robin dugout, a prancing man with toed-in steps, head down, a sheet of paper in his hand. The fans saw him and began to roar, and Roush waved his free hand without looking up. From the Titan dugout came Chub Fowler, the line-up in his hand, too, and Needy heard Roush shoot a word at Fowler. The Titan manager's face flushed hot and angry. Roush, Needy knew then, hadn't changed.

Needy moved away from the cluster at the plate, so that Roush would have to see him. He wanted that part over quickly. But Roush, head down, pushed by as though he knew he had the center of the stage. He was a showboat, Needy knew, and then, in his grudging heart, he added, *but a hell of a ballplayer.*

Roush stopped and nodded curtly to McQuinn and Carlson and Jankowicz. "Good afternoon, you blind bats," he said softly. Then he turned to Needy. He put his hands on his hips and said, "Hello, choke-up."

Needy felt his throat tighten and he knew the flush was rising to his temples.

McQuinn pushed past Jankowicz, coming chest to chest with Roush. "Cut it," he said quietly, but there was a bristling quality to his voice. "Cut it, I say. I won't stand for your language."

Roush didn't budge a half inch. His voice was as low as McQuinn's, but rasping and hard. "Listen," he said, "when you bums yell play ball, I'll watch my tongue. But right now you're just guests in this house, and my boss owns this house. Until that first pitch comes in, this game is in the hands of the club owners. Not you." He whirled on Needy again, and the venom lay in his throat. "Choke-up Needy, the yellowest umpire ever to call 'em wrong. Too chicken to call 'em as he sees 'em." Then he spun away and stalked off.

McQuinn roared this time. "Roush! Come here." And Roush turned, wide-eyed. "The ground rules," McQuinn said.

Roush waved his hands. "Whatever you say, Mac. We won't need any rules today." And he minced to the dugout.

McQuinn turned to Chub Fowler. He said, "I'm sorry, Chub. The smiling little skipper is off to his usual start."

Fowler growled and handed McQuinn his line-up. "Maybe we'll rub some of it off," he said, and he ambled to the visiting dugout.

Needy watched Fowler, and then he looked at McQuinn, and he froze. The big umpire was staring at him with icy blue eyes. "You're a major-league umpire, Needy," he said. "Act like one."

Needy nodded and tried to say something, but his voice failed him, and then McQuinn waved the three of them to their bases before he bent to the plate, whisk broom in his gnarled hand.

The field was empty except for the four umpires, and then the Robins poured from the dugout, Roush leading them, and the fifty-two thousand fans got up and roared. They stayed standing as the PA system crackled and the announcer said, "Ladies and gentlemen, our national anthem."

But Needy barely heard it. He turned to center field to watch the flag go up into the blue sky, and he remembered. . . .

It hadn't been an important game, though Needy knew now how important it really was. And, more than that, how important they all are, the 10–2 games between a first-place team and a cellar team, and a 2–1 affair between two clubs battling for the lead. To an umpire, they're all the same. Needy knew it now.

It was the end of September, and Roush's club had already clinched the Association flag. They were playing at home, three days before the season would end, most of the regulars resting, but Roush still in there. Roush's team was losing 6–1, though Roush had started one double play and pivoted like a flying ghost on two others, and now, in the bottom of the ninth, with two out, he had hit the ball to the center-field wall for a triple.

It was a hot day, Needy remembered, fearfully hot, and it had been a hot month, a hot summer. Needy was behind the plate, weighted down with mask and protector. Somebody had once said an umpire takes hell, but that the hours couldn't be beat. That was before night ball, Needy thought, and hot days like this.

So he leaned in behind the catcher, the ball-and-strike indicator telling him it was two out, one out away from the dressing room and a quick beer, and the pitcher missed twice with curve balls, as Roush pranced down the line from third base.

Nobody was watching very closely, most of the fans having gone home in the seventh inning when Roush's pitcher was hammered for four runs. Not that there had been many to begin with. Maybe twelve hundred, Needy thought. No more than five hundred still remained.

So, when Roush started down the line and seemed to stumble, Needy hoped he'd come in all the way, for he'd surely be out, and the game would be over. The pitcher hadn't started his motion, but Roush had had a bad start. Then the batter suddenly put his hand to his eyes and stepped out of the box. Four or five times that day, swirling spirals of dust had attacked home plate, and Needy had been forced to call "Time," each time a batter stepped out.

But somehow, as his hand went up and he started to say "Time," he saw Roush continue down the line, and he saw the pitcher quickly throw to the plate. The catcher took the toss, blocked off Roush and put the tag on the runner.

There was a feeble cheer from the stands, and five hundred people slowly began to walk across the field to the exit gates. Roush got up and looked at Needy. He jabbed the edge of his hand against his own throat. "You choke-up rat," he said, "why didn't you call time?"

Needy hadn't said anything, but he knew Roush was right. He had quit on his assignment. It wasn't important whether Roush stole home or not; it was only important that Needy call it as he saw it. And he had seen the batter step out before the pitcher went into action toward the plate. He knew it and Roush knew it, and maybe the batter knew it, but he hadn't seemed to care.

Roush cared. It was baseball, and baseball was life and blood to him. Needy knew he, too, should have cared. He should have called time even then, with the five hundred fans scattered all over the diamond, paper falling to the grass, the bags being ripped up by the ground-keepers. He should have waved his hands and roared until he had controlled them, and then resumed play.

But he hadn't. He had just walked past Roush, trying to reason that it hadn't mattered, that the ball game wouldn't have changed, that the team standings wouldn't have changed. He tried to forget it. . . .

And standing here at second base in Robin Field, the flag flapping against the blue sky, he knew he had never forgotten it.

Nor had Roush. The ball came spinning out from behind the plate, and Roush had it, tossing it to his second baseman, and then turning to Needy.

"Choke-up," he whispered to the umpire. "Chicken minor-leaguer."

Needy knew he didn't have to take it. The game was still not in the umpires' hands, but he was a human being being abused. There wasn't much he could do. But he could answer Roush, fire a hot word at the shortstop to let him know he was alive and fighting back.

Instead he moved behind the bag and slightly to the left of second base, as the first Titan moved in and McQuinn bellowed, "Play ball!" And just as quickly, Roush seemed to forget all about Needy, close to the bag. He bent slightly, his body swaying, his arms hanging, knees slightly hinged, and Needy watched his mouth move and a flow of words waft to the pitcher's mound. The game began.

Needy had heard it said that a major-league baseball game is unlike any minor-league game, no matter the quality of play. Now he believed it. A cloak hung over the field, a shimmering wave of electricity that coursed through the action, crackled in the air with every pitch, rose and fell with hits and outs. And behind the cloak was the booming that whooshed from the stands, like a heavy hand or the ocean rolling in. It was lightning and thunder, Needy thought, the sizzling atmosphere on the diamond and the roaring from the stands.

The Titans scored first. In the fourth inning, the Titan batter, a man named Jewell who batted left-handed and choked up on his stick three inches, pulled a line drive down the first-base line past Rogers, the Robin first baseman, and into the corner where the Robin bull-pen crew sat beneath a sun canopy.

The Robin right fielder raced to the line and into foul territory, took the rolling ball with his gloved hand, whirled and threw into second base. It was a fine throw, but Jewell hooked to the center of the diamond and grabbed off the inside edge of the bag. Needy bent to the play, head through the low cloud of dust, and he spread-eagled his hands.

Instantly Roush was at him, feet stamping, voice raised in indignant clamor, but Needy stood firm and when Roush wouldn't quit, he turned his back and walked away. It was not a serious beef, Needy knew, because Roush knew as well as he that Jewell had beaten the throw. So Roush growled and kicked dirt and went back to his position, and Needy grinned. Roush had played it four-square, fighting a close call against his team, but watching his tongue. Maybe, Needy thought, the Robin manager was going to let bygones be bygones.

The next hitter was Thomas, another left-hander, and though the Robin pitcher threw on the outside, Thomas still dragged his bunt down the first-base line, moving Jewell to third.

And Mayo, the Titans' No. 4 hitter, the league's home-run king and stolen-base leader, hit to the edge of the center-field wall, where Earl Rider had just enough room to make the catch. Jewell sauntered home and the Titans led 1-0.

It stayed that way into the seventh, a 1-0 game that was taking longer to play than any 1-0 game Needy had ever seen. The pitchers violated the twenty-second rule on nearly every pitch, and Needy knew how foolish the rule was.

When Mayo came up, there was always a short conference, and even after it ended, the Robin pitcher would lean in for a full thirty seconds, his eyes boring a path to the plate, trying to find that groove past Mayo's lunging bat. And Earl Rider had the Titan pitcher in the same grip, the long look, the signals shaken off again and again, catcher Festrun calling time and insisting on a pitch while the fans muttered and buzzed and called down their timeless hue.

In the seventh, Roush came up with one out. He slashed two bats at the grass, talking as he minced forward, and then he threw one behind him, and dug himself in.

The Titan pitcher threw, a quick white blur, and Roush was flat on his back. The mutter from the stands grew thick and ugly. But Roush was up, wiping himself off, snarling an obscenity that McQuinn behind the plate pretended he didn't hear. And Roush drilled the next pitch past the Titan pitcher's left ear and into center field.

At first base, Roush pointed his finger at the pitcher, and the Titan came down from the mound two steps to hurl a word at the Robin manager. McQuinn then hustled forward, waving his arms. And time dragged, while the sun faded, dipping to the lip of the stands over first base, lengthening the shadows.

Roush led off from first and taunted the pitcher with three quick steps down the line, drew a throw, and then started his lead again. On the second pitch, he went.

Festrun came out of his crouch with the ball in his clenched fist and he threw, true and swiftly, to the second baseman covering the bag. Needy drifted over, eyes searching, and Roush came in, one leg high. The tag was made and Needy started to go up with his right hand, but then the ball came squirting out of the glove, rolling toward the shortstop. Needy broke off his call and dropped his hands down low, yelling, "Safe, safe!"

The second baseman rolled to his feet and called "Time!" and held up his dripping red wrist.

The Titan doctor came out and cleaned the dirt from the spike wound, and then started to lead the infielder away. But the Titan insisted he could play, and the doctor shrugged, slapped on a piece of plaster and walked away, shaking his head.

Then the second baseman turned to Needy and said, "He kicked me, you know."

Needy nodded. "I guess he did, son. Nothing I can do about it. Kick him back next time," and Roush laughed out loud.

It was part of the game Needy didn't like, but there was nothing anybody ever did to remedy it. It was the way the game was played. There were rules about interference and roughness, but the line could seldom be drawn. So the umpire ignored the contact and watched the bases.

Now Roush led away, and the Titan pitcher threw four times to big Rogers, wasting one, and Rogers swung and missed three times.

The Titan pitcher then took off his glove and wiped his hand with a towel that he directed from the dugout, when Earl Rider took his bent-over stance, waving a big brown bat. And on the first pitch, Needy heard the pitcher groan with the delivery. It was what Casey Stengel liked to call a dead fish, a fast ball, down the pipe, waist high, thrown to Rider's strength.

The ball disappeared over the right-field wall, clearing it by about forty feet, and the Robins led, 2–1.

They stayed that way through the eighth, and Needy looked at his watch and saw that two and a half hours had gone by as they came into the ninth. The public-address announcer made his usual statement about fans' not being allowed on the playing field until all players had reached the dugouts, and the fans made a derisive sound.

It was then Needy realized that the game was nearly over,

that Roush was not riding him any more than he was the other umpires. Needy felt suddenly that the problem had somehow resolved itself. He gave a short little laugh, and Roush, twelve feet away, looked at him cold-eyed, his mouth mocking and twisted. Needy felt the afternoon chill, and he knew he was wrong. It wasn't resolved. It wouldn't be until he and Roush had tangled again.

The first man in the ninth was a pinch hitter for the Titan pitcher, a red-faced man with a plug of tobacco in his cheek and the grinning self-confidence of a man who believed no pitcher on earth could get him out. He was Joads, who couldn't catch fly balls and couldn't throw, so he didn't play regularly, but who hit close to .350 in his two hundred at bats each season.

The Robin pitcher tried to curve Joads, but the ball hung on the inside corner, and Joads stroked it off the wall, where the right fielder made a swift recovery, and Joads lumbered into first, the grin still splitting his wide red face. Then he lumbered off again, for a pinch runner, and Roush spoke sharply with his pitcher.

Finally Roush called his catcher, a man named Camps, to the hill and they talked until McQuinn pushed his way to the mound.

Needy heard the big umpire say, "What's it to be, Roush? You sticking with him or you calling in the reliefer?"

Roush said, "I dunno. That's a real tough one."

McQuinn flushed and towered over Roush. "Don't con me," he said. "Make up your mind. I won't stand for any stalling."

Roush said, "Who's stalling? I'm trying to think. Get your beef off me, and I'll be able to figure it out."

McQuinn said quietly, "I'll give you fifteen seconds, Roush."

Roush stared at the sky and squinted, and Needy could see the Robin manager's lips moving. Needy tried to hide his grin. Roush was actually counting off the seconds.

Then he stopped and said, "I got it. It's the reliefer." He waved to the bull pen with his right hand, and the right-handed knuckleball thrower strolled in, carrying his jacket, and began to warm up.

Needy watched from behind second, marveling that Camps could catch such a thing as the reliefer threw. Every one was a knuckler, writhing in mid-air like a drunken butterfly. Then

McQuinn held up his hand for the game to pick up where it had stopped, a Titan on first, nobody out, the ninth inning, and the Robins leading, 2–1.

The knuckler got Lark, the Titan lead-off hitter, to go for a chest-high floater, and the Titan hit it straight up in the air. The ball disappeared in Camps' mitt, and there was one out.

But Jewell, who hadn't been stopped all afternoon, singled to right field and the Titan runner fled past Needy into third.

The thunder was two-edged now, the Titan fans who had braved the river and crossed into enemy territory, and the Robins, upset and grumbling as the lead teetered.

Roush raised his hands and yelled "Time!" and turned to the bull pen. He wanted a left-hander to pitch to Thomas.

The sun fell over the edge of the stands, and the field lay in shadow, but lightning still hovered over the players' heads. Needy felt himself waiting with the fans now, impartial as ever concerning the game's outcome, yet intensely interested.

He watched the left-hander, a stocky hurky-jerky man named Lombardo, pitch curve balls to Thomas, but they were breaking too much and too soon, and on six pitches the bases were loaded.

Again Roush stopped the game, and a third time he signaled to the bull pen. The hitter was Mayo, the big, fleet Titan who could do everything so well. And when time was in again, Needy saw that Roush had his team playing halfway. Roush wanted to cut off the tying run at the plate, but he wasn't all the way in. The double play could still be made, though Needy knew that Mayo was as fast a man getting down the line as anybody in baseball.

The new pitcher eyed the bases, Thomas coming off first. The other Titan runners drifted away, and Roush kept darting toward second, feinting Jewell back to the bag. Roush's mouth was still moving, the words flowing to the mound, and Needy felt them hang like drones in the air.

"Come on, boy," Roush was saying. "Come on boy; nobody hits." Then the reliefer took a deep breath and threw hard to Mayo.

It was a fast ball, Needy thought, on the inside, and Mayo started to lunge. The pitch broke. It had not been a fast ball at all, but a curve, thrown hard and loose, fooling the big Titan.

But Mayo somehow got a piece of it, hitting it on a high bounce past the mound, headed for the hole between second base and Roush. Needy moved in toward the bag from behind, seeing Thomas hurtling down the line, Mayo bulleting his way toward first and Roush gliding over, surefooted, a swift ghost on the brown dirt.

The thought crossed Needy's mind that Thomas would be an easy force, once Roush came up with the ball, but the winging Mayo would be a different story. Then Needy banished the thought; his problem lay at second, not first.

Roush reached to his left with his gloved hand while on the dead run eight feet from second base, and then he plucked the ball out with his right hand, leveled his arm back and threw like a rifle to first, a split second before his foot hit second base, kicking dust high into the air.

It was then that Needy's ankle buckled under him and he fell, sprawling heavily while the picture of Roush making his throw before he touched second became frozen-fixed in his mind. Needy never knew that big Rogers, at first, stretched into the diamond while Mayo leaped for the bag. Nor did Needy hear the ball spank into the first baseman's glove, umpire Carlson booming, "He's out!" All Needy heard was the thunder pounding out from the stands as he rolled to his feet to make his call.

But nobody was watching him, the players fleeing to the dugouts, and fifty-two thousand people starting to pour onto the field. Even Roush was gone. Only Thomas was near, sitting on second base, staring up at Needy, openmouthed.

For Needy stood stock-still, arms spread-eagled, yelling, "Safe, safe, safe!" He knew why Thomas couldn't believe the call. Roush had him beaten by five full steps. But Roush had taken the chance that Needy wouldn't have the guts to make the insane call he was now making. Roush had thrown the ball before his foot touched second, and the force play had never been made.

Needy knew it, and he knew why it had happened. He'd have bet his life on it. Roush had seen what he had seen. The shortstop knew that Mayo, moving like a whippet down the first-base line, would beat the throw unless he got rid of the ball right away. The tying run was thundering homeward.

It was McQuinn who finally noticed Needy, still standing

at second, arms held out and low, the time-honored sign of a man being called safe.

The big ump charged to second base and said, "What's the matter, man? Are you crazy?"

Needy looked at his chief. The park cops were in a tight cordon at the foul lines, keeping the fans from trampling the young infield grass, but they couldn't keep them from roaming all over the outfield. It was a swirling, still roaring throng, most of them happy, all of them knowing they had seen a fine game, and glad to be on their way home.

"I'm sorry, Mac, but the man is safe."

McQuinn looked at him peculiarly and said, "Roush touched the bag. I saw the dust rise up."

Needy shook his head stubbornly. He thought, *What am I getting into?* The field was strewn with debris. It was like that day five years ago, except a thousand times worse. He said, "He touched the bag after he got rid of the ball. Thomas is safe."

McQuinn started to rub his jaw and then he began to grin, and finally he started to laugh out loud, a bellowing laugh that brought tears to his eyes. "I swear," he said, "if you weren't standing here, I wouldn't believe it. Now what do we do?"

Needy said, "We get the game going again."

McQuinn turned and yelled, "Carl, Janko, come here! This crazy pup's starting a rhubarb and we'll have to back him up!" The two umpires raced to second and scratched their heads as McQuinn filled them in.

Thomas suddenly got up from his perch on second base and said, "Excuse me, but if I'm safe, is time still in?" He was ready to keep running.

McQuinn roared, "Hell, no! I call time right now!"

Thomas began to yell to the near-empty Titan dugout. "Hey, I'm safe, I'm safe!"

Needy said, "And your club is leading, three-two."

McQuinn howled, "Now, what the devil does that mean?"

Carlson grinned. "I get him, chief. He means the men on second and third. They both scored. As a matter of fact," he said, winking at McQuinn, "I noticed Jewell touch home plate in case you didn't. The lad's right. The Titans are ahead, three-two."

"And probably piling out of their uniforms this minute," Jankowicz said. "What happens now?"

Needy said, "You boys wouldn't want me to change my decision, would you? Because," he said, "I won't, you know."

A handful of Titans began to drift onto the field. The word began to spread through the filing throng and Needy heard the first ominous mutter.

Somebody said, "Whaddya mean, the game's not over? Sure it is."

"No," somebody else said, fifteen feet from second. "That new jerk of an umpire says Thomas ain't out. They ought to mobilize the bum."

McQuinn turned to Needy. "All right, bum, take it from here."

Needy said, "It's very simple. The rules don't cover it, but you're in charge. Make an announcement over the PA that the game isn't over, that you'll give everybody—fans and players— a half hour to get back in their seats and to their positions, and that the game will continue."

Carlson said, "We could have 'em play it off some other time."

Jankowicz grinned. "No," he said. "That's too easy. I like the lad's idea. . . . Go on, Mac, make the announcement."

"Not me," McQuinn said. "Don't pass the buck to me. Let the lad do it."

Jankowicz said, "Go to it, boy. I must say you've got guts. Are they going to love you here!"

Needy shook his head. He knew it didn't matter. Love him or hate him, it didn't matter. Respect him. That was all. He started to walk to the Robin dugout to ask where the PA mike was. It would have been very easy to make the out call, he knew. But he had never even thought of it.

And thirty minutes later, before a crowd gone blood-mad as it heaped abuse on Needy, Tad Roush led his ball club back onto the field.

The shortstop took his post, raised two fingers in the air and called, "Two out, men, two out! We'll get it back!"

Then Roush turned, before his pitcher threw, and said to Needy, "Welcome to the big league, you blind bat." He was grinning. Needy ignored him, to watch the ball game.

The Pitcher

ANDRE DUBUS

They cheered and clapped when he and Lucky Ferris came out of the dugout, and when the cheering and clapping settled to sporadic shouts he had already stopped hearing it, because he was feeling the pitches in his right arm and watching them the way he always did in the first few minutes of his warm-up. Some nights the fastball was fat or the curve hung or the ball stayed up around Lucky's head where even the hitters in this Class C league would hit it hard. It was a mystery that frightened him. He threw the first hard one and watched it streak and rise into Lucky's mitt; and the next one; and the next one; then he wasn't watching the ball anymore, as though it had the power to betray him. He wasn't watching anything except Lucky's target, hardly conscious of that either, or of anything else but the rhythm of his high-kicking windup, and the ball not thrown but released out of all his motion; and now he felt himself approaching that moment which he could not achieve alone: a moment that each time was granted to him. Then it came: the ball was part of him, as if his arm stretched sixty feet six inches to Lucky's mitt and slammed the ball into leather and sponge and Lucky's hand. Or he was part of the ball.

Now all he had to do for the rest of the night was concentrate on prolonging that moment. He had trained himself to do that, and while people talked about his speed and curve and change of pace and control, he knew that without his concentration they would be only separate and useless parts; and instead of nineteen and five on the year with an earned run average of two point one five and two hundred and six strikeouts, going for his twentieth win on the last day of the season, his first year in professional ball, three months short of his twentieth birthday, he'd be five and nineteen and on his way home to nothing. He was going for the pennant too, one-half game behind the New Iberia Pelicans who had come to town four nights ago with a game and a half lead, and the Bulls beat them Friday and Saturday, lost Sunday, so that now on Monday in this small Louisiana town, Billy's name was on the front page of the local paper alongside the news of the war that had started in Korea a little over a month ago. He was ready. He caught Lucky's throw, nodded to him, and walked with head down toward the dugout and the cheers growing louder behind it, looking down at the bright grass, holding the ball loosely in his hand.

He spoke to no one. He went to the far end of the dugout that they left empty for him when he was pitching. He was too young to ask for that, but he was good enough to get it without asking; they gave it to him early in the year, when they saw he needed it, this young pitcher Billy Wells who talked and joked and yelled at the field and the other dugout for nine innings of the three nights he didn't pitch, but on his pitching night sat quietly, looking neither relaxed nor tense, and only spoke when politeness required it. Always he was polite. Soon they made a space for him on the bench, where he sat now knowing he would be all right. He did not think about it, for he knew as the insomniac does that to give it words summons it up to dance; he knew that the pain he had brought with him to the park was still there; he even knew it would probably always be there; but for a good while now it was gone. It would lie in wait for him and strike him again when he was drained and had a heart full of room for it. But that was a long time from now, in the shower or back in the hotel, longer than the two and a half hours or whatever he would use pitching the game; longer than a clock could measure. Right now it seemed a great deal of his life would pass before the shower. When he trotted out to the mound they stood and cheered and, before he threw his first warm-up pitch, he tipped his cap.

He did not make love to Leslie the night before the game. All season, he had not made love to her on the night before he pitched. He did not believe, as some ballplayers did, that it hurt you the next day. *It's why they call it the box score anyway,* Hap Thomas said on the bus one night after going hitless; *I left me at least two base hits in that whorehouse last night.* Like most ballplayers in the Evangeline League, Thomas had been finished for a long time: a thirty-six-year-old outfielder who had played three seasons—not consecutively—in Triple A ball, when he was in his twenties. Billy didn't make love the night before a game because he still wasn't used to night baseball; he still had the same ritual he'd had in San Antonio, playing high school and American Legion ball: he drank a glass of buttermilk, then went to bed, where for an hour or more he imagined tomorrow's game, although it seemed the game already existed somewhere in the night beyond his window and was imagining him. When finally he slept, the game was still there with him, and in the morning he woke to it, remembered pitching somewhere between daydream and nightdream; and until time for the game he felt like a shadow cast by the memory and the morning's light, a shadow that extended from his pillow to the locker room, when he took off the clothes which had not felt like his all day and put on the uniform which in his mind he had been wearing since he went to bed the night before. In high school, his classes interfered with those days of being a shadow. He felt that he was not so much going to classes as bumping into them on his way to the field. But in summer when he played American Legion ball, there was nothing to bump into, there was only the morning's wait which wasn't really waiting because waiting was watching time, watching it win usually, while on those mornings he joined time and flowed with it, so that sitting before the breakfast his mother cooked for him he felt he was in motion toward the mound.

And he had played a full season less one game of pro ball and still had not been able to convince his mind and body that the night before a game was far too early to enter the rhythm and concentration that would work for him when he actually had the ball in his hand. Perhaps his mind and body weren't the ones who needed convincing; perhaps he was right when he thought he was not imagining the games, but they were imagining him: benevolent and slow-witted angels who had followed him to take care of him, who couldn't understand they could rest now, lie quietly the night before, because they and Billy had all next day to spend with each other. If he had known Leslie was hurt, he could have told her, as simply as a man saying he was beset by the swollen agony of mumps, that he could not make love on those nights, and it wasn't because he preferred thinking about tomorrow's game, but because those angels had followed him all the way to Lafayette, Louisiana. Perhaps he and Leslie could even have laughed about it, for finally it was funny, as funny as the story about Billy's Uncle Johnny whose two hounds had jumped the fence and faithfully tracked or followed him to a bedroom a few blocks from his house, and bayed outside the window: a bedroom Uncle Johnny wasn't supposed to be in, and more trouble than that, because to get there he had left a bedroom he wasn't supposed to leave.

Lafayette was funny too: a lowland of bayous and swamps and Cajuns. The Cajuns were good fans. They were so good that in early season Billy felt like he was barnstorming in some strange country, where everybody loved the Americans and decided to love baseball too since the Americans were playing it for them. They knew the game, but often when they yelled about it, they yelled in French, and when they yelled in English it sounded like a Frenchman's English. This came from the colored section too. The stands did not extend far beyond third and first base, and where the first-base stands ended there was a space of about fifty feet and, after that, shoved against each other, were two sections of folding wooden bleachers. The Negroes filled them, hardly noticed beyond the fifty feet of air and trampled earth. They were not too far down the right-field line; sometimes when Billy ran out a ground ball he ended his sprint close enough to the bleachers to hear the Negroes calling to him in French, or in the English that sounded like French.

Two Cajuns played for the Bulls. The full name was the Lafayette Brahma Bulls, and when the fans said all of it, they said Bremabulls. The owner was a rancher who raised these bulls, and one of his prizes was a huge and dangerous-looking hump-necked bull whose gray coat was nearly white; it was named Huey for their governor who was shot and killed in the state capitol building. Huey was led to home plate for opening-day ceremonies, and after that he attended every game in a pen in foul territory against the right-field fence. During batting practice the left-handers tried to pull the ball into the pen. Nobody hit him, but when the owner heard about it he had the bull brought to the park when batting practice was over. By then the stands were filling. Huey was brought in a truck that entered through a gate behind the colored bleachers, and the Negroes would turn and look behind them at the bull going by. The two men in the truck wore straw cowboy hats. So did the owner, Charlie Breaux. When the Cajuns said his first and last names together they weren't his name anymore. And since it was the Cajun third baseman, E. J. Primeaux, a wiry thirty-year-old who owned a small grocery store which his wife ran during the season, who first introduced Billy to the owner, Billy had believed for the first few days after reporting to the club that he pitched for a man named Mr. Chollibro.

One night someone did hit Huey: during a game, with two outs, a high fly ball that Hap Thomas could have reached for and caught. He was there in plenty of time, glancing down at the pen's fence as he moved with the flight of the ball, was wait-ing safe from collision beside the pen, looking now from the ball to Huey, who stood just on the other side of the fence, watching him. Hap stuck his arm out over the fence and Huey's head; then he looked at Huey again and withdrew his arm and stepped back to watch the ball strike Huey's head with a sound the fans heard behind third base. The ball bounced up and out and Hap bare-handed it as Huey trotted once around the pen. Hap ran toward the dugout, holding the ball up, until he reached the first-base umpire who was alternately signaling safe and pointing Hap back to right field. Then Hap flipped him the ball and, grinning, raised both arms to the fans behind the first-base line, kept them raised to the Negroes as he ran past their bleachers and back to Huey's pen, taking off his cap as he approached the fence where Huey stood again watching, waved his cap once over the fence and horns, then trotted to his position, thumped his glove twice, then lowered it to his knee, and his bare hand to the other, and crouched. The fans were still laughing and cheering and calling to Hap and Huey and Chollibro when two pitches later the batter popped up to Caldwell at short.

In the dugout Primeaux said: "Hap, I seen many a outfielder miss a fly ball because he's wall-shy, but that's the first time I ever seen one miss because he's *bull*-horn shy." And Hap said: "In this league? That's nothing. No doubt about it, one of these nights I'll go out to right field and get bit by a cottonmouth so big he'll chop my leg in two." "Or get hit by lightning," Shep Caldwell said. In June lightning had struck a center fielder for the Abbeville Athletics; struck the metal peak of his cap and exited into the earth through his spikes. When the Bulls heard the announcement over their public-address system, their own sky was cloudy and there were distant flashes; perhaps they had even seen the flash that killed Tommy Lyons thirty miles away. The announcement came between innings when the Bulls were coming to bat; the players and fans stood for a minute of silent prayer. Billy was sitting beside Hap. Hap went to the cooler and came back with a paper cup and sat looking at it but not drinking, then said: "He broke a leg, Lyons did. I played in the Pacific Coast League with him one year. Forty-one. He was hitting three-thirty; thirty-something home runs; stole about forty bases. Late in the season he broke his leg sliding. He never got his hitting back. Nobody knew why. Tommy didn't know why. He went to spring training with the Yankees, then back to the Pacific Coast League, and he kept going down. I was drafted by then, and next time I saw him was two years ago when he came to Abbeville. We had a beer one night and I told him he was headed for the major leagues when he broke his leg. No doubt about it. He said he knew that. And he still didn't understand it. Lost something: swing; timing. Jesus, he used to hit the ball. Now they fried him in front of a bunch of assholes in Abbeville. How's that for shit." For the rest of the game most of the players watched their sky; those who didn't were refusing to. They would not know until next day about the metal peak on Lyons's cap; but two innings after the announcement, Lucky went into the locker room and cut his off. When he came back to the dugout holding the blue cap and looking at the hole where the peak had been, Shep said: "Hell, Lucky, it never strikes twice." Lucky said: "That's because it don't have to," and sat down, stroking the hole.

Lafayette was only a town on the way to Detroit, to the Tigers; unless he got drafted, which he refused to think about, and thought about daily when he read of the war. Already the Tiger scout had watched Billy pitch three games and talked to him after each one, told him all he needed was time, seasoning; told him to stay in shape in the off-season; told him next year he would go to Flint, Michigan, to Class A ball. He was the only one on the club who had a chance for the major leagues, though Billy Joe Baron would probably go up, but not very far; he was a good first baseman and very fast, led the league in stolen bases, but he had to struggle and beat out drag bunts and ground balls to keep his average in the two-nineties and low three hundreds, and he would not go higher than Class A unless they outlawed the curve ball. The others would stay with the Bulls, or a team like the Bulls. And now Leslie was staying in this little town that she wasn't supposed to see as a town to live in longer than a season, and staying too in the little furnished house they were renting, with its rusted screen doors and its yard that ended in the back at a woods which farther on became a swamp, so that Billy never went off the back porch at night and if he peered through the dark at the grass long enough he was sure he saw cottonmouths.

She came into the kitchen that morning of the final game, late morning after a late breakfast so he would eat only twice before pitching, when he was already—or still, from the night before—concentrating on his twentieth win; and the pennant too. He wanted that: wanted to be the pitcher who had come to a third-place club and after one season had ridden away from a pennant winner. She came into the kitchen and looked at him more seriously than he'd ever seen her, and said: "Billy, it's a terrible day to tell you this but you said today was the day I should pack."

He looked at her from his long distance then focused in closer, forced himself to hear what she was saying, felt like he was even forcing himself to see her in three dimensions instead of two, and said: "What's the matter, baby?"

"I'm not going."

"Not going where?"

"San Antonio. Flint. I'm staying here."

Her perspiring face looked so afraid and sorry for him and determined all at once, that he knew he was finished, that he didn't even know what was happening but there would never be enough words he could say. Her eyes were brimming with tears, and he knew they were for herself, for having come to this moment in the kitchen, so far from everything she could have known and predicted; deep in her eyes, as visible as stars, was the hard light of something else, and he knew that she had hated him too, and he imagined her hating him for days while he was on the road; saw her standing in this kitchen and staring out the screen door at the lawn and woods, hating him. Then the picture completed itself: a man, his back to Billy, stood beside her and put his arm around her waist.

"Leslie?" and he had to clear his throat, clear his voice of the fear in it: "Baby, have you been playing around?"

She looked at him for such a long time that he was both afraid of what she would say, and afraid she wouldn't speak at all.

"I'm in love, Billy."

Then she turned and went to the back door, hugging her breasts and staring through the screen. He gripped the corners of the table, pushed his chair back, started to rise, but did not; there was nothing to stand for. He rubbed his eyes, then briskly shook his head.

"It wasn't just that you were on the road so much. I was ready for that. I used to tell myself it'd be exciting a lot of the time, especially in the big leagues. And I'd tell myself in ten years it'd be over anyway, some women have to—"

"*Ten?*" Thinking of the running he did, in the outfield on the days he wasn't pitching, and every day at home between seasons, having known long ago that his arm was a gift and it would last until one spring when it couldn't do the work anymore, would become for the first time since it started throwing a baseball just an ordinary arm; and what he could and must do was keep his lungs and legs strong so they wouldn't give out before it did. He surprised himself: he had not known that, while his wife was leaving him, he could proudly and defensively think of pitching in his early thirties. He had a glimpse of the way she saw him, and he was frightened and ashamed.

"All right: fifteen," she said. "Some women are married to sailors and soldiers and it's longer. It wasn't the road trips. It was when you were home: you weren't here. You weren't here, with me."

"I was here all day. Six, seven hours at the park at night. I don't know what that means."

"It means I'm not what you want."

"How can you tell me what I want?"

"You want to be better than Walter Johnson."

From his angle he saw very little of her face. He waited. But this time she didn't speak.

"Leslie, can't a man try to be the best at what he's got to do and still love his wife?" Then he stood. "Goddamnit, who *is* he?"

"George Lemoine," she said through the screen.

"George L*emoine*. Who's George L*emoine?*"

"The dentist I went to."

"What dentist you went to?"

She turned and looked at his face and down the length of his arms to his fists, then sat at the opposite end of the table.

"When I lost the filling. In June."

"*June?*"

"We didn't start then." Her face was slightly lowered, but her eyes were raised to his, and there was another light in them: she was ashamed but not remorseful, and her voice had the unmistakable tone of a woman in love; they were never so serious as this, never so threatening, and he was assaulted by images of Leslie making love with another man. "He went to the games alone. Sometimes we talked down at the concession stand. We—" Now she looked down, hid her eyes from him, and he felt shut out forever from the mysteries of her heart.

All his life he had been confident. In his teens his confidence and hope were concrete: the baseball season at hand, the season ahead, professional ball, the major leagues. But even as a child he had been confident and hopeful, in an abstract way. He had barely suffered at all, and he had survived that without becoming either callous or naive. He was not without compassion when his life involved him with the homely, the clumsy, the losers. He simply considered himself lucky. Now his body felt like someone else's, weak and trembling. His urge was to lie down.

"And all those times on the road I never went near a whorehouse."

"It's not the same."

He was looking at the beige wall over the sink, but he felt that her eyes were lowered still. He was about to ask what she meant, but then he knew.

"So I guess when I go out to the mound tonight he'll be moving in, is that right?"

Now he looked at her, and when she lifted her face, it had changed: she was only vulnerable.

"He has to get a divorce first. He has a wife and two kids."

"Wait a minute. *Wait* a minute. He's got a wife and two *kids?* How *old* is this son of a bitch?"

"Thirty-four."

"God*damn*it Leslie! How dumb can you be? He's getting what he wants from you; what makes you think he won't be smart enough to leave it at that? God*damn*."

"I believe him."

"You believe him. A dentist anyhow. How can you be married to a ballplayer and fall for a dentist anyhow? And what'll you do for money? You got that one figured out?"

"I don't need much. I'll get a job."

"Well, you won't have much either, because I'm going over there and kill him."

"Billy." She stood, her face as admonitory as his mother's. "He's got enough troubles. All summer I've been in trouble too. I've been sad and lonesome. That's the only way this could ever happen. You know that. All summer I've been feeling like I was running alongside the players' bus waving at you. Then he came along."

"And picked you up."

He glared at her until she blushed and lowered her eyes. Then he went to the bedroom to pack. But she had already done it: the suitcase and overnight bag stood at the foot of the bed.

He picked them up and walked fast to the front door. Before he reached it she came out of the kitchen, and he stopped.

"Billy. I don't want you to be hurt; and I know you won't be for long. I hope someday you can forgive me. Maybe write and tell me how you're doing."

His urge to drop the suitcase and overnight bag and hold her and ask her to change her mind was so great that he could only fight it with anger; and with the clarity of anger he saw a truth which got him out the door.

"You want it all, don't you? Well, forget it. You just settle for what you chose."

Scornfully he scanned the walls of the living room, then Leslie from feet to head; then he left, out into the sun and the hot still air, and drove into town and registered at a hotel. The old desk clerk recognized him and looked puzzled but quickly hid it and said: "Y'all going to beat them New Iberia boys tonight?"

"Damn right."

The natural thing to do now was go to Lemoine's office, walk in while he was looking in somebody's mouth—*It's me, you son of a bitch*—and work him over with the left hand, cancel his afternoon for him, send him off to another dentist. What he had to do was unnatural. And as he climbed the stairs to his room he thought there was much about his profession that was unnatural. In the room he turned off the air conditioning and opened the windows, because he didn't want his arm to be in the cool air, then lay on the bed and closed his eyes and began pitching to the batting order. He knew them all perfectly; but he did not trust that sort of perfection, for it was too much like confidence, which was too much like complacency. So he started with Vidrine, the leadoff man. Left-handed. Went with the pitch, hit to all fields; good drag bunter but only fair speed and Primeaux would be crowding him at third; choke hitter, usually got a piece of the ball, but not that quick with the bat either; couldn't hit good speed. Fastballs low and tight. Change on him. Good base runner but he had to get a jump. Just hold him close to the bag. Then Billy stopped thinking about Vidrine on base. Thing was to concentrate now on seeing his stance and the high-cocked bat and the inside of the plate and Lucky's glove. He pushed aside the image of Vidrine crouching in a lead off first, and at the same time he pushed from his mind Leslie in the kitchen telling him; he saw Vidrine at the plate and, beyond him, he saw Leslie going away. She had been sitting in the box seat but now she walked alone down the ramp. Poor little Texas girl. She even sounded like a small town in Texas: Leslie Wells. Then she was gone.

The home run came with one out and nobody on in the top of the third inning after he had retired the first seven batters. Rick Stanley hit it, the eighth man in the order, a good-field no-hit third baseman in his mid-twenties. He had been in the minors for seven years and looked like it: though trimly built, and the best third baseman Billy had ever seen, he had a look about him of age, of resignation, of having been forced—when he was too young to bear it well—to compromise what he wanted with what he could do. At the plate he looked afraid, and early in the season Billy thought Stanley had been beaned and wasn't able to forget it. Later he realized it wasn't fear of beaning, not fear at all, but the strain of living so long with what he knew. It showed in the field too. Not during a play, but when it was over and Stanley threw the ball to the pitcher and returned to his position, his face looking as though it were adjusting itself to the truth he had for-gotten when he backhanded the ball over the bag and turned and set and threw his mitt-popping peg to first; his face then was intense, reflexive as his legs and hands and arm; then the play was over and his face settled again into the resignation that was still new enough to be terrible. It spread downward to his shoul-ders and then to the rest of him and he looked old again. Billy wished he had seen Stanley play third when he was younger and still believed there was a patch of dirt and a bag and a foul line waiting for him in the major leagues.

One of Billy's rules was never to let up on the bottom of the batting order, because when one of them got a hit it hurt more. The pitch to Stanley was a good one. Like many players, Stanley was a poor hitter because he could not consistently be a good hitter; he was only a good hitter for one swing out of every twelve or so; the other swings had changed his life for him. The occa-sional good one gave the fans, and Stanley too by now, a surprise that always remained a surprise and so never engendered hope.

His home run was a matter of numbers and time, for on this one pitch his concentration and timing and swing all flowed together, making him for that instant the hitter of his destroyed dream. It would happen again, in other ball parks, in other seasons; and if Stanley had been able to cause it instead of having it happen to him, he would be in the major leagues.

Billy's first pitch to him was a fastball, waist-high, inside corner. Stanley took it for a strike, with that look on his face. Lucky called for the same pitch. Billy nodded and played with the rosin bag to keep Stanley waiting longer; then Stanley stepped out of the box and scooped up dust and rubbed it on his hands and the bat handle; when he moved to the plate again he looked just as tense and Billy threw the fastball; Stanley swung late and under it. Lucky called for the curve, the pitch that was sweet tonight, and Billy went right into the windup, figuring Stanley was tied up tightly now, best time to throw a pitch into all that: he watched the ball go in fast and groin-high, then fall to the left and it would have cut the outside corner of the plate just above Stanley's knees; but it was gone. Stanley not only hit it so solidly that Billy knew it was gone before looking, but he got around on it, pulled it, and when Billy found it in the left-center field sky it was still climbing above James running from left and LeBlanc from center. At the top of its arc, there was something final about its floodlit surface against the real sky, dark up there above the lighted one they played under.

He turned his back to the plate. He never watched a home run hitter cross it. He looked out at LeBlanc in center; then he looked at Harry Burke at second, old Harry, the manager, forty-one years old and he could still cover the ground, mostly through cunning; make the pivot—how many double plays had he turned in his life?—and when somebody took him out with a slide Billy waited for the cracking sound, not just of bone but of the whole body, like a dried tree limb. Hap told him not to worry, old Harry was made of oiled leather. His face looked as if it had already outlived two bodies like the one it commanded now. Never higher than Triple A, and that was long ago; when the Bulls hired him and then the fans loved him he moved his family to Lafayette and made it his home, and between seasons worked for an insurance company, easy money for him, because he went to see men and they drank coffee and talked baseball. He had the gentlest eyes Billy had ever seen on a man. Now Harry trotted over to him.

"We got twenty-one outs to get that back for you."

"The little bastard hit that pitch."

"Somebody did. Did you get a close look at him?"

Billy shook his head and went to the rubber. He walked the fat pitcher Talieferro on four pitches and Vidrine on six, and Lucky came to the mound. They called him Lucky because he wasn't.

"One run's one thing," Lucky said. "Let's don't make it three."

"The way y'all are swinging tonight, one's as good as nine." For the first time since he stepped onto the field, Leslie that morning rose up from wherever he had locked her, and struck him.

"Hey," Lucky said. "Hey, it's early."

"Can't y'all hit that fat son of a bitch?"

"We'll hit him. Now you going to pitch or cry?"

He threw Jackson a curve ball and got a double play around the horn, Primeaux to Harry to Baron, who did a split stretching and got Jackson by a half stride.

He went to his end of the bench and watched Talieferro, who for some reason pronounced his name Tolliver: a young, big left-handed pitcher with the kind of belly that belonged on a much older man, in bars on weekend afternoons; he had pitched four years at the local college, this was his first season of pro ball, he was sixteen and nine and usually lost only when his control was off. He did not want to be a professional ballplayer. He had a job with an oil company at the end of the season, and was only pitching and eating his way through a Louisiana summer. Billy watched Lucky adjust his peakless cap and dust his hands and step to the plate, and he pushed Leslie back down, for she was about to burst out of him and explode in his face. He looked down at the toe plate on his right shoe, and began working the next inning, the middle of the order, starting with their big hitter, the center fielder Remy Gauthreaux, who was finished too, thirty years old, but smart and dangerous and he'd knock a mistake out of the park. Low and away to Gauthreaux. Lucky popped out to

Stanley in foul territory and came back to the dugout shaking his head.

Billy could sense it in all the hitters in the dugout, and see it when they went to the plate: Talieferro was on, and they were off. It could be anything: the pennant game, when every move counted; the last game of the season, so the will to be a ballplayer was losing to that other part of them which insisted that when they woke tomorrow nothing they felt tonight would be true; they would drive home to the jobs and other lives that waited for them; most would go to places where people had not even heard of the team, the league. All of that would apply to the Pelicans too; it could be that none of it applied to Talieferro: that rarely feeling much of anything except digestion, hunger, and gorging, he had no conflict between what he felt now and would start feeling tomorrow. And it could be that he simply had his best stuff tonight, that he was throwing nearly every pitch the way Stanley had swung that one time.

Billy went to the on-deck circle and kneeled and watched Harry at the plate, then looked out at Simmons, their big first baseman: followed Gauthreaux in the order, a power hitter but struck out about a hundred times a year; keep him off balance, in and out, and throw the fast one right into his power, and right past him too. Harry, choking high on the bat, fouled off everything close to the plate, then grounded out to short, and Billy handed his jacket to the batboy and went through cheers to the plate. When he stepped in Talieferro didn't look at him, so Billy stepped out and stared until he did, then dug in and cocked the bat, a good hitter so he had played right field in high school and American Legion when he wasn't pitching. He watched the slow, easy fat man's wind-up and the fastball coming out of it; swung for the fence and popped it to second, sprinting down the line and crossing the bag before the ball came down. When he turned he saw Talieferro already walking in, almost at the third-base line. Harry brought Billy's glove out to the mound and patted his rump.

"I thought you were running all the way to Flint."

In the next three innings he pitched to nine men. He ended the fifth by striking out Stanley on curve balls; and when Talieferro led off the sixth Billy threw a fastball at his belly that made him spin away and fall into the dust. Between innings he forced himself to believe in the hope of numbers: the zeroes and the one on the scoreboard in right center, the inning number, the outs remaining for the Bulls; watched them starting to hit, but only one an inning, and nobody as far as second base. He sat sweating under his jacket and in his mind pitched to the next three Pelicans, then the next three just to be sure, although he didn't believe he would face six of them next inning, or any inning, and he thought of eighteen then fifteen then twelve outs to get the one run, the only one he needed, because if it came to that, Talieferro would tire first. When Primeaux struck out leading off the sixth, Billy looked at Hap at the other end of the bench, and he wanted to be down there with him. He leaned forward and stared at his shoes. Then the inning was over and he gave in to the truth he had known anyway since that white vision of loss just before the ball fell.

Gauthreaux started the seventh with a single to right, doing what he almost never did: laid off pulling and went with the outside pitch. Billy worked Simmons low and got the double play he needed, then he struck out the catcher Lantrip, and trotted off the field with his string still going: thirteen batters since the one-out walk to Vidrine in the third. He got the next six. Three of them grounded out, and the other three struck out on the curve, Billy watching it break under the shiny blur of the bat as it would in Flint and wherever after that and Detroit too: his leg kicking and body wheeling and arm whipping around in rhythm again with his history which had begun with a baseball and a friend to throw it to, and had excluded all else, or nearly all else, and had included the rest somewhere alongside him, almost out of his vision (once between innings he allowed himself to think about Leslie, just long enough to forgive her); his history was his future too and the two of them together were twenty-five years at most until the time when the pitches that created him would lose their speed, hang at the plate, become hits in other men's lives instead of the heart of his; they would discard him then, the pitches would. But he loved them for that too, and right now they made his breath singular out of the entire world, so singular that there was no other world: the war would not call him because it couldn't know his name; and he would refuse the grief that lurked behind him. He watched the final curve going inside, then breaking down and over, and Lucky's mitt popped and the umpire twisted and roared and pointed his right fist to the sky.

He ran to the dugout, tipping his cap to the yelling Cajuns, and sat between Hap and Lucky until Baron flied out to end the game. After the showers and good-byes he drove to the hotel and got his still-packed bags and paid the night clerk and started home, out of the lush flatland of marsh and trees, toward Texas. Her space on the front seat was filled as with voice and touch. He turned on the radio. He was not sleepy, and he was driving straight through to San Antonio.

Reflex Curve

CHARLES EINSTEIN

It was not for nothing that Sam Lewis, the pitcher, was known through the unfeeling medium of the sports pages as Six-Inning Sam. Six innings was his ball game, lately. It was as far as he went. Three starts in a row now, they had got him out of there in the sixth, and two of the three times the Lions had lost the game. The fact that he still took his regular starting turn was a tribute neither to him nor to the Lions' faith in him; it merely indicated the condition of the Lion pitching staff in general.

Sam was big and black-haired and genial: a young man of thirty-one who had been raised on a fictional-sounding street called Gravity Avenue in Carbondale, Pennsylvania, and had never quite lived it down. He had a fair fast ball, a recent and not altogether dependable slider, a good curve, and control.

"It wasn't for your control," Himmerling would tell him, "I'd have you out of here, Dimple." Himmerling was the playing manager of the Lions. He did not particularly like Sam Lewis, and called him Dimple because, when Sam smiled, which happened too frequently to suit Himmerling, a dimple formed in his right cheek. Himmerling had his problems, too. They never spelled his name fully in the box scores. It always appeared as H'm'l'g.

But neither the apostrophes in his name nor the dimple in Sam's cheek plagued Himmerling now. As of the moment, the Lions led Boston 3 to 1, Boston had men on first and third with one out and the menacing Legs Kelly at bat. Sam Lewis was pitching, and the scoreboard, certain as the angel of death, said it was the sixth inning. Himmerling waved his glove for time and went from first base to the mound.

"I'm going to cut a phonograph record," he said to Sam, spitting into the brown dirt to the side of the pitching rubber. "It's going to say, 'Don't throw him the curve ball, Dimple.' I'm going to play it every time we get to the sixth inning."

Sam tugged at his cap. Though he would not voluntarily stroll on the window ledges of hotel rooms or set fire to himself in bed, as had other big-league players of his own generation, still there ran through him the makings of a character. With Sam it was a kind of optimistic placidity; in the most mortifying situations, he could always contemplate the morrow, and it made him sort of a walking *non sequitur*. Irrelevantly, it occurred to him now that the season was hardly begun, and there was time—time for the Lions to get up out of fifth place, time for Sam to win some ball games, time perhaps to realize a pennant dream. The Lions were not a great team. But, like the New York Yankees of 1951, they were playing in a bum league.

Out loud, he said now, "Funny thing. One of the writers was telling me that, with my looks, I should be on television."

"I got news for you," Himmerling said. "You are on television. A million little boys are watching you, praying to hell you throw something besides the curve."

"Curve's my favorite," Sam said.

"His favorite, too," Himmerling said, indicating Kelly, the Boston batter. "Throw him something else, you want to do me a favor. Roll it at him." The manager turned to address the catcher, Birnbaum, who had joined the conference at the mound. "How's he look to you, Birn?"

Birnbaum had neglected to remove his mask. "Okay," he said, talking through the metal bars. "He looks great."

"That's what you said last time when he was going to pitch to Kiner," Himmerling said, unhappily. "Remember?"

"It's all right," Birnbaum said comfortingly. "Now and again you got to figure Kiner for the long ball."

"Yeah," Himmerling said, "but not for a line drive into the center-field bleachers. You know how to pray, Birn? Maybe you better face the east, face Mecca like the Mohammedans. It's the sixth inning. Dimple, here, is pitching. Need I say more."

"I often wondered about that." Birnbaum was still talking through his mask. "About facing east and facing Mecca at the same time. What happens if you live east of Mecca?"

"It's all right," Himmerling said. "They got a town called East Mecca. How about it, Dimple? You going to throw him the fast ball?"

"No," Sam Lewis said. "He figures I'm going to throw the curve because he thinks I expect him to think I'm going to throw something else so I'll throw the curve instead. Then at the last minute he changes his mind. So I'll throw the curve."

"Makes sense," Birnbaum said. "Tell you what. I'll signal for the fast ball and you throw the curve anyway. Then we can all go crazy."

Hughes, the plate umpire, came to the mound. "All right, girls," he said. "I'll serve tea."

"We're talking," Himmerling said.

"You want another pitcher?"

"I ain't got another pitcher."

"Then knock it off," Hughes said. "Play baseball."

Himmerling and Birnbaum moved, with elaborate lack of haste, back to their positions. Legs Kelly stepped into the batter's box, waving his bat like a cow switching flies. Sam went up on the rubber. Birnbaum signaled helplessly with open palm, and Sam nodded briefly, stretched, checked his runners, and threw the fast curve without a windup, watching the ball go just as he wanted it to, seeing it break off sharply, a foot in front of the plate.

Legs Kelly hit it. Swinging into the curve, he hit it far toward center, and high. Sam's legs carried him automatically in the direction of third base, to back up on a throw, but less than halfway there he knew there would be no throw. He turned and saw the ball slicing off to the right, falling back behind the right fielder and into the sixth or seventh or maybe it was the tenth row of seats in the right-field stands, fair by thirty feet, a home run.

Himmerling took him out. Sam licked his lips and went toward the dugout, not looking up except to show a brief, sad, close-up smile for the television camera back of first base. In his mind's eye, he could see the morning papers. *Six-Inning Sam,* the lead in the Tribune would begin.

The Chronicle and the News ran their stories that way, but he was wrong about the Tribune. The Tribune began even more succinctly. *Same old Sam,* said the first paragraph, in its entirety.

"Same old Sam," he said to himself, aloud, waving his razor at the soapy white face in the mirror. "I have an idea for you, Dimple. You don't mind if I call you Dimple?" The face in the mirror acquiesced. "All you got to do is talk to Frick. Get him to change the rules. Make all games five innings long. Then"—he stroked his right cheek with the razor—"then, Dimple, you'd probably get knocked out in the fourth. What are you going to do?"

The telephone rang, and he went soapily to answer it. "It will be a strange and beautiful young lady," he said to the ringing telephone. "She will have a sultry voice, and I will ask her to marry me."

It was indeed a sultry voice that asked if this were Sam Lewis, the pitcher.

"Yes," Sam said into the telephone. "Do I know you? Are you strange and beautiful? Will you marry me?"

"No, three times," the voice said. "My name is Edna Langdon and I work for the Chronicle. I wondered if I could come up."

"Ah," Sam said. "The press. You can, indeed. May I order something from room service? A Coke?"

"That would be nice," the sultry voice said, "but don't plan on too much of an orgy. All I want is an interview."

"Come upstairs," Sam said. "I will give you an exclusive interview, after which I may jump out the window and end it all. You can write 30 to the story of Sam Lewis, pitcher."

"We don't use 30 in the newspaper business any more," the voice named Edna Langdon said. "We use those funny little things on the typewriter I don't know the name of. I'll be right up."

Sam Lewis hung up the telephone for a moment, then picked it up again and got room service and ordered two Cokes. They arrived simultaneously with Edna Langdon of the Chronicle.

"That is a nice pair of legs you have there," Sam Lewis said, conversationally.

The bellhop from room service said, "I beg your pardon?"

"The lady," Sam said. He signed the check.

"Oh," the bellhop said, and looked carefully at the lady. "She does, at that." He nodded and departed.

The girl in the doorway looked at Sam. "Would you like to call the manager for his appraisal?" she said. "Or the little man on the elevator?"

"No," Sam said. "No, I don't think so. Are you married?"

"Why, no," Edna Langdon said. "But any time you say. Meanwhile, I am twenty-seven years of age, born in Dayton, Ohio, five feet five, weight one eighteen, hair auburn all the time, hips thirty-four, waist twenty-four. Does that do it?"

"Not completely," Sam Lewis said. "Didn't you leave something out?"

Edna Langdon blinked at him. "What, for instance?"

"Collar size," Sam said. "Sit down, Edna. May I call you Edna? You have a baseball writer named George Johnson—may his children be born wearing sneakers—and I always call him George."

"He has a name for you, too," the girl said. She sat down on the side of the bed and crossed her legs in a silken sweep that left Sam baffled and aware. "George filled me in on you. He said you would make good copy for the Sunday supplement, if you are still with the team Sunday. He said you are tall and dark and handsome and ought to be optioned to Fort Worth, whatever that means."

"Good old George," Sam said. He sat himself in an armchair that afforded a commanding view of his beauteous inquisitor and doodled a dagger on the copy of the Chronicle in his lap. "Do you know anything about baseball?"

"Only what I read in the papers," the girl replied. "As far as I can find out, baseball is the one occupation in which nothing is called by its right name. A pitcher isn't a pitcher. He is a slab artist who toils on the hill. Why is that?"

"I used to know," Sam said. "All I know for sure now is that it's a lucky thing they've been knocking me out in the sixth inning. It would be awful to go through life known as Five-Inning Sam."

Edna began to take notes. In the expectation that she might recross her legs, or uncross them, or perhaps even smile gently at him, Sam dared not look away. She wore a pastel-blue summer frock, and her hair fell to her shoulders. Her eyes were dark brown and serious, and Sam wondered achingly if she were in love. He did not often wonder this of anyone.

Indeed, she *was* smiling at him. Sam felt like stout Cortes, silent upon a peak in Darien. "You," the young lady from the Chronicle said softly, "have a dimple."

"Oh, my," Sam said. "I've known you ten minutes and I'm falling in love with you. Isn't it strange? It doesn't even happen on television."

"It does on the half-hour shows," Edna said, but she was still smiling, and she let him look at her. "I'm sorry," she said, after a pause. "I wish I wasn't doing this story."

"It's all right," Sam said helpfully. "I'll make it as easy for you as possible."

"Well, then," Edna said, "you might as well know. The title of this magnificent story is going to be Six-Inning Sam—the Handsome Flop. So if you want to make it easy for me, you'd better make a pass at me or do something else I'll resent, so I won't like you. I'd feel better if I didn't like you."

"Anything to oblige," Six-Inning Sam declared slowly. He stood up and went over to the bed. He held her face with his hands and bent his head and kissed her, first on the eyes, then on the tip of her nose, and then on her mouth. He found her lips languorous and warm and not unwilling, and it was a sensation such as he had not known before.

At length, her arms went up about his neck and, balance lost, they tumbled on the bed. Edna drew away and sat up, her hand at her hair, looking down at him. "You," she said.

"You had better call me Sam," Sam said. He lay there and

looked up at her. "Or Six-Inning, or something. I'm sorry. I was only trying to help."

"Why aren't you a better pitcher?" the girl said to him, shaking her head slowly.

"I used to be. I won fourteen games last year. Seventeen the year before. Twenty-two in forty-nine."

"What happened?"

"They're hitting my curve ball," Sam said. "A curve ball, for your information, is a ball that curves. You're beautiful."

She made a face at him. "George the baseball writer told me every batter in the league expects you to throw the curve. Why don't you throw something else?"

"Like what?"

"What else is there to throw?"

"Fast ball, slow ball, slider, spitter."

"That sounds nice."

"What sounds nice?"

"Spitter." She said it gingerly.

"It was outlawed thirty years ago," Sam said. He sat up. "Anyway, I think this. So they're expecting my curve; so what? Sooner or later they'll figure I'm just so dumb and I'll change my big pitch to something else. So then I throw the curve and they're not expecting it. See?"

"No," Edna said. "All I know is you keep on losing. And it's always the sixth inning. George the baseball writer says you're a psycho."

"Donald the baseball writer, on the Tribune, said the same thing last Tuesday. In print."

"Well," the girl said, "how would you—Sam, don't make that dimple at me—how would you explain it?"

Sam dimpled. "Coincidence."

"Is that all? Nothing else?"

"Certainly. Suppose I took a fat lead into the sixth inning. Do you think I'd blow it?"

"I asked George the baseball writer," Edna said seriously, "what would happen if the Lions went into the sixth inning ahead of the other team by a score of forty to nothing. He said it was an unusual thing for the Lions to score forty runs in an entire season, but he said if you were pitching, then they'd lose forty-one to forty."

"That's assuming Hawthorne could put the fire out," Sam said bitterly. "Hawthorne is my relief pitcher."

"Don't you like Hawthorne?"

"I don't know him well enough. All I ever do is give him the ball."

"Well," the girl said, gazing distractedly at her notes, "not knowing anything about baseball, I'd say maybe you ought to throw something besides the curve when you get yourself into a bad situation."

"Not if the curve's my best pitch."

"But they've been hitting it. George the baseball writer—"

"George the baseball writer hasn't hit it. The only thing George the baseball writer ever hit was his wife, who is an underweight midget. Honey, pitching is ninety per cent brains." Sam tapped his temple significantly. "You've got to outguess them."

Edna shook her head in wonderment. Then she stood up. "I don't know," she said. "I think maybe we'd better continue this interview some other time. I have to collect my thoughts. George the baseball writer told me I had no business in the newspaper game, and I'm beginning to think he was right."

"As much could be said for George the baseball writer," Sam said. He rolled off the bed and stood up. "We have a night game tonight. Have supper with me?"

"I suppose." She sighed. "Sam . . ."

"Ma'am?"

"I'm afraid you're crazy, like they said."

"And you're lovely."

"And you're handsome, and I'm going to have to write a nasty story about you, just like they said I would."

"In that case," Six-Inning Sam declared, "I'd better get you real mad."

"Yes," Edna said, moving into his arms, "so kiss me one more time."

Outside the ball park, early editions of next morning's papers already were on sale. Sam bought one without thinking about it, steeped as he was in the magic of the single lamb chop he had had for supper, and the memory of Edna in the candlelight. She had told him softly that he was, indeed, a bum; that his reputation was that of a domesticated animal; that perhaps he should get mad once in a while, and that would solve his problem.

Now Sam glanced casually at the sports headlines. What he saw made him stop where he was and read it all.

LEWIS LACKS GUTS, SAYS H'M'L'G, the headline read. Even in this moment, Sam was comforted to see that Himmerling still could not get his name spelled fully in the headlines. But it was slack comfort. The reason Sam was losing, said the story, was that he had no guts. Who said so? Himmerling, the manager. He would, Himmerling had told the press that afternoon, trade Sam off for a used bat boy at the earliest opportunity. A trade, indeed, was brewing with Midland City. Sam shuddered involuntarily and read on.

The tail end of the story was, as it could on frequent occasion be in the local press, the most interesting. *Himmerling's outburst*, it said, *was viewed in some quarters* (what quarters? Sam wondered) *as a masterpiece of psychology aimed at shaking the easygoing right-hander out of the mental doldrums. Himmerling is known to subscribe to the school of thought that says a manager is a manager off the field as well as on, and that the occult art of psychology is his to practice even as is the art of changing pitchers at the right moment.*

Himmerling's problem (the story went on) *is twofold: first, he must convince Lewis that the sixth inning is no different from any other inning; second, he must convince Lewis that his curve ball has become the biggest sucker pitch in the league; third, he must see to it that Lewis develops a substitute delivery.*

There is nothing, Sam said to himself, reading the last paragraph a second time, like a twofold problem with three folds. Sam folded the paper and went into the clubhouse.

Pregame banter was at a minimum. Himmerling avoided Sam. So did practically everyone else. Sam went out to the bull pen with a third-string catcher named Wasser and sat down to watch the game. Wasser had not broken into the line-up yet this season, and there seemed no reason to believe he would rupture this record.

"Wasser," Sam said, "are you speaking to me tonight?"

Wasser shifted his tobacco within his ample cheek and blinked at Sam. "Why not?"

"That does it," Sam said.

Burke was pitching for the Lions against Boston this evening, and he could have been called Two-Inning Burke. Boston got him out of there in the second, and Hawthorne, the wrong-arm, went in. He went all right until the fifth, when Himmerling yanked him for a pinch hitter. The pinch hitter put a triple into the wrong field, and two runs scored, and it was a tie game at 4 and 4. Walsh, no kin to the great Spittin' Ed, went in to throw for the Lions in the Boston sixth, and Sam, suddenly alone with Wasser in the bull pen, got up to get heated. He had to heat fast. Walsh walked the first man, fed the second one a double, and then let Legs Kelly work him for a walk.

That made it none out and bases loaded, and Himmerling, in a motion born of despair, waved his right hand toward the bull pen. A roar, one part hope and three indignation, went up from the stands as Sam Lewis ambled toward the hill.

Himmerling met him there with the ball in his hand.

"Of all the people I was hoping not to see," he said.

"Good evening," Sam said. "I see it's the sixth inning."

"Yes," Himmerling said, "and we are about to lose another. Hawthorne can't come in to relieve you tonight, buddy boy. Hawthorne's already been in. So if they score twenty-five runs on you, you'll still be in. Did you read the papers?"

"Only the obituaries."

"Read 'em again tomorrow," Himmerling advised, and went darkly back to first base.

Sam took his warmup throws and went to work on the Boston pitcher. The pitcher was up there to bunt, and he was determined to die bunting. This he did. He squirted three foul and went unhappily back to the bench. That brought up Wells, the lead-off man. Sam got ahead of him, at one-and-two, and, with Wells looking for the waster, slipped the fast curve over the corner for strike three.

Two out, and the crowd was buzzing now, with him instead of against him. Facing Jolley, the Boston third baseman, Sam worked with the care he always used against a left-handed hitter. The count went full, to three-and-two. Birnbaum, the catcher, came out to say something, and Himmerling came over from first.

"Don't throw that curve ball," the manager said.

"He can't throw the fast ball," Birnbaum said. "This guy grew up on fast balls."

"I don't care what you throw," Himmerling said to Sam, "but, Dimple, don't you throw that curve. He's set for it."

Sam smiled placidly. "That's just it."

"Oh—oh," Himmerling said.

"Throw him a slow ball," Birnbaum advised.

"You crazy?" Sam said.

"Newhouser used to do it."

"I'm not Newhouser."

Hughes, the plate umpire, came out. "It's always fair weather," he observed, "when good fellows get together."

"I'm talking to my pitcher, prune face," Himmerling said. "You object?"

"Yes," Hughes said. "On two accounts. The talking and the prune face."

"Sam says he isn't Newhouser," Birnbaum said.

"I never said he was," the umpire said. "Play ball. One more prune face and you're all out of here."

"Ah," Himmerling said, and went back to first base. Sam waited for Birnbaum to get back behind the plate. After all this, he said to himself, there is one pitch this batter will not expect. And I am going to fog it by his nose.

He checked his runners, stretched quickly and threw. The ball darted in, hung for no more than an instant, snapped off as a perfect curve ball should and bent inward toward the left-handed hitter.

Jolley, the Boston batter, went for it. There was the sound of a pistol crack, followed by the sharper, ringing noise as the ball caromed high off the scoreboard in right field.

Six-Inning Sam stood there, watching the runners race around the bases. Midland City, he said quietly to himself, here I come.

Midland City, there he went. Himmerling swung the trade within twenty-four hours. Sam talked to Edna once on the telephone before he went.

"You're a bum," she said to him. She was crying.

"I love you," Sam said.

"Leave me alone," she said.

Sam went to Midland City.

There (and it baffled him) they were glad to see him.

Gottwald, the manager, had him in the bull pen from the start. "I'm saving you for the Lions, Sam," he said.

"I shall take that literally," Sam said. It was a bad joke. He had read it on a sports page somewhere.

"Don't you want to start against them?"

"I'll start against anyone."

"All right. The Lions. What about the curve ball?"

"What about it?"

Gottwald shrugged. "Who knows?"

"Is it as good as ever?"

"I think so," Gottwald said. "But they're expecting it. You got to confuse them."

"All right," Sam said. "Did I tell you I was in love?"

"Sometimes it makes a difference."

"She isn't talking to me."

"Who blames her?"

"I don't know," Sam said, in despair, and went home to dream about Edna. In his dream, he struck Edna out with a slow ball.

He woke up in a sweat and consulted the Midland City papers, whose baseball writers, in a ten-strike of originality, had fastened upon him the nickname of Six-Inning Sam. Midland City was in fourth place. The Lions, not climbing so much as the top teams were falling, were now up in third place. It was that kind of league. Anyone had a chance to take it all. Even Midland City.

Sam waited his turn. The Lions arrived in town, and it came. The press made much of the fact that he was making his first Midland City start against the team that had traded him away because he had no guts. It appealed to the local fans. Curiously, Sam found it appealed to him, too.

He let his curve do the talking for him. He used just enough of the other stuff to keep the hitters honest, but his fast curve was the baby. Sam could not remember when it had worked so well: when the break had been so sharp, so controlled, so impossible for a batsman to anticipate.

It was the top of the fourth before they got a hit off him. Birnbaum got it, dropping a Texas leaguer back of short and legging it to second when it fell in. But Sam struck out the next man, to get out of the inning, and in the Midland City half of the fifth he put down a cold bunt sacrifice to help push a run around and put his club ahead, 1 to 0.

Gottwald, the manager, said, "All right, Sam. You know what inning this one coming up is."

"Okay," Sam said. "I'll stiff 'em. Then I'll be known as Seven-Inning Sam."

"You read the papers too much," Gottwald said. "They're all crazy. I see where some dame in one of the papers in your old town said last Sunday you're potentially the greatest pitcher in baseball."

Sam thought for a moment. "I shouldn't have kissed her."

"Yeah," Gottwald said, and spat over the bat rack. "Himmerling told me before the game that she got fired for it."

Sam picked up his glove and went out to pitch. It was the sixth inning, and he was acutely conscious of it. The stands, he knew, were as conscious as he; and so were his teammates, for, with one out, a ground ball went at medium speed through the hole for a single to left and then the second baseman gummed a double-play grounder behind him, and there were men on first and second, and Himmerling, the Lions' manager, was at bat.

Himmerling grinned. "For once," he called, "I'm glad to see you out there."

Sam threw him the curve for called strike one, then came back fast outside for a ball. He took a bad call low for ball two, then got strike two with his curve. Himmerling was still waiting. Sam missed inside with his slider, and it was three-and-two, and Himmerling stepped out of the batter's box.

"Dimple," he called. "I hear you turned lover-boy in your old age! Conned some broad into thinking you was the greatest pitcher since Alexander. Come on, Dimple, cross me up! Throw me the curve!"

Sam stood there, hunched slightly forward, waiting for Himmerling to step back in. His catcher squatted to give the signal, and Sam shook his head no. This would be his pitch to call, to throw. Would Himmerling expect—actually expect—the curve?

Sam eyed his runners and looked back at the plate, where Himmerling stood waving his bat in slow, steady arcs. Coldly now, suddenly, Sam realized he was angry. But it did not affect his thinking. All these weeks he had been playing disastrous guessing games with the batters, he had overlooked one thing: he, the pitcher, knew what the pitch would be; the batter did not.

He grinned a little; steadied, kicked, and threw. From behind, his arm came fogging through, all the power of his strong shoulder behind it. His body carried around blazingly in the direction of the plate. And at the very moment of release, his fingertips drew swiftly back.

The slow ball seemed to creep from his hand. It floated toward the plate, turning almost not at all as it went. Sam thought he could read the manufacturer's imprint on the ball as it traveled. He saw Himmerling, dug in, suddenly shift his stance and prolong his timing to meet the lazy throw.

Then Himmerling leaned toward the ball and swung, and the roar of the crowd danced in Sam's ears as he saw the ball fly past his head. Almost dimly, he realized Himmerling had not hit it. Himmerling had struck out. The catcher had whipped the ball down to second to catch the runner off base. Sam turned and saw the second baseman putting on the tag for the double play. He turned back toward the plate and saw Himmerling sitting there in the dirt.

Back at the hotel, the operator told him there was a long-distance call waiting for him. It was Edna. She said to him, "I'm a heel."

"Well, I don't know," he said. "I finally got mad. You told me to throw something else, and I heard about that piece you did, and it got through my thick head. Anyway, I had a dream where I struck you out with a slow ball."

"That was nice of you."

"It was unusual," Sam said. "I heard about your tough luck."

"What tough luck? They saw the box score of today's game and offered me my job back."

"You going to take it?"

"Unless something better comes along." Her voice was warm in his ear. "I think I'm in love with you, Sam."

Sam said, softly, "Wow."

"You might tell me you love me," she suggested.

"I was busy making a dimple," Sam Lewis said.

The Natural

BERNARD MALAMUD

On the train, en route to his tryout with the Cubs,
Roy Hobbs encounters Harriet Bird, a gorgeous
brunette; Max Mercy, a syndicated sportswriter
who would ruin a man's life for a scoop; and Walter
(the Whammer) Wambold, the American League's
leading hitter. The train makes an unscheduled
stop, and the Whammer challenges Roy to pitch to
him. Encouraged by his catcher-companion, Sam
Simpson, veteran scout for the Cubs, Roy strikes
out the Whammer on three pitches, winning the attention of Ms. Bird, unaware that her idea of fun
is shooting champion athletes with silver bullets
and dancing naked around their bodies. From the
novel *The Natural*.

About a hundred yards ahead, where two dirt roads crossed, a
moth-eaten model-T Ford was parked on the farther side of the
road from town, and a fat old man wearing a broadbrimmed
black hat and cowboy boots, who they could see was carrying a
squat doctor's satchel, climbed down from it. To the conductor,
who had impatiently swung off the train with a lit red lamp, he
flourished a yellow telegram. They argued a minute, then the
conductor, snapping open his watch, beckoned him along and
they boarded the train. When they passed through Eddie's car
the conductor's face was sizzling with irritation but the doctor
was unruffled. Before disappearing through the door, the conductor called to Eddie, "Half hour."

"Half hour," Eddie yodeled and he got out the stool and set
it outside the car so that anyone who wanted to stretch, could.

Only about a dozen passengers got off the train, including

Harriet Bird, still hanging on to her precious hat box, the Whammer, and Max Mercy, all as thick as thieves. Roy hunted up the
bassoon case just if the train should decide to take off without
him, and when he had located Sam they both got off.

"Well, I'll be jiggered." Sam pointed down about a block
beyond where the locomotive had halted. There, sprawled out at
the outskirts of the city, a carnival was on. It was made up of
try-your-skill booths, kiddie rides, a freak show and a gigantic
Ferris wheel that looked like a stopped clock. Though there was
still plenty of daylight, the carnival was lit up by twisted ropes
of blinking bulbs, and many banners streamed in the breeze as
the calliope played.

"Come on," said Roy, and they went along with the people
from the train who were going toward the tents.

Once they had got there and fooled around a while, Sam
stopped to have a crushed cocoanut drink which he privately
spiked with a shot from a new bottle, while Roy wandered over
to a place where you could throw three baseballs for a dime
at three wooden pins, shaped like pint-size milk bottles and set
in pyramids of one on top of two, on small raised platforms about
twenty feet back from the counter. He changed the fifty-cent
piece Sam had slipped him on leaving the train, and this pretty
girl in yellow, a little hefty but with a sweet face and nice ways,
who with her peanut of a father was waiting on trade, handed
him three balls. Lobbing one of them, Roy easily knocked off the
pyramid and won himself a naked kewpie doll. Enjoying the
game, he laid down another dime, again clattering the pins to
the floor in a single shot and now collecting an alarm clock. With
the other three dimes he won a brand-new boxed baseball, a
washboard, and baby potty, which he traded in for a six-inch
harmonica. A few kids came over to watch and Sam, wandering
by, indulgently changed another half into dimes for Roy. And
Roy won a fine leather cigar case for Sam, a "God Bless America"
banner, a flashlight, a can of coffee, and a two-pound box of
sweets. To the kids' delight, Sam, after a slight hesitation, flipped
Roy another half dollar, but this time the little man behind the
counter nudged his daughter and she asked Roy if he would now
take a kiss for every three pins he tumbled.

Roy glanced at her breasts and she blushed. He got embarrassed too. "What do you say, Sam, it's your four bits?"

Sam bowed low to the girl. "Ma'am," he said, "now you see how dang foolish it is to be a young feller."

The girl laughed and Roy began to throw for kisses, flushing each pyramid in a shot or two while the girl counted aloud the kisses she owed him.

Some of the people from the train passed by and stayed to watch when they learned from the mocking kids what Roy was throwing for.

The girl, pretending to be unconcerned, tolled off the third and fourth kisses.

As Roy fingered the ball for the last throw the Whammer came by holding over his shoulder a Louisville Slugger that he had won for himself in the batting cage down a way. Harriet, her pretty face flushed, had a kewpie doll, and Max Mercy carried a box of cigars. The Whammer had discarded his sun glasses and all but strutted over his performance and the prizes he had won.

Roy raised his arm to throw for the fifth kiss and a clean sweep when the Whammer called out to him in a loud voice, "Pitch it here, busher, and I will knock it into the moon."

Roy shot for the last kiss and missed. He missed with the second and third balls. The crowd oohed its disappointment.

"Only four," said the girl in yellow as if she mourned the fifth.

Angered at what had happened, Sam hoarsely piped, "I got ten dollars that says he can strike you out with three pitched balls, Wambold."

The Whammer looked at Sam with contempt.

"What d'ye say, Max?" he said.

Mercy shrugged.

"Oh, I love contests of skill," Harriet said excitedly. Roy's face went pale.

"What's the matter, hayfoot, you scared?" the Whammer taunted.

"Not of you," Roy said.

"Let's go across the tracks where nobody'll get hurt," Mercy suggested.

"Nobody but the busher and his bazooka. What's in it, busher?"

"None of your business." Roy picked up the bassoon case.

The crowd moved in a body across the tracks, the kids circling around to get a good view, and the engineer and fireman watching from their cab window.

Sam cornered one of the kids who lived nearby and sent him home for a fielder's glove and his friend's catcher's mitt. While they were waiting, for protection he buttoned underneath his coat the washboard Roy had won. Max drew a batter's box alongside a piece of slate. He said he would call the throws and they would count as one of the three pitches only if they were over or if the Whammer swung and missed.

When the boy returned with the gloves, the sun was going down, and though the sky was aflame with light all the way to the snowy mountain peak, it was chilly on the ground.

Breaking the seal, Sam squeezed the baseball box and the pill shot up like a greased egg. He tossed it to Mercy, who inspected the hide and stitches, then rubbed the shine off and flipped it to Roy.

"Better throw a couple of warm-ups."

"My arm is loose," said Roy.

"It's your funeral."

Placing his bassoon case out of the way in the grass, Roy shed his coat. One of the boys came forth to hold it.

"Be careful you don't spill the pockets," Roy told him.

Sam came forward with the catcher's glove on. It was too small for his big hand but he said it would do all right.

"Sam, I wish you hadn't bet that money on me," Roy said.

"I won't take it if we win, kiddo, but just let it stand if we lose," Sam said, embarrassed.

"We came by it too hard."

"Just let it stand so."

He cautioned Roy to keep his pitches inside, for the Whammer was known to gobble them on the outside corner.

Sam returned to the plate and crouched behind the batter, his knees spread wide because of the washboard. Roy drew on his glove and palmed the ball behind it. Mercy, rubbing his hands to warm them, edged back about six feet behind Sam.

The onlookers retreated to the other side of the tracks, except Harriet, who stood without fear of fouls up close. Her eyes shone at the sight of the two men facing one another.

Mercy called, "Batter up."

The Whammer crowded the left side of the plate, gripping the heavy bat low on the neck, his hands jammed together and legs plunked evenly apart. He hadn't bothered to take off his coat. His eye on Roy said it spied a left-handed monkey.

"Throw it, Rube, it won't get no lighter."

Though he stood about sixty feet away, he loomed up gigantic to Roy, with the wood held like a caveman's ax on his shoulder. His rocklike frame was motionless, his face impassive, unsmiling, dark.

Roy's heart skipped a beat. He turned to gaze at the mountain.

Sam whacked the leather with his fist. "Come on, kiddo, wham it down his whammy."

The Whammer out of the corner of his mouth told the drunk to keep his mouth shut.

"Burn it across his button."

"Close your trap," Mercy said.

"Cut his throat with it."

"If he tries to dust me, so help me I will smash his skull," the Whammer threatened.

Roy stretched loosely, rocked back on his left leg, twirling the right a little like a dancer, then strode forward and threw with such force his knuckles all but scraped the ground on the follow-through.

At thirty-three the Whammer still enjoyed exceptional eyesight. He saw the ball spin off Roy's fingertips and it reminded him of a white pigeon he had kept as a boy, that he would send into flight by flipping it into the air. The ball flew at him and he was conscious of its bird-form and white flapping wings, until it suddenly disappeared from view. He heard a noise like the bang of a firecracker at his feet and Sam had the ball in his mitt. Unable to believe his ears he heard Mercy intone a reluctant strike.

Sam flung off the glove and was wringing his hand.

"Hurt you, Sam?" Roy called.

"No, it's this dang glove."

Though he did not show it, the pitch had bothered the Whammer no end. Not just the speed of it but the sensation of surprise and strangeness that went with it—him batting here on the railroad tracks, the crazy carnival, the drunk catching and a clown pitching, and that queer dame Harriet, who had five minutes ago been patting him on the back for his skill in the batting cage, now eyeing him coldly for letting one pitch go by.

He noticed Max had moved farther back.

"How the hell you expect to call them out there?"

"He looks wild to me." Max moved in.

"Your knees are knockin'," Sam tittered.

"Mind your business, rednose," Max said.

"You better watch your talk, mister," Roy called to Mercy.

"Pitch it, greenhorn," warned the Whammer.

Sam crouched with his glove on. "Do it again, Roy. Give him something simular."

"Do it again," mimicked the Whammer. To the crowd, maybe to Harriet, he held up a vaunting finger showing there were other pitches to come.

Roy pumped, reared and flung.

The ball appeared to the batter to be a slow spinning planet looming toward the earth. For a long light-year he waited for this globe to whirl into the orbit of his swing so he could bust it to smithereens that would settle with dust and dead leaves into some distant cosmos. At last the unseeing eye, maybe a fortune-teller's lit crystal ball—anyway, a curious combination of circles —drifted within range of his weapon, or so he thought, because he lunged at it ferociously, twisting round like a top. He landed on both knees as the world floated by over his head and hit with a *whup* into the cave of Sam's glove.

"Hey, Max," Sam said, as he chased the ball after it had bounced out of the glove, "how do they pernounce Whammer if you leave out the W?"

"Strike," Mercy called long after a cheer (was it a jeer?) had burst from the crowd.

"What's he throwing," the Whammer howled, "spitters?"

"In the pig's poop." Sam thrust the ball at him. "It's drier than your granddaddy's scalp."

"I'm warning him not to try any dirty business."

Yet the Whammer felt oddly relieved. He liked to have his back crowding the wall, when there was a single pitch to worry about and a single pitch to hit. Then the sweat began to leak out of his pores as he stared at the hard, lanky figure of the pitiless pitcher, moving, despite his years and a few waste motions, like a veteran undertaker of the diamond, and he experienced a moment of depression.

Sam must have sensed it, because he discovered an unexpected pity in his heart and even for a split second hoped the idol would not be tumbled. But only for a second, for the Whammer had regained confidence in his known talent and experience and was taunting the greenhorn to throw.

Someone in the crowd hooted and the Whammer raised aloft two fat fingers and pointed where he would murder the ball, where the gleaming rails converged on the horizon and beyond was invisible.

Roy raised his leg. He smelled the Whammer's blood and wanted it, and through him the worm's he had with him, for the way he had insulted Sam.

The third ball slithered at the batter like a meteor, the flame swallowing itself. He lifted his club to crush it into a universe of sparks but the heavy wood dragged, and though he willed to destroy the sound he heard a gong bong and realized with sadness that the ball he had expected to hit had long since been part of the past; and though Max could not cough the fatal word out of his throat, the Whammer understood he was, in the truest sense of it, out.

The crowd was silent as the violet evening fell on their shoulders.

For a night game, the Whammer harshly shouted, it was customary to turn on lights. Dropping the bat, he trotted off to the train, an old man.

The ball had caught Sam smack in the washboard and lifted him off his feet. He lay on the ground, extended on his back. Roy pushed everybody aside to get him air. Unbuttoning Sam's coat, he removed the dented washboard.

"Never meant to hurt you, Sam."

"Just knocked the wind outa me," Sam gasped. "Feel better now." He was pulled to his feet and stood steady.

The train whistle wailed, the echo banging far out against the black mountain.

Then the doctor in the broadbrimmed black hat appeared, flustered and morose, the conductor trying to pacify him, and Eddie hopping along behind.

The doctor waved the crumpled yellow paper around. "Got a telegram says somebody on this train took sick. Anybody out here?"

Roy tugged at Sam's sleeve.

"Ixnay."

"What's that?"

"Not me," said Roy.

The doctor stomped off. He climbed into his Ford, whipped it up and drove away.

The conductor popped open his watch. "Be a good hour late into the city."

"All aboard," he called.

"Aboard," Eddie echoed, carrying the bassoon case.

The buxom girl in yellow broke through the crowd and threw her arms around Roy's neck. He ducked but she hit him quick with her pucker four times upon the right eye, yet he could see with the other that Harriet Bird (certainly a snappy goddess) had her gaze fastened on him.

They sat, after dinner, in Eddie's dimmed and empty Pullman, Roy floating through drifts of clouds on his triumph as Harriet went on about the recent tourney, she put it, and the unreal forest outside swung forward like a gate shutting. The odd way she saw things interested him, yet he was aware of the tormented trees fronting the snaky lake they were passing, trees bent and clawing, plucked white by icy blasts from the black water, their bony branches twisting in many a broken direction.

Harriet's face was flushed, her eyes gleaming with new insights. Occasionally she stopped and giggled at herself for the breathless volume of words that flowed forth, to his growing astonishment, but after a pause was on her galloping way again —a girl on horseback—reviewing the inspiring sight (she said it was) of David jawboning the Goliath-Whammer, or was it Sir Percy lancing Sir Maldemer, or the first son (with a rock in his paw) ranged against the primitive papa?

Roy gulped. "My father? Well, maybe I did want to skull him sometimes. After my grandma died, the old man dumped me in one orphan home after the other, wherever he happened to be working—when he did—though he did used to take me out of there summers and teach me how to toss a ball."

No, that wasn't what she meant, Harriet said. Had he ever read Homer?

Try as he would he could only think of four bases and not a book. His head spun at her allusions. He found her lingo strange with all the college stuff and hoped she would stop it because he wanted to talk about baseball.

Then she took a breather. "My friends say I have a fantastic imagination."

He quickly remarked he wouldn't say that. "But the only thing I had on my mind when I was throwing out there was that Sam had bet this ten spot we couldn't afford to lose out on, so I had to make him whiff."

"To whiff—oh, Roy, how droll," and she laughed again.

He grinned, carried away by the memory of how he had done it, the hero, who with three pitched balls had nailed the best the American League had to offer. What didn't that say about the future? He felt himself falling into sentiment in his thoughts and tried to steady himself but couldn't before he had come forth with a pronouncement: "You have to have the right stuff to play good ball and I have it. I bet some day I'll break every record in the book for throwing and hitting."

Harriet appeared startled then gasped, hiding it like a cough behind her tense fist, and vigorously applauded, her bracelets bouncing on her wrists. "Bravo, Roy, how wonderful."

"What I mean," he insisted, "is I feel that I have got it in me—that I am due for something very big. I have to do it. I mean," he said modestly, "that's of course when I get in the game."

Her mouth opened. "You mean you're not—" She seemed, to his surprise, disappointed, almost on the verge of crying.

"No," he said, ashamed. "Sam's taking me for a tryout."

Her eyes grew vacant as she stared out the window. Then she asked, "But Walter—*he* is a successful professional player, isn't he?"

"The Whammer?" Roy nodded.

"And he has won that award three times—what was it?"

"The Most Valuable Player." He had a panicky feeling he was losing her to the Whammer.

She bit her lip. "Yet you defeated him," she murmured.

He admitted it. "He won't last much longer I don't think—the most a year or two. By then he'll be too old for the game. Myself, I've got my whole life ahead of me."

Harriet brightened, saying sympathetically, "What will you hope to accomplish, Roy?"

He had already told her but after a minute remarked, "Sometimes when I walk down the street I bet people will say there goes Roy Hobbs, the best there ever was in the game."

She gazed at him with touched and troubled eyes. "Is that all?"

He tried to penetrate her question. Twice he had answered it and still she was unsatisfied. He couldn't be sure what she expected him to say. "Is that all?" he repeated. "What more is there?"

"Don't you know?" she said kindly.

Then he had an idea. "You mean the bucks? I'll get them too."

She slowly shook her head. "Isn't there something over and above earthly things—some more glorious meaning to one's life and activities?"

"In baseball?"

"Yes."

He racked his brain—

"Maybe I've not made myself clear, but surely you can see (I was saying this to Walter just before the train stopped) that yourself alone—alone in the sense that we are all terribly alone no matter what people say—I mean by that perhaps if you understood that our values must derive from—oh, I really suppose—" She dropped her hand futilely. "Please forgive me. I sometimes confuse myself with the little I know."

Her eyes were sad. He felt a curious tenderness for her, a little as if she might be his mother (That bird.) and tried very hard to come up with the answer she wanted—something you said about LIFE.

"I think I know what you mean," he said. "You mean the fun and satisfaction you get out of playing the best way that you know how?"

She did not respond to that.

Roy worried out some other things he might have said but

had no confidence to put them into words. He felt curiously deflated and a little lost, as if he had just flunked a test. The worst of it was he still didn't know what she'd been driving at.

Harriet yawned. Never before had he felt so tongue-tied in front of a girl, a looker too. Now if he had her in bed—

Almost as if she had guessed what he was thinking and her mood had changed to something more practical than asking nutty questions that didn't count, she sighed and edged closer to him, concealing the move behind a query about his bassoon case. "Do you play?"

"Not any music," he answered, glad they were talking about something different. "There's a thing in it that I made for myself."

"What, for instance?"

He hesitated. "A baseball bat."

She was herself again, laughed merrily. "Roy, you are priceless."

"I got the case because I don't want to get the stick all banged up before I got the chance to use it."

"Oh, Roy." Her laughter grew. He smiled broadly.

She was now so close he felt bold. Reaching down he lifted the hat box by the string and lightly hefted it.

"What's in it?"

She seemed breathless. "In it?" Then she mimicked, "—Something I made for myself."

"Feels like a hat."

"Maybe a head?" Harriet shook a finger at him.

"Feels more like a hat." A little embarrassed, he set the box down. "Will you come and see me play sometime?" he asked.

She nodded and then he was aware of her leg against his and that she was all but on his lap. His heart slapped against his ribs and he took it all to mean that she had dropped the last of her interest in the Whammer and was putting it on the guy who had buried him.

As they went through a tunnel, Roy placed his arm around her shoulders, and when the train lurched on a curve, casually let his hand fall upon her full breast. The nipple rose between his fingers and before he could resist the impulse he had tweaked it.

Her high-pitched scream lifted her up and twirling like a dancer down the aisle.

Stricken, he rose—had gone too far.

Crooking her arms like broken branches she whirled back to him, her head turned so far around her face hung between her shoulders.

"Look, I'm a twisted tree."

Sam had sneaked out on the squirming, apologetic Mercy, who, with his back to the Whammer—with a newspaper raised in front of his sullen eyes—had kept up a leechlike prodding about Roy, asking where he had come from (oh, he's just a home town boy), how it was no major league scout had got at him (they did but he turned them down for me) even with the bonus cash that they are tossing around these days (yep), who's his father (like I said, just an old semipro who wanted awful bad to be in the big leagues) and what, for God's sake, does he carry around in that case (that's his bat, Wonderboy). The sportswriter was greedy to know more, hinting he could do great things for the kid, but Sam, rubbing his side where it pained, at last put him off and escaped into the coach to get some shuteye before they hit Chicago, sometime past 1 A.M.

After a long time trying to settle himself comfortably, he fell snoring asleep flat on his back and was at once sucked into a long dream that he had gone thirsty mad for a drink and was threatening the slickers in the car get him a bottle or else. Then this weasel of a Mercy, pretending he was writing on a pad, pointed him out with his pencil and the conductor snapped him up by the seat of his pants and ran his freewheeling feet lickity-split through the sawdust, giving him the merry heave-ho off the train through the air on a floating trapeze, ploop into a bog where it rained buckets. He thought he better get across the foaming river before it flooded the bridge away so he set out, all bespattered, to cross it, only this queer duck of a doctor in oil-skins, an old man with a washable white mustache and a yellow lamp he thrust straight into your eyeballs, swore to him the bridge was gone. You're plumb tootin' crazy, Sam shouted in the storm, I saw it standin' with me own eyes, and he scuffled to get past the geezer, who dropped the light setting the rails afire. They wrestled in the train until Sam slyly tripped and threw him, and helter-skeltered for the bridge, to find to his crawling horror it was truly down and here he was scratching space till he landed with a splishity-splash in the whirling waters, sobbing (whoa whoa) and the white watchman on the embankment flung him a flare but it was all too late because he heard the roar of the falls below (and restless shifting of the sea) and felt with his red hand where the knife had stabbed him . . .

Roy was dreaming of an enormous mountain—Christ, the size of it—when he felt himself roughly shaken—Sam, he thought, because they were there—only it was Eddie holding a lit candle.

"The fuse blew and I've had no chance to fix it."

"What's the matter?"

"Trou-ble. Your friend has collapsed."

Roy hopped out of the berth, stepped into moccasins and ran, with Eddie flying after him with the stuffed wax, into a darkened car where a pool of people under a blue light hovered over Sam, unconscious.

"What happened?" Roy cried.

"Sh," said the conductor, "he's got a raging fever."

"What from?"

"Can't say. We're picking up a doctor."

Sam was lying on a bench, wrapped in blankets with a pillow tucked under his head, his gaunt face broken out in sweat. When Roy bent over him, his eyes opened.

"Hello, kiddo," he said in a cracked voice.

"What hurts you, Sam?"

"Where the washboard banged me—but it don't hurt so much now."

"Oh, Jesus."

"Don't take it so, Roy. I'll be better."

"Save his strength, son," the conductor said. "Don't talk now."

Roy got up. Sam shut his eyes.

The train whistled and ran slow at the next town then came to a draggy halt. The trainman brought a half-dressed doctor in. He examined Sam and straightened up. "We got to get him off and to the hospital."

Roy was wild with anxiety but Sam opened his eyes and told him to bend down.

Everyone moved away and Roy bent low.

"Take my wallet outa my rear pocket."

Roy pulled out the stuffed cowhide wallet.

"Now you go to the Stevens Hotel—"

"No, oh no, Sam, not without you."

"Go on, kiddo, you got to. See Clarence Mulligan tomorrow and say I sent you—they are expecting you. Give them everything you have got on the ball—that'll make me happy."

"But, Sam—"

"You got to. Bend lower."

Roy bent lower and Sam stretched his withered neck and kissed him on the chin.

"Do like I say."

"Yes, Sam."

A tear splashed on Sam's nose.

Sam had something more in his eyes to say but though he tried, agitated, couldn't say it. Then the trainmen came in with a stretcher and they lifted the catcher and handed him down the steps, and overhead the stars were bright but he knew he was dead.

Roy trailed the anonymous crowd out of Northwest Station and clung to the shadowy part of the wall till he had the courage to call a cab.

"Do you go to the Stevens Hotel?" he asked, and the driver without a word shot off before he could rightly be seated, passed a red light and scuttled a cripple across the deserted street. They drove for miles in a shadow-infested, street-lamped jungle.

He had once seen some stereopticon pictures of Chicago and it was a boxed-up ant heap of stone and crumbling wood buildings in a many-miled spreading checkerboard of streets without much open space to speak of except the railroads, stockyards, and the shore of a windy lake. In the Loop, the offices went up high and the streets were jampacked with people, and he wondered how so many of them could live together in any one place. Suppose there was a fire or something and they all ran out of their houses to see—how could they help but trample all over themselves? And Sam had warned him against strangers, because there were so many bums, sharpers, and gangsters around, people you were dirt to, who didn't know you and didn't want to, and for a dime they would slit your throat and leave you dying in the streets.

"Why did I come here?" he muttered and felt sick for home.

The cab swung into Michigan Avenue, which gave a view of the lake and a white-lit building spiring into the sky, then before he knew it he was standing flatfooted (Christ, the size of it) in front of the hotel, an enormous four-sectioned fortress. He hadn't the nerve to go through the whirling doors but had to because this bellhop grabbed his things—he wrested the bassoon case loose—and led him across the thick-carpeted lobby to a desk where he signed a card and had to count out five of the wallet's pulpy dollars for a room he would give up as soon as he found a house to board in.

But his cubbyhole on the seventeenth floor was neat and private, so after he had stored everything in the closet he lost his nervousness. Unlatching the window brought in the lake breeze. He stared down at the lit sprawl of Chicago, standing higher than he ever had in his life except for a night or two on a mountain. Gazing down upon the city, he felt as if bolts in his knees, wrists, and neck had loosened and he had spread up in height. Here, so high in the world, with the earth laid out in small squares so far below, he knew he would go in tomorrow and wow them with his fast one, and they would know him for the splendid pitcher he was.

The telephone rang. He was at first scared to answer it. In a strange place, so far from everybody he knew, it couldn't possibly be for him.

It rang again. He picked up the phone and listened.

"Hello, Roy? This is Harriet."

He wasn't sure he had got it right. "Excuse me?"

"Harriet Bird, silly."

"Oh, Harriet." He had completely forgotten her.

"Come down to my room," she giggled, "and let me say welcome to the city."

"You mean now?"

"Right away." She gave him the room number.

"Sure." He meant to ask her how she knew he was here but she had hung up.

Then he was elated. So that's how they did it in the city. He combed his hair and got out his bassoon case. In the elevator a drunk tried to take it away from him but Roy was too strong for him.

He walked—it seemed ages because he was impatient—through a long corridor till he found her number and knocked.

"Come on in."

Opening the door, he was astonished at the enormous room. Through the white-curtained window the sight of the endless dark lake sent a shiver down his spine.

Then he saw her standing shyly in the far corner of the room, naked under the gossamer thing she wore, held up on her risen nipples and the puffed wedge of hair beneath her white belly. A great weight went off his mind.

As he shut the door she reached into the hat box which lay open next to a vase of white roses on the table and fitted the back feathered hat on her head. A thick veil fell to her breasts. In her hand she held a squat, shining pistol.

He was greatly confused and thought she was kidding but a grating lump formed in his throat and his blood shed ice. He cried out in a gruff voice, "What's wrong here?"

She said sweetly, "Roy, will you be the best there ever was in the game?"

"That's right."

She pulled the trigger (thrum of bull fiddle). The bullet cut a silver line across the water. He sought with his bare hands to catch it, but it eluded him and, to his horror, bounced into his gut. A twisted dagger of smoke drifted up from the gun barrel. Fallen on one knee he groped for the bullet, sickened as it moved, and fell over as the forest flew upward, and she, making muted noises of triumph and despair, danced on her toes around the stricken hero.